M.J. VIGNA

DEADLY DEADLY

Book 2

Trail's End

ISBN: 1546929894
ISBN-13: 9781546929895

This prologue is a brief refresher for the readers of the first book of Deadly Deadly. It is highly recommended that you read the first book. It is a rich epic full of adventure, action and emotion.

PROLOGUE

In the first book of "Deadly Deadly" We are introduced to Deadly, a huge Texas Longhorn Bull, and the humans and animals that make up his world.

It is the relationship between Deadly and trail boss Joe Bob Grady that propels this story forward. Together, this unusual partnership is an indomitable force and a blessing for the beautiful Grace Cecile McNamara.

Grace Cecile McNamara, who prefers to be called Ceci, hires Joe Bob Grady to drive her small but special herd of Hereford cattle to her ranch in Texas.

The journey is treacherous from the beginning. With extreme wilderness, historical storms, Indians and evil men, the trail crew face and battle constant danger.

Deadly becomes a hero as he consistently rescues Ceci, Grady and the herd from the many perils that befall them.

First he sniffs out a deadly nor'easter and alerts Grady in time to get the drive to safety.

Next, when Cecile is alone in camp and attacked by two men Deadly hears her screams, runs to the camp and gruesomely mauls her attacker.

After this attack Cecile is very injured and allows Grady to care for her. It is during this time that their fondness for each other begins to grow.

Reginald, one of only two bulls that Cecile has procured to grow her herd, is separated from the herd after the nor'easter. He stumbles upon a wild herd and is attacked by a wild range bull who gores out his eye. Deadly hears the battle and the painful screams when Reginald is injured. He rushes into battle, killing the wild bull. The valuable Hereford bull is saved albeit without one of his eyes.

During the attack on Cecile one of the bandits escapes. Considering him a danger Grady has Bear track the man down and they find his entire crew.

They recognize the group as the men who attacked and robbed a fort they had sheltered at, and suspect the men are now trailing them.

Grady decides to capture the men and hold them as prisoners until they can be turned into the proper authority.

All goes well for a time but the outlaws finally engineer an escape and Grady learns a tough lesson about the depth of the leaders depravity. The escapees kill several of Grady's cowboys, also much of the food supplies for the humans, cattle and horses are destroyed.

A record winter storm of driving ice and freezing temperatures forces them to find a canyon in the Chiricahua Mountain and take shelter.

Grady realizes he must journey the few days to Janos with Deadly and return with supplies in order to survive until they can get the cattle safely out of the mountains.

With Grady leaving for Janos there are only four people including Cecile to care for the herd and each other while he is gone.

Grady is desperate to make the turnaround as quickly as possible as the lives of the people under his charge and the herd are depending on him.

Grady hurriedly rides from camp on horseback with Deadly following with haste, traveling dangerously fast on rugged downhill trails. The horse takes a wrong step and breaks a leg, throwing Grady into a ravine. Badly injured with a concussion and broken shoulder Grady manages to mount and tie himself to Deadly. He points him down the familiar trail to Janos, and relies on Deadly as he floats in and out of consciousness.

Exposed to the elements he becomes extremely ill with pneumonia and lapses into full unconsciousness after nearly drowning when Deadly has a standoff with wolves, in a stream, and the saddle falls underneath Deadly, dunking Grady who is tied to the saddle into the water. Grady uses his last reserves to release himself from the saddle, shoot his gun to scare off the wolves, remount and tie himself back onto Deadly.

Deadly arrives in town with an unconscious Grady tied to his back. It is weeks before Grady wakes up and realizes it may be too late to rescue his responsibilities.

He meets Candace Murray who is a saloon owner and has been caring for Grady during the weeks he was unconscious. Upon awakening he also meets Juan Aviles, who is Cecile's majordomo. Concerned for her wellbeing Juan had traveled to Janos to meet up with the trail drive and make sure his charge was safe.

Both Grady and Juan are driven to get back up the mountain, especially after they learn that the escaped outlaws that killed some of Grady's crew have regrouped with the intent to find the herd and steal the treasures in Cecile's trunk.

With Grady bedridden it is left to Juan to hire help and supplies for the return rescue trip. Fear overshadows their efforts when they learn the outlaws have gotten a head start.

Meanwhile in the mountain canyon Cecile has taken seriously ill from exhaustion, bitter cold and hunger. When Grady did not return the crew assumes the worst and since they are trapped they fear that Cecile will not survive.

When the outlaws find the canyon Little Bear rides to Cochise holdout for help.

Grady's group also arrives. They are finally able to overpower the outlaws but it is not without more horrific losses to Grady's main team.

Grady finds Cecile hovering near death. They work on bringing her back from the brink. Grady realizes his feelings for Cecile are very strong.

The first book ends with Cecile gaining enough strength to be able to begin the decent down the mountain and on to Janos. With Grady still unable to lead the drive due to his injuries he gives his command to Deadly, who knows the trail as well as Grady, to "lead them out."

Grady tucked the covers around the sleeping woman in his arms. He studied her precious face. He saw exhaustion, worry wrinkles, frostbitten skin, chapped and cracked lips.

Guilt flooded his conscience. He had accepted the responsibility of driving her small herd to Texas.

He had originally told her no. He didn't drive less than a thousand head. She had agreed to the set price for a thousand head, wanting only a safe delivery of her small herd, which was less than one hundred. She had been told Joe Bob Grady was honest and reliable. He had finally accepted the job.

He came close to reneging when she insisted she travel with her herd. He warned her the trail would be difficult, hard for a man, too strenuous for a woman. Agreeing to pay the requested trail fees, she insisted on her right to travel with her precious herd.

Now as he looked down at the ravaged face of Grace Cecile McNamara, he didn't see that proud beautiful woman who rode a prancing Arabian stallion down the main street of San Diego.

He felt he had failed this woman laying in his arms. She looked like a child, a very ill child. It would take several days to reach Janos and a doctor.

He laid his head back. He was so tired, hardly well enough to function. He was still recovering from a severe concussion, a dislocated shoulder, and a difficult struggle with pneumonia.

The two invalids lay under heavy furs, a canvas cover to keep them warm and protect them from the snow flurries that continued to fall as the small herd and crew climbed out of the canyon that had sheltered them for many weeks while they waited for Grady's return.

His return to the canyon was almost too late due to his illness and recovery. A band of outlaws, intent on stealing the treasures Cecile had in her trunk, beat Grady's rescue team to the canyon by a few hours. Little Bear, one of Grady's crew, a half Navajo Indian, prevented the outlaw attack by enlisting the aid from a camp of Apache that lived in those mountains.

Grady was uncomfortable with his weak body. He wanted to be on his horse helping to herd the cattle but realized he was not ready to climb into a saddle, much less apply the strenuous effort to stay on a working horse.

The herd and his crew, including Cecile, had been left in a canyon high in the Chiricahua Mountains. He struggled with the effort to regain some strength. The struggle only created more loss of health. He was relieved and grateful when he met Juan and realized he had help to return to the canyon and rescue those hopefully still alive.

He enlisted Juan to gather supplies, wagons, and a couple of drovers to make the trip. With Candy's help with supplies and her team and wagon, Juan was able to hire the help. He also obtained another wagon loaded with grain and necessary bad-weather gear.

Deadly Deadly, Grady's longhorn bull, friend, and partner, was eager to return to the canyon and find his friend Trumpeter, Cecile's Hereford bull. He would not make the trip without Grady's participation and had to see Grady lifted into the back of Candy's wagon and hear Grady call out, "Lead them out, Deadly," before he took his place ahead of the small rescue wagons and began the tedious and treacherous path back up the mountain.

Lance and Glancy, the two young men hired for the job to help with this rescue, were sons of a Spanish woman who ran a bar and a very large cattle ranch outside of Janos. They were young, and Juan had tried to dissuade her from offering their help. Herding a hundred cattle was an easy job, but if they were to run into outlaws, he did not want to return her boys to her in a pine box.

After testing their skills with both pistol and rifle, he had finally agreed. He found the boys efficient in all the tasks set before them, and Lance, the eighteen-year-old, was always ahead with camp jobs before anyone asked.

Glancy, sixteen years old, was given the job of driving the grain-wagon team and was remarkable at this job for one so young.

Finally they were beginning their decent out of the mountain canyon to begin their journey to Janos.

The Indian, Little Bear, had ridden on ahead to scout the trail and clear fallen trees and other hazards. Gimpy Lou was driving the four-horse grain wagon, and Glancy was helping drive the herd. Juan watched the boys gather the herd into a group and move it down the mountain. He was working the drag. They would work this way until they came to a spot to halt the herd and let Deadly hold them, while they rode back and attached ropes to the wagons to break their downhill effort to plunge down the mountain.

Strange as it may seem to rely on a bull to take part in the work required in getting this herd down the mountain, Little Bear and Gimpy Lou knew they could absolutely depend on Deadly from past experience. They would work this way all the way down the side of the mountain. It was tedious and dangerous in the falling snow and freezing weather.

Candy had put some rocks behind the wheels to stop her wagon from rolling on down, but she still had to encourage her blacks to stand still. Lou's wagon with its heavier load and four-mule team was a worry to her, behind her wagon. If the heavier wagon broke loose, it would take them both down. She decided to let the men take his wagon down first when they came back to move wagons.

Her passengers had gone to sleep. She saw Little Bear work his way past the herd and come toward her. He was a handsome man. She had teased him a lot, and they were getting to know each other. She figured he was coming back to talk with her.

He smiled as he passed her and, riding by, stopped by Grady. "Boss."

Grady opened his eyes and nodded to let Bear know he was awake.

"We got company on the ridge," Bear reported.

"Red or white?" Grady shifted Ceci and removed his arm from under her.

Bear grinned and said, "Red."

Grady rose up on his elbows and asked, "Paint?"

"No, hungry, hunting. They've had no luck. Big game gone down mountain, little game gone to dens." Bear took his fur hat off and ran his fingers through the thick black hair before putting the fur back on.

"They saved us big time. If they hadn't helped us, we would probably be dead. They should have taken a cow or two."

"Why didn't they?" asked Grady, leaning up on his elbows. They were getting tired and painful leaning on them. "Why wouldn't they accept a cow?"

Bear replied, "They believe the white buffalo is sacred. They've never seen Herefords before. Because there are so many look-alikes, they think they are special. They are not sure they are sacred, but they won't take a chance to kill one. The calves were already dead."

Candy had been listening, and she spoke up. "The two calf carcasses couldn't have gone far to feed the camp. What about a horse? You eat horse, don't you, Bear?"

He grinned, dimples showing. "No, remember I'm half-white. I know they would ordinarily eat anything, but now with the army after them, as soon as this weather breaks, the entire clan will cross over into Mexico. The army will be chasing Cochise and will take out on any of them to get to Cochise.. The Indians will be needing all their horses, and my guess is they would not eat any horse we gave them."

He thought for a moment and then said, "I think a mule would do it. Mules are stubborn and hardheaded. Give Indians lots of trouble."

Grady lay back off his aching elbows and said, "We've got some mules in the remuda. Cut them out a couple."

"I'll tell Lance. I go tell them before they ride on. I'll be right back." He kicked up his horse and ran to catch up with the herd. He gave Lance the order to cut out a couple of mules and deliver them to Grady. He told Juan to keep the herd moving slowly while he fetched an Indian to come get the mules. "We'll catch up with you." He waved, and digging his heels he hurried his horse past the herd and went to meet the four Indians setting their mounts. They were watching the small herd of special cows come down the trail.

Candy wrapped her reins around the brake handle and climbed off the wagon. They hadn't even begun this trip and she was stiff already. She stamped her feet and swung her arms.

Grady, using his sore arms, raised himself to a sitting position, his back against the driver's seat.

Candy said, "We packed so fast in Janos to get started to the canyon that I didn't separate much. Didn't have time—I just tossed supplies into

4

the wagon. I know I threw in a fifty-pound sack of beans and one of flour. We only used enough for the trip up and a couple of days in the canyon. I'll take some pans and divide up enough for us for four more days. We'll be going downhill. Be faster going back. Once we get back to the saloon, I'm stocked there."

Grady thought about her suggestion and agreed. "Lou can help you sort it out. Go ahead."

She hurried back to the grain wagon.

Grady tried to turn his body to see the herd. All he could see were disturbed ground and trees. He turned back to check on Ceci and found her eyes open. She was studying his face. She coughed, and it sounded deep in her chest. He fumbled with the covers and tucked them around and under her chin. The snow flurries had slowed some. She had a fever, and the soft flakes melted as they hit her face. Afraid the melted snow would get the furs wet, he pulled up the canvas top cover Candy had spread across the entire pallet for that purpose.

She smiled and tried to talk. She was very hoarse. "Where are we?"

"Practically where we were an hour ago. We came onto some of Bear's Indian friends who helped us rescue you. They wouldn't accept any of the little red cows, so we are giving them a couple of mules and some food supplies. We owe them much more—you can't put a price on saving you. All we can do to thank them is help hold off their hunger."

Just then Bear returned. An Indian nearly hidden in hide and furs was with him. Grady said to Bear, "Candy's getting some food supplies together, go on back to Lou's wagon."

Bear spoke to the Indian, and the Indian followed him to where Candy was struggling to tie two gunnysacks together. She smiled at him as he took over and pulled the ties tight and then tossed the heavy bags over the horse in front of the Indian. Lance rode up with the two mules and handed the lead ropes to the Indian.

Bear spoke in their language, and the Indian turned, kicked his horse, and rode back to the ridge whooping and hollering, two fat mules stubbornly pulling back on the lead as the Indian dragged them to meet the other Indians, who quickly had the mules racing with them or feeling a whip to encourage faster travel. Their joyful yipping echoed over the mountain as they hurried to their camp, taking back a meal on four hooves.

Bear swung Candy around and gave her a big hug. She returned the hug with a quick kiss.

"You're too much, gal. Thanks for doing that." He hugged her again and then mounted his horse and hurried to catch up with the herd.

Candy thanked Lou for his help. They had divided beans and flour, salt and sugar, and a slab of bacon. She went back to her wagon. Checked on Grady. He had scooted back down in the covers and pulled the girl back into his arms. She thought she could hear him humming.

Removing the rocks, she took her seat, untied the reins, and cracked her whip. The black team strained into the harness. The wheels had already begun to freeze. The wagon jerked loose and pulled forward. She reined the team to the left and moved team and wagon over so Lou could go around her. She had to wait for the crew to lower the grain wagon down to where Deadly held the waiting herd. It was snowing a little harder. She was miserable, rubbing her hands together to warm them. She wondered how many more interruptions they would have. Shit! So far all they had done was climb out of the canyon.

The young boys continued directing the small herd down the mountain, while Juan and Bear came back and helped the smaller wagon until it reached where Lou sat with the grain wagon. The boys settled the herd, left Deadly in charge, and came back to help with the grain wagon.

This was the system the rest of the day. Except for the struggle to keep the herd and horse remuda from bolting down the mountain, the rest of the day was uneventful.

Annoyed at the effort to keep the herd together and traveling at a slower pace, Deadly often stopped and grazed. A slow pace for the Herefords was a crawl for him. Occasionally he left Trumpeter and Reginald to lead the herd, and he turned back to walk beside Candy's wagon, where his friend Grady was. He didn't understand this arrangement. He hadn't understood it on the way back up the mountain. Never had Grady not been on his horse and in control of the herd.

Grady was aware of Deadly's confusion. When the longhorn would walk alongside the wagon, Grady talked to him, repeating trail commands, words the Bull was familiar with. When Grady's soft command told Deadly to take care of the herd, the longhorn would resume his leadership.

He knew if Grady were on a horse, this drive would get on down this trail. He didn't understand this unusual behavior but appreciated Grady talking to him and occasionally reaching out of the wagon to playfully grab a longhorn and hold it for a short time and then let go.

Deadly had just picked up his pace to head back to the herd when a commotion began. He sped up and came onto the herd. They had reached a small meadow. The herd, tired, irritable, and hungry, had stopped to graze and began to spread out. One cow had left the herd, with Glancy riding to head her off. She leaped into a run, and Glancy kicked his horse up to head her off from falling into a ravine that ran along the side of the meadow.

Juan, Lance, and Bear were standing above the ravine looking into it. Lance handed Bear his horse's reins and disappeared into the ravine.

Candy stopped her wagon and, while putting on the brakes and shoving a stone under the front wheels, disturbed Grady, who sat up, saw the little herd out of control, and called out to Deadly, "Deadly, bed them down. Make camp." He repeated the order several times, and Deadly went to work. Using horns and blocking progress, the herd realized they could stop and graze. Deadly circled, set the perimeter, and stopped by Trumpeter. Curious, he watched the men.

Candy wrapped her reins around the brake handle. Got a lead rope and tied the team to Lou's grain wagon. She quickly put a small measure of grain in nose bags for each horse to insure they stayed put and ran to where the men were looking into the ravine.

The drop-off was only about a dozen feet deep, but it had been a catastrophe for the horse and rider that had fallen into it.

Glancy had kicked his horse into a run to turn the cow before she fell into the ravine. It was close. Both cow and rider were at top speed when Glancy cut in front of her. She turned and ran back to the herd. The weight of horse and rider and the speed traveled caused the edge of the ravine to cave in.

Running hard, their collision with the bottom of the ravine broke two legs on the horse. Glancy's right leg was under the horse. He was unconscious. Lance slid down the side of the dirt ravine and hurried to his brother.

The horse, in pain, continued to thrash in an attempt to regain his feet. Lance immediately realized the horse had broken both front legs. Thrashing, the horse was rolling on Glancy.

Lance pulled out his pistol. A shot rang out and echoed down the ravine. The thrashing stopped.

Bear called out, "How's the kid?"

Lance did not answer right away. With his heart hammering in his chest, he felt for the throb of a pulse in Glancy's neck. His brother was alive! He checked his arms. No broken bones there. He ran his hand over Glancy's head. He located a bump already swelling. His hand came away bloody.

The relief Lance had over Glancy being alive was short-lived as he answered Bear, "He's out cold. There's a head wound. One leg is caught under the horse. I'll need help to move the horse."

Before Lance could finish that request, Bear was sliding down and landed beside him. Bear studied the position of the horse and the trapped boy.

"Can't roll the horse over the boy. Going to be much harder to lift the horse and slide the boy out." Bear lifted the horse's top back leg and tested the weight. The horse wasn't going to move. He was summer fat, healthy and heavy.

Grady had gotten himself out of Candy's wagon and slowly made his way to stand beside Lou, Candy, and Juan Aviles. Hearing Bear, he answered, "Can we hook a rope to the horse and use a horse up here to lift some of the weight off the boy?"

Bear answered, "Might help. Lou, come help us, and Juan can throw us his rope!" Bear felt the boy's head and found a large swollen bump. His worry was that Glancy's neck or back was broken.

Juan hurried back to the wagons to get his horse. He untied his reins and climbed aboard. Loosening his lariat, he returned to the ravine and stopped a dozen feet back from the edge. All they needed was another horse and rider on top of them. He ran the lariat through the hole under the saddle horn and then around the horn and handed Grady the bulk of the rope.

Grady, testing each step, got close enough to toss the rope over the edge.

"Rope coming down," he called.

"Toss it," Bear answered.

Grady threw it down. He waited to hear if it fall where it was needed.

Wasn't long before Bear called back, "Got it. Give us a few minutes. I'll holler when I've got it fastened."

"OK," Grady answered. He was breathing hard, and his legs had begun to shake.

Candy, always monitoring Grady's energy, having nursed him through pneumonia, concussion, and dislocated shoulder, recognized his effort to stand. She reached forward and carefully pulled him back from the ravine. She put one of his arms across her shoulder and gently escorted him to a nearby boulder.

"Sit down before you fall down," she ordered.

Used to her gruff orders, he smiled and sat on the boulder. Impatient, he called out, "Bear, will it work?"

"Hold on, boss. I got to get the rope under the horse. Lance and Lou are trying to lift his rear enough to work it under and tie together on top. When that's done, I've got the head. Lance has the back feet and Lou the tail, hopefully to use as a rudder. Tell Juan, when I give the word to back up slow and easy. If it looks wrong, I'll yell, hold it!"

Bear was quiet for a while and then he called Candy, "Candy, can you make it down here?"

"Coming," she answered. He could hear debris sliding as she slid down the ravine wall.

She went to his side, where he was studying the position the kid was in. "You think you can pull Glancy out if we get the weight off?" he asked.

"I think I can. He's tall but skinny. I don't think he weighs more than I do," she answered.

"We don't know the seriousness of his injuries. I need you to slide your arms under him and pull from his underarms. Let his head rest on your shoulder and try to keep his head and neck as level with his body as you can." Bear gave her these directions. She was a strong young woman, but she was still a woman.

His words worried her. "You're afraid his neck is broken?" she asked.

"Don't know—can't take a chance." He spoke to Lance and Lou, "Get ready!"

"Juan?" he called,

"Yo!" Juan answered.

Bear gave Juan directions. "Stretch out your rope until you feel it tighten a little. Let me know when you get there. I'll holler if I need you to stop."

He watched the rope begin to rise. The slack began to disappear over the edge of the ravine. It stopped rising, and Juan called out, "OK!"

Bear answered, "I'll count to three. On three you pull slow and don't let up unless I yell whoa!"

"Gotcha. Let's get this done," Juan answered.

Bear began, "One, two, three." Juan moved his horse back, tightening the rope, and felt his horse hesitate when it felt the weight on the other end. A soft kick, and the horse continued backing.

As the rope tightened, Bear lifted the dead horse's head, and Lou used the horse's tail to keep it from swaying. Lance could do little to lift. The horse was too heavy, but he kept the rear from rolling.

They felt the dead horse move, and the rear lifted slowly. As the horse lifted off of Glancy, Candy tugged, and Glancy began to slide from under the horse. Suddenly the boy came to a halt.

Candy yelled, "Stop, stop."

Juan pulled up his horse, Lou cussed, and Lance tried to see what was wrong.

Candy, her scared voice trembling, said, "His boots caught in the stirrup."

Bear called out, "Can you hold it there, Juan?"

"I'm not going anywhere," Juan replied.

"Hold steady. I'll have to let loose the head. I have to find something to put under the horse to hold it up enough to free the boot." Bear slowly let the weight of the horse's head down. The muzzle reached the ground, and he let loose.

"Bear?" Grady called.

"Yeah, boss?"

"Did you undo the cinch? If not, do so. Drag the saddle with the boy. You pull him out and have Candy drag the saddle out with him." Grady shifted on the boulder he sat on. He was getting tired, and the weather had drenched his clothes. He felt useless. He should be down there helping.

"Why didn't I think of that?" Bear answered.

Grady chuckled, "You're the Indian, and I'm the chief. Tell us when you're ready."

Bear struggled getting the cinch unfastened. The savage drop into the ravine and the pressure as the horse had thrashed had tightened the leather.

10

It was taking too long. Bear pulled the knife kept in his boot and severed the leather. To keep the longer end from catching, he cut the cinch away.

"OK, let's get this done." He moved to take Candy's place with Glancy, and she grabbed the saddle horn and prepared to pull.

As they moved into position, Glancy groaned. They stood ridged as they watched him try to open his eyes.

His eyes fluttered, and his next groan was one of pain. His arm moved as he tried to lift a hand to his head. Eyes clenched shut and then opened.

Candy reached out and brushed his hair out of his face. "Glancy honey, can you open your eyes?"

He turned his head in the direction of her voice and tried to open his eyes. It took a couple of minutes before he could open them and keep them open. As they cleared, he recognized the three around him. He stuttered, "My leg hurts." Tears rolled down his cheeks.

Bear spoke up, "Can you move your arms?"

Glancy moaned, "It hurts—my head hurts." He sobbed but managed to move one arm. The other was penned under him.

Candy pulled that arm out carefully so as not to move him in case the neck was damaged. The hand on that arm had one finger broken and possibly more. He was able to move the arm, and the movement of his head back and forth as he fought the pain assured them the neck was not broken. A later inspection would be made of his back.

The three released held breaths. Bear was the first to speak. "Glancy's awake and moving his head. Neck seems good. Juan, let's get this horse off him. Give me a moment. I'll give you a three count."

"Gotcha," Juan answered. His horse was starting to get restless. He was responsible for bringing this kid on the drive. Tension relaxed some as he learned there was no broken neck. He prayed there would be no more serious injuries. Taking a crippled boy back to Carmella was not an option.

Bear said to his three helpers, "I'll give the count of three. We all do our jobs until the horse looks high enough to drag Glancy free." He got behind the boy and carefully worked his hands under both arms. Candy took hold of the saddle by the horn, ready to pull with Bear.

"OK, one, two, three." The dead horse continued the slow lift upward. A little space appeared above boy and saddle.

"Whoa! Juan, whoa," Bear yelled. Glancy and saddle were pulled free. Bear released the boy's foot from the stirrup. Glancy screamed from pain. Bear called up to Juan, "You can let the horse down, Juan. Good job."

As the horse was slowly lowered down, Lou let go of the tail and moved over to inspect Glancy's leg. Grady called out, "Am I going to have to come down there?"

Bear answered, "That's all we need is another invalid in our way."

Grady answered back, "Then tell me what's going on."

Candy spoke up, "Lou's checking his leg. Give us a minute to check the boy out."

Lou moved about Glancy, lifting arms, checking out fingers. Two were broken and beginning to swell.

He came back to the leg. The boy was in such pain that Lou took his time to carefully cut away his pant leg. All four gasped as they saw the bone punched thru the skin, tearing a great bloody gash.

Lance stepped away and placed a hand over his face, embarrassed to have anyone see his emotion. He had been holding up since the start of Glancy's accident, but the rock in his gut exploded when Lou exposed his brother's leg. He had been silently praying that little injury would be found. Once he saw the wound, he knew his brother was in serious trouble, and tears poured behind his hand.

"What! What!" Grady yelled.

Lou answered, "Bad break. Could be broke in two places."

"Oh shit!" Grady spat. He lay back on the boulder and looked up, snow still falling softly. He stared at the fading light. It would soon be dark. He was damp from snow melting from his body heat.

He sat back up and yelled, "Dark is closing in, Lou. You need to give the kid a knockout dose before you try to set it. Bear, you need to take over. We'll need a fire in the ravine and one up here. Candy, get us a meal going and some broth for the kid. Juan, help me get back to Ceci and then see the herd is settled for the night."

Everyone moved quickly to follow Grady's orders. First Candy moved over to Lance and grasped him around his shoulders. "Look, hon," she said, "I know you're worried, but we can deal with a broken leg—just looks bad now, but we need to be happy he didn't break his back or neck."

Surprisingly with that comment there seemed to be a lifting of everyone's spirits, and they each buckled down to their jobs with fervor.

Firewood was gathered, and the two fires crackled. Lou heated some water and made a warm drink of diluted coffee with a spoon of honey and a strong dose of sleeping powder.

Candy decided not to tackle a difficult meal. She made a pot of oatmeal and a pan of hot biscuits.

Lou gave Glancy the knockout drink and figured it would take about an hour to work. He spent that time moving things around in the grain wagon, preparing a bed for the boy. He found a pair of branches approximately the same size and whittled to make a satisfactory brace after setting the leg. He searched Candy's medicine box for clean rags to bind the braces to the leg. After inspecting the break more closely, he found he just had to deal with one break. It was severe, but he hadn't been sure he was experienced enough to repair two breaks. He had repaired many breaks through the years on many cattle drives, but he had never seen one as bad as this one. He had gotten his name of Gimpy Lou due to a leg injury of his own. He wanted to do a good job on the kid. As bad as the break was, the kid would probably have a limp.

Grady was exhausted. Fine fix for a trail boss to be so weak—he had to sit and watch his crew work. He couldn't even get back to his wagon without help. He had to lean on Juan's arm to get back. He used up all his reserve to crawl into the wagon and join Ceci under the covers.

She had slept through this catastrophe. His arrival back under the covers woke her.

"Where are we?" Her question was accompanied by a series of coughs.

They had not traveled much farther from the spot where she had asked this question before.

"We are making camp. Candy will have a meal ready soon." No sense worrying her tonight with Glancy's injuries.

"I need to relieve myself," was accompanied with more coughs. She got them under control and said, "Sorry."

Grady hesitated. There was no way he could carry her out to the trees so she could have some privacy. "It's OK, but I'll need to get help. Can you handle Bear carrying you?"

She started coughing again, got it under control, and answered, "I'd be more comfortable with Juan. He has taken care of me all my life."

Lance was walking by with a load of firewood. Grady stopped him. "Take Juan's place with the herd and send Juan to me."

"Yes, sir." Lance dropped the wood in reach of the campfire. At the nearest tree he untied his horse and rode to the herd, happy to stay busy in order to keep his mind from focusing solely on his brother.

Juan rode to Candy's wagon and learned of the chore he was summoned to perform. Grady helped him uncover Ceci and move her to the tailgate where Juan could lift her into his arms.

Juan was not a young man but an active old gentleman, used to hard work, and he could toss grain sacks about with the youngsters. He teased Ceci, "You've gained a few pounds since the last time I carried you around."

Ceci laughed, struggled not to cough, and said, "Juan, I was only five years old. I'm sorry. I hate being so helpless."

"It's all right, honey. You'll be up and around in no time." He settled her by a tree she could grab if she got unbalanced. He walked away and turned his back to give her a little privacy.

Juan soon had Ceci back in the wagon. Grady took over, tucking her back in the covers. He heard Lou call Bear and Lance to help him set Glancy's leg. He and Ceci snuggled close and dozed off to be wakened later with the offer of oatmeal, biscuits, and honey.

Lou was still feeling relief that there was only one break. Although it was bad, it could be set. If it had been a double break, the chances that Glancy could have gangrene set in before they could get him to Janos and a doctor increased immensely. If gangrene set in, he would probably lose the leg.

Lance had tears in his eyes as he held his brother tightly in his arms. Lance had him in a bear hug with his arms crossed in front of Glancy and hands securely locked together. Bear had the job of pulling until the bones meshed. He had taken off his boots and had a stocking foot placed between Glancy's legs carefully but secure enough that Glancy's body remained firm. Lou was ready to help shift the bones and hopefully settle them to meet where the break had occurred.

It was a hard struggle. Perspiration dripped from Bear's face, as the strain to pull the break apart was a concentrated effort to keep the boy from sliding to him while he struggled to stretch the leg into position.

Luckily the bones meshed back together properly. Lou poured whiskey over the opened wound, pulled it together with a few stitches, and poured honey on it. He covered it with clean rags, put the two branches on each side of the leg, and began wrapping it tightly with clean rags. He wrapped the rags from the knee to the foot and then ran the wrap under and over the foot to keep the wraps from traveling up the leg.

The three men sat back, looked at each other, and let out a collective breath. Lance, with tears still running down his cheeks, asked, "You think it will hold?"

Lou answered, "We'll have to keep an eye on it. It's a makeshift bandage. Needs a plaster cast to keep it in place. We still got some rough ground to go over. I made him a bed behind me in the grain wagon where I can keep an eye on him."

Bear took out his tobacco, rolled Lou a smoke, and gave it to him. He took out his pipe, filled and lit it. Bear let out the smoke with a sigh. Lance picked up Glancy's injured hand and studied the broken fingers taped together and secured to a stick.

The brothers were young, Lance eighteen and Glancy sixteen. Neither had acquired the cigarette habit.

Little Bear, always juggling his Indian blood and his white blood, sometimes just needed some quiet time. So far, this first day, struggling to get out of the canyon with both herd and humans had been delayed by Indians, invalids, and now a serious accident. Lance and old Gimpy Lou were exhausted. The emotional drain on Lance was understandable. His tears were now drying on his cheeks, evidence of the love for his little brother. Old Lou was just feeling his age, and now he had the added worry of responsibility for the injured boy. It would still take three, possibly four more days to get off this mountain and get the boy to a doctor. Anything could go wrong, including the very real possibility that gangrene would develop.

Bear knocked the pipe against his bootheel and dropped the ashes into the fire. Making sure the pipe was free of embers, he put the pipe in his shirt pocket and fastened the button to secure it. He addressed the tired men, "Let's get this kid up to the wagon while he's still out."

Lou threw his cigarette stub into the fire and got to his feet, both hands on his hips while he stretched aching muscles and waited for further instructions. Lance carefully laid the boy's wounded hand across his chest, pulled the other arm, and secured both together with his bandana.

Bear moved to the boy's head and reaching under Glancy's arms secured the boy so he could lift him. He directed Lance to take the good leg and keep it high enough so as not to drag as they worked to climb the side of the ravine. Lou he told to take the bad leg, hold it above the knee, and with the other arm raise the injured lower leg to keep it from hitting the ground.

This uphill climb was not done standing up. Bear leaned his back on the uphill dirt wall and with his bootheels began a steady upward push a couple of feet at a time. He waited after each push for Lance and Lou to carefully move up with their burden. When he reached the top of the ravine he stepped to solid ground and said, "I'm going to pull him on up and take him in my arms. You guys just keep him steady while I pull him up." Quickly Glancy was safe in Bear's arms, and the Indian walked slowly to the grain wagon.

Lou and Lance caught up with him, climbed into the wagon, and helped position the boy on the pallet Lou had made for him.

Bear said, "Good job, both of you. It won't be long before the powder wears off. He's going to be in a world of hurt. You two had better eat. Candy's got hot biscuits and honey. Lou, you fix the kid up with some broth and another dose of sleeping powder. I'll put out the fire in the ravine." But first he needed some grub. He walked away, toward the campfire and some of Candy's hot biscuits and honey.

He passed on the oatmeal. Filled his metal camp plate with four of Candy's large biscuits, dripping with honey, and slid back down the ravine. He added another log to the embers of the fire built to provide light to work on Glancy. He pulled another log closer and sat and ate his biscuits slowly. He stared into the flames of the fire and realized just how tired he was. He had worked steady. As the strongest, he had taken on the job of the trail boss. This was his first chance to sit, eat a meal, and enjoy some quiet time.

He undid the button on his shirt pocket and withdrew his pipe and tobacco. Filled the pipe with tobacco and returned the tobacco to the pocket. He used a twig, one end lit by the fire, to light the tobacco in the pipe. He drew in the first pull of smoke. His body relaxed. He flicked the twig into the fire and watched it burn and turn into ashes.

Watching the flickering flames and chewing on the pipestem as much as drawing and expelling the smoke, he enjoyed the quiet around him. His eyes began to droop, and he jerked and shook his head to clear it. He had been daydreaming and forgot for a moment where he was.

He looked at the dead horse, and it brought his mind back to the present. Sad—the animal was going out to pasture way before its time. The fire was flickering and throwing light flashes on the collapsed dirt behind the horse. At first he didn't register what he was seeing. It looked like there was an opening at the top of the dirt pile.

He rose and knocked the pipe out on his bootheel. Checked to make sure the pipe was out and returned it to his pocket. He walked around the dead horse and stopped before the avalanche of dirt. He was between the pile of dirt and the fire. He had to move sideways so the fire could continue to cast light on the small opening at the top of the loose dirt.

He looked around and found a small branch. Put one end into the fire, and when it caught, he went back to the avalanche of dirt. Evidently the horse had broken through the lip of what looked like a cave. The dirt pile had nearly hidden the entrance.

Curious and a little excited, he was to explore the cave. Physically and mentally exhausted, he knew moving the dirt would be a major undertaking. It was too dark to mess with tonight. It could be the home of a bear or possibly snakes. Using caution was the best plan, that meant waiting until tomorrow when there was light and backup.

He kicked some dirt on the fire, climbed out of the ravine, and joined Candy, Juan, and Lance seated around the cook fire. Exhaustion was on all their faces. He sat on a log by Candy and took her hand in his. They sat watching the flickering fire and the steam rising from a pot of beans, which would cook most of the night. It would be the main dish for that much-needed good meal.

Candy brought Grady a bowl of oatmeal, sweetened with honey and four biscuits. Two lightly smeared with honey and two without. She was learning Grady's and Deadly's morning and evening rituals. She helped Grady sit up so he could share his oatmeal with Ceci. "I'll pick up your bowl and utensils in a bit."

She returned sooner than planned. She had prepared a rag doubled and smeared with mentholated salve and warmed by the fire. She unfastened Ceci's shirt and placed the warm poultice against her skin.

Ceci breathed in the medicated fumes that rose. She closed her eyes to avoid the sting and obediently swallowed several spoonfuls of sweetened oatmeal. With her eyes closed, she was soon back to sleep.

Grady finished the oatmeal. He ate his two biscuits, saving Deadly's two for when he showed up. The bull would find him. This nightly ritual was established over many nights on trail drives.

Bear helped Candy clean the pots and pans. Lance gathered enough wood to burn through the night. Lou spread his bedroll under the grain wagon, away from the softly falling snow. Glancy was deeply drugged. Best if he slept. Lou would care for him if needed.

Deadly came out of the darkness. He knew Grady was in the wagon. He was confused that his friend did not mount his horse and move about. But he approached the wagon and found Grady sitting up. Waiting for him. He could smell the biscuit odor all through the camp.

Grady spoke softly to the big longhorn. He gave him a biscuit and scratched the bony skin between the dual horns. Grady rubbed the broad area between Deadly's eyes and offered the second biscuit. The bull's long rough tongue swept the biscuit into his mouth.

Deadly left to rejoin the herd. Bear took the bull's place beside the wagon and with voice lowered so as not to disturb Ceci said, "Boss, looks like there's a cave in the ravine. The horse broke through the top of it. Too dark to check tonight."

"Animal cave?" Grady brushed the snowflakes off his face.

"Could be. If so, it's too close to our camp," Bear answered.

"Better warn Lance and Juan. Set up night watch. Leave Lou out of it. He's got his hands full with the kid."

"Night, boss."

"Night, Bear." Grady rubbed the cold flakes of snow off his face again and tried to study how intense the snowfall was. Flakes were slowly drifting down. Flakes were light. Weather could go either way—could be a freezing cold or, hopefully, go away.

18

He pulled the canvas cover over both of their heads. It protected the pallet and its two occupants from wet weather. Ceci's even breathing said she was asleep. He listened to it and thought over the day's trials. Just a day's travel from the canyon, and already tragedy had struck.

All they needed to add to their problems was a bear attack. He drifted off to sleep to the soft sound of Cecile's breathing.

The soft snowfall had not lessened during the night. A foot of snow accumulated.

Candy woke hearing camp noise. Lance dropped a load of wood on the simmering coals of the night's fire. He tossed some smaller sticks on the coals, and soon the fire recovered. He threw some larger logs on it and went in search of more wood.

She hadn't had much sleep. There was a friendship growing with Little Bear. She had looked forward to having him join her after the camp quieted down. She had planned to put their bedrolls away from the light of the campfire, but Bear had told her about the cave and requested she bed down close to the fire.

She had heard him tell Lance and Juan about the cave and gave them orders to share night watch.

Bear stretched out beside Candy for a few hours. Glancy awakened around three in the morning. The drug was wearing off, and the pain in the broken leg was intense. Lou was up and down with the kid. He prepared another cup of weak coffee laced with whiskey and a small sprinkle of sleeping powder.

The disturbance by Lou working about the fire to warm the kid's drink woke both Candy and Bear. He decided to get up and take over the watch. When Juan and Lance were relieved of duty, they also bedded down close to the fire. Their tired snores ended her sleep.

She spent the last couple of hours of rest trying to decide what she was going to do once they reached Janos. She had lost her bartender to the spreading rumors of a civil war. Several of her girls had taken the stage out, heading to the East to earn a better living in the camps that followed the soldiers.

She could hang in there. She could hire some girls from Mexico. The building belonged to her, and she was heavily stocked with whiskey and wine. She could pack up the booze and go to the East herself, but that would be a huge expense.

Janos was a small town. She had struggled to build up her saloon business there. She was not rich enough to just pack up and go elsewhere. She was tired. This trip to help Grady had sounded like a break from the tedious running of a saloon. It had turned into the trip from hell.

Candy had not anticipated run-ins with outlaws, Indians, flying bullets, Indians scalping the outlaws. In addition to dealing with a couple of invalids, there was now a kid to care for. Lou had that job, but she had evidently inherited the job of camp cook. Between cooking, taking care of Grady and Ceci, and driving a wagon, she had little time to care for herself.

She knew it wasn't fair to resent Little Miss Muffet, but she did. She resented the concern Grady lavished on the girl. She had, early in his illness, realized a romantic closeness with Grady was out of the question. They had formed a friendship. Out of that friendship and concern for his health, she had tackled this trip.

So far all she had to show for her concern were blisters on her hands and feet, stiff muscles, and several large bruises. What she really looked forward to was her bathtub at the saloon. The tub was a luxury she had splurged on. It was ordered from an outfit back east and had taken four months to be delivered by western freighters.

She stretched her arms up, out of the fur cover, and straightened her legs. She didn't have to test for stiff joints and muscles. They screamed, "Here we are!" Her body had been in this condition for days. She groaned. Sick Ceci, weak Grady, injured Glancy. Gimpy Lou in charge of Glancy and driving the grain wagon. Juan and Lance in charge of the remuda and herd. Bear was everywhere, in charge of everyone because Grady was down.

The thought of Little Bear brought a smile to her lips. He was the one good thing this trip had given her. A decent, handsome man liked her! As least

21

for the duration of this trip, he was hers. She decided to enjoy her one pleasure while she could and worry about her next step once they reached Janos.

She forced her muscles to work, climbed out of her bedroll, and slowly made her morning trip to the woods. When she returned, she stopped at the supply wagon and quietly tried to find the coffee. It would have to be oatmeal again. Sometime during the day, she would have to get herself and the supplies organized. They all needed a decent meal.

Little Bear saw that Candy was up putting the coffeepot onto heat. He walked over to the grain wagon and grabbed a couple of shovels. Getting Lance's attention, he tossed him a shovel and motioned him to follow.

Juan saw them leave. He rolled over, closed his eyes, and dozed. Breakfast would be ready soon, and then he would have to get up. His first chore would be to check the herd.

Bear slid into the ravine and approached the cave-in cautiously. He wasn't really expecting a bear. Given all the commotion of the day before that created the closure of the cave, it surely would have scared any animals away. Still, there were always snakes.

Working together, Bear and Lance soon had the loose dirt cleared from the opening. It was dark inside the cave. Bear sent Lance to get some branches and light one at the campfire.

When Lance returned, they took it slow. Bear went first while holding the burning branch with Lance following carrying the extra branches in case they needed them. They found the cave was quite large. Bear was watching where he put his feet.

Lance whispered, "Hey, Bear, look at the drawings on the walls."

Bear lifted the flare and saw the drawings carved into the stone. They were Indian symbols. These carvings were old. Centuries possibly. Bear's grandfather, who was a Navajo, had schooled him in much of his culture, including their Athabaskan ancestors of the Navajo and Apache. The symbols on the walls resembled many of those still practiced by his people. It told a story, but there were some symbols he didn't recognize.

His flame was about to go out. Lance touched a branch to the fire, and when it caught, Bear pulled his eyes away from the symbols and studied the rest of the cave. There were scattered bones from human skeletons that had been disturbed by animals, proving that at times animals used the cave. He used his foot to move aside some bones. He was uncomfortable walking on bones that might represent dead ancestors. He mumbled, "Forgive me, Grandfather."

He raised the branch. Enough light shone for him to see a pile of things stacked against the back wall of the cave. He moved the branch back and forth across the wall, and at times a shimmer sparkled and disappeared as the light from the flare passed over it. He lifted the flame to expose the ceiling. The occasional sparkle repeated itself.

Lance, impatient, moved past Bear and knelt down by the pile. It was clothes thrown down in a heap. Careful not to startle rodents or snakes that might hide there, he used one of the branches and stirred the pile. Only a stinkbug, large in size, scampered across the cave floor. Using the branch, he picked up a garment and lifted it toward the burning branch light.

"Hey, look at this, Bear. It looks like part of a uniform." Lance held it so Bear could see it.

Taking his eyes off the walls, Bear moved closer and watched Lance drop the object to the side and pick up another rag that turned out to be a pair of soldier's pants.

Bear said, "Looks like more than one. Try to count them."

Lance kept pulling pieces out until he was sure this was the clothing of three soldiers. The clothes had been dumped on three army saddles and bridles. An army saddlebag was still attached to one of the saddles. They could see *Army* engraved in the leather.

Bear put his hand on Lance's shoulder and spoke softly, "We've got to get out of here. Loosen that saddlebag. Hand it here and put everything else exactly as we found it, and hurry up."

He studied the symbols carved into the rocks. He spoke as he moved from one drawing to the next. "Some I do not recognize. Which tells me my ancient grandfathers were here. 'The Deni' (the People) are hanging upside down—it is the symbol for death. If it were a horse upside down, it would be a dead horse. This a warning for any Deni, which means us."

He pointed to another symbol. "That's an enclosure. It means a place for a special ceremonial event."

Bear hesitated for a moment at the next symbol. He swallowed and whispered, "That's the symbol for the Great Spirit. The one under it means protection."

He looked at Lance and said, "This cave is sacred ground, and the Great Spirit protects it."

Lance nodded he understood. Bear turned back to the wall and said, "I'm not sure about this one. I know the circle is the sun and the lines around it represent the north, south, east, and west. I don't know why the star. My guess is it means night and day."

He continued to the last symbol. "The opposing arrows mean war. Well, I guess that's clear. We are standing on sacred ground protected by the Great Spirit, night and day. If found here, we are dead!"

As they left the cave, Bear handed a shovel to Lance. Bear picked up the other one and began to shovel back the dirt that they had just removed from the cave entrance. As he worked, he talked.

"The bones were too old to be soldiers. Probably ancient tribal chiefs. We just stumbled on sacred ground. We've got to get out of here." His hurried shoveling encouraged Lance to work steady beside him.

They piled the dirt to look like the horse had caved it in. Lance put out the fire and shoveled dirt over the ashes. His voice trembled as he said, "That was scary. What about the soldiers?"

Bear used a branch and swept it over all the footprints as he replied, "That ought to do it. Indians should be in their tepees, waiting out this weather. The snow should cover some of our tracks. We want them to believe the horse hid the cave. The soldiers' bodies were not important to the Indians. Hungry animals soon devour a body left in the wilderness. Uniforms left on them would identify them as army. With no identification, bodies can be anyone. The Indians took their possessions and probably their scalps. The clothes and tack were hidden here, the scalps will be hanging on their staffs."

Bear grabbed up the army saddlebag and said, "Let's get out of here."

Breakfast was ready. Lou was getting a bowl of oatmeal for Glancy. He doctored it with honey. He made a weak cup of coffee laced with a knockout powder. He saw Bear watching him and said, "We ain't hardly got this herd on the road. We still got at least three days to get off this mountain. Kid's in a lot of pain—best he sleeps through it."

Bear nodded his agreement. He walked as far as Candy's wagon with Lou. He stopped by Grady and saw that Ceci was awake. Grady was spooning oatmeal in her mouth. She smiled at Bear between bites.

He smiled back at her and spoke to Grady, "Cave, Indian hideout. Used many years. Symbols on wall. Soldiers' uniforms hidden there. Serious business this cave. We need to get away from it. They could be watching us. We been lucky so far we haven't lost our scalps. I brought out this army saddlebag. It might have orders or some way to identify those three men." He handed the bag to Grady. Grady put the saddlebag in a corner and pulled the canvas windbreaker over it to keep it dry.

Grady said, "When we get a break and are stopped, I'll take a look at it."

Bear stood for a moment thinking and said, "Boss, there're gold streaks showing all over the wall and ceiling. They glitter when the light hits them. There's one symbol I wasn't sure about. It was the sun with the star in it. The sun could represent the gold, and the stars mean night and day."

Grady took a deep breath and said, "I don't know about you, Bear, but I'm really fond of my scalp. If you are right, we'd better get a move on. The tribe that protects that cave finds out we were even near it, then we aren't safe. I know they wouldn't think twice about killing us to keep it secret. What about Lance? Did he notice?"

Bear shook his head. "I don't think so. I didn't point it out. He's a bright young man though."

"Let's get the hell out of here." Grady slid down and drew the windbreaker over his head. His hair was snow damp. Cecile had drifted off to sleep.

Bear saw Lance had saddled his horse for him. He got a tin bowl and filled it with oatmeal. He gave Candy a hug and without words climbed on his horse. While eating he headed down the trail to help move the herd.

They worked steadily all day. The small herd of Herefords and the loosely hobbled remuda horses were beginning to settle into the routine. They quit scattering when they were halted. By the day's end, they had settled into a calm holding pattern and waited patiently while the men tied onto the wagons and lowered them down to the waiting herd. Then the men moved the cattle and horses down the mountain.

It was tedious work, and Deadly was irritated. His tail was switching. He did his job. Halted the herd and worked to keep them bunched until the wagons caught up. By the end of the day, when Grady ordered him to "bed them down," he did so gladly and left the herd in Trumpeter's charge, while he visited the wagons.

Deadly found Grady sitting on a log by the night's campfire. Lance had built the fire a short distance from Candy's wagon. Juan had carried Cecile and settled her on a blanket where she could sit up and lean against the log Grady sat on.

Deadly took his place behind Grady. He closed his eyes and chewed his cud. He would relax and wait for his biscuit. Enjoy the comfort of the fire and time spent with his friend.

When he returned to the herd, he would be on duty again. Many dangers could disturb the small herd during the dark of night. Night noises could frighten them, cause a stampede, a runaway herd. Wild animals, the banging of pots and pans, a sudden storm with lightning and thunder were all a threat. A herd of cattle or horses were like small children, afraid of the sounds in the dark.

Deadly was a veteran of many trail drives. Just because this herd was small, they were still cattle, and because they were smaller in size, probably feared predators more than the larger range cattle.

Grady gave Deadly his biscuits. He stood and scratched the hard bone between the horns. He moved along the big bull's backbone, scratching, and reached the rump, Deadly's favorite scratching spot, a place where he could not reach. As Grady scratched his rump Deadly began to sway his hind end showing his pleasure. Satisfied that he had given Deadly enough attention Grady gave him a final pat on his shoulders. Time to go back to work.

He spent most of his night circling the herd. Touching noses. Herding a stray back to the safety of the herd. Assuring the herd he was taking care of them. A few were still grazing. Many stood with closed eyes, chewing their cuds. Grass secured in the pockets of their cheeks to be made more digestible, a soothing activity before bedding down.

Some had already settled to the ground. The old Hereford bull Trumpeter was down. His legs were folded under him. His eyes were closed, and he was also chewing his cud. The old bull suffered from age. His entire body was muscle sore from the downhill travel, especially his legs from constantly braking his downhill descent.

Soon one of the drovers would bring him his evening feed. A portion of dried oats and a small serving of hay. He was always too tired to graze. He didn't get up to eat. He took turns eating and resting.

Deadly stood near him and discouraged any of the hungry cows from stealing Trumpeter's feed. Reginald was the worst grain thief. With only one eye—the other gouged out in a fight with a vicious range bull—he sometimes didn't see Deadly standing by. A ball-tipped horn would remind Reginald that Deadly was on guard.

Candy provided Grady with a small pail of warm water. He carefully washed Ceci's face and hands. He used the water and washed his hands. They smelled a little like longhorn bull. Juan carried her back, and Grady helped settle her under the protection of the covers.

Leaving the canyon both of them were cocooned under a pile of furs and canvas, with their heads under the canvas, as a shelter from the falling snow. Grady and Cecile were both recovering from serious ailments. Both tired easily and napped often. A rut and the jolts of the wagon would wake them. Sometimes the jar was violent. The wagon running to the end of the lariats that kept the wagon from running away came to a sudden halt with a bang.

Scary, a runaway imagined. Thumping hearts needed to settle down. Grady was constantly pulling Cecile close to him to keep her from slamming into the wagon seat where Candy was struggling with the team.

They comforted each other, sharing childhood stories, getting acquainted. They had not had much time to get to know each other on the active trail drive. Now with the restricted circumstance of illness, they talked to relieve boredom and the secret desire of each to know more about the other.

This was the end of the second day on the downhill trail. Candy had outdone herself. She had managed to organize the supplies whenever her wagon waited its turn to move down the trail.

She had a pot of small white beans, with hunks of potatoes floating in them. There was a pan of flour-dusted fried beef strips and a skillet of beef gravy and pan bread. Each got a small serving from a jar of stewed tomatoes.

Quiet filled the air as everyone filled their hungry bellies. Juan and Lance took turns keeping an eye on the cattle and horse herds while they enjoyed the great meal. Lou having settled Glancy grabbed his tin and fed himself.

Little Bear had been searching for burnable wood. He had taken his shirt off to work with his ax to turn dead tree limbs into usable fire logs. Candy took the opportunity to quietly admire his lean, muscular build enhanced by the sheen of sweat from his hard work. He was a beautiful specimen of a man, she thought to herself.

Bear put his shirt back on for dinner. Added his sheepskin vest and grabbed his tin plate and filled it.

Candy added coffee grounds to the metal coffeepot with water. She set it on the grate that rested on some boulders. She tossed a couple of logs into the fire under the grate. It wouldn't take long for it to come to a boil.

She filled her tin and sat beside Bear. All was quiet except for sounds of hungry people enjoying a great meal.

Grady fed Cecile from his tin. He cut the meat into small pieces. Her throat was still sore, and she coughed some. She did better with the beans and potatoes mashed with gravy added. This gruel slid down her throat easily.

When she had enough, she laid her head on Grady's shoulder and watched her crew. They were all filling empty stomachs. This was her crew. It was strange to remember. This was her herd and crew.

She was so weak, so ill. It was strange—she felt so worthless. They all looked tired. They were all working so hard taking care of her and her herd. Grady, still recovering himself, was caring for her. They had all become dear to her, even the newcomers, Candy and Lance. Glancy also, but she had hardly met the boy before his injury. Like her, he was now confined to a wagon.

When Ceci quit eating and laid her head on his shoulder, Grady fed himself. Having been ill for so long, being fed only gruels and soup, he was really enjoying tasting the red meat, beans, and potatoes.

As they finished eating, Candy poured coffee for all. Grady shared his cup with Cecile. The warm fluid felt good on her sore throat.

Grady broke the silence. "How's the kid?"

Lou answered, "Pretty bad. Wagon bouncing keeps him unsettled. I've kept him drugged, but his pain is severe. It's not just the broken bone. There was a lot of skin and muscle damage. He's running a low fever— nothing to worry about yet. I'm going to try to get some mashed-up dinner down him. Then I'll drug him again."

Grady shook his head and said, "We're a sorry bunch. Half of us need a hospital. I'm sorry you're all carryin' the load."

Old Lou said, "It is what it is. You been taking care of some of us for years so let us look after you, you've earned it. You're looking a lot better tonight. You'll be on your feet in no time."

"Thanks, Lou. I'm feeling a lot better, but I think it's because we are all back in charge of our lives. Thanks to all of you—a timely rescue." Grady looked each in the eyes.

They accepted the thanks. Candy refilled coffee cups and, not directing the question to anyone in particular, said, "You think we'll make it to Janos in two more days?"

Grady shook his head and said, "I have no idea. I was out of my head on the way back to you, and we were going uphill, wagons loaded on the trail back up to the canyon. Had to take longer going up, but it's been mighty stressful going down. I can't tell if we're going faster or slower. What do you think, Juan?"

Juan thought a moment, took a sip of his coffee, and said, "I'm planning on making it in two days, but the herd's slowing us down. It's taking a lot of our time to keep both the horses and the herd controlled. Ordinarily downhill would go faster, but doing the work of moving the herd and then the wagons, I'm just not sure."

Cecile had a fit of coughing. Grady asked Juan, "Can you take her back to the wagon? This is her first outing. She's got to be exhausted."

Juan got right up and, with Bear's help, got her in his arms. He made a trip to a tree and gave her time to relieve herself.

Grady made his own way back to the wagon and helped Juan move her into place under the warm covers.

Candy came with another warm compress treated with Mentholatum. She opened Ceci's blouse, removed the old compress, and placed the warm compress on Ceci's chest. She refastened the blouse. Cecile tried to thank her, but another coughing fit stopped her. Candy patted her shoulder and went back to clean up the supper mess.

Lou fixed a bowl of gruel and fed Glancy. The boy was groggy from all the drugs, but surprisingly he was hungry. He groaned or caught his breath every time he tried to move. He ate until he was comfortable. He downed some coffee with both some whiskey and a little of the drug. Lou was aware they were running out. Whiskey might end up being all they had left to get the boy to the doctor.

Lou was satisfied. The boy had eaten. Best medicine for him, strength to fight the pain. Lou lit a cigarette, sat on the tailgate of the grain wagon, and studied the falling snow. It had slowed. The storm waging on the mountaintop was behind them. He took some time to himself to think of his dead son. Murdered by the thieves they had caught and were trying to bring to the law. His heart was broken, and he felt so lost. Some tears leaked from Lou's eyes.

He'd be damned if he was going to lose this young man under his care. He didn't want to see another mother or father go through the pain he was experiencing. Ain't no parent should ever have to go through what he was enduring.

Candy had flapjacks, pure cane syrup, and hot coffee for breakfast. They were spending another day going down the mountain. The effort was rigorous and demanding; everyone needed energy to endure the day.

The day's travel was much the same as the day before. She had a pot of stew meat and potatoes cut up ready to go on the campfire for dinner with biscuits and honey.

The snow ceased about midday. The wagons were moving easier over dirt than snow.

All breathed a sigh of relief. It was the end, hopefully, of damp clothes and frozen trails. Camp atmosphere was happy for the first time that night.

They were getting in a routine. The next morning they got things together quickly. Candy sped up breakfast by making oatmeal and biscuits. They were all hoping to reach the valley floor by evening and Janos sometime the next day.

The night before, Glancy had wakened with a high fever. Lou had removed the bandages and braces to find a faint odor of infection. He had washed the wound out with more of Candy's stock of whiskey. Cut some fresh limbs to keep the leg steady and wrapped it again. Using the last of the sleeping powder, added to warm water, laced with honey, Glancy was still knocked out as breakfast was hurried and the wagons were moving downhill.

Once they were under way, Grady spent some time walking about on weak legs. Too much downtime. He knew he had to get more physical exercise. He had weeks of inactivity to overcome.

Cecile seemed better. She was coughing less and sat up whenever the wagons were on hold. During the wagon stops, Candy visited with Grady and Ceci. With Ceci able to communicate more easily, Candy could see why Grady was so taken with her. Candy had to agree that Cecile McNamara was a very special lady.

In the afternoon the downhill journey became more difficult than the previous days. There were several steep areas with large boulders and rocks that had to be negotiated very carefully. The travel was terrifying for Candy, and it took all of her attention to keep her matched black team of horses on their feet.

The accident happened late in the day. Everyone was tired, including the horses and the herd. Juan, Lance and Bear had already lowered the grain wagon down to the herd. They had just tied their lariats to the back of Candy's wagon.

Candy had taken off her brakes, and lifting her reins, slapped them on the backs of the team to let them know they could move on. The men's lariats had drawn taut, and the wagon was pulling hard to go rushing downhill when Juan's lariat tied to the right side broke.

Bear's rope was tied to the left side of the axle. Lance had his rope tied close to the middle under the tailgate. He was the swing rope. It was his job to keep the wagon going wherever the trail went.

The right side of the wagon loosed suddenly and swung the right front end into the right black gelding. Spooked, he sprang forward dragging his teammate, causing the wagon to swing and hit him again. The downhill momentum pulled the rope Lance had wrapped around his saddle horn and held in his left hand. The braided lariat tore up the palm of his hand and caused him to let go. Bear was the only one still in control of the wagon.

Bear was instantly aware of what had happened. He was yelling "whoa!" and at the same time urging his horse to hold. His horse stopped and braced his legs. The weight of the wagon and the added panic of Candy's team were pulling rider and horse down the hill. Bear kept his head and was trying to get in control.

Candy lost one of her reins and was hanging on to the wagon seat. Her feet were braced against the front of the wagon.

The team and wagon were in a downhill runaway. The one rope was stretched tight by Bear, causing the wagon to drag crookedly, plunging to the right. The gelding barely dodged a large boulder. The wagon crashed into the huge rock. A loud crack, and the front right wheel splintered into kindling, and the nose of the wagon on the right front plowed into the dirt. It slowed the downward momentum, and the back right wheel slammed against the boulder and halted.

The sudden halt threw Candy from the wagon seat. She landed on a shoulder beside her left gelding. The sudden stop had thrown him to his knees, and he was struggling to get up.

Bear, observing from behind, calculated the next disaster coming would be Candy rolling under the horse's hooves without quick action.

With his heart in his throat he yelled to Juan and Lance, "Get control of the horses. Get their heads." The two men obeyed.

Bear swung off his horse, patted his neck, and told the paint horse to hold. He ran to Candy, grabbed her under her arms, and pulled her away from the team and wagon. She screamed at the movement. The shoulder was damaged. He didn't have time to investigate. He hurried to the team and unhooked them from the wagon.

Lance moved the team to some close trees and tied them. He spent a few moments calming them and inspected for injuries. There was no blood or open wounds. But he bet that right gelding would be plenty sore in the rear from the wagon's assault. He went to help Bear and Juan jam some rocks about the left wheels. The right side wasn't going anywhere.

Bear went to Candy. "I'm sorry, hon. Let me take a look." Carefully he unbuttoned her blouse and slid it slowly off her shoulder. It was totally dislocated and under the collarbones. Tears were running down her face. Just moving the blouse had really hurt. He carefully pulled the shirt up. He didn't button it.

She wiped the tears away with her good arm and said, "Go help Grady and Ceci. I'll be all right."

Grady and Cecile had been thrown forward into the wagon seat and then slammed into it again when the wheel smashed and the wagon plowed into the ground. At the first awareness of trouble, Grady pulled her tight against himself. He prevented her from hitting the back of the wagon seat, but his head, already damaged and trying to recover from a concussion, slammed into it twice.

He tried to shift Cecile toward the tailgate when a dizzy spell hit him, and his head ached so bad that he sat back and closed his eyes. Bear and Juan took over. Juan pulled the canvas cover off and put it on the ground a short distance from the wagon and the boulder that had stopped it. Bear gathered Cecile up and carefully deposited her on the canvas.

Grady was trying to move to the tailgate; every move he made slammed him with dizziness and nausea. Bear could see he was hurt pretty bad. There was a gash on the right side of his head. It was bleeding. Bear helped him reach the tailgate and then to the canvas. He sat by Cecile and lay back with a groan.

Bear went back to Candy. He helped her stand, and with one arm around her waist, careful not to touch her shoulder, he helped her settle to the canvas by Grady and Cecile.

Bear stood back and looked over the people and shattered wagon. The near catastrophe seemed to be over. He breathed a sigh of relief and decided what had to be done first. He had to get these people down the mountain to the other wagon.

Grady opened his eyes in a tight squint, looked at Candy, and said, "Candy, are you all right?"

"Hell no! That scared me shitless, and I've broken my shoulder. It hurts like hell." She was holding her arm against her chest to keep from moving it.

Grady let out a shaky laugh. "That's my Candy." Her coarse language told him she might be hurt and scared but she was a fighter.

Cecile saw the streak of blood running down Grady's head. "You're bleeding!" she said and tried to sit up.

Not wanting to stress or alarm her Grady reached over, grabbed her arm, and stopped her from sitting up. "Be still. It's just a small bang. Let's all just relax and figure out what we do next. Bear, you got any ideas?"

Lance, Juan, and Bear gathered around the three on the ground. They were all gradually calming down. Lance had wrapped his rope-burned hand in his bandana. Juan was holding the broken end of his lariat, the rotten break that had created this accident.

Bear studied the two men and said, "It's a good thing Lou was already down to the herd. Lance, your hand hurts. How bad?"

"Pretty bad, but it's just a rope burn. I'll put some ointment on it when we get to the grain wagon." He was afraid the hand was pretty torn up from the rough-braided lariat, but this wasn't the time to complain too much.

"Take your horse and go tell Lou what's holding us up. We should have caught up by now and they'll be worryin'."

"Yes, sir. I gather we're not going on any further today? I'll get some wood and get a fire started. Lou can put some kind of dinner together." He smiled and waited for further orders.

Bear returned the smile. "OK, tell Lou to fix a couple of pallets close to the camp. Juan and I will be right behind you with Grady and Miss Ceci."

Lance was mounted and down the mountain as Bear turned to Candy and said, "I hate to leave you here by yourself. I'll be right back for you. We're going to have a half-dozen trips back and forth to clean out the wagon and bring the horses down. You're next. Can you handle the wait by yourself?"

She said, "Leave me your pistol. I don't want to be wolf bait." She cringed when she released her bad arm and took the pistol he handed her.

He looked into her eyes and saw the pain in them. "I'll be right back. Don't move. You hear me? Don't move."

"OK, boss, I'm in pain here. You're wasting time. Go!" She smiled weakly.

He bent over, avoided touching her shoulder, and gave her a gentle kiss. Seeing her get tossed from the wagon and then nearly stomped by a horse had scared Bear. The accident made him realize that his feelings for this sharp-tongued, funny lady had definitely deepened beyond friendship.

Bear hoisted Cecile on Juan's horse behind him. She wrapped her arms around the old gentleman and she laid her head on his back.

Grady sat up slowly to keep the dizziness controlled. He spoke to Cecile, "Are you going to be all right?"

Ceci said, "I can do this. You take care of yourself."

Grady and Bear watched as Juan and Cecile started down. Juan was walking his horse slowly, but they were soon out of sight. Bear turned to Grady. "Think you can get in the saddle?"

Grady gave a weak smile and said, "Guess I'll have to. Don't care to walk it."

Bear went to get his horse. He was glad he had chosen his paint gelding that morning for the day's work. The paint was trained to carry anything Bear loaded on him. It would be a job to get Grady in the saddle. He ground tied the paint close and helped Grady stand. He teetered for a moment and, taking Bear's arm, steadied himself. He took the two steps to put himself in position to mount. Many, many years of climbing into a saddle came to his aid. He reached for the horn with his left hand and lifted his left foot to the stirrup. The leg was weak and missed and hit the ground. Grady laid his head on the saddle and waved Bear back.

Bear had anticipated Grady's weakness. He stopped and waited for Grady to resume his effort. Grady stood and turned the stirrup so the boot could slide into it, and with a desperate lift, his right hand went to the back of the saddle. It was an effort, but the boot hit the stirrup. He threw his right leg over the horse and settled himself in the saddle. He made it, and it felt good, his first time on a horse in weeks of illness. It would have been more enjoyable if he weren't so dizzy, which made him nauseous.

Grady removed his boot from the left stirrup and Bear used it and swung up behind him.

Grady gathered up the reins and gave the paint a small kick. The ride down the mountain seemed long because the horse carrying two robust men was not as surefooted. They took their time and let the horse test each step.

They reached camp not far behind Juan. They found Cecile on a blanket a safe distance from the fire. Lance had collected firewood and started the fire. He helped Lou find the meat for a stew and put water on for coffee.

Bear unloaded Grady by Cecile and helped him lie down. She threw part of her bedroll cover over him, and this time she ran her arm under and around his neck and settled his head on her shoulder.

Bear mounted his horse and headed back uphill to collect Candy. Lance followed to bring the black geldings down. Juan had gone to check on the herd.

It felt really good, his head resting on Cecile's shoulder, but he knew it was too much weight so he waited for his head to settle down and then rose up on one elbow and shifted her into his arms. He brushed a curl of black hair out of her face and studied her closed eyes. She was pale, worry lines on her forehead. He thought she was asleep, but in a hoarse voice she said, "I guess this is one of those jams?"

He smiled, recalling the conversation they had after they had captured six outlaws and had them tied to a wagon. They had many miles yet to drive the herd. Adding six outlaws was like adding a load of nitroglycerin. She had said then, "This is a real jam." And he had answered, "Yes it's a big hell of a jam!"

He took her small hand in his. "Today could have gone a lot worse than it did."

Cecile answered, "Well, it scared me pretty bad. Now I have a huge headache added to a sore throat, and my chest hurts. Are you all right? I heard you hit that wagon seat a couple of times." She opened her eyes.

Grady raised her hand to his lips and kissed it. "I know exactly how you feel. It scared me bad also. The head banging didn't help my concussion, but I'm glad we're both alive. We almost ended up in the valley below." He kissed her hand again and tucked the covers under her chin.

Old Lou came over with a cup of coffee. "I put some honey in it. We're out of drugs. I'll have some meat-and-potato stew ready soon. Anything I can do for you?"

"Thanks, Lou. We'll get this down. I think we'll close our eyes and try to relax and recover our bravery. This was pretty scary." Grady helped Cecile sit up and held the cup for her so she could sip the warm, sweet drink.

Lou disappeared behind the grain wagon. Grady heard him talk to Glancy. The boy answered, but his voice was too low to hear. Cecile lay back down, closed her eyes, and was quickly asleep. Grady downed the rest of the drink, set the cup aside, and joined her.

Bear and Lance headed back up the mountain. They let their horses choose their speed, it was more important to prevent any more accidents.

Lance went directly to the black geldings, untied them, and climbed back in his saddle. Man, did his hand hurt. Blood had soaked the bandana. The geldings were still nervous. They pulled against the ties that held them together. He would have to use his good hand to manage them. He wrapped his horse's reins around the saddle horn and prayed they would all make it safe down to the camp.

Bear tied his horse and went to Candy. He felt like crying himself when he saw tears rolling down her cheeks. Her mouth was set, teeth gritted.

She was slumped forward, resting herself with her good arm braced on her knee.

He was afraid to touch her. He knelt down on one knee and said, "You are in way more pain than the shoulder. What hurts?"

She tried to smile. It came out as a grimace, "You're wrong, it's just the shoulder. I had to relieve myself. Have you ever tried to do that job with one arm?"

"I told you not to move," he growled.

"Nature called, I answered." Another tear rolled down her cheek.

"Well, I'm afraid to move you now. You are in such pain—it's not going to be a picnic getting you on the horse." He ran his fingers through his thick black hair and stood up.

She struggled to raise herself back upright, once again holding the injured arm against her chest.

"I can do it. I can jerk that arm back in place, but it will hurt like hell. You will probably pass out. It could take hours for you to come to. Even then we still have to get you on the horse. I wanted to get you down to camp so Old Lou could help me. We could give you a drug and make setting it easier. Less painful." He knelt back down and looked into her pain-filled eyes.

She said, "I'd rather make the trip now. My broken wagon is depressing and it's getting dark. And this rock is hard." She tried to slide forward off the rock. No hands and arms to help herself. "Help me get on the horse."

Bear slid his arm around her waist and tried to move her slowly off the boulder and onto her feet. Then he swung her into his arms and carried her to where his horse was tied.

"Now this is going to take some doing. I'm going to lift your legs up. Try to swing your right leg over the horn onto the saddle. Then I'll shift and push your body upright into the saddle. "Think you can do it?"

"Yes, I'll try," she said through clinched teeth.

Bear talked to his horse, thankful, once again, he was riding his own paint horse. He spoke quietly. "Whoa boy, good horse. Easy now." He raised her hips and legs up.

She lifted her right leg over the horn and onto the saddle. He used both hands at her waist and moved her upright on the saddle. She was whimpering. He had tried to avoid her arms and shoulder. He asked, "Are you all right?"

"Hell no! Will you please get me out of here!"

He swung up behind her and with one arm around her waist, kissed the top of her head, gathered up the reins, and guided the paint down the mountain.

That late afternoon in camp was a quiet one—that is, anyone awake was silent, but when Candy arrived in camp, her husky voice raised in discomfort, it awoke those who had drifted off.

Bear got her off the horse and deposited her on the blanket by Grady and Cecile. Lou, Lance, and Juan gathered around to see how she was.

Bear said, "Lou, her shoulder is totally out of the socket, under the collarbone. She's going to need some knockout powder now. We need to give it time to work."

Lou answered, "Sorry, Bear, drug's all gone. I used it on the kid."

"Well, darn," Candy said. "Get me some whiskey. I packed plenty. It's on the grain wagon somewhere." Lance went to look for it and soon joined them with a full bottle.

Grady said, "Get us some cups. I think we could all use it tonight."

Cups were passed around, and even young Lance sipped his share.

While the crew sipped, Candy chugged. After three refills, she was slurring her words. She was getting pretty free of pain. She said, "Lesh gi' dish done."

Bear had to turn his head and try to stuff down a chuckle at her inebriation. It was a slight reprieve from the serious gravity of the situation.

Lance wrapped his arms around her. Pinning her good arm, Bear raised her injured arm. Rotated the shoulder and pulled. Candy screamed. Everyone heard the pop as it settled into place.

She whimpered. Under her breath she said, "Oh dear, oh shit, oh crap, that hurt. Give me another shot of wishkey."

Lou poured. It disappeared down her throat. She dropped the cup and fell back on the blanket.

Old Lou fetched a bedroll, and Grady helped him spread it over her. Lou said, "I needed to tape that arm to her chest to keep her from moving it for a few days. Oh well, she needs the sleep more. I'll do it in the morning.

Stew's warm; biscuits are done. Deadly should be showing up. He smells em, ya' know."

Lou was right. They were all getting their plates full when the big bull entered the light of the campfire. Grady put a small serving of stew in a cup for Cecile. She sat up and fed herself. He loaded his bowl with stew and grabbed a tin. Filled it with his two biscuits, another for Cecile, and two for Deadly. He honeyed hers. Deadly settled behind Grady as was his habit and enjoyed his biscuits and time with his people, especially Grady.

Grady, Bear, Juan, Lance, and Old Lou cleaned out the stewpot. They sat and rolled smokes. Bear took out his clay pipe. They smoked quietly for a while. Lance closed his eyes. Not yet a smoker, he rested, as cigarettes fell to the ground and were mashed out. Grady spoke, "Well now, hasn't this been a day?"

No one answered, but all nodded in agreement.

Grady continued, "What's the order for tomorrow?"

Bear knocked the ashes out of his pipe and put it away. "We need to empty Candy's wagon and load everything on the grain wagon. That includes all the invalids." He smiled to soften those words.

Grady smiled. He looked skyward and said, "It's quit snowing. I hadn't even noticed."

They all studied the still air. Juan drew in a deep breath and said, "The air's even a little warmer."

Grady said, "I guess we have to leave Candy's wagon here."

Bear answered, "Two wheels destroyed. No way can we repair them. It's important to get these sick people off this mountain."

Lance opened his eyes and said, "I can come back with a couple of wheels and a team and get it back to her. In the spring I can get Grady's grub wagon and the bull carrier, if someone hasn't stolen them or used them for firewood. I don't trust those Indians." He smiled at Bear.

Bear smiled back, no slur intended. He saw Lance still had the bandana around his hand and said to Old Lou, "Lance needs that hand looked at."

Lou rose wearily and said, "Come on, kid, let's have a look." They both headed to the grain wagon. Lou was talking under his breath. "If this keeps up, we're not going to have any medicine to doctor with."

As if on cue, they all scattered. Juan made a last trip to check the herd.

The following day was uneventful. The herd traveled obediently, and in the early afternoon a few miles from town, the weary group was met by Cecile's vaqueros who had arrived in Janos, while Juan was on the trek to fetch Cecile to help on the final leg of the journey.

The weary and banged-up travelers were more than happy for the help. Juan gave orders to his vaqueros, and they took over bringing the herd into town.

The herd stayed bunched and did not bolt as spectators lined the street. Cecile's Arabians, on the other hand, knew they were on display and decided to show off their breed by prancing and cutting up all the way to the stockyard. Lance had been smart to tie them on a lead, as they put on a lively exhibition of their fiery spirits.

It was a sorry crew that followed the herd through town. Candy had ridden on the grain-wagon seat with Lou. She pointed out the doctor's house, which also was his office. Bear dismounted and carried Glancy in and put him on a bed at the doctor's request. Lou stayed with the boy and helped the doctor remove the makeshift bandages.

Juan had ridden on with his men to see that the herd was settled. Bear drove the grain wagon another block and parked in front of Candy's saloon. He put on the brakes, climbed down, and lifted his arms to help her down.

He held her for a moment, kissed her softly, and said, "Doc will be over after he gets Glancy cleaned up and settled."

At that moment Della, one of Candy's working girls, came out of the saloon doors and hurried down the stairs. She was going to hug Candy but saw the bandaged arm and stood ringing her hands. Excited, she said, "Oh my gosh, were you shot?"

Candy answered, "No, just dislocated my shoulder. I sure am glad to see you. I figured all my girls would be gone."

"No, ma'am," Della said. "I was afraid to leave the saloon alone. Some of the drifters in town tried to steal the whiskey. I threatened to shoot them with the shotgun. I've kept the doors locked. I'm so blessed you're back. I was really getting scared something had happened to you. I didn't know how long I could hold thieves off. And I don't mind tellin' you I was also scared to death being alone."

Candy, smiling through her pain, used one arm to hug her. "Good girl. Thank you. I'm glad you were not hurt. You could have been injured protecting my building. I owe you a lot for that."

Taking Della's hand, she walked her to the back of the wagon, where Grady and Cecile had sat up and were waiting patiently.

Candy said, "You remember Grady, don't ya?"

Della nodded and seeing the bandage on his head said, "Mr. Grady, what happened to your head?"

He answered, "Got caught in the same wagon accident Candy did."

Candy turned to Cecile and said, "This lady is Grace Cecile McNamara. She's the lady we went to rescue. Miss Cecile, this is Della Rankin. I'm going to turn you over to her if agreeable with you. She will help you get a warm bath and put you to bed. The doctor is helping Glancy. It could be a while before he can come look after us."

Candy asked, "Della, can you care for Miss Ceci?"

"Yes, ma'am, I'll go get water on heating." She turned and ran up the stairs and disappeared into the saloon.

Candy turned to Bear. Put her good arm around him and laid her head on his chest. "Thank God she stayed on. With this shoulder I don't think I could manage any of this."

Bear put his arms around her and spoke to Grady, "I'll carry Miss Ceci up and deposit her in a room, then I'll come back and get you, boss."

Grady chuckled, "You keep babying me, and I might get to liking it. You take care of Ceci. I'll get myself into the saloon. I might even help myself to a shot of that whiskey."

Bear swung Cecile up in his arms and carried her into the saloon. Candy followed and watched him as he got his patient to her room. She was enjoying being able to observe him without him knowing. She was surprised to note the butterflies she had as she admired him from behind. "Oh lordy," she thought, "you are fixin' to get your heart broken." She had been unlucky in love, and she wasn't expecting that to change.

Grady climbed carefully out of the wagon, walked slowly to the stairs, and using the guardrail climbed the four stairs to the porch. He walked carefully to one of the many chairs and lowered himself into it. Using both his hands, he rubbed his aching head, careful of his bandaged injury. He massaged his neck and closed his eyes. He clasped his hands in his lap and laid his head back on the chair back. He soaked up the restful feel of stillness. No more wagon jarring and head banging.

Bear came back and took a chair next to Grady. He stretched out his long legs and drew in a deep breath. He said, "This has been one hell of a trail drive."

Grady answered, "I planned on this drive to be my last, but I didn't expect it to be as loaded with danger as it turned out to be. I have to agree. Glad I'm retiring." Grady opened his eyes, looked down the street toward the stockyards and saw Juan headed their way.

The old man climbed the stairs and dragged a chair over to Grady's other side. He said, "Lance took off to tell Carmella about Glancy. I imagine they'll be back pretty quick. I couldn't get Deadly into the stockyard. Remembering how he was when you were sick here, I just left him out."

"Thanks, Juan. We'll put him up later if he causes any trouble." Grady saw the exhaustion in Juan's and Bear's faces. "We can worry about things after we've gotten cleaned up, had a good meal, and placed the gear into a corner of the saloon. Then we can take the grain wagon down and give the herd some grain."

Juan drew his brown papers from his pocket and his tobacco from another. He talked while he rolled a cigarette. "They are tossing some hay to the herd now and will report to me when finished. It won't take the boys long to empty the wagon." He finished rolling the tobacco and placed the cigarette in his mouth. Tired himself, it took a few minutes before he lit it.

Grady continued, "The saloon will be our camp for a few days while we get organized, if Candy's willing. Juan, I can't tell you how grateful I am that you came to our rescue. What a relief to finally have Ceci and her herd safe here in Janos for a spell."

"Senor Grady, I also am very relieved to have my godchild safe. When I hear the stories of the problems you had, I know you saved her many times. She is such a willful child. Brave like her father. I am grateful she had you and your crew taking care of her."

Grady held out his hand, and the two shook hands. He said, "If you agree, I'll turn the herd over to you and your vaqueros. I don't have many of my crew left."

"Of course, Senor. You need to gain some strength. Do not worry about the herd. They are now in my hands."

Grady liked the idea of relaxing and regaining his strength. He laid his head back on the chair and drifted off to sleep.

Bear sat quiet for a while, and then he went down to the stockyard to see how Juan's cowboys were doing. Juan waited quietly and smoked his cigarette. When the vaqueros and Bear returned, he quietly motioned them into the saloon. It wasn't long before they were unloading the wagon.

Della, with Cecile's help, got the weakened girl into the tub of warm water. It was heavenly. Ceci relaxed into its comfort. Della poured some bath salts into the water. Its flowery fragrance was wonderful. It brought back memories of her own bathtub at her hacienda. Home! What a wonderful word, *home*. There were times in that mountain canyon, waiting for Grady's return, that she feared she would never see Hacienda de Ciela again.

Della settled her in a bed with clean sheets. In a clean nightgown, she was instantly asleep.

Della had water heating for Miss Candy's bath while she settled Cecile to bed. Candy welcomed Della's help to get her out of the filthy clothes she wore. She said, "Throw all these rags away."

Della replied, "Yes, ma'am, they smell bad."

It was with some pain to the injured shoulder, using one arm to hold on to the side of the tub, she lowered herself into the water. It felt so good.

It was worth every penny and the four months it took for delivery for this luxury.

She closed her eyes, leaned back, and rested her head on the back of the tub. She let her body sink down until both shoulders were covered with the heated water.

Candy heard Della moving around. Felt and smelled the bath salts the young girl poured into the water. Her eyes closed, she spoke, "Della, please keep adding some hot water. I just want to lie here and soak awhile. Would you please lay out some clean underclothes, my silk hose, and my blue calico dress? I'll call you when I'm ready to get out. Thank you so much for staying and taking care of things while I was away. I hope you'll stay awhile and help me. I don't think I can do much with this shoulder."

"Yes, ma'am, I'll stay as long as you need me. I've never been away from Janos. It scared me to think of traveling all that distance. I'm not partial to the work the other girls were off seeking, and caring for a multitude of soldiers is terrifying. If you hadn't come back, I figured to just stay on, change the name to Della's. That terrified me also. I'm relieved you made it back safely. Really, Miss Candy, you're the closest thing I have to a family. I just don't know what I'm going to do if you leave."

Candy chuckled. Della was the youngest of the girls she hired for the upstairs business. "I intend to leave Janos. At the moment I don't have a direction. Stay with me, and I'll provide for you until I decide what I'm going to do."

"Oh! Thank you, Miss Candy. I'll go lay out your things and give you soak time. While you relax I'll get a bed ready for Mr. Grady. If it's all right with you, I'll put him back in his sickroom."

"That's fine, Della." Candy was much relieved that Della would help her get through the days while she was slowed down with the damaged shoulder. She settled to enjoy the warm water. Della poured some more hot water in the tub, and Candy heard her leave, shutting the door behind her.

Juan was tired. He had also just come off that difficult and exhausting trip. He had the advantage of his vaqueros, fully rested and full of vigor. Staying seated on the porch by Grady he directed his team to unload the food supplies from the grain wagon into the saloon kitchen. Other items—supplies, bedrolls, coats, and so on—were put in a corner of the saloon.

Old Lou stayed with Glancy until the boy was doctored, bathed, and put to bed.

Glancy settled in bed, Lou hurried to the saloon and started a meal. He located a large roast pan, tossed in a rump roast, and had one of Juan's vaqueros peel plenty of potatoes and onions. They joined the roast.

Candy wanted to go to bed and pass out. Instead, with Della's help she managed to get dressed. Della combed her hair and braided it in one long braid down her back. A pair of low-heeled shoes and her arm in its sling, she added a touch of rouge to her lips and cheeks. She descended the stairs and found Old Lou busy in the kitchen.

She went to him, gave him a one-armed hug, and said, "Bless you, Lou. I've been no help. What can I do now?"

Embarrassed but pleased by the hug, he said, "I just threw together what I could find. 'T'ain't much but plenty of it. Looks like we're feeding an army. Besides our gang, there's Juan's vaqueros and maybe Lance, Carmella, and the older son. I think Lance called him Ed."

Candy picked up a spoon and dipped some gravy out of the roast pan. She blew on it to cool, took a sip, and said, "Oh, that's good. You're doing great. I'd like to make some pies, but that's out with one arm."

"Don't you fret, Miss Candy. Juan and I have things in control. Those vaqueros of his are doing most of the work. Juan's on the porch with Grady. Grady's sleeping."

"Good heavens!" She turned to check on Grady then stopped and said, "There're jars of peaches in the pantry. Be a good substitute for pies."

She found Grady just where Lou said he was. She pulled a chair close to Grady and studied his face. He looked peaceful. Worry lines had relaxed. She drew a deep breath, then sat back. She rested her good arm in her lap and looked down the street toward the doctor's house. No one was in sight, but three saddled horses were tied to the hitching rail. She figured Carmella, Lance, and the older son, Edward, had arrived to check out the damage to Glancy.

She would like to know how the boy was. She had hated to return one of Carmella's boys to her damaged. However, they were all lucky. They had all met a dangerous hail of bullets and a serious trail accidents and survived.

It shouldn't be too long before the doc headed her way. She studied the other buildings in Janos—such a small town. Why had she settled in such a small town? She answered herself. It was all you could afford at the time. You did all right. You don't owe anyone. You have a large stock of bar drinks. The building's yours, but I doubt you could find a buyer for it. If it weren't for this pending war, she would still be getting by. But what now? She really didn't want to do this saloon business anymore. She hated dealing with working girls. Well, that had been handled. Except for Della, they were all gone. Grady reached over and took her hand. It surprised her. She came quickly out of her daydream. His head still remained leaning on the hard chairback. His eyes were open and met hers.

He said, "Where were you? You have a frown wrinkle across your brow that I've never seen before."

She smiled and replied, "I had just studied your face and found it very peaceful. What's next, Grady?"

He squeezed her hand slightly and withdrew his to the arm of his chair. Not moving his head, he said, "I'm so grateful to be here. We're a sorry, exhausted bunch, but at least at this moment Cecile's safe and her herd's safe. I guess, with her people here, my job's done. It's not really finished until we reach her ranch, but she's in safe hands now. What's up with you?"

"That's what I've just been sitting here wondering. This war thing is apparently going to get serious. I just know what I'm not going to do. I'm not going to stay here. Without the army's protection, the Indians will be on the warpath. Janos is a direct path between Texas and Mexico. I guess I'll just start packing up. I'll see where that leads."

She reached over, patted his hand, and asked, "Head hurting? You haven't moved it while I've been here."

"Hurts like hell," he replied. "Feels like I've got a concussion all over again."

"Doc should be over soon. He will have something to quiet the pain." She rose and said, "I'll have Della heat you some bathwater. She'll get you when it's ready. A warm bath and some clean clothes will help. She has your bed ready. Don't worry about Cecile. She's already bathed and asleep in her bed."

Grady reached for her hand to keep her from hurrying away. "Candy, I know I've said this before, but I really want you to know this. You saved my life. I've never met a finer lady. I'll always be grateful. I won't forget it. If you ever need my help, just ask."

Candy squeezed his hand lightly and bent over and kissed his forehead. With head high she went inside to find Della.

Grady shut his eyes tight and opened them. The old noggin really hurt. Keeping his head still, he moved his eyes only, and studied the buildings across the dirt road. He saw the army's border outpost, and he remembered the army saddlebag Bear had found in the cave. He had read over the formal papers in it.

They read like a closure of army border outposts. The Regular Army's frontier missions were being interrupted by the onset of the civil war. The regulars were being replaced by volunteers, who would report to outposts in New Mexico.

The orders were dated, and the outpost he observed across the road had already closed. Candy was right. This town would probably be in the path of the Apache. She was wise to move out.

He saw Deadly headed his way. He wasn't surprised. The big longhorn bull was skilled at breaking out of enclosures and hunting Grady down. He smiled. He was glad to see Deadly. He leaned forward, braced his hands on the arms of the chair, and rose slowly to his feet. The pain in his head increased, but it wasn't accompanied by nausea, thank goodness. He pulled the chair to the porch rail where he could talk to Deadly.

The bull took a stance by the rail and was careful not to bang a long horn into the porch. He was satisfied to stand at rest and chew his cud. Grady scratched the hard bone between the two horns and laid his aching head back on the chair.

The two, content to be together, were found later by Little Bear. He said, "Della has a bath ready for you. I'll help you up the stairs."

Grady said, "I'm really uncomfortable being so helpless. I hate to admit it, but I'd welcome the use of your arm to lean on." He used his arms and raised himself out of the chair. He gave a final pat to Deadly and said, "Fella, you did a good job of getting us here. You deserve a rest as much as any of us." Grady ended with a scratch under Deadly's cheeks and took Bear's arm. They reached the stairs in this manner, and there Grady steadied himself by using both Bear's arm and the stair railing. Bear guided him to the room where the tub waited.

He sat on a chair that Della had placed close to the tub for him. He said, "Thanks, Bear, I can handle it from here."

"You sure, boss?" Bear was concerned about Grady undressing himself and climbing into the tub.

"I'll just take my time. I'll holler if I get stuck. I would like to ask a favor of you." Bear waited.

Grady continued, "Can you keep an eye on Deadly? He's used to this place. He spent some time here while I was ill. There's a barn out back where Candy keeps her black geldings. If you throw some hay back there, hopefully he'll stay back there most of the time. Don't pin him. He breaks out, as you know. Just watch and warn people to stay away from him. He will hang out by the porch. If you bribe him with biscuits, maybe you can take him back to the barn. Maybe?"

"I doubt it," Bear said. "Trumpeter's with the herd. If I bring Trumpeter up and pin him, maybe Deadly will stay back there with him. I will warn everyone to leave him alone."

"Thanks, Bear." Grady began unbuttoning his shirt.

The undressing, the careful climb into the tub, bathing, redressing in the clean robe provided, and exiting the bath closet was exhausting. He found Candy waiting to help him to his bed. He hesitated to use her good arm to brace as he was afraid he would fall and drag her down with him. He asked her, "Are you sure?"

"Take my arm, Grady. Use the wall with the other hand, if you need it. How's the head?"

He answered, "Hurts like hell. How's your shoulder?"

"Hurts like hell," she answered. They both got a chuckle out of that. She tucked him in bed and said, "Doc will be here soon."

Candy went back downstairs. She gave orders where needed. Helped Lou with supper and showed the Mexican cowboys where to find plates, utensils, and serving bowls. She sent Bear to get his bath. Della was already heating water for Juan.

As things got under control, she went to the porch and sank tiredly into a chair. Lance, Carmella, and Ed came out of the doctor's house. Lance untied their horses, and the group walked to Candy's. Lance tied their horses to her hitch rail, and the three Smiths climbed the stairs and joined Candy.

All four sat quiet for a while. Candy spoke first. "I'm really sorry, Carmella. Sure wasn't part of the plan to get your son hurt. I know Grady is feelin' low about his injury. What did Doc tell ya?"

Carmella drew in a deep breath and sat up a little straighter. "It's a very bad break. The problem is the open wound. Torn muscles clear to the bone. Doc says he can't plaster over the wound."

"But how's the break going to heal?" Candy asked.

"Doc's got a brace. The kind used to brace a weak leg. He's going to try to adapt it to keep the leg steady. The wound had begun to fester. He had to cut away a lot of the damaged flesh. Glancy won't be able to stand on the leg until the infection is cured and begins to heal. That's the hardest part of recovery. He's bedridden while we fight the infection. If it gets under control, Doc said he might not lose the leg. If not, he'll have to take it off at the knee." She had a damp handkerchief in her hand and brushed away tears rolling slowly down her cheeks.

Juan had come quietly on the porch, in time to hear Carmella's report. He stood behind her with both hands laid on her shoulders in a friendly offer of sympathy. He had not wanted to accept the boys for the rescue mission to the canyon for Cecile. He feared bringing them back to her, possibly dead, and now this terrible injury was a reality and he felt guilty. Without their help, his godchild had been in danger, and he had risked her boys to save his lady patron.

Carmella reached to pat Juan's hand on her shoulder. She knew the remorse and guilt he felt for Glancy's injury. They clasped each other's hand, and Carmella gave his a small squeeze. She had been the one who had insisted the boys should accompany them. They all had known the danger. Lance had told her about the trip, and about the attack at the campsite. He told her about Glancy's accident, the crew's efforts to rescue the boy, and the constant care to get him back to Janos. Juan released her hand and took a chair.

Carmella wiped her cheeks again and continued, "Doc gave him a powder. It knocked him out. He'll be out all night. We're headed home. Lance needs to get cleaned up."

"We've got supper nearly ready—won't you stay?" Candy invited.

"No, thanks, not tonight. We'll be back in the morning. Doc wants to keep him for a few days so he can be sure the infection is controlled. I'd appreciate a meal for us tomorrow. I'll bring some pies."

"Of course, you and the boys are always welcome. We have all been stressing for days over Glancy's injury. I know it's much more stressful for you. You don't need to bring anything, just yourself." Candy leaned back in her chair. She was running out of energy.

"We'll do the pies. I'll set my cook to them tonight. It won't put any stress on me. It will help me take my mind off of worrying. Doc told me Mr. Lou's care is the reason he has a chance to keep his leg. I will forever be grateful to him and all of you." Carmella smiled and rose from her chair.

"Pies would be grand." Candy reached over and took Carmella's hand and continued, "This arm doesn't work well without its partner, and we have a large crew to feed. I don't know how long they will all be here. We will have to wait and see what the doc says." She released Carmella's hand.

"He said to tell you he would be over as soon as he gets Glancy's leg braced. We're out of here. I'll help you all I can tomorrow." She and her sons mounted their horses and rode out of town. Candy went to check on Lou.

The chairs were soon filled with Juan and his vaqueros. Bear arrived and said, "Juan, your water's ready."

Juan rose, and Bear took his chair. It wasn't long before Juan returned, refreshed in clean clothes. Candy joined them, and Juan introduced his vaqueros.

Gesturing to the oldest of the four, Juan said, "This is Fernando Ortega. Fernando is our number-one *segundo*. He keeps a tight rein on the young vaqueros that work at Hacienda de Ciela. His wife, Maria, has control of the hacienda. Its efficient running is credited to her.

"This youngster," he continued, indicating the youngest of the four, "is Jalo Ortega, Fernando's oldest son.

"Beside him is Paco Mendoza, top bronc rider and horse trainer at the rancho.

"And this young man," he finished, indicating the fourth vaquero, "we keep around because he plays an exciting guitar. He also works the cattle, but he's much more skilled with the guitar. He's a little shy, but if we coax him, maybe he will play for us after our meal. His name is Garcia Santos."

Bear stood and shook hands with the four and said, "This is your hostess, Miss Candace Murray. I'm Little Bear. You can call me Bear, and I would really look forward to hearing you play. We've just come off a long, hard, and dangerous trail drive. A little music would be a blessing."

Bear noted how solid and sinewy all of the vaqueros were, including the older gentleman. There was not a pinch of fat on any of the handsome men. They were not thin, but any bulk was from muscles, and this only came from hard work.

Bear was relieved to find he would be able to rely on these men, given the worn-out and injured condition of Grady's crew.

They chatted for a while until the doctor arrived.

Candy introduced him. "This is Dr. Emery Wilson."

She didn't bother introducing the bunch. She could tell the doctor was tired, so she took his arm and led him upstairs to the patients waiting for him.

Candy was first, and Della helped her shed the calico dress off her shoulders so the doctor could see the deep blue and purple bruising. It was dark and angry and ran around the shoulder and down the arm. She didn't have to tell him it had dislocated.

Against Candy's pleading protests, he taped her upper arm to her side by running the tape around her body. The lower arm he put into a sling designed so that she would need help to remove it.

She had Della show him to Cecile's room and return to help her change her clothes. With her arm taped to her body, the only garment she could wear was a large men's shirt.

Not having a men's shirt, she sent Della to raid Bear's bags. She found one clean shirt that was large enough to do the job and still loose enough to be comfortable.

Buttoned across her arm and chest, it left the empty sleeve arm dangling. She pinned the sleeve out of the way and Della helped her finish the ensemble with a skirt that hung respectably to the floor. She looked in her mirror and laughed. Della looked over her shoulder and joined the laughter. Candy's turned to tears, and Della put her arms around her waist and softly hugged her.

Candy said, "No more pretty dresses for a while." The doctor wanted her to remain in this immovable discomfort for at least a week and possibly longer. He said she would need some exercises after the tape was removed to keep the muscles from forming painful scar tissue.

"Oh well," she said to Della, "what you see is what you get. No more fancy saloon owner."

She caught the doctor as he left Cecile's room and directed him to Grady, who lay on the bed. He had placed a pillow over his face to block the sunlight from his eyes and muffle the noise from the saloon.

Grady heard them enter, removed the pillow, and started to sit up. The doctor told him to lie still and said, "I warned you not to make that trip. You were not well enough."

Grady put his left hand over his eyes and held out the right one to shake hands with the doctor. "Good to see you too, Doc."

"Forget that shit. I don't know why I'm even seeing you. You don't listen to a thing I tell you."

Grady felt like a bad little schoolboy who was going to have his hands slapped with a ruler.

"I know Doc, but my mind was too full of worry for Cecile and my crew. I couldn't rest 'cause I just couldn't quit thinkin' about all the problems they coulda run into on that mountain," he replied. "As it turned out, my imaginings weren't too far off from reality." He gave Doc an "I told you so" face and leaned back and crossed his legs.

Doc knew when he was beat, so he just scowled and asked, "So what's bothering you the most?" He admired Grady's tenacity. The doctor set his bag on the foot of the bed and took out his stethoscope to listen to Grady's chest.

Grady asked, "Have you checked Cecile? How is she?"

"Try to keep quiet while I check you." The doctor closed his eyes and concentrated. He expected a lot of racket coming from a congested chest. It was acting normal. He folded up the instrument and stuffed it back in the bag. He frowned and said, "I expected to hear a buzz saw. It's better than when you left here. So what's ailing you?"

Candy spoke up. "It's his head. I told you about the accident that dislocated my shoulder. It threw him into the wagon seat headfirst."

The doctor did a check of each eye, both ears, throat. Used the fingertips of both hands to inspect Grady's scalp. Found the swollen lump. Grady whined as the fingers pressed and explored its size and sensitivity.

He pulled a chair up and sat down. He was tired. He wasn't a young man and the hours treating Glancy had tired him out, both physically and emotionally. He pulled his bag onto his lap and searched for a bottle of laudanum. Once found, he set it on the table by the bed and said, "The concussion you had did enough damage. You sure didn't need to add to what was already bad enough."

Grady took his hand away from his eyes. The doctor continued, "Not much I can advise. The laudanum may help quiet the pain some. If not, we may need to give you a sleeping powder and knock you out for a few days. I'll check you tomorrow. We'll see how the laudanum works. You mostly need to stay still and rest the head. You keep beating yourself up and you could end up with some constant headaches."

Candy, standing at the foot of the bed, said, "Some good news about Cecile would probably help him to relax and rest his head. How is she, Doc?"

Doc closed his bag and said, "The girl's in a pitiful state. Undernourished. Chest has some congestion. Looks like she's recovering from a really bad sore throat. She needs rest and some regular meals more than anything. I gave her a bottle of cough syrup. Mix up some soda and salt water and have her gargle often."

Before Grady could ask any more questions, Candy said, "How long for bed rest Doc? Both of them still have a wagon trip to San Antonio."

"Well hell, Candy. Won't make no difference what I tell him. He don't mind me anyway. But for that girl's sake, stay at least a couple of days and let her get some decent sleep and regular meals."

Grady reached for the laudanum, unscrewed the top, and swallowed a couple of large mouthfuls.

Doc reached over and took it away from him, "That ain't whiskey! Try using a spoon for an accurate dose."

Grady grinned and said, "I sure have missed you, Doc."

"I don't know why. You don't pay attention to anything I tell you."

The doctor rose and Candy followed him into the hall. She took his arm, and he steadied her down the stairs. She said, "Supper's ready, join us."

"Don't mind if I do. Busy day. I'm weary. Look forward to a good meal if it includes an after-dinner alcoholic beverage."

"You betcha, Doc. That sounds good to me too." Candy introduced Dr. Emery Wilson to her guests.

All but Grady and Cecile enjoyed the supper hour. She was knocked out on cough medicine and Grady on a couple more swallows of laudanum.

After their meal they all helped Old Lou clear the table. Then choosing either an alcoholic drink or coffee they retired to the porch. Candy brought out some light army blankets that had been rescued from the Border Patrol's campgrounds by Della when the men evacuated. Laundered and hung outside they smelled of soap and fresh air. She passed them around. The temperature was dropping lower each night.

Garcia ran his finger lightly over the strings, tuning a few, and soon the soft strum of the guitar was joined by Fernando's violin. Paco and Jalo's voices blended in harmony.

They all enjoyed the music and watched the stars come out. The temperature was dropping. They were all tired. It was hard for Candy to believe that she'd been high up on the mountain this morning and now she and the crew were safe in Janos.

Doctor Wilson was the first to break up the gathering. He headed for home to check on Glancy. Juan and his vaqueros disappeared upstairs to beds assigned to them by Della.

Bear and Candy remained on the porch. She moved from the porch chair into Bear's lap.

He covered them both with a blanket and carefully wrapped his arms around her. She laid her head on his shoulder. They remained quiet for a while. It had been a long busy day. For Candy a painful one. The arm taped to her body was extremely uncomfortable and it also made her feel claustrophobic.

Bear whispered in her ear, "You are quite a lady Miss Candace Murray."

She turned her head, gave him a soft kiss, and said, "I don't feel like a lady. I feel lost. Too much has changed in such a short time. I've lost control."

He kissed her cheek and answered, "What can I do to help?"

"That's the problem. I don't know what to do. Where am I headed? You will be gone with Grady. I'll miss you so much." Tears filled her eyes and she tucked her head back into his shoulder to hide her embarrassment. She didn't have a right to burden him. They had come together on the trail drive. She had no reason to expect more from him. She was a saloon girl. There was a lot of baggage with that title. She had no right to expect more than the time spent on the trail.

Bear was quiet. He didn't know what to say. Had Candy just expressed a fondness for him? He hadn't expected a relationship with this white woman. As a half-breed, life could turn ugly in white communities with a breed's familiarity with a white woman. He had accepted the fact that once they reached Janos their brief interlude would be over.

She shifted in his arms, and he tightened his hold on her. He said, "Stay here. Let me hold you for a while. I need to arrange some thoughts. We haven't had much time today to be alone together. Let me hold you while I can. I need to answer you. Just sit still while I think this through."

She was afraid he wanted to tell her good-bye. If he did, she would lose it! Her nerves were stretched to the limit. It was enough that her body was confined in this tape. She felt helpless. They had just come off that awful trail drive. She had not slowed down all day. She was exhausted and ready to explode. She couldn't stand to say good-bye.

Bear could feel the tension in her body. He kept her from leaving his lap and said, "I care for you. I expected you to end this relationship when we reached Janos."

Candy used her hand to wipe tears from her eyes and replied, "I expected you to just ride on with Grady. It's tearing me up."

He turned her head and kissed her softly. She returned the kiss, and pulling back she said, "What are we going to do?"

"We'll figure it out. As long as we both feel that we are not ready to end this relationship, we have an understanding. The way I see it, we'll have a few days to rest our minds and our bodies. We are both too tired tonight to address such a serious decision."

He released her from the blanket and she stood. He lifted her into his arms, carried her upstairs, and deposited her on her bed. He kissed her and said, "Get some sleep. I'm going to check on the herd. We'll work things out."

Della came in and helped her get dressed for bed.

Bear ran into Juan, who had also checked on the herd. He turned and walked back to the saloon with him. Juan went up to bed, and Bear returned to the chair on the porch. He wrapped a blanket around himself. Heavy thoughts would keep him awake for a while.

With the help of the laudanum and exhaustion, Grady finally slept. Grady's head reminded him of having a hangover.

It was dark when he woke. A dull ache had overcome sleep. He started to reach for the laudanum and stopped himself. Not good to depend on the drug. Knowing Dr. Wilson from his previous illness, he knew the man would not give him another bottle. He would give him a knockout and put him to sleep for a few days. He would probably wake up to find everyone gone. That's not going to happen!

With a hangover, it helped to stay still and not move his head. He tried that. Didn't work. The pain was steady. Better after the syrup and sleep but still very uncomfortable. He closed his eyes and thought about Cecile and the last month on the trail. Huddled together under canvas and covers to keep warm, they had a chance to exchange tales of their lives before meeting in San Diego. The trail drive was hard work with little time to learn each other's personal history.

They had acquired respect and a mutual attraction to each other on the trail drive. He often returned his thoughts to the kiss she had given him as he rode out of the canyon to Janos for supplies and hired help. An accident on the way gave him a concussion, a dislocated shoulder, and pneumonia. He struggled to get well enough to return and rescue his crew and the herd. His biggest worry was Grace Cecile McNamara. He had feared he would not make it in time to save her herd from the hardships of winter up in the mountains. He had planned to get to Janos, load up supplies, and turn right around. Instead he came into Janos unconscious on Deadly's back and stayed that way for a few weeks.

They arrived back in the canyon up in the mountains in time to help battle outlaws. He had found Cecile rapped in bedrolls, feverish and delirious. As he was still recovering and too weak to ride a horse himself, the two invalids had been transported in Candy's wagon. He had held her safe in his arms. Kept her covered. Her throat so sore she could hardly swallow broths. He had spoon-fed her.

This was the first night in days she was not in his arms. No wonder he was having trouble sleeping. She was safe and just down the hall from him. He missed her. Holding her close to help cushion her from the rough wagon's jolting felt right. His head hammered as he realized part of his discomfort was missing Ceci. He reached for the laudanum and, following Doc's orders, used the spoon and swallowed just one spoonful of the thick syrup. With her on his mind, he drifted back to sleep.

Voices woke him. Light was just barely showing. Must be early. It sounded like the voices were Cecile and Della. He tossed back his covers and swung his legs to the floor. His head pounded and a dizzy spell warned him to stay seated until it passed. He didn't want to end up on the floor, so he waited.

The two young ladies seemed to be getting along well. He heard Cecile laugh. Good! She was better.

He rose carefully and moved slowly into the hall to Cecile's open door. She was sitting up, sipping on a cup of what he figured was coffee. She saw him, and holding the cup with one hand, she motioned him to enter with the other.

Grady's stomach did a somersault seeing Ceci's beautiful face.

When Cecile looked up at Grady she soaked in his presence. Seeing his face gave her a flush and butterflies in her stomach. She thought to herself what a strong and handsome face he had, with just enough softness to it to make him appear friendly and approachable.

Della pulled a chair close to the bed, and he sat down. Cecile held out her hand, and he took it in his and said, "You look better. How do you feel?"

She set her cup on the tray in her lap. A little hoarse, she answered, "I think I'm going to live." She smiled and continued, "I'm hungry. I'm really hungry. Della just asked me what I felt like eating. Won't you join me?"

"Sounds good to me if it's not too much trouble for Della."

"No trouble Mr. Grady. That nice Mr. Lou has coffee ready and is frying bacon. I believe eggs and biscuits is the direction he's headed. I can bring you a cup of coffee. When breakfast is ready I'll bring you both a tray. Miss Cecile has requested two poached eggs and a biscuit. What would you like Mr. Grady?'

Cecile groaned and said, "Oh, that sounds so good."

Della removed the pan of water with a washrag floating in it. She had brought it warm for Cecile to sponge bathe. Before she left the room, she said to Grady, "I put some honey in Miss Cecile's coffee to help calm her cough. How do you prefer yours, sir?"

"Black's good, Della. Thank you. Breakfast sounds even better. Double the bacon and eggs and bring me four biscuits, please."

Della left, and Cecile laughed, "Habits are hard to break. You ordered extra biscuits because you always share with Deadly."

Grady grinned and replied, "I never gave it much thought, but you're right. I always stick a couple in my shirt pockets. If he's there for breakfast, we share."

Della was back with Grady's coffee. They were still holding hands when she hurried back down the stairs to help Lou feed the gang.

Bear brought Trumpeter to the corral behind the saloon. He threw in some hay and dumped some grain on top. Hungry, Deadly readily entered the corral and joined Trumpeter. Bear fastened the corral gate and left the two friends to their meal.

Deadly was comfortable through the night. He spent most of it standing over the sleeping old bull. He took turns dozing and chewing his cud until daylight. He had become familiar with this routine during Grady's previous illness. He knew Grady was in the building. The wait had lasted days, and restlessness and concern had driven him to work on the corral's latch. He had mastered it then.

As this morning's sun began its rise, habit urged Deadly to find Grady for breakfast biscuits. He had last seen him on the porch of the building. Knowing the secrets of the corral latch, he had it opened quickly and went directly to the saloon porch.

Trumpeter followed Deadly and waited with him by the porch. He soon got bored and wandered around the building grazing on what grass he could find. He often returned to touch noses with Deadly. Hearing the cattle bellowing from the stock yard, he ambled down the road to answer the call of his ladies.

That's where Bear found Deadly when he walked out with his coffee to sit on the porch. He could see old Trumpeter standing by the herd at the stockyard. He went back in and returned with a biscuit for Deadly.

He sat and enjoyed the morning quiet. No hurry—neither bull was going anywhere. When he finished his coffee he would go get Trumpeter and fasten him back in the corral. Wouldn't do any good to put Deadly with him. The longhorn would stay close to the porch and by Trumpeter, in the corral.

After their shared breakfast, Grady could tell Cecile was tired. After a good meal, she should sleep for a while. He talked to her about things that were unimportant so that he could keep his tone even and help lull her to sleep. After her meal she lay on her side so she could see Grady more easily. He watched as her eyes became drowsier. He enjoyed being able to stare at her without an excuse. Storytelling was the perfect excuse to be able to study her face without any awkwardness. She was a beauty, or at least that was how he saw it. He smiled when her eyes finally gave up and closed.

He returned to his room. His travel bag had been brought to him. Any clothes in it had days of trail dirt on them. He looked around and spotted clothes folded on the room's dresser. He recognized them as the clothes he had been wearing when he arrived in Janos, weeks ago, ill and out of his head with fever.

Grady dressed carefully, continuing to move slowly so as not to aggravate the head and bring on the dizzy spells and nausea. He actually felt a lot better. His head still ached but not as much. A good night's sleep and a decent meal seemed to have helped.

The saloon was empty. Sounds of pans banging and voices came from the kitchen. He found Juan's youngest vaquero cleaning up the breakfast mess.

Lou spotted Grady and said, "Morning, boss. Sure am glad to see you on your feet. Did I send up enough breakfast?"

"You sure did. It was grand. Thanks, Lou. Where is everyone?" Grady picked up a clean cup. "Is there any coffee left?"

"Yes sir." Lou took the cup and poured it full from the pot on the large wood cook stove. He answered Grady, "Juan and his boys are at the stockyard. He said something about checking out the grain wagon. The wagon belongs to Carmella. He's already figuring out how we're going to get this herd to Cecile's ranch. All our wagons are in the canyon. I believe he's thinking of buying hers or borrowing it. He was going to look it over and see if it needs any repairs."

"I'm glad Juan's working on things. I believe part of this headache is from worrying about trying to put this trail drive back on the trail." He took the cup of coffee and asked, "Where's Bear?"

Lou answered, "Bear's on the porch. Miss Candy's still in bed. She wore herself out yesterday. We're letting her sleep in."

"I'll go join Bear."

When Grady stepped out on the porch, he was immediately aware of the frost in the air. After the freezing cold in the mountains, it had felt almost balmy yesterday sitting on the porch. In reality winter was closing in on this small town.

Bear was leaning back in a chair with his feet on the rail. Deadly stood close and greeted Grady with a low bawl.

"B-r-r," Grady said as he walked to the rail and gave Deadly one of the biscuits out of his shirt pocket. He pulled a chair over and sat where he could rub the bull's head and neck.

"Morning, boss." Bear was taking turns drinking his coffee and smoking his clay pipe. "Thought you would spend the day in bed."

"My body wanted to. But my aching head is going to hurt wherever I am. Thought I'd try staying up awhile. Doc gave me some laudanum. It helped some. He threatened to knock me out with sleeping powder, so I need to overcome these ailments."

He rolled a smoke and continued, "A lot of this headache is coming from worry. There's still some six hundred miles to reach Cecile's ranch. That's another month herding those slowpoke cows. It usually takes a large herd of a thousand or more to travel ten to twelve miles a day. As we found out, this small herd is worse. They are small cattle with short legs. Travel time is naturally longer. Add their determination to stop and graze constantly. They need to be pushed to fifteen miles a day to make it in a month. Not going to happen. It would kill them."

Grady paused, lit the cigarette, and took in a drag. Let the smoke out, lifted the coffee to his mouth, and took several swallows. The coffee was getting cold. He tossed the rest over the rail to the dirt between Deadly's front feet.

Bear saw that Grady's hand holding the cigarette was shaking. He said, "I thought with Juan and his boys here that the drive on to San Antonio would be their worry."

"And I am grateful they arrived in time to rescue us. But you know as well as I do what a fiasco putting that herd on the trail again is going to be, and that's not counting on Trumpeter. His travel carrier is still in the mountains. I see he's down at the stockyards. What happened—Deadly turn him loose?"

Bear grinned. "Yeah. I put them both in the corral out back. This is where I found them this morning. I'll put Trumpeter back in the corral. I'll leave Deadly loose." He dropped his feet to the floor and knocked his pipe free of ashes. He put it back in a shirt pocket.

Grady dropped his half-smoked cigarette to the floor, stepped on it, then kicked it off the porch. He gave Deadly the other biscuit from his pocket and said, "The worst of it is, that sick woman has to be driven another six hundred miles in this weather. Let's move into the saloon where it's warmer. I don't relish another bout of pneumonia." He gave Deadly a final pat and stood slowly, mindful of the vertigo that threatened.

"I'll go get Trumpeter and put him up. Give me time to toss the two bulls some hay, and I'll join you. I could use a cup of hot coffee. Lou usually keeps a pot on the stove." He moved into a slow jog. He sat on the porch long enough last night and again this morning to feel the cold in his muscles.

Grady stood in front of the potbellied wood stove that heated the saloon. The heat warmed his legs until he had to move away some and turned to warm his hands. It felt so good to feel warm. He wasn't looking forward to heading out on the trail again. However, Juan and his boys did not know the trouble they were going to have moving this herd. And no way was he going to leave Cecile's care in their hands. They would need his guidance.

When Bear came back, they chose a table where they could be comfortable from the heat of the potbellied stove. Lou saw them come in and brought them each a hot cup of coffee. He disappeared back into the kitchen.

Bear took a few minutes to warm his hands on the hot cup. He sipped some to warm his insides and said, "How is Ceci? What did the doctor say?"

"She's very undernourished, congested lungs, bad sore throat. We knew all that. He says if she eats properly and gets some rest, she will heal. You know as well as I do that putting her in a wagon for another month is totally unpredictable. We have no control over winter weather." His head throbbed. He leaned back in the chair and rubbed the muscles in his neck and the base of his skull. "Good news is she ate a good breakfast this morning, so her appetite seems good."

Bear sat on the porch thinking for about an hour last night. He wasn't sure this was the right time to bring his thoughts up. Instead he said, "You're not much better off than she is. Why don't you stay here for the winter?"

"I thought about it. I don't believe Ceci will do it. You know how stubborn she can get. She has a ranch to run. She's not going to let that herd get out of her sight. She's already been away from her ranch for months, and Juan, her main ranch foreman, has been away for a month, and half of his crew is here. They have to travel on. I'll be lucky to get them to hang out a few days." He drank the last of his coffee and pushed the empty cup to the center of the table.

Bear did the same and said, "Have you given any thought to what's best for you? We've talked about Old Lou and me going on to your ranch with you and helping you add onto your cabin over the winter. I don't think you are in any condition to do that. You need some healing time also."

"I don't have an answer for that yet. It's all going around and around in my head."

Stamping feet announced the arrival of people. Carmella and Lance came in the door. They came over to the table, and Bear introduced Carmella to Grady. Lance went to the kitchen to find Lou. He wanted to know where to put half a dozen pies he had in his wagon.

Lou gave directions, and Lance carried in two pies at a time. After the last pie trip, he made one more and brought in a large package of beef ribs. Then he joined his mother, Grady, and Bear.

Candy appeared on the stairs. She looked uncomfortable in her men's shirt penned across her chest and arm. Della had braided her hair. She had added some rouge to her cheeks and lips to hide her pale face.

As she looked down the stairs at Grady and Bear, she couldn't help but notice the differences and the similarities. Bear was dark with bronzed skin and black hair, long and tied behind his head with a leather strip. His face was chiseled with a square jaw. He usually looked serious.

Grady was light with sandy curly hair. His face and anything exposed to sun was tanned, but she knew after nursing him that in most places he was fair of skin. They were both the same in that they were both more than easy on the eyes. They were also about the same height at about six feet tall, she figured. Both of them were muscular in a sinewy way.

The thing she liked most about both of them was that they were good, solid men. In her line of business, she hadn't had the honor of meeting such men. They made a good team, dark and light, both honorable and dependable.

She took the chair next to Bear, and he took her free hand in his.

Carmella gave an update on Glancy. He was holding his own. So far no indication of infection. "Doc said he could have visitors today early. He's been sleeping in the afternoon."

Juan joined them. They spent most of the morning getting better acquainted. Juan brought up the subject of Carmella's wagon. "Can we buy or rent your wagon?"

She smiled and said, "I wondered how you were going to continue on with all your wagons on the mountain. Glancy has been telling me about the trip. He is so excited to have me share that adventure. It takes his mind off the leg pain. I got fearful when he told me about the confrontation with the evil ones. You could have all been killed. Thank you, Jesus, and please, Jesus, help my boy heal. The wagon's yours. I'll pick it up when we go to the city."

They all said amen, and Grady hurried to let Carmella know they were all thankful their rescue efforts had been on time. He said, "Your boys are fine young men. We couldn't have succeeded without your help, and your boys did a man's stand-up job the entire trip."

Grady breathed a sigh of relief and said, "Now all we need is a wagon for Trumpeter."

Juan looked puzzled and said, "Don't you think, now that we are off that mountain, he can keep up?"

"That mountain was easy for him. All downhill and long rests while you lowered wagons. He won't make it another six hundred miles in cold weather being driven at a speed needed to reach your ranch by Thanksgiving. I don't think you know what that bull means to Cecile. She will risk her health to protect him, and she won't let him out of her sight." He shut up. His head hurt, and he was talking to a man who knew Cecile better than all of them.

Juan hung his head, and all were quiet waiting for him to agree or disagree. When he looked up, his attention went to Carmella. He said, "I thought I saw some kind of covered traveler out by your barn. What is it? Would it work, and if so, can we buy it?'

She hesitated for a moment. Then she smiled and said, "That's what it's made for. I had it built special to haul bulls or horses to and from breeding and sales. I won't be needing it for a while. I can pick up two just as easy as one." She excused herself and went to help Lou in the kitchen.

Juan watched her as she walked out. "I hope I'm not taking advantage of her. She's really stepped up to help us."

"Sorry if I spoke out of turn, Juan. This headache's got me a little cranky. Let's talk to Cecile and suggest she offer Carmella some future Hereford bull calves to improve her meat on the hoof. If Carmella's not comfortable with that, I've got enough money with me to pay her for the use of her wagons. Hell, it's money Cecile gave me to drive her herd, and I'm still responsible to get them all to your ranch."

Carmella split her time between helping Lou put together a barbecued-rib dinner complete with potato salad and corn bread and making short trips to check on Glancy and often resting at the table conversing with Bear and Grady.

Juan hung out with Carmella. He enjoyed her company and helped her where he could. Lance went to join the vaqueros at the stockyard. Grady grew tired and went back to bed, leaving Bear and Candy to talk quietly by themselves.

Bear put another log in the potbellied stove. He returned to his chair. Candy had a frown on her face. He said, "What's bothering you? Is there a problem?"

The frown relaxed. She chuckled and replied, "I've got a million things crowding my head. My thoughts just now were what items and furniture I want to take with me. I can't even decide that because I don't know where I'm going. That led to acquiring a wagon. That led to what size wagon, which led to not knowing until I decide what I'm going to take or leave, which led to the need for boxes to pack small things. I'll have to have them made. I can't order them until I have an idea what I'm taking, which brought me back to the question of where the hell I'm off to."

Bear smiled and said, "If that's all that's on your mind, I have an answer for most of it."

She sat forward to listen to him and said, "Tell me. I need some ideas."

Bear hesitated and collected his thoughts. He picked up her hand in one of his, and his other hand softly ran his fingers over the back of her hand. When ready he said, "I talked some with Grady this morning. He's got a list of problems that out match most of yours.

He continued, "We had talked about Lou and me wintering at his ranch. He only has a one-room cabin on the property. He wants to build a barn and add a room to the cabin. He also has a lot of unbranded cattle. It would keep us bachelors busy until spring."

He hesitated again, arranged his thoughts, and continued, "Those plans were made while we were still on the trail. Since then a lot has changed. He's not able to work. Doubt if he can recover enough to winter in a one-room cabin. He may decide to take Miss Cecile home and winter at her ranch."

Candy held her breath, waiting for Bear to say what she wanted to hear.

He said, "if that's the direction he takes, Old Lou and I can hang out here with you. Lou can make boxes. I'll find a wagon—make it if I have to. Shame of it is, there's a grub wagon and a supply wagon and Trumpeter's cart back in the canyon."

Candy let out her breath. Excited, she said, "No, you don't! You're not going back to that freezing hell canyon. I can afford to buy a wagon."

"Don't get too excited," he warned her. "I have to know what Grady needs to do. I gave him my word, and if he decides to go on to his ranch, he's going to need Lou and me until he gets on his feet. However, you can begin to inventory your rooms. Make a list of things you would like to take. You can always add or remove things later. Make a list of items you definitely want to leave or sell. The list will give you an idea of how many boxes you'll need. Tomorrow I'll see if I can find a wagon, and whether I go or stay, at least you will have some direction."

It wasn't exactly what Candy was hoping to hear from Bear. She had a yearning to be near him for an unforeseeable time and wanted Bear to feel the same way. Her pride would not allow her to show him her disappointment, however.

Oh well, she thought, at least he is thinking about staying longer and helping me. That was a start, and she would be happy for it.

While Bear and Candy were planning her move. Grady had taken a swallow of laudanum and passed into a fitful sleep. When he woke from his nap, he thought for a moment that it was breakfast time, as he was hearing Cecile and Della talking and giggling like best friends. Clearing his head, he realized it was nearly suppertime. He hadn't shaved that morning, so he grabbed his toothbrush and his shaving gear and, walking slow, made it to the indoor privy.

When finished, he dropped off his belongings at his room. He didn't hear Della, so he walked to Cecile's open door and looked in. She was sitting up, brushing a head of shining black hair. It was parted and hung equally pulled forward on each side of her head. It was so long that the ends landed in her lap. She had always kept it controlled on the trail.

She looked up and saw Grady standing in the door and motioned for him to come in. He dragged a chair close, sat down, and reached to take a strand of hair in his fingers. It ran through his fingers like spun silk.

"Beautiful," he said and sat back and motioned for her to continue. "Don't let me stop you. I like to watch you brush your hair."

She continued brushing and said, "I haven't taken very good care of it on the trail. There were times when I felt like cutting it all off. It felt wonderful yesterday as Della helped me give it a good soaping."

"I'm glad you didn't cut it. It's beautiful." He unconsciously massaged the back of his neck and head. Cecile noticed he winced and closed his eyes while he rubbed her neck.

"You are still hurting?" She stopped brushing. A worried frown formed on her brow.

He stopped massaging and settled his hands in his lap and said, "It's not as bad. Gives me some hope that maybe with rest and time it will go away. We need to talk. I'm worried about you. Doc says you need to rest and get some good meals in you. You need a few weeks to recover. A wagon trip right now is not advisable."

Her jaw dropped. She stared in surprise at him. Defiance flashed in her eyes. She closed her mouth. He could hear her teeth grind. She swallowed and said, "I'm going home, Grady!"

He knew this would be her response. "That sounds final." She just glared at him.

"Just listen to me a moment. I've made this trip with a herd many times. You have another month of trail to get to your ranch. You're still helpless. You can't ride a horse. You'll have to make it in a wagon. At this time we don't have a second wagon. We're borrowing Carmella's supply wagon. It's still winter cold. Grass is frozen. We have to haul grain. The herd's already suffering from poor feed and needs recovery time. We're going to need two wagons, or you're going to have to share the supply wagon with the grain. We both know how that was. If we find a second wagon, that means two drivers. I haven't even mentioned Trumpeter. We don't have enough men to drive wagons and herd cattle. Who's going to take care of you?"

Anger had left her face, and she whispered, "Aren't you going with me?" She studied him. His face registered shock.

He came out of it. "That's one of the problems. I've been taking care of you for several months after that outlaw handled you. I'm not ready to turn you over to anyone. But I have to be reasonable. I can hardly take care of myself. In an emergency I'd be worthless."

She spoke soft, "If you get me home, we can both rest and recover together."

She was pleading. She watched while he thought about what she said. He swallowed and said, "That doesn't quite sound respectable."

She grinned and said, "You could marry me."

His eyes grew as large as billiard balls. He tried to tell if she was serious or kidding. He said, "Are you proposing marriage to me?"

"If you'll have me." Nervously she returned to brushing her hair.

Grady stood, leaned over, and put a hand behind her head. His other hand lifted her chin. He lowered his mouth to hers. A soft, gentle kiss turned into a serious need. It took effort to leave her sweet lips and settle back in his chair.

She licked her lips and said, "Do I take that kiss as a yes?"

"Well, I gotta say that never in my wildest dreams did I imagine that the most amazing woman I have ever had the pleasure of knowing would propose to me! Actually, I was planning to do just this when I had a ring to give you. You've kind of jumped the gun. Yes! Thank you. I would be honored to be your husband."

She smiled. She looked like a little girl. Excited, she set her brush on the small table by the bed and said, "About the ring. I would really love to have you place my mother's rings on my finger. I would feel she was sharing my wedding and my happiness with her."

"I like that. I'll find another way to express my love. For now, it looks like our future is planned. We'd better work on the here and now." He rubbed the tight muscles in his neck.

"You know," Cecile said, "we've spent hours talking in the back of that wagon, but since you just kind of said that you loved me, exactly when do you think you first started to care for me?"

"Oh, that's easy," he chuckled. "The first time you stepped off the wagon and expertly cracked your bullwhip."

Cecile blushed. "Really? You liked that, huh? If I'd known, I would have done it a lot more often to impress you."

"Everything you do impresses me, ma'am." Grady looked seriously at Cecile, squarely in the eye. "Just to leave no doubt, I want to declare right now, Miss Cecile McNamara, that I love you." He grinned and said, "I even love you more than that darn bull of mine."

"Oh, you!" Cecile playfully smacked his shoulder. "Well, that is an honor because I know you love Deadly. Just so you know, I first started growing fond of you after that horrible man damaged my chest and you had to help me with that awful burning balm. You were so uncomfortable and sweet about caring for me. That's when I first started to lose my heart to you." Cecile's eyes moistened. "I love you too, Grady."

They wrapped each other in a long hug. Cecile had her head buried in Grady's neck, breathing in his scent. Suddenly she pulled away, full of emotion. "I want to go home." Tears gathered in her eyes.

"Don't cry, we'll get there. Do you feel like a trip downstairs for dinner?"

"I'd love it. I'm so tired of bed. Can I wear my robe? Candy gave me one. It's beautiful."

He stood, leaned over, kissed her softly, and pulling away said, "You look beautiful in whatever you wear. I'll send Della up to help with your hair, and Bear will have to carry you down the stairs. I'll carry you over the ranch threshold after we are married."

Everyone was gathered in the saloon except Carmella and Lou, who were finishing up the meal. Jalo was bringing plates and silverware. A table was set up buffet-style. Everyone could serve themselves, cold tea and water were for the taking.

Juan caught sight of Cecile in Bear's arms coming down the stairs. He rose and quickly went to take her hand and kiss it. He looked years younger as his eyes grew bright. He was so glad to see her up. She held to his arm, walked over to where Grady sat, and took the seat beside him.

Her vaqueros came to her one at a time, bowed down, kissed her hand, and greeted her warmly.

Grady watched this spectacle and for the first time really realized what a fine, respectable woman cared for him. Had asked him to marry her. She was a fit bride for a king, and she wanted to marry a cowboy.

She knew what Grady was thinking, as each of her vaqueros knelt down to her. She reached over, took his hand, raised it to her lips, kissed it, and settled their two hands clasped by her side. She had just staked a claim. He smiled, raised their two hands, and returned the kiss to hers.

Carmella came from the kitchen, perspiration sparkling on her brow. Juan brought her over and introduced her to Cecile. Cecile thanked her for helping with her rescue. She said, "I will forever be in your debt. After dinner please tell me how Glancy is doing."

Lance came in with a huge platter of barbecued ribs, followed by Lou with a steaming bowl of late-summer corn on the cob. There was already potato salad at the table. Jalo arrived with corn bread cut in squares. He set it down by a bowl of fresh churned butter.

Plates were filled. Juan fixed Cecile a plate. Grady managed his own. Juan gave a moving prayer. Thanking God for the rescue of his patron. Asking a speedy recovery for the ill and injured. He gave a special blessing for Glancy's recovery. Amens were expressed.

There was plenty of chatter as they visited and filled their stomachs with this spectacular meal.

Grady caught Cecile sitting quietly, her fork at rest. She was running her eyes over this gathering. There was such love in her face as she looked at each person at the table. Her people were her family. Old Lou and Bear her heroes. For days on the trail, they had cared for her and her herd. Her new friends, Candy, Carmella, and Della, she also gathered into her heart. She ended looking at each face in succession with Grady's, who had been watching her. He gave her hand a squeeze. She smiled, lifted her fork, and resumed eating.

After the meal, Della cleared the table with Jalo's help. Pie was cut. Hot coffee took its place where tea and water had set.

Grady stood and using his coffee spoon tapped his water glass for everyone's attention. They all stopped what they were doing and waited.

He cleared his throat and said, "I'd like to add another blessing to Juan's prayer. I feel that we are among our family. Some are hers, and I consider Bear, Lou, and Candy mine. We would like to announce our intention to marry."

Everyone talked at once. Questions were asked. Grady held up his hand and the room went silent. He smiled and said, "I'm kind of new at this. I'll let Ceci answer questions. We just arrived at this decision today. We've yet to make plans."

All were quiet and looked to Cecile. She ducked her head, taking a moment to collect her thoughts. Juan cleared his throat, stood, and said, "You are my godchild and my patron. I have taken care of you since you were born. I've known this day would come. I am proud of you. I respect and approve of this man who will take over the care of you." He sat back down.

"Juan, you are like a father. You will never get rid of me. You will walk me down the aisle and help me become a good wife to this man."

The vaqueros cheered and clapped their hands. Candy asked, "Have you set a date?"

Grady was about to shake his head. Cecile spoke up. "Things are so unsettled now. Our country is talking war, Abraham Lincoln will soon be our president, there's a long trail ahead of us. I don't want to wait a long time. If we can get to the rancho by Thanksgiving, it would give me time to plan a Christmas wedding." Then she remembered Grady. She looked at him, raised her eyebrows, and said, "Does that make sense?"

"Makes sense to me," he answered.

They all started to talk. The women took turns congratulating the two.

Candy stood up and announced, "Well, this has just turned into an engagement party, and we need to toast this handsome couple. I'm gonna step outside to my cellar and find the best bottle of whiskey I own so we can do this proper!"

An appreciative smile lit up Ceci's face. "That is so kind of you, Candy, but we don't want you to use up your best supply on us."

"Nonsense," replied Candy. "You all have been the kindest people I have been around in a long time, and, well, you feel kinda like family to me too. I own more booze than I know what to do with now that everyone is leaving Janos, and we are not gonna miss this important moment!"

Candy scooted back in her chair, stood, and headed toward the kitchen and back door that led to the cellar.

Happy conversation and well-wishes continued while the table awaited Candy's return.

Della had started to toss a few biscuits and breads out the kitchen door to the big bull when Deadly had first brought Grady into town, unconscious, many weeks ago. This heroic bull that had carried an almost dead man into town, strapped to his back, had enchanted Della. The bull then refused to budge from the yard, somehow sensing Grady was nearby, while Grady fought for his life. It didn't take long for Deadly to know by the smells and time that goodies would be coming to him soon.

Now that Grady was on his feet, he also knew to hang out on the front porch, by the hitching rail, for Grady to appear with biscuits and scratchings.

As Candy stepped outside with the cellar key in hand, she ran into Deadly standing by the back door, knowing that it was time for some leftovers to come his way. She smiled at the bull and said, "Sorry, Deadly, I shoulda known you'd be out here waiting for some goodies. I'm sure Della will be out with something soon, she has a real soft spot for you. Your best friend just announced some great news, so we got some celebratin' to do."

Deadly dropped his head and swung it back and forth, making it appear as though he understood every word.

He watched while Candy stood over the cellar doors working to undo the lock with her keys. She then threw the doors open and walked down into the cellar.

Deadly stood quietly waiting either for Della to throw him a tasty treat or for Candy to come back out of that hole she had just walked into. Whenever a part of his human herd or animal herd got separated from the group, he instinctively kept an eye on them until they returned to their group, especially the females.

Deadly wasn't comfortable having Candy down in that hole, his senses told him to watch out for her. He became agitated when he heard her voice change into a loud, sharp tone.

Candy was inside the cellar, bent over and searching for her special whiskey, when she heard glass bottles clinking together and drunken mutterings coming from the far corner of the cellar.

"Dammit, Toothless!" Candy exclaimed. "If that's you, I am gonna have you tarred and feathered!"

More garbled mutterings came from the corner. Candy stood and walked over to the dark corner without any apparent fear. As she approached the area, she saw a dark shape on the floor, leaning into the corner of the wall. Her foot hit an empty bottle and sent it skittering.

"I'm show shorry, Mish Cann'ee." The drunken man slurred his apology.

"You better be more than sorry, Toothless!" Candy, using her loudest and angriest voice, hoped to make an impression on the extremely inebriated man. "I told you if I caught you sneaking down here one more time, you'd really be sorry! Now get up and get upstairs right now! I have had it with you drinkin' all of my booze, so I brought me a special friend here just to deal with you since you won't listen to me!"

On many occasions the man known as Toothless would hide out in the back waiting for someone to unlock and open the cellar. He would then, quiet as a mouse, sneak down the stairs and hide until whoever had opened and went into the cellar left. He would then drink himself into oblivion until, usually the following day, someone would come open the cellar again to retrieve potatoes, onions, jams, or booze. Once, it was three days before the cellar was opened for supplies and he was found.

Deadly was quite worked up by the time Candy led Toothless out of the cellar. He was snorting and pawing the ground. After the incident with Cecile and the outlaw who had attacked her, he was much more alert with strangers until he watched how Grady responded to them. He learned that when he had protected Cecile, after she had screamed for help, he had done the right thing because Grady had praised him and given him extra biscuits. Cecile had even petted him, hugged him, and talked to him in a sweet, nice voice.

He had heard Candy yelling, and now she was coming out of the hole with someone he did not know. As he watched them come up, he continued to paw the ground. He put his head down, blew hard through his nose, and again swung his giant horns back and forth, although this time it was done very aggressively. He was clearly signaling "Watch out!" to the man with Candy.

Candy's sharp tone had not changed as she brought Toothless out of the cellar. She heard Deadly before she saw him. One look told her that he was reacting to the tone of her voice.

She inwardly felt honored that Deadly considered her as part of his herd family, or whatever it was that made him want to protect her.

Toothless, the drunken man, also saw the gigantic monster only a few yards away. His eyes nearly blew off his face as he turned in fright trying to get behind Candy and go back down into the cellar.

Candy didn't want to see old Toothless get hurt, so in a soft voice she said, "Oh no you don't," while gently but firmly grabbing his shoulders. "Listen, old man, I'm gonna let you go. I'll call my bull off of you, but only this time. If I catch you in my cellar one more time, I am determined to let this bull have his way with you." Candy flicked her eyes over to Deadly and could see he was quickly calming down as she changed the tone in which she spoke.

The shock that Toothless had over seeing Deadly ready to take a piece out of him sobered him up some, he was literally scared speechless. Toothless vigorously shook his head up and down in agreement to Candy's demand.

When they finished climbing up the cellar steps, Candy turned Toothless to face her. "Toothless, you are going to quietly turn away from Deadly and walk calmly out of here. Do you understand me?"

Toothless's head bobbed quickly up and down, his face was formed into a mask of terror.

"OK then," Candy said, exhaling the breath she had been holding, "I am going to go over and distract Deadly, while you get out of here."

Deadly had settled quite a bit by the time Candy approached him. "Deadly, I think there is a chance you just scared a man sober. There's a chance old Toothless may never take a drink again."

When Candy turned around to make sure Toothless had cleared the area, he was nowhere to be seen.

Everyone heard Candy come back in. She was laughing loudly and shouting, "That bull is a miracle worker!" All eyes turned toward the swinging door that led to the kitchen, waiting to see what Candy found so hilarious. As she swung through the door with a bottle of whiskey in hand, she giggled out, "We've got more than a wedding to celebrate! I think we get to celebrate the future sobriety of old Toothless! At the very least we get to celebrate him not sneakin' in my cellar and drinkin' all my booze!"

Candy had been laughing so hard when she came in that she had tears streaming down her face. She set the bottle on the table, grabbed her belly, and started laughing all over again.

"Sorry, folks, but each time I think of the look on that old man's face when he saw Deadly, well, it's just about the funniest thing I've ever seen."

Knowing that Deadly was involved naturally piqued Grady's curiosity. "Candy, why don't you get ahold of yourself and tell us all what happened?"

While she poured everyone a shot of whiskey for a toast, Candy gave them all a rundown of the trouble she'd had with the town drunk ever since she opened her place. Many at the table knew Toothless already. Soon the whole table was chuckling and smiling, Cecile said, "I guess we have to chalk up one more thing we owe to Deadly. He sure is special. I hope he will accept me into the family, or I'm in real trouble."

Once again the table broke out in laughter. It was a cheerful table that raised their glasses to toast Grady and Cecile's marriage announcement. It was suggested by Candy that they also do a toast to Deadly. Everyone agreed, so Candy started around the table again pouring shots.

When she got to Cecile's glass, Cecile placed her hand over it. "I think I shouldn't take another one, not while I'm recuperating."

"Nonsense." Candy grabbed the small shot glass underneath Cecile's delicate hand. "Both you and Grady can do for a few shots of this. Consider it your dose of medicine tonight. You'll both get a good night's sleep, and Grady, it will help you save on the sleeping potion the doc gave you."

Cecile relinquished, and with that they all raised a glass to Deadly. After the second toast everyone loosened up and the talk got happier and louder.

Grady looked around the table at the smiling faces. The whiskey had helped to ease the pain in his head, and for the first time in months he felt a slight sense of well-being. He was engaged to the most amazing woman he had ever known. It was hard for him to believe that a fine woman like Cecile wanted him for her husband. He felt like the luckiest man alive.

He was also grateful to be warm, and it put his mind at ease to know that all the people around this table that he cared about had full bellies and were safe, at least for the moment.

The conversation stayed lively for a while. Grady began getting tired. He noticed Cecile had quieted down and imagined she was exhausted. He motioned Bear over and asked him to get her up to bed.

Everyone said their good-nights to them as Grady followed them up the stairs along with Della. Bear sat Cecile on her bed and left. Grady gave her a kiss good-night and then let Della take over helping her ready for bed while he went to his room.

Too tired to remove his clothes, Grady took off his boots, lay on the bed, and pulled covers over himself. He skipped the swig of laudanum as the whiskey was still working. He expected to spend the night hashing over the day's surprises. This morning when he had gotten out of bed, he was a bachelor. He was going to bed a man betrothed to an angel.

The occupants of the saloon's beds were up and out early. Juan's crew were off to the stockyard to work on Carmella's supply wagon. They wanted to make sure it was in good repair, and they had to find grain to sack and load on it.

Carmella had insisted they take her supply wagon. She refused to accept a fee. She had laughed at Grady's surprised thank-you. She said, "I'm not giving it to you. It's a loan. It will give me another reason to attend your wedding. I'll take it back with me."

Grady had wakened early and listened to the early-morning breakfast noise. Fully dressed he pulled on his boots and carefully, clinging to the stair rails, made his way to a chair near the potbellied stove. He had noticed Cecile's door closed as he passed it. She had to be exhausted. Doc had ordered rest, so he decided to go straight downstairs.

He greeted those who passed and watched the men and women grab a hurried meal and disappear in different directions.

Bear came in, filled a cup with coffee, and joined Grady where he sat and watched the comings and goings.

Grady said, "I feel so useless. Had a little break from my head bangin', but this morning it's back in full bloom. I'm tired of this."

Bear chuckled and answered, "Does kind of feel like we're being left out. Juan's in charge. You're right. We're not going to hold that bunch here."

"I was going to suggest they stay a few days for Cecile's sake. I guess I'll give that up."

Grady eyed Bear's cup of coffee. Bear got up and poured coffee, black, in a clean cup and set it before him.

Grady had a bewildered look on his face, but he thanked Bear for the coffee.

Bear said, "I thought we would have a few days to work things out."

Grady's thoughts shifted to Bear. "What's up?"

"Remember we made plans for after we delivered this herd to winter at your cabin? Lou and I agreed to help with some work. But illness and your wedding may change those plans. My guess is you'll stay at Cecile's hacienda until after the wedding."

Grady closed his eyes and tried to envision these changes. Bear waited until he opened his eyes. Grady hesitated and said, "That sounds like the best plan. I still want the two of you to go to the ranch. Hopefully I'll be able to travel with you. The wedding will give me time to think this over."

"Changes things," Bear said. "I think it best we all wait until after the wedding to make other plans. Candy is determined to leave Janos. She could use Lou and me. She wants to go to your wedding. I think we can get her packed up and all meet at Cecile's ranch for the wedding."

They both sat quiet for a moment while Grady thought about this change. He decided Bear's suggestions were good. Bear and Lou would be uncomfortable hanging out at Cecile's hacienda, and Candy had more than earned some help.

He said, "I'm agreeable, Bear. I really need to travel on with Juan. I'm not ready to abandon Cecile. I can take care of her. I'll take Deadly with us. He knows the trail even in bad weather. However, I need Lou. We still don't have the wagon problems solved. The stock wagon from Carmella that is providing transportation for Trumpeter is fully enclosed and would keep the weather off of us if Cecile and I confiscated it. As you know, Trumpeter is first on all our lists for protection. So we need to do a quick search through town and see if we can buy another wagon. If we get lucky and find one, I'm going to need Lou to drive it. He also has some doctoring experience in case Cecile gets worse."

Bear finished his coffee and said, "I'll saddle my horse and go scouting." They shook hands, and he left Grady to worry over this trail drive that was not fully in Grady's command.

After his talk with Grady, Bear realized he would have to wait on a wagon for Candy. He saddled the paint and set off to ride around the small town. Whenever he spotted a wagon that would work, he found the owner and offered to buy it. He was turned down on the first two. After a couple of hours, both he and the paint were getting tired and he frustrated. He realized not many families had a wagon and those who did didn't want to sell.

He was ready to call it quits and head back to the saloon when he spotted what looked like a box with large steel-rimmed wheels. The box was black with lettering on the sides: Moore Mortuary, Burials $1.25.

The black box was behind a run-down old house that needed a paint job and yard care. He turned the paint horse in and stopped by the box. He swung down and tied the horse to one of the wheels. He walked around the box and stepped off a size of six feet wide and eight feet long. Definitely large enough for a coffin or a mattress. It would be perfect for two ill travelers.

He went to the door of the run-down house. He knocked and waited. No one came. He banged harder. He heard someone say, "I hear ya. I'm coming."

The door opened on squeaking hinges, and a little old lady looked up at him. Her eyes widened as she saw an Indian standing there. She reached to her right and pulled a shotgun into her arms, its barrel pointing at him.

"Whoa, hold on, I'd just like to buy your black wagon," he said.

Her eyes blinked. She took her time looking him over. Bear stepped back so as not to scare her. She stepped out the door and saw the paint horse tied to her wagon.

"Whatcha offering?" She moved the shotgun in both arms across her chest.

"What are you asking? If you're willing to sell it. I have to talk to my boss."

"How about a million dollars?"

Bear caught his breath, stepped back, and put his hands back up and said, "Whoa?"

She chuckled. Her serious little face changed to having laugh wrinkles. She lowered the shotgun and turned around. She said, "Come on in, my legs are tired." She led him to a small neat parlor and motioned him to sit on an old but clean settee decorated with crocheted doilies. She sat in what looked like her favorite old rocking chair. She laid the shotgun across her lap. An old valise on the floor beside the rocker spilled over with yarns.

She watched him as he surveyed her neat little house. When his eyes came back to hers, she said, "Whatcha want that hearse for? I didn't think Indians did white men's burials."

He smiled and answered, "You're right, we don't bury our people in the ground. We put them on raised piers where they have fresh air and can see the Mother Sun."

She nodded her head, smiled, and said, "I like that. Think I'll request a pier burial in my will. You didn't answer me. Whatcha want with my hearse?"

Bear was enjoying himself. This bright little woman reminded him of his grandmother. He told her about the herd at the stockyard. "My boss is ill. The herd has to be trailed to a ranch near San Antonio. It's winter. The weather is bad. He's just recovering from pneumonia. Your hearse would keep the weather off him."

She nodded again, laid the shotgun beside the rocker, and got up. She steadied herself and looking Bear in the eye said, "I need some tea. Water's hot—just be a minute."

He watched her walk out. He wanted to hurry this along. But he didn't want to blow the chance of obtaining her hearse. She was probably lonely, and this was a social hour for her. In just a few minutes, she was back with a tray. Two large mugs of hot water floated loose tea leaves, and beside the mugs was a saucer of cookies. She set the tray on a stool and slid the stool between them.

She sat down, drew in a deep breath, and told Bear the story of the hearse.

"My father was a mortician. We lived in New York. Business was good. We lived in a nice house. Always had plenty to eat.

"My father took in young men to apprentice in his business. Most young men disliked working with the dead. It was often hard to hire someone to help in the business. I often had to work with my father. When Mr. Wilbert asked if he could apprentice with my father, we learned right away that he chose to apprentice as a mortician because he was poor. He didn't have a family so he needed a roof over his head, and at least one meal a day.

"My father agreed. Mr. Wilbert worked hard to learn the business. Often I would find him on his rest breaks sitting on the porch, daydreaming. After a year Mr. Wilbert stayed on working for my father because he didn't have the money to start up his own mortuary.

"I often joined him on the porch and learned of his dreams. He wanted to go out west. I listened to his stories of free land, but I had learned about the savage Indians and discouraged him. I married Mr. Wilbert. That's what I always called him.

"We had one child, a son. Little Willie was twelve years old when my father died of a bad heart. I learned that he also had a bad gambling habit. He left me with a lot of debts. Mr. Wilbert was a skilled student. We could have continued on in the business, but he convinced me that now was a good time to move the business out west. At that time even though it scared me to pack up and travel, it was also exciting. New lands to explore.

"We barely had enough money to buy supplies. We packed our belongings in the hearse. With a tent and our two horses, we headed west.

"We camped in towns. Earned a living working with the towns' morticians. Often the town had no mortician and the local doctor performed that job. I did many jobs. Waitressing or housecleaning. When we had earned enough to buy supplies, we continued.

"When we got to San Antonio, it was a year after we left New York. I had had it! I told Mr. Wilbert no more!

"I wanted a house to settle down in. He wasn't happy with my decision, but he tried to grant my wishes. He hired on with a freight hauler that serviced many small communities. He covered the signs on the hearse and was hired to fulfill the smaller provisions needing delivery.

"We were still living in our tent. I house hunted and soon realized it would take us months to earn rent money.

"Mr. Wilbert came back from a freight run to Janos. He was excited about the small town. Houses were cheap here, and he had seen several abandoned ones we could fix up. He could still work for the freight company and maybe set up a mortician's business in Janos. It sounded like my dream was to come true.

"He convinced me to pack up our tent with all our possessions. I had no idea how far it was to Janos. It took us three weeks of steady driving. We had to kill game for food. I was so upset. He kept telling me it was going to be a good move.

"When we reached Janos, I was so disappointed. We had left a thriving city. It had places I could work. Mr. Wilbert was a good mortician. We could have built a business there. Janos was small and unruly. It had one local doctor. The people were nice but most as poor as us. They were lucky to grow their own food. It would be a year before we would see any produce from a garden.

"We found this house. It had been abandoned a long time. We had tools. We had brought my fathers with us. Mr. Wilbert patched holes in the roof. I cleaned and painted when I could afford the paint. We had no furniture, but I finally had my house.

"The local minister and some of the church family shared garden vegetables. Mr. Wilbert hunted. We had deer meat and rabbits. Little Willie went to school. The class was small and had children of several ages.

"It took us several weeks to settle in our house. Mr. Wilbert came home one day with this rocker I'm sitting in. It had a broken leg. I was getting pretty good with the tools. I fixed it. my first piece of furniture.

"Mr. Wilbert was getting restless. He was anxious to return to San Antonio. We needed some steady income."

She sat back in her chair and drank the last of her tea, leaving tea leaves in the bottom of her mug. She set the mug on the tray and said, "I'm getting ahead of myself."

Bear had gotten caught up in her story. With this hesitation he realized he had been here longer than needed. He was about to make good-bye words when she continued.

"One day Mr. Wilbert came home with a worn saddle and bridle. He shared his plan with me. The horse would make faster time than the hearse and the team, and he would have less cost for care and feed for one horse. The owner of the freight business had other setups. He would just hire on as a driver. He packed a bag, taking some of the dried deer jerky. He kissed me good-bye. Warned me that it could be many months before he saw me because of the distance to Janos. He surprised me by putting ten dollars in my hand.

"That was the last time I saw Mr. Wilbert. I knew when he left that I had to care for Little Willie and myself for many months until his return. Thank goodness I looked for work immediately.

"The saloon Miss Candace owns now was owned by a man. He was not a nice man, but he had odd jobs at times. There was no other source of income in Janos. I used my hearse and cut wood and hauled it. I did laundry for the saloon. I refused to work the upstairs beds, but I washed the sheets and cleaned. I learned to work the bar. Wages and tips were small, but when working at the saloon, I could take home leftover food.

"I became the town's mortician. I had learned enough from my father and Mr. Wilbert to do the work. I used my hearse and earned my way."

She sat still for a moment. Bear saw a tear roll down a wrinkled face. Then she said, "And now you want to buy my hearse?"

Bear shook his head to dispel the story she had told. His mind returned to the parlor in her little house. He had asked to buy the only thing she had counted on all her life.

He answered, "I'm sorry. I can see you rely on that hearse. It's always been there for you." He rose to leave.

She stopped him. "I want twenty-five dollars and two cords of wood."

He was surprised. "Are you sure you want to sell It?"

She answered him, "I'm by myself. Little Willie died in a gunfight. I'm worthless. I can't cut wood no more. Got no horse to pull the wagon. I need wood. I no longer need the hearse. If it serves your purpose, I'm proud to let you have it."

Bear smiled and said, "Forgive me. I failed to introduce myself. I am Little Bear of my mother Rising Star's clan. I am Navajo. I have worked for the Grady Trail Drives for three years. I will talk to him about the purchase of your black wagon. I will return to buy it or to let you know if we decide not to get it. Thank you, Mrs. Wilbert."

She stood, steadied herself, and said, "I quit using Mr. Wilbert's name after he abandoned me. I use my father's name." She offered her hand to shake and continued, "I am Metta Mabelle Moore. I prefer Belle."

Bear took her small hand in his and said, "It's an honor to meet you, Miss Belle."

She followed him to the door, stood on the porch, and watched him ride the paint horse down the street.

Bear found Grady at the same table as when he left. He learned Grady had spent the afternoon visiting with Cecile. They had both taken a nap. Grady had woken first and made his way back downstairs.

Grady was drinking coffee. Bear went to the kitchen and found the coffeepot keeping warm on the back of the wood stove. Lou wasn't around, but a large pot of beans was also simmering on the stove. He got a cup, filled it, and joined Grady.

"I gather you've been wagon hunting." Grady acknowledged him.

"Yes, sir. I met an interesting little old lady. She reminded me of my Indian grandmother."

Candy came down the stairs and, seeing Bear was back, joined the men to hear Bear's report.

Bear told them about Belle's hearse. When he finished, he said, "I think it will be just what you need. It's light enough to pull easily and sturdy enough to make the trip."

"From what you've told me, it's quite old." Grady was concerned. Whatever vehicle they used, he didn't want it to break down halfway to Cecile's ranch.

"I'll take it to the blacksmith by the stockyard and have it checked out. The wheels are wooden with steel rims; they looked good to me. It's been sitting for some time, so it will need greasing. I want him to test the axle. Not my expertise." Bear got up and put another piece of wood in the stove.

Grady wished he could see this wagon before taking it on, but he trusted Bear's judgment. In his condition he would be forced to rely on others at times. This was one of those times. He asked, "What kind of horsepower do we need?"

Bear remembered his surveillance of the hearse and said, "It has a one-horse hookup now, but I saw the double yoke they used to carry them from back east to San Antonio. After the husband left, she only had one horse. It won't take much to switch back to a team. We've got plenty of harness saved from the wagons left in the canyon."

Candy knew Belle, and she said, "I had forgotten about that hearse. Belle used to work at this saloon for the previous owner. After I bought it, she occasionally stood in for my bartender. Been a while since I used her. She got too old to handle rowdy alcoholics. She took up handwork. Knit sweaters, crochet doilies. I let her set up on the porch during the summers

84

to sell her things. I never really thought about how she made it through the winter. Poor old gal."

Grady waited until Candy finished her reminiscing about Belle and then asked her, "Is my cash still in your safe?"

Candy had found a money belt on Grady when he had first arrived on the bull, delirious with fever. He had left the canyon on horseback with money to purchase food supplies and hire some riders; half his crew had been killed by outlaws. The crew left behind in the canyon needed supplies and help to get the herd down to Janos. He had counted on enough grass and water to provide for the herd until he got back. The crew would have to butcher a cow if needed to tide them over till he returned. His plan was thwarted when his horse broke its leg and he was severely injured.

If Candy had not nursed him back to health weeks after his arrival, he would have died from a concussion, dislocated shoulder, and severe case of pneumonia.

Juan had arrived from Cecile's ranch and found the Smith boys to help drive the herd. Candy had furnished the supplies. He had not yet repaid the money as planned. He was going to pay Candy and the boys, but as yet all the funds should be in the safe.

She answered, "It should be. I haven't had time to check out my office or the safe. I'll go up now, and I hope no one broke into either while I was away on our rescue mission. Do you want it all?"

"No, I'll need to settle up with you and pay the boys their wages. Just bring me the twenty-five for the hearse."

The office was on the second floor next to her bedroom. The door was locked. It didn't show signs of having been jimmied. Della and her shotgun did a good job protecting things. The safe was locked, and it opened to reveal that all stored in it was as she left it.

She breathed a sigh of relief as she counted out twenty-five dollars from Grady's stack. She locked back up, went downstairs, and laid the bills on the table before Grady.

He didn't bother to count them. He handed them to Bear and said, "What about the wood?"

Candy spoke up. "We'll have to buy it or pay someone to cut and deliver. We can check with Carmella. She usually has some of her ranch crew stocking up for the ranch and the bordello." She turned to Bear and said, "Tell Belle that Candace Murray will be responsible for the wood. I think she will trust my word."

Grady said, "We need to get that hearse now. Juan is not going to hang around here, and we don't know what repairs the thing will need."

Bear cut in, "It wouldn't hurt to leave a couple of days after the herd. With a lightweight wagon pulled by a team, it won't take you long to catch up. That would give both of you a couple more days' recovery time and allow us to make repairs or changes to the hearse."

Grady agreed and said, "Find Lou before you go. Tell him I need to see him. You need to get a wagon horse and harness and go get that hearse."

Bear left, and Grady asked Candy to wait so they could discuss what he owed her and to retrieve the money needed to pay the Smith boys. When that was settled, she rose to go back to the safe and get the boys' wages. When she returned to the saloon with the money, Lou was just coming in to join Grady. She gave the cash to Grady and left the two men to conduct whatever business Grady had for Lou.

Grady told Lou about the wagon Bear had located and informed Lou of the decision to accompany the herd to Cecile's ranch. He said, "Cecile refuses to let the herd go without her. We know that she has always refused to turn the Herefords over to anyone. So! I need to run some things by you."

Lou shifted in his chair. Took his hat off, set it in the chair next to him, and waited for Grady to continue.

"It's not looking like I'm going to be well enough to go on to my ranch in bad winter weather. The added surprise of a Christmas wedding creates the need to remain at the hacienda until after the holidays. I know you and Bear had planned to hang out with me over the winter. I've already talked with Bear. He's going to stay here and help Candy pack up. She's determined to move out of Janos."

Grady had been feeling the headache getting stronger and knew he was going to have to lie down for a while before dinner. He continued, "Is there any coffee?" He massaged his neck and the back of his head.

Lou got up and hurried to the kitchen. He always kept a pot warm on the wood cook stove. He returned with two cups and set Grady's before him. He sat and waited for Grady to continue. He was afraid he was going to be let go.

"Anyway, Bear thinks he can get Candy packed up and make it to the wedding at Christmastime. They will travel in Candy's packed wagon." He took some more sips of the hot coffee, rubbed his head, and continued, "I need you to stay with me and stay on the payroll."

"Hell yes, boss! I didn't think you were going to make it to your ranch. Just tell me what you need me to do."

"We are going to use the wagon Bear found to carry Ceci and me to her ranch. Bear is picking up the wagon now and will stop by so we can see what we're dealing with. I want you to be our driver. You and I will care for Ceci. I need you, Lou; you have some doctoring. I know it's more for animals than humans, but you're good. You can see to it we have the supplies and medicine our wagon needs to keep her well. Does this sound all right with you?"

"Hell yes, boss. I've been worrying about Miss Ceci. I know how sick she was in that canyon. I watched over her there, and I can do it now.

"OK, here's what I need you to do. First, pick a good harness team out of the remuda, move them here to Candy's barn. Bring me the proper harness and some oil. I can manage cleaning and mending it right here. You need to start concentrating on loading us up. It's a small wagon, so check it out when Bear gets here to figure how much we can carry. We will leave a couple days after the herd. Might take us a couple of days to catch up. We'll need to carry food for a few days in case of delays and breakdowns. Check with Juan at supper to get an idea of the herd's departure."

Grady drank his coffee and pushed the cup to the center of the table. He said, "Lou, you and I are going to put our plans on hold until after the wedding in December. That will give me some time to build some strength and figure things out. I want you to stay with me at Ceci's. Will you do that?"

Tears pooled in Lou's eyes. He said, "Boss, I miss my boy. I'm pretty lost with him gone. I'm grateful you need me. You're kind of the only family I have."

Grady's memories flashed to the bloody youngster shot by the outlaws with a shotgun. He had to blink his eyes to keep them from tearing up. Denny had been a good boy.

"That's pretty much how I feel also, Lou. I plan on you being best man at the wedding." Grady offered his hand.

A tear rolled down Lou's cheek. He took Grady's hand in a firm shake and said, "I'd be honored, son."

Grady realized Lou called many of the younger trail hands "son." He felt this use of the word was closer to Lou's heart. Having gone many years without a father, Grady was touched. He gently squeezed Lou's hand.

Lou grabbed his hat and went to check his pot of beans. After he did a few chores in the kitchen, he sorted through the pile of harness in the corner of the saloon. He made sure it was complete with bridles, reins, and all the extras needed to dress a team. He took them to Grady and piled them close enough for his boss to reach them.

He went back to the kitchen. Peeled a dishpan full of potatoes. Quartered them and dropped them in the beans. Next he mixed up dry ingredients for biscuits. When dinner was about ready, he would add the liquid and bake.

Grady waited for Lou to bring water to clean the leather and oil to soften it. When he realized Lou had forgotten, he decided to check on Ceci. He climbed the stairs and went to her opened door.

She was sitting up, leaning against a pile of pillows. Her eyes were closed, and she had a smile on her face.

She was so beautiful. She still had some skin suffering from the harsh weather on the mountain, but it was healing. The nourishing food and the rest she was getting were doing their job. He spoke softly, not wanting to startle her. "I hope you are thinking of me."

Her eyes opened, and she said, "You were included. I was dreaming of home and the wedding. It's so much fun to have happy thoughts. I spent so many hours in the canyon fearing I would never see home again."

He pulled a chair close, kissed her, and settled into the chair. Grady said, "It's been many years since I had a home. I was sixteen when my dad died and I took to the trail. The last few years, I looked forward to settling down on my land in Texas. I planned on building a home." He smiled as he said this. He didn't want her to think their marriage would interfere with his plans.

She sobered. She realized she had been so caught up in her desires and plans that she hadn't considered the dreams he might be giving up. She reached to him, and he took her hand. She said, "I don't want you to give up that dream. I have been hoping you would love my home and want to live in it with me."

Grady kissed her hand and said, "I'm sure I will love your home. We are not going to worry about this until after our wedding. We have a month's travel ahead. It will give us time to organize our future. Just keep thinking about our wedding plans. I'm going to go down and clean harness. Bear has found us a wagon. It will take you home. Keep that thought. Lou has dinner about ready. Do you want to join us later?"

"Yes, send Della to help me. I want to try walking down. I must get out of this bed. I intend to walk whenever the wagon stops for the night. Remember how I worked to recover from that disgusting man's hands on me? I can do this. I would like to arrive at the hacienda on my feet. Well enough to plan this wedding. Then there're the Herefords. You think Deadly was a challenge meeting Trumpeter and Reginald? You haven't met a challenge until you meet Diablo." The worry lines crossed her forehead.

Diablo? Probably one of her Spanish fighting bulls, thought Grady. She had told him of the Toro Bravo bulls bred by her father and her promise to keep them bred pure. He had forgotten them. Taking Deadly and the two Hereford bulls into Diablo's territory could be a serious challenge.

He could tell her mind was active. She was getting some color back in her cheeks. He kissed her and left her to her thoughts. She was right. She needed to get her legs useful, but he didn't want her to overdo it and bring on the sore throat and fever. Muscles weak from inactivity. He knew all about that, clinging as he was now to the stair rail and forcing his weak leg muscles to carry him down the stairs.

When he reached his table and the pile of harnesses, he saw that Lou had brought a pan of soapy water, rags, and some lubricating oil. Sorting the things into organized piles, he began on the bridals.

Bear knocked on Belle's door. When she answered, he gave her the money and told her Candace Murray would be responsible for supplying the firewood. He asked if it was all right for him to take the hearse now.

She stepped out on the porch and saw the horse he brought already harnessed and ready to attach to the wagon.

He said, "I need to make some small changes to get it ready for my boss to leave. The herd will leave before him to give me time to get it trail ready. I'm not traveling with the herd. I'm staying to help Candy pack up. She's determined to leave Janos after I get my boss on the road. I'll personally see you get your wood."

Belle said, "I don't blame her for getting out of this town. What I should have done. I'll miss her. She's helped me often. I see you brought a horse. Go ahead and hook up. I'll sit here in the porch swing and watch the old buggy go."

Bear knew it would be like watching an old friend drive away. He remembered the double hitch and said, "Ma'am, we need the team hookup. I'll see you get another half cord of wood for it."

"Sounds like a good deal to me, so go ahead. I got no more use for it anyway. I'd just end up cutting it up for firewood." She rocked the swing and watched Bear hitch the horse.

When he finished, he slid the team yoke into the hearse. It stuck out a bit. He couldn't shut the doors. It was steady, it would ride as far as the blacksmith. When he finished, he walked to Belle and offered his hand. She put her wrinkled little hand in his. He shook it softly and said, "Thank you, Miss Belle. We'll take good care of it for you."

"Thank you, Mr. Bear. I'm sorry to see it go, but it's better than watching it rot in the yard."

Bear pulled the horse up in front of the saloon. Tied the horse to the hitch rail. Hurried up the stairs and stuck his head in the saloon door. Grady was still sitting at the table where he had left him. He said, "Boss."

Grady looked up, and Bear said, "Hearse is here. Want to see it?"

Grady set aside the harness he had been working on. Stiff from sitting, Grady got up, stretched tight muscles, and went out to the porch. Bear sat in a chair. Grady sat next to him. His first thought as he studied the hearse was, how many dead people had occupied the hearse.

He cleared his head and with an experienced eye looked over the wagon. It looked sturdy. The blacksmith would do a closer inspection. He said to Bear, "Looks good, however, my first thought was, how many customers has it carried over the years?"

"Yeah." Bear leaned his chair back and lifted his feet to a porch rail. "That's been my first thought every time I see it."

Grady was quiet, thoughtful, and finally said, "Won't do. I don't want Ceci to have that thought every time she sees it or when she's in it."

Bear agreed, he nodded and said, "I thought of covering it with canvas. Make it warmer."

"She would wonder what we were hiding, and a good wind could blow it off." Grady had acquired a habit of massaging his aching head and neck. The pain had slowly subsided, but worrying over a subject caused the dull pain to intensify. He said, "It needs a coat of paint."

Bear laughed and said, "Where do you think you are? There is a small emporium, but it's mostly a wish-list freighter drop-off. The owner gets orders. He makes lists and gives them to the driver. The items arrive months later, *if* the freighter has enough orders to make a Janos delivery."

Grady smiled and said, "Are you forgetting? I'm one of those freight drivers when I'm not pushing a herd. And I know a couple of those drivers that have Janos on their route."

"I can check and see if the emporium has any paint or whitewash. It's a good thing you've decided to leave a few days after the herd. Hope it gives me time to get all these changes made."

"Cecile's coming down for dinner. I don't want her to see this black box. Please take it on to the blacksmith's."

Laughing, Bear dropped his feet to the porch, "Yes, sir. I'll be back for dinner."

Bear unhooked the horse and, leaving the hearse for the Smithy, returned the horse to the remuda at the stockyard. It didn't look as if anyone was around, but he heard laughter coming from the hay barn. Lance and Jalo, close in age, were getting to know each other as they threw hay to the herd.

They both came out of the hay barn dragging a bale of hay. Bear saw they were racing to see which one reached the Herefords first. Lance was a little ahead. Jalo was a year younger than Lance, but he was larger in size and catching up with Lance fast. Laughter was slowing both down. They reached the pen together.

Still laughing, each dropped to sit on his bale. Fighting for breath, they hadn't seen Bear and were startled when he said, "Looks like a tie to me." He walked over to the corral rails and, with one booted foot on the bottom rail, leaned his arms on the top rail and looked over the little white-faced cows.

They were pushing each other aside, crowding in anticipation of the hay to be thrown to them. The boys were getting their laughter under control. Bear lingered, checking out the small herd. He had spent many a mile eating their trail dust and taking care of them. They looked restless being penned, but he could see that the rest and a few good meals were showing a vast improvement in their condition. It had been a bedraggled herd that had come out of that canyon. He was relieved to see them looking so much better.

Bear turned to face the young men. He leaned back against the corral fence.

Lance was grinning at him and said, "I didn't see you. We were having a race. The winner gets to have the others' dessert tonight."

"Doesn't sound like a good bet to me," Bear chuckled. "Old Lou's not stingy with seconds."

"Yeah," Lance said, "but Jalo don't know that. I was going to bet chores on the next two bales. I let him catch up to me on this one. Setting him up, you know?"

"You dirty snake!" Jalo pulled off his hat, reached over, and slapped Lance with it.

Lance dodged away. Jalo lost his balance and fell off his bale.

Now all three were laughing. Bear enjoyed these two. He hadn't known Jalo long. He had gotten to know Lance pretty well when they were trailing out of the canyon. He was a good young man, always carrying his load and more. It had been a while since Bear had heard laughter.

Bear asked, "Where is everyone?"

Lance sat back down on his bale of hay. Jalo brushed the dirt off his pants and sat back on his bale.

Lance answered, "We were all taking a break before dinner. We met in Juan's room and played some poker. Jalo and I were losing so they made us feed tonight. We left them still playing cards."

Jalo spoke up. "We saw you drive by in a hearse. What's that all about?"

Bear told them the plans for the hearse. He said, "I wanted to talk to the smithy about checking it out. Seems I missed him. Guess it will wait till morning. I have to hunt for paint in the morning also."

"Paint?" Lance looked puzzled. "What you need paint for?"

Bear explained Grady's desire to cover the faded black hearse before Cecile saw it. He said, "He doesn't want her to worry about traveling in a buggy that used to carry dead folks."

"I don't blame him," Lance said. "That's the first thought I had when you drove by. I was wondering who just died."

Jalo agreed by nodding his head. He put his hat back on and was about to stand when Lance said, "What color you going to paint it?'

"Don't suppose I'll have much choice," Bear answered. "Do you know if the emporium carries paint?"

"Didn't a few years ago when Ma wanted to paint the barn. She wanted that red barn color. She had to order it from back east, where most paint their barns that dark red. Took three months to get it, and she had to pay up front before Mr. McKee would order it." Lance got up, took out a pair of wire cutters, and cut the baling wire.

Bear was tired. He hadn't stopped more than a few minutes since coming to town. Lance saw the weary expression on Bear's face. He and Bear had carried the most strenuous workloads coming off the mountain. The Indian had earned Lance's respect. Maybe Lance could help him. He said, "I think he keeps whitewash. You could do the inside white."

Bear straightened up off the corral and said, "The inside's in pretty good condition. The hearse is lined with cedar inside. It's damaged a little. Belle used the hearse to haul firewood. The cedar's dry, but it still puts out a pleasant smell. Whitewash or paint might get overpowering in that enclosed area."

That thought gave Bear another job to fix. There was no air circulation without opening the doors. The occupants, especially the two recovering, would be unable to escape body odor and medications. He would need to cut a window that could be opened to let in fresh air.

The best spot for that would be behind the driver's bench designed so the driver, Lou in this case, and Grady could talk.

Bear had been lost in thought. He realized Lance had been talking to him. He held up his hand to silence the young man. "Sorry, I was working something out. I didn't hear you. Start over."

Lance said, "I know we've got paint stored. Ma didn't know how much we would need. To keep from running out and reordering, she doubled her order. I don't know if paint spoils. I'll see if I can find it. That is if you want red?"

"Oh, hell, Lance. It will make for a good conversation topic and laughs. It will stand out for miles. But it seems the best we can do. I know Grady will be grateful, anything to keep Miss Ceci from knowing this was a hearse."

Lance grinned and said, "I think I heard Candy's dinner bell. We'd better throw feed and go eat."

Bear pulled out a bale of hay and fed Grady's remuda horses.

The next morning, after Lou made oatmeal, biscuits, and coffee and put them on the wood stove to stay warm, he made a trip to see the hearse. His first thought, like everyone else, was how many dead people the old hearse had seen over the years.

He opened the double doors and viewed the empty space. There was a musty cedar scent. Looked to be about six feet wide, eight feet long, and five feet tall. Not much to work with. A couples mattress would just fit. No room elsewhere.

There was a six-foot-by-one-and-a-half-foot space under the driver's bench. Add a small catch rail around it, and he could store some things in that space. Some low rails around the roof of the hearse would carry food supplies, extra covers, clothes, and winter wear. To be usable it would need a canvas tie-down tarp to cover the roof's necessary load.

Bear helped himself to a bowl of oatmeal, buttered several biscuits, grabbed a mug, and filled it with coffee. With his breakfast gathered, he chewed on a biscuit while he walked to the blacksmith shop and found Lou inspecting the hearse.

The doors to the wagon were open so he set his bowl and mug to one side and sat beside his breakfast. He said, "Good morning, Lou. What you think?"

Lou said, "Ain't much room. I have a few suggestions." He drug over an empty nail keg. Turned it upside down and sat on it. He rubbed his gimpy leg, cold weather made it ache.

Bear picked up his mug and swallowed the coffee that was quickly cooling in the cold morning temperature. He put the mug down and worked on the oatmeal while Lou gave him the suggestions for creating a buggy that could carry the items needed to care for Grady and Cecile.

When Lou finished, he left in a hurry to get back to the kitchen for breakfast cleanup. He carried Bear's empty dishes with him.

Bear sat and mentally envisioned the additions Lou had requested. He was getting a faint musty odor from the old cedar interior wood. This enclosed wagon definitely needed a window.

He would cut the window out and use the cutout as the door. He could use leather hinges and put a slide bar on the inside for closure.

Lou had not asked for it, but he could put a small six-inch shelf a foot down from the ceiling on Cecile's side. It would keep things from falling on her and give her a place to put girly things she might need to get to.

On Grady's side up close to the ceiling he would add a rifle rack. Above each of their heads, on the front wall just under the ceiling, he would put hooks for their pistols. Everything in easy reach. Just in case. After all, this red wagon was gonna stand out like a sore thumb.

One last thought. He would extend the side rails on the roof three feet out over the driver's area and add a canvas awning to shield Old Lou from rain or blazin' sun.

The blacksmith showed up. Bear left him to inspect the hearse while he went in search of lumber to do the additions.

Grady passed Cecile's closed door and noticed Candy's door was also closed. He made his way slowly down the stairs and found Juan and his vaqueros. They had helped themselves to breakfast and were seated in the saloon eating.

Grady went to the kitchen and helped himself to oatmeal and coffee. He buttered two biscuits and put two extra biscuits in his pocket for Deadly. He joined Juan and his crew. A good time to share travel plans. He told Juan about the wagon they had located and that he and Cecile planned to leave a few days after the herd to give her more recovery days.

Juan was vastly relieved to learn his godchild agreed to take more time to recover. She had insisted they get back on the trail immediately. He was happy to accommodate her wishes, but he had been worried sick about her condition. Knowing Grady was putting her well-being first gave him great peace of mind. So far, this man was proving to be an admirable match for his fine lady.

Juan said, "I want to give the herd a couple more days of feed and rest. They need care as bad as the humans brought out of the canyon. Now that I know space is not needed for passengers, I can carry more cattle feed in the wagons. We will leave in two days."

In better spirits Juan and his crew left to begin the loading and care of the wagons. Wheels needed greasing before they could add feed and supplies.

Lance came into town midmorning driving a team pulling the traveler wagon Carmella was loaning them to carry old Trumpeter. He also had a five-gallon can of red barn paint and half a dozen paintbrushes. Beside him in the shotgun seat was Glancy. Against her better judgment Carmella had been talked into letting him ride to town with Lance. The boy had gotten so restless at the ranch knowing all the excitement was going on in town. The ranch foreman and Lance had loaded him bodily into the driver's seat.

He had some pain as he adjusted the broken leg encased in brace bars, but he gritted his teeth and smiled for fear Carmella would make him get down and stay home.

When Lance pulled up to the saloon, Bear gathered the boy in his arms and carried him to a chair next to Grady. Candy was up, and she directed Bear to bring down one of the smaller single beds. She moved tables together and set the bed up close to Grady where they could visit and Glancy could see people coming and going from the saloon doors and kitchen door.

There was a glowing happy look on Glancy's face as all who came and went stopped to greet the boy and visit with him. Grady gave him an oiled rag and a bridle to work on.

Lance drove the cattle hauler to the blacksmith and parked it where the smithy could get to it when he was ready. He was working on three wagons at once. The traveler just needed wheels greased. Jalo threw hay in to cushion the floor in case Trumpeter fell.

Bear turned the paint and brushes over to Juan, who in turn put the vaqueros and Lance to painting the hearse. In an hour there was no depressing black hearse. In its place was a very red wagon.

Lance and Jalo were in stiches laughing, joking, and teasing Bear. The hearse now looked like a traveling salesman's wagon or a calling card for ladies of the night.

Bear was surprised the painting was finished so fast. He hadn't yet added the roof rails. He would have to paint them himself.

Lou was busy gathering medical supplies. He would also need a few pots and pans. He got them from a pile in the saloon of cooking utensils he had salvaged from the grub wagon, which was still up in the canyon. He would have to put some hooks on the little wagon to hang them.

He packed up all the remaining salvaged supplies in a trunk and asked Juan to find room for them on the supply wagon. They would need them once they were all together on the trail again.

Carmella arrived in early afternoon in the family buggy. She brought more pies and a big pot of Mexican chili. When she saw the bed set up for Glancy and noted how happy he was, she gave Candy a heartfelt hug and said, "Thank you, thank you."

Candy replied, "Well, thank you for the desserts and letting Glancy join us! We've all worried about him, and it's better getting to see him."

Grady looked up from oiling the harnesses, smiled, and thanked Carmella for the red paint.

She said, "I'm just glad I had it. I hated to send a five-gallon can. I knew it would be too much but that's the way it came, and I wasn't sure it was still good."

Grady set the harness reins down so he could visit with Carmella.

She said, "I'm really worried for you all to travel now. I wish you had more protection."

Grady studied her face and saw the worry in her expression. He asked, "Do you know something I don't know?"

She settled her hands in her lap and said, "Probably not. I forgot you make a business of traveling into Indian territory. You probably deal with them all the time, however, the frontier army has not been able to control the raids, and with the refusal of a Republican-controlled Congress to provide essential aid in fighting the Indians, it's at a standstill. I wasn't so bothered when the Border Patrol was stationed here in Janos, but now that they have been reassigned," she continued, "there's another problem you need to be aware of."

Lou came in with a tray of coffee mugs. He set one down in front of Grady, Carmella, and Juan. He handed Glancy a cup of tea with a spoon of honey in it. He set a cup for himself and sat to hear Carmella's news.

She began by saying, "We get our news from the freighters that deliver our supplies from San Antonio. They always bring us a stack of newspapers. It's old news by the time we get them, but it's new news to us. We learned of Lincoln's bid to run for president. That news was overshadowed by a Texas paper reporting the talk of Texas seceding from the Union.

"It seems the east-Texas cotton farmers, members of the Cotton Kingdom, depend on slave labor. Over the late summer, a series of fires in the cities around the state aroused fears that an abolitionist plot was afoot and a slave uprising might be at hand.

"A vigilante committee was formed, and they were lynching Negros and Northerners across Texas.

"Before the Border Patrol moved out, they advised us to warn travelers entering Texas to be on guard, not only from the vigilantes but from the slave owners protecting their slave property."

Carmella looked Grady in the eye and said, "Maybe I'm worried over nothing, but I've been expecting a load of hay and lumber. The freighter is a week late. I know deliveries are not a strict science. They're often late, especially if they have to wait till they have enough orders to justify the trip, but I know the stockyard also ordered hay and grain for the winter. That delivery should be here by now." She drank her coffee and waited for someone to speak.

Grady played with his empty coffee mug and setting it aside said, "It's true we don't get much news when we're on the trail, but we do follow most of the Butterfield Stage route from Texas to San Francisco, and they leave news along their stops. The storm we ran into detoured us off the stage route.

"I was aware of the slave controversy, but I hadn't heard of this vigilante uprising. Being a cattleman and a lone cowboy I never thought much about slavery. If this uprising is serious, we have seven rifles between us and about as many pistols, and we don't have any slaves.

"Little Bear is an Indian and a free man, as he has a white father. He also is the one who deals with our Indian encounters. We've run into more unrest, especially with the Apache. I predict Indians are going to be on the warpath if this civil war ignites. With the army's withdrawal, they are bound to increase raids in an effort to regain some of the lands settlers have claimed. Reminds me to have Bear pick up ammunition at the emporium."

Juan, with a worried look, said, "This war everyone is talking about. Part of our rancho is in Texas. It was a Spanish land grant. Cecile's family has lived there many generations. Texas is a new state. Most of our rancho is in Mexico. When part of Mexico became Texas, Cecile's father had to begin paying for the acreage, and I believe he even had to pay a fee for each acre he wanted to keep. My question is, why is Texas part of this war? It's a new state, and we are in the western half of the Union."

Grady answered him, "It doesn't seem to go by East or West. The way I understand, it goes by the strong slave states, Mississippi, Florida, Alabama, Georgia, Louisiana, Kansas. Because eastern Texas is next to Kansas and uses slave labor in the cotton fields, it becomes part of the Confederates who are talking secession.

"Even if many of us ranchers building a new life in this state don't own slaves, it helps me understand the divide between the Texas men who are joining the union and the Texas men talking secession. Our state is probably the only state divided like that."

Carmella said, "I wish you would explain that to Lance. He's driving me crazy. He thinks this war is an adventure. He wants to join."

"For sure it's not going to be an adventure. More of a nightmare," Old Lou said. "He needs to stay at home in Janos and raise beef. If this war develops like we hear, both sides are going to need food. They can't fight on an empty belly."

"You're right, Lou." Grady rubbed his neck. The headache was coming on. "That's my thinking and the main reason I'm retiring from the trail business. I intend to beat the brush and get a herd together. I may be trailing beef to New Orleans in a year."

Juan pushed his chair back and stood. "Speaking of cows, I'm going to see how the boys are doing on the wagons and get the livestock fed."

Carmella stood and asked, "May I walk with you? I haven't had time to see this herd."

Juan took Carmella's arm and helped steady her down the porch steps. He shifted to holding her hand as they walked. They were becoming good friends, comfortable with each other.

As the small group watched them walk away, it became clear that something more than friendship could be developing between the mature couple. Their calm and gracious personalities complemented each other.

Grady returned to his harness mending. It was nearly finished.

Old Lou said, "I'm sure glad Carmella brought that pot of chili. I'll make some corn bread." He gathered up the dirty dishes and went to the kitchen.

Candy had sat quietly during all the disturbing talk of Indian raids and war rumors. She saw Glancy had shut his eyes and gone to sleep while the adults talked. She said to Grady, "I sure hate all this war talk. We've all had enough drama and hardships. We don't need Indians and vigilantes."

"Amen," Grady said.

She rose and said, "I'm going to walk down and join Carmella. I want to see what Bear's done with the hearse. You'd better go up and rest while we're gone and Glancy is napping."

Grady didn't answer her as she pulled on a sweater and left. He needed a break and a spoonful of laudanum. He wanted to check on Cecile.

He visited with her, and they both took a nap while holding hands.

Voices from downstairs woke Grady. Glancy was talking with Lou. The old man had been his nurse after his injury on the trail, and they had formed a close friendship. Lou was taking a break and visiting with the boy.

Grady joined them. Lou went to the kitchen and brought back a piece of buttered corn bread and mug of coffee for both of them.

Loud voices and laughter made them aware people were coming. They expected to see Carmella and Candy returning. They were surprised when the saloon doors flew open and strangers walked in. There were four large men. Their leader removed his hat and slapped the dust out against his pants. In a loud voice, he said, "Grady, how the hell are you!"

Surprised, Grady took a closer look and recognized the man as he crossed the room, his hand held out.

"Dizzy, is that you! What the hell are you doing in Texas?"

"My family all live out here. My mom's ill. She's convinced she's going to die. I just packed up my freight wagons and moved back. I'm picking up a few jobs until she's gone."

"I'm sorry, man. This is not a little jaunt out to Janos. How bad is she?"

"She perked up some since I showed up. I think she's pulling my leg. I borrowed some of my family. We've been taking turns driving night and day. We made it in half the time. Anyway, I'm a lot closer here than in Frisco."

Lou came in from the kitchen, drying his hands on his apron. He saw the man talking to Grady and recognized him as one of the freighters Grady had hired on with in those years before trail driving cattle.

He was a big man, and the first thing you recognized when meeting him face-to-face was one eye did its own thing. It never joined the other eye, and you had a hard time knowing which eye was looking at you. He got his nickname Dizzy as a kid in school. It had stuck with him.

"Hello, Lou, you still hanging out with this bum?" Dizzy grabbed Lou and hugged him.

"I ain't hanging out with him. He just keeps following me around. How the hell are you, Dizzy?"

"I'm hungry. This place serve any food?" Dizzy grinned and pulled out a chair at Grady's table.

Grady motioned for his companions to drag up chairs and sit.

Lou said, "I must'a known you was coming. I got dinner fixin'. There's a crew of us. I'll ring the dinner bell when I'm ready. I'll bring you a cup of coffee and some corn bread to hold you over."

Dizzy dropped his hat to the floor by his chair. His companions did the same. He introduced the three as Jimbo, his brother, and Ace and Elvin. They were his sisters kid, his nephews.

Grady shook their hands and asked, "How many wagons you driving?"

"Just one. It was loaded, mostly with hay and grain. Several tons and some lumber for Miss Carmella," Dizzy answered.

Lou came in with an iron skillet of sliced corn-bread, hot coffee, butter, and honey. Hungry men grabbed saucers, and the corn-bread disappeared.

Grady was confused. One freight wagon didn't need four men. "What's up, Dizzy? These guys must be riding shotgun for you."

"You got that right. I'm chicken, man, when it comes to Indians, but what really scares me shitless is white men shooting anything that moves and men, black and white, hanging by their necks."

"Vigilantes?" Grady asked.

"That's what they call themselves, but they are just thieves wearing bandanas to me." Dizzy's walleyes crossed and separated, each going its own way.

His companions hadn't said a word, but their nodding heads agreed with Dizzy's words.

"Be serious, Dizzy. How bad is it? I've got a herd headed to San Antonio in a couple of days. What do I need to know?" Grady just realized Glancy was hearing all of this. He wasn't saying a word, but his eyes were as big as saucers.

Grady motioned to the boy and said, "This is Glancy, Carmella's boy."

Dizzy said, "Howdy, boy. Met your mom at the stockyard. Looks like you broke your leg, sorry for your luck, son."

Dizzy turned back to Grady and said, "We left the wagon at the stockyard. We'll unload their hay and grain tomorrow and take Carmella's out to her ranch and unload. That's how I knew you were here. I saw those pretty little cows." A low chuckle broke out at the table.

"Everyone I talked to told me you were driving seventy or so Hereford look-alikes. I told them they was nuts. My old pal Grady only trails two thousand head." He was laughing as he spoke.

Grady smiled, "You may think it's a joke, but this is the toughest herd of cows I ever drove."

"Those little bitty cows?" Dizzy's eyes glistened as they shifted back and forth.

Cecile, holding on to the stair railing, appeared, and Grady met her on the landing. Taking her arm, he helped her over to introduce the men. They all stood. Grady pulled another chair over for her and said to Dizzy, "We'll continue this discussion after dinner."

Dizzy understood. No troublesome talk when the ladies were present.

Candy and Carmella returned. Carmella went to the kitchen to help Lou. Candy found Della and asked her to provide soap, water, washcloths, and towels in the bathtub room. She invited the men to wash up. Dinner was ready. She went to the porch and rang the dinner bell. Soon the saloon was full.

Carmella's chili went over big. Lou filled several iron skillets with cornbread. Pies and coffee ended the meal.

Carmella, with help from Bear and Lance, loaded Glancy in her buggy and left for home. Lance stayed to join the men with cigarettes and beer that Candy graciously donated. She poured a strong shot of whiskey for herself as well.

Della helped Cecile return to her bedroom.

The freighters were tired. They had driven their loaded wagon night and day, taking turns handling the six-mule team. They planned to return the same way.

Grady was quiet as all the men discussed the unrest that the talk of war was causing. Thieves, outlaws, and Indians were common problems, but the unexpected introduction of vigilantes was a new danger.

He motioned Dizzy to join him on the porch. It was uncomfortably cold, but he wanted to ask Dizzy for a favor.

They didn't sit. Grady said, "Dizzy, I know I'm going to ask you a serious favor. I won't blame you if you turn me down. Could you please travel with us? It would mean no night travel and would extend your travel to twice the time."

Dizzy took a drag on his cigarette and thought about Grady's request. Both men were quiet, and then Dizzy talked out his thoughts.

"I don't like the idea of a month out here. If I push night and day, I can do it in two weeks. I probably have orders waiting for me. I've just been killing time because of my mom. I'm not really doing serious business. I was extremely uncomfortable taking this job and more so involving my family in a job that could possibly get them killed." He sat on a chair and drew smoke in and let it out. It curled over his head.

Grady sat down, studied the overcast skies, and felt the winter's cold chill his chest. He should not stay long in this cold. He was afraid his friend would say no. It was a lot to ask of him.

Dizzy continued, "When are you leaving?"

"The herd is leaving day after tomorrow. Old Lou, Cecile, and I are going to leave in three or four days. We figure on catching the herd in a couple of days. My concern is traveling alone, just one wagon with an old man driving and an ill woman and myself. What you don't know is I nearly died a few weeks ago and I'm still recuperating from pneumonia."

Dizzy dropped his cigarette, stepped on it, kicked it off the porch, and said, "Why aren't you leaving with the herd?"

"You met Cecile. She also has been sick. It's a long story, but it's Doc's orders to give her a couple more days of rest and nourishment."

"I see your concern. As a unit, you're traveling with one old man and two sick people. You need your head examined. And what's this I hear about marriage to that lady? How did you get so lucky?" Dizzy was chuckling.

Grady drew in a breath and with a shy smile said, "That's the first thing I wonder about every morning when I get up and the last thing at night. I'll try to explain our travel decision. Those boys driving the herd are Cecile's vaqueros. Juan is her ranch foreman. He came searching for us when we didn't show up at her ranch. Long story. Tell you about it another time. That Hereford herd is the most important concern, and getting them back home as quickly as possible is a necessity. Half of her crew is driving that herd. Her ranch has been left with a skeleton crew."

Dizzy cleared his throat and said, "They could have waited a couple more days."

Grady said, "True, but the only way I could get Cecile to mind the doctor was this compromise. And the doc will have to give us a release before I'll let her leave here."

"Henpecked already." Dizzy took off his hat, ran his hand through his hair, put it back on, and said, "Well, that kind of throws a wrench in what I was thinking. Tell you what. You get that doc over here tomorrow and see if you can get some idea of the girl's health. If he gives you a reasonable time limit—say, three days after the herd leaves—I don't like it, but I can wait to leave. How does this sound? I'll send my wagon with Ace and Elvin with the herd. Jimbo and I will hang out with you and get you to the herd. At that time I'll reassess things. I'd like to get us all further away from this range of mountains. Too many Apache hang out up there.

Grady reached to shake Dizzy's hand and said, "Thanks, buddy. I'll owe you big-time."

"Hell yes, but let's wait to see if we all get back alive. You understand, my offer depends on the doc's word. I won't wait no week."

Dizzy and his family had their bedrolls. They moved tables together to create floor space. After everyone left for their beds and the building got quiet, they crawled in their bags, and musical snores soon announced exhausted men glad for a great meal and a roof over their heads.

Morning came early. Everyone had plans to solidify. Lou, with Jalo's help, produced trail-driver flapjacks.

Juan's crew transferred hay and grain from Dizzy's wagon to the supply wagon headed for San Antonio. The hay had been ordered for the stockyard, and Grady paid the stockyard for it.

Dizzy's crew unloaded the rest of the stockyard's hay and planned to drive Carmella's order out to her ranch.

Carmella had invited the freighters to stay at the bordello. She had eight cabins that circled the main lodge house, where her housemaid served meals and beer. The meals and beer were on her, but the company of the young ladies would be settled by the girls.

When Dizzy's family finished unloading the stockyard's hay, they walked into the saloon and sank tiredly into chairs at Grady's table. Candy offered them beer, which they gladly accepted.

Grady had finished the harness, and Bear had taken it to Candy's barn and hung it, where it would wait until they harnessed up and pulled out.

Grady sipped on a mug of coffee and visited with Dizzy.

Dizzy said, "We're headed out to Carmella's to unload her hay and lumber. It was really kind of her to put us up for the night. Jimbo's staying here. He plans to hang out with Lou. He likes to cook and so figured he could help out. He's a married man—has a daughter. He doesn't girl around no more. It's different with Ace and Elvin. They are still looking for the right woman." He was teasing his nephews.

Grady said, "How about you, Dizzy? I remember you're quite the lady's man."

"That's only because I'm a rich booger. They like my money." He cracked a giant smile with googly eyes going in different directions. "I have to help the guys unload the hay. I'll spend the night out there. I'll be in in the morning. The boys will stay and come in when the herd's ready to move out. Jimbo and I will stay here until you're ready to travel."

"Doc's coming over later today. I'll have some answers for you tomorrow," Grady said. The freighters shook Grady's hand and filed out of the saloon.

Grady was upstairs in his room packing up. He didn't have much to pack, but he didn't want to hold up Lou, who was carrying the load of getting the hearse ready to move out. Thanks to Della and Candy, he had clean clothes, and he had found a bar of soap, toothbrush, and small jar of salt and soda left on his bedside table.

Doc Wilson knocked on his door and stepped into his room. "Come on in, Doc. You finished with Cecile already?"

The doctor answered, "First things first, sit on the bed and let me check you out."

Grady did as he was told. He knew the man would not give him any information on Cecile until he was good and ready.

The doctor went through the ritual exam, eyes, ears, throat, and chest. He lingered over listening to his chest. He stood up, reached over, pulled a chair facing Grady, and sat down.

He said, "How are you feeling? That chest sounds a lot better."

Grady said, "Head still aches. Legs still weak, but I can tell daily I'm getting there. Think I'll be able to ride a horse in a few days."

"I wouldn't rush it. That's several hundred pounds of muscle and a headful of his own meanness. Set a routine you can stick with and give those leg muscles a chance to improve. Oh, hell, you're not going to pay any attention to anything I tell you. You'd better pay attention to what I tell you about that girl though."

Grady sat up straight. He was holding his breath. He said, "Please no bad news."

"No, son, she's doing remarkably well considering the way she was when she got here. But she's still fighting the throat. Her chest is better, but she's still coughing. I can tell she's been pushing herself to get on her feet. She can do that later. Don't get me wrong, she needs some daily exercise, but don't you let her fool you into letting her push herself. No walking alongside the wagon until she's gotten rid of the cough and no horse riding unless an emergency, and keep her from lifting heavy objects—that includes her saddle."

Grady let out his breath and relaxed his back. "Can we get on the trail?"

The doctor sat back, drew a deep breath, and said, "I'd like to keep her here another week, but she won't have it. I'd set my foot down, but I've watched you put that hearse together. Having her out of the weather could be the answer, but cold's going to be your enemy. Keep her warm! Her head covered. Just pray you don't break down. I don't think she'll stay here more than another two days."

Candy stuck her head in and said, "Stay for supper, Doc? Chicken and dumplings."

"My, my, that sounds good. Don't mind if I do. I've got a patient to see, but I'll surely be back." He took a bottle of laudanum out of his case and set it on the bed table. He said, "That's not whiskey, use a spoon." He rose, gave Candy a hug, and waved at Grady.

Candy asked, "What's the verdict? He going to let her take off?"

"Sounds like she's in charge. Two days—that's all she'll agree to." Candy shook her head and said, "You're going to have your hands full with that one. I'll be downstairs if you need me."

Grady continued to sit on the side of the bed. He eyed the empty bottle of laudanum and the full bottle. His head was pounding. He wanted to grab the bottle and swallow it all. Instead he put it in his pack. A cup of coffee would have to do. Getting them on the trail was going to require a lot of patience. He needed to settle up with Candy. He would do that tonight. He owed her his life. That he couldn't repay. He would always be in debt to her for that.

He owed her for supplies and the use of her wagon and the team used to rescue the herd in the canyon. He realized she had shut down the saloon and forfeited any profit from customers. She had fed them, housed them, and donated alcoholic beverages when needed. He didn't know how to figure this. She might not let him pay her. If so, he would wait until they left and leave money in his room.

Two mornings later seemed to come quickly. The last two days had been days of vast confusion. Meals eaten on the run. The final pile of Grady's trail equipment had been packed in trunks and loaded on the supply wagon. Cecile's trunk had also been added. The corner of the saloon looked empty. Lou had even swept the floor, adding to the ghostly appearance.

Grady and Dizzy sat on the porch, watching the hustle and trying to stay out of the way.

Deadly arrived and stood next to Grady. Grady, expecting the bull to come, had sat close to the rails so he could feed Deadly his morning biscuits and talk to him using soothing words. Deadly always looked forward to hearing Grady's kind voice, his eyes turning soft and tranquil.

While Grady carried on his conversation with Deadly and Dizzy, they all watched down the street while Trumpeter was loaded. Deadly, watching his old friend climb easily inside the roomy cattle traveler, decided all was well and refocused on his treats, and with the swipe of a long red tongue the two biscuits disappeared.

Deadly recognized the gathering excitement of a trail drive. He watched the activity and enjoyed Grady scratching the hard bone between his horns.

Dizzy's wagon was coming down the road. It passed Doc's house and pulled up in front of the saloon. Two of the mules were tied to the back of the wagon. Without a load they didn't need the extra team. Instead, Dizzy and Jimbo would ride them while traveling with Grady.

Dizzy sat forward and said, "What the hell!"

Ace was driving the team, while Elvin rode shotgun. It was the two passengers behind the bench sitting among a pile of pillows and blankets that caused Dizzy's exclamation. Two young ladies, wearing fur hats, wool coats, and snow gloves, pulled a blanket up under their arms and waited for Dizzy to explode.

Ace had a sick grin on his face, and Elvin wouldn't look Dizzy in his floating eyes.

Dizzy stood up and laid his hands on the porch rail. He leaned out to talk in a very controlled voice. He said, "Tell me these ladies just needed a ride into town?" His eyes crossed. He closed them and waited for an answer.

Ace cleared his throat and said, "They need a ride to San Antonio."

Dizzy opened his eyes, and they went wild, crossing and uncrossing. He said, "Not going to happen."

Ace tried to sound confident. He said, "Come on, Dizzy. Carmella's shutting down the brothel. She's going to start running a ranch. She knew you would throw a fit. She said to ask that you please take the girls. She sent half a beef, garden veggies, potatoes, and squash. She even sent flour, sugar, coffee, and two bottles of whiskey and a barrel of beer. It's not like we don't have plenty. They won't be any trouble, and Wyvon the brunette says she can cook."

Dizzy shut his eyes again, and his face grew red with anger. He opened his eyes, and one of them stared Ace in his eyes. He said, "You have no idea what trouble is until you travel with women."

Ace answered, "They promised to be good, and Elvin and I will keep them corralled."

Dizzy turned to the woman closest to him and said, "This ain't no stagecoach. This is a freight wagon. It's a long dirty trip to San Antonio. It's too hard for women. You stay here."

The woman he had spoken to said, "Mr. Dizzy, we have to get to San Antonio to even ride a stagecoach. We can't earn a living here. We really need to go with you. I promise we'll try to be helpful."

Dizzy sat back down. He pulled out his tobacco and papers and rolled a cigarette. Everyone sat quiet, waiting for his answer.

He smoked. He drew in and blew out. It looked like steam coming off his head. He said, "Elvin, put those two mules and me and Jimbo's saddles out back in Miss Candy's barn."

Noise had increased at the stockyards. They were ready to open the gates and let out the horses, under Jalo's supervision.

Bear came jogging to the saloon. He yelled, "They are getting ready to head out."

Grady rose, went down the steps with Deadly following, and joined Bear. They went to watch the horses and cattle pour out of the pens.

Dizzy said to Ace, "This is a bad thing. This is on you. I'll tell you just how bad it is when I catch up with you on the trail." He threw down his cigarette stub and ran to catch up with Grady.

Ace grinned. Elvin climbed back to the driver's bench. They were relieved to get away from Dizzy. Ace flicked the reins and said, "Git up. Giddap." The freighter's whip cracked over the mules. The four-mule team gave a plunge, and the wagon moved with some speed to the stockyard. Ace didn't slow down at the yard. He urged the mules to pass the confusion going on there. He didn't care to eat herd dust all day. He would keep his wagon way in front.

Fernando drove the supply wagon. A four-horse team pulled it. His job was to reach a campsite, get a fire going and supper started. He fell in behind Ace.

Jalo had tied Miss Cecile's Arabian stallion and mares to the supply wagon. As soon as the supply wagon got far enough out of town, he let the remuda out. The horses were wearing loose hobbles to keep them from taking off. Horses were fast travelers. Jalo's job was to keep them calm and close enough so that Juan and Paco could get a fresh horse when needed.

When the dust from the horses settled, Juan opened the gate to release the Herefords. They excitedly exited out of the pen and began to scatter to freedom. Juan and Paco immediately began using their lariats to enforce discipline to get them bunched. Grady yelled, "Deadly, lead them out."

Deadly trotted to the front of the herd. This was more like it. He had watched Trumpeter be loaded. Saw the supply wagon pull out with the horses and leave town. Deadly shook his head, sniffed the air, and settled into a strong walk, one the small Herefords could sustain.

Reginald, with his one blind eye, was confused. He was glad when Deadly stepped out in front. He respected Deadly. The longhorn had saved him from the wild brush bull that had ripped out his eye. He took a place beside Deadly, where his good eye could keep him alongside the big bull.

The little herd soon fell into a comfortable pace. They remembered the miles traveled. They weren't beginners anymore.

The last to move out was Trumpeter. He was riding in style in Carmella's cattle traveler. His driver, Garcia, had his guitar in its case under the driver's bench. His job was to keep the traveler steady. It wouldn't do to have the old bull fall, so he avoided holes when possible and made sure there were no sudden stops or starts.

The street became quiet again as the trail drive left Janos and headed for San Antonio.

Candy, Della, and Lou had watched the herd leave from the saloon porch. They watched Grady, Bear, and Dizzy walk back from the stockyard.

Candy said, "Whew, I'm exhausted just watching." They all nodded in agreement.

Lou counted heads, Bear and Candy, Grady and Cecile, Dizzy and Jimbo, Lou and Della. Eight for breakfast. Then he saw Lance coming into town. Nine for breakfast. He headed for the kitchen. He already had coffee warm on the stove. They all filed in, grabbed a mug, and found a table and chair.

They visited. Lance was sorry he was too late for the departure and wanted to hear all the details.

Lou outdid himself. The breakfast buffet included bacon, fried potatoes, scrambled eggs, biscuits, butter, honey, and coffee.

When breakfast was over, they scattered. Grady took a tray with a loaded breakfast up to Cecile. She had chosen to stay in bed while her herd left town. She wished she was with them, but she was wise enough to realize she would be a burden.

Bear and Lance harnessed a horse and pulled the hearse to the barnyard behind the saloon. Bear had a few more jobs to do on it. Lance just hung out and helped when he could.

Lou worked around in the kitchen and continued to gather necessary trail supplies.

Candy and Della decided on the mattress to be used in the wagon. They collected bedding, towels, soap, and rags. Candy went through her rag drawer and added them for Lou. Extra rags on a trail drive were always welcome.

The day was a quiet one. Carmella did not come. Dizzy and Jimbo played cards and walked the town, visiting and sharing news from San Antonio.

Lou, busy organizing the wagon, put a pot of beans on for supper, gathered ham and sandwich-making materials, and put them on the table used for buffets. Satisfied people could fend for themselves, he went on with his packing.

Bear finished the rails on the roof of the wagon. Lance grabbed a brush and the red paint. Soon the little wagon was all one color. Lance cleaned his brush and then hammered the lid on the paint.

Lance and Bear built a couple of sandwiches each and joined Grady at his table.

Bear said, "Wagon's done. Mattress loaded. Lou's getting it set up for you. He even set a mason jar in your corners between the mattress and the wall. You each have your own jar at hand, and it has a lid so it won't spill when it's filled with water or coffee."

Grady smiled and said, "Man's a genius. I saw him go by a while ago with my pistol and rifle. What's that about?"

Bear chuckled and said, "I put some hooks above your head near the ceiling, and he hung both your and Cecile's pistols on them. Your sidewall up high is a rack for your rifle. In case of an emergency you can grab it quick."

"You know, Bear, I've sat around on my rear for two weeks watching everyone come and go. I've come to the conclusion that I'm not as important as I think I am. Either I've trained you guys right or I'm just not needed."

"Two weeks! Is that all it's been since we came off that mountain? I've lost track of time." Bear pushed his empty plate aside and leaned back in his chair.

Grady noticed Lance was silent, eating, his eyes locked on the plate before him. He wasn't hearing their conversation, he was miles away. Grady said, "What's up, Lance?"

Startled, Lance looked up. His mind returned to the saloon and the two men looking at him.

He stuttered and said, "S-Sorry, sir, I didn't hear what you were talking about."

Grady said, "I realize that, boy. Why are you so quiet? Not your nature. What's on your mind?"

Lance blurted out, "Can I go with you to San Antonio?"

Startled, Grady said, "Is this about going to war?"

Lance swallowed, pushed his plate back, and said, "Yes, sir."

"How about you get us some coffee while I digest your request?"

"Yes, sir." Lance took their dirty dishes and headed for the kitchen.

Grady looked at Bear. Bear shrugged his shoulders. When Lance came back, he sat and, looking Grady in the eyes, waited for an answer.

Grady met Lance's eyes and saw dogged determination. He hadn't known Lance long. In the time spent with him, he knew two things. The young man wasn't lazy, and he was years older, mentally, than his age of eighteen.

Grady picked up his mug and continued studying Lance over the top of it. He set it down and said, "I like your company, son. You'll always be welcome with me. You came to my rescue and did a stand-up job of it. Let's take a minute and sort this out.

"Your ma's worried about you. She said something to me of your desires to join. Tell me what's motivating you." Grady rubbed his neck.

"Sir, my pa died when I was twelve. Indians killed him." He paused and looked at Bear. Bear smiled and nodded for him to go on.

"I've worked that ranch and that brothel since he died. I must have wanderlust because I can't wait to get away from this town, that ranch, and especially that brothel."

Lance continued, "I'm afraid I'll end up killing one of those drunk customers. If I'm going to kill someone, it might as well be in a war."

Grady's face changed. He looked hard into Lance's eyes and said, "Is killing your incentive?"

"No, sir! I didn't mean it that way, Mr. Grady. I'm a middle son. My brother Ed is the man of our family. He likes ranching and business, keeping books and stuff. Glancy's the baby. Spoiled pretty bad. I'm the one who punches cows and mops the brothel's floors and takes care of the baby. I'm not a businessman, Mr. Grady. I just feel my future is out there somewhere."

Grady saw himself in this young man. After his parents had died, he was left to decide his path. He wanted to see the world. He caught wagon trains and worked for freighters up and down the West Coast.

They sat quiet for a few moments while Grady put together a thought. Then he said, "This civil war is a bad thing. I think about it a lot. Especially if I had to decide which side to fight on. I don't think I could kill a man who had been my friend just because he was on the other side. That's what this Union and Confederate war is all about." He paused and said, "You picked a side?"

"No, sir, I'd have to give it some thought," Lance said.

Grady continued, "Let me throw an idea at you. Mind you, it's just an idea. I'm not giving you a direction. I like the idea of young men joining the army. It gets them away from home but also has the army looking after them while they learn a job and get to travel. Don't get me wrong, there's the possibility they'll get killed. That's a pretty big deterrent."

Grady waited for Lance to digest that thought.

Grady turned to Bear and said, "I'm going to give him a suggestion that you need to think about and correct me if I'm wrong or you have a better plan."

Bear nodded, and Grady continued, "I've stopped at army forts all along the Pacific-coast trail. I have a few good friends, some are officers. Rumors are the regular army units are being ordered east. Lance, that means our West Coast, rampant with angry Apache, is going to be left open to Apache attacks."

Grady paused and looked at Bear. Bear nodded, and Grady continued, "There's an officer named Canby who's started raising regiments of New Mexico volunteers and militia to replace army units."

Lance looked at Bear. Grady was talking about fighting Indians.

Bear, looking serious, said, "My tribe is of the Navajo. My mother and her family live in New Mexico. Our tribe has warred against our cousins, the Apache, for many years. My father was an officer stationed in New Mexico. That's how he met my mother. Our tribe is one that the government wants to put on a reservation. It will happen. It is inevitable. This volunteer army's job will be to protect us and the settlers from the Apache. You and I have a lot in common. Our fathers were killed by Indians."

Grady spoke up. "You don't have to join an army. This Wild West is opening up. You know cattle. You could hire on to any of the big ranches. I say this because I've noticed you have a vast amount of experiences you can draw from. If you decide you want to be an army man, I think you would make a stand-up Indian fighter. You are aware and have participated living in Indian country. It's a choice. Fight with the North or the South, killing each other, or fight to protect the homes of people such as yours."

It was a heavy subject. Grady sat back and waited for Lance to say something.

Lance backed his chair and stretched his long legs under the table. He laid his head back on the chair and studied the ceiling, and then he drew his legs under the chair, sat up, and said, "Makes sense to me. I like what you said about all the options I have." He grinned and said, "I can even mop floors."

Both Grady and Bear laughed.

Grady said, "Hell yes, but let me give you something else to think about. Your mom is planning on coming to our wedding at Christmas. Bear and Candy will be packed and coming at the same time. Safety in numbers. It is Indian territory. You can help them. It will give you time to put yourself together. Make time to convince your mom that you are serious about making a life change.

"By then you should have a better idea the direction you want to go. Also, Bear will be going on to my ranch, which is farther north from San Antonio. You could have the safety of another hundred miles from Cecile's ranch to San Antonio. It will give me time to find out more about the volunteers. If you decide to go that way. Son, here's the important thing. Be sure your mother knows you are leaving."

Lance nodded and said, "Yes, sir. The way I understand it, I can go on with you now if I want. Or I can wait and go with Bear. Brace my mom now or have time to work on it."

"That's about it. My head hurts. All this heavy problem solving. I'm going to take a nap." Grady got up, patted Lance on his shoulder, and went upstairs.

They sat quiet for a few moments, and Lance said, "What do you think?"

Bear said, "When I was a young boy, my grandfather sent me to a mountaintop to seek a vision. He gave me no food—just my water bag and my bow and arrows. I was frightened. There were wolves and mountain lions in those mountains. I was to stay night and day until I had a vision. Grady has just given you time to have a vision. A clearer idea of who you are and who you want to be." Bear continued, "While you are seeking your vision, you can help me get Candy packed. You can make wooden boxes to pack in."

Lance laughed and said, "That's better than mopping floors. I'd better get on home. I'll see Grady tomorrow and let him know if I want to go with him or stay and seek my vision."

It was not a nice quiet day on the beginning of this trail drive to reach Cecile's ranch.

Juan was the only one who had experience with driving the Herefords. He had supervised bringing them out of the canyon and down the mountain to Janos. He wasn't surprised when some darted out of the herd and wandered off. Some stopped to graze, and others kept trying to turn back to the barns.

Paco was cussing. His horse was dripping sweat. Juan sent him to pull a fresh horse out of the remuda.

Deadly knew exactly the habits of these little red cows. Traveling the deserts of California in tornado weather and flooded gullies, up and down over mountain ranges, he had helped to keep the disobedient little herd on the trails. He knew that in a day or two the drovers would get some control. Today, however, he had to stay in front and lead them on the trail. It was one he knew well, having traveled it many times coming and going with Grady.

Fernando, driving the supply wagon, was sure the freight wagon driven by Ace would kick up a lot of dust. He resigned himself to expect it, but it didn't happen. Not carrying a load, the four-mule team Ace drove stretched out and was soon far ahead.

Ace and Elvin, flirting with the women, let the mules set their own pace. They settled into a fast walk.

The young blond lady's name was Ellen and the brunette was Wyvon. They were relieved they had gotten past the man with the scary eyes. So relieved, that spirits were high, and Fernando could hear laughter and teasing between the four passengers far ahead of him.

The four had paired up. Wyvon with Ace and Ellen with Elvin. Ellen thought it fun their names both began with *El*. She kidded him. She said they were soul mates. Elvin was a shy young man, but the kidding pleased him.

The girls talked all the time. They whispered and giggled. They were so excited to have a way to San Antonio. Away from the small unexciting town of Janos. What an adventure they were having!

As the day wore on, Ace realized they had traveled out of sight of the supply wagon. He pulled up the horses and gave the girls a chance to take a short walk to relieve themselves.

When the supply wagon came into sight, Elvin took over the reins and drove the team. Ace realized he had been so entertained by the girls that he had forgotten the danger of Indians and outlaws. He had allowed them to get too far ahead of help in case they were attacked.

Ace was rattled by how easily he quit being careful, so he cautioned his passengers and reminded them to all keep constant lookout. Elvin was told to keep ahead of the supply wagon but not to let it get out of sight again. His warning and the mention of Indians quieted the girls.

Sobering with the warning, the girls soon got tired, lay down, and pulled the covers over their heads and napped.

The quiet was welcome after the ceaseless chatter. Ace climbed over the women and closed his eyes. He hadn't expected to sleep, but soon he drifted off to the sound of mule hooves hitting the dirt.

The day was long, boring, and dusty. Weather was unsettled. Clouds rolled in. Temperature dropped.

Deadly, aware the weather was changing, looked for a higher rise to bed the herd down. Juan, having accompanied Deadly before, knew his habit of calling a halt. Juan rode ahead and let Fernando know to circle and set up camp.

Garcia backed Trumpeter out of the cattle traveler and led him to the herd. He would graze and rest with the herd and be fed some grain when he returned to the traveler in the morning.

Garcia detached his team and hobbled them. They immediately went past the herd and joined the remuda horses, happy for a break. Garcia got his guitar and walked past the herd to the campsite.

Jalo shortened the hobbles on the remuda horses and joined Fernando at camp. He helped find wood for the morning fire and helped Fernando cut up some potatoes, carrots, and onions to add to the beef in a pot simmering on the fire. Fernando added salt and pepper. A stew would be ready when the hungry men finished their chores.

Still a distance ahead but in sight, the freight wagon had camped. Ace walked back to check in with Juan. He reported they would make their camp where they stopped. It would give the women some privacy and less competition for their attentions. He told Fernando not to plan for them. They had their own provisions.

All the men were quiet around the fire that night. They were tired, dusty, and hungry. They didn't need to guard the herd. Both cattle and horses were happy to stop, rest, and graze.

Juan, being cautious, gave his crew orders for guard duty anyway. Indians were silent night marauders and always took advantage of weary drovers.

It sprinkled a little but quit as the clouds drifted on and stars lit up.

The first day's trail drive was over.

The two days after the herd left, the occupants of the saloon were busy with last-minute preparations. Getting the occupants of the little wagon ready to travel was the priority.

Meals were kept simple, cooked, and left to warm on the iron stove. The kitchen managed to get cleaned between other chores. There was also last-minute laundry and packing.

The night before they were to leave, with Candy's help, Lou served steak, baked potatoes, and molasses baked beans. Candy brought out a bottle of peach brandy. They toasted to a safe journey, and Candy toasted to Grady's and Cecile's engagement again and included a guarantee to be there for their wedding at Christmas.

Cecile hardly slept. She tossed and turned. In the morning she was going home. She said it over and over, "Home." There were many times driving her small Hereford herd from San Diego to Texas she had feared failure.

Shaking off the depressing memories, she turned her thoughts to the busy days ahead. The month of travel Grady said it would take the herd to reach her hacienda. She wished it were over. She was impatient to get home.

She expected to find many problems waiting for her to solve. It had been months since she had left her rancho's supervision in Juan's and the vaqueros' care. Ramone, her brother, had little to do with running the cattle business. He was handicapped and spent most of his time in a wheelchair.

Juan would have told her if anything had happened to him, but he had been away from the hacienda for more than a month. She hoped Ramone was safe.

Her mind shifted to the little Hereford herd. She wanted to prepare the pasture where she intended to graze the herd close to the casa. The Bravo herd, in it now, would have to be moved to another fenced pasture. Her thoughts came to an immediate stop. She caught her breath as she remembered her Bravo Toro black bull, Diablo.

Diablo was bred for fighting the matadors in the arenas. Bred for an aggressive personality. There was no way he would welcome the three bulls arriving in a few weeks. Trumpeter, Reginald, and Deadly would be most unwelcome. She must remember to send one of her vaqueros ahead when they got close to home to have Diablo penned in his special iron-reinforced corral.

These thoughts made her nervous. She got up and paced around the room for thirty minutes until she began to chill. She brushed away her anxiety. There were days of travel ahead, she had plenty of time to figure things out.

Determined to think good thoughts, she climbed back in bed and turned her mind to the wedding.

Grady had suggested she plan for their wedding and not worry about their plans after marriage. She knew there would be some struggles to make their union work. She smiled. Grady didn't realize planning a wedding was hard work, but he was right, it was more fun than stressing over their future.

She drifted off to sleep planning her wedding dress.

Noises woke her. She opened her eyes to see Della moving about. Cecile's satchel had been packed yesterday. The clothes she was wearing to travel had been laid out.

Della said, "Time to get up, Miss Cecile. I brought you a pan of warm water and a washcloth. You freshen up, and I'll be back with your breakfast." She left the room.

Cecile got up. She used her chamber pot. She wrung out the cloth floating in the warm water and pressed it to her face. It felt so good. She dunked the cloth several times. Repeatedly wrung it out and pressed it to her face. It helped her to wake up.

She climbed back into bed, sat up against her pillows, and smoothed her covers to make an even spot to place her breakfast tray. Della arrived with a loaded tray. Bacon, scrambled eggs, fried potatoes, biscuits, and coffee.

"My goodness," Cecile said, "I'll never get all this down."

Della answered, "You'd better try. Remember you'll be on the trail all day. No telling when they will stop to camp. Lou fixed plenty of eggs and bacon so he can make sandwiches to carry. I'll be back to help you bathe and dress."

She didn't think she could eat all of it, but she surprised herself and ate all but half the potatoes.

Della moved quickly when she came back. She set the breakfast tray aside.

Talking as she fetched Cecile's robe and slippers, she said, "It will be a while before the men will be ready to pull out. I woke you early so you can get a tub bath. Let me help you with your robe."

Della helped her down the hall to the room with the tub and said, "Let me help you off with your robe. Hurry, the water will get cold."

"Della, you're a wonder. I'm going to miss you." With Della steadying her, she climbed into the warm water.

Della said, "I figured it will be a few weeks before you get home to your own bath. At least you'll start off clean and comfortable. Don't dawdle now. I'll bring your clothes and help you dress."

Early in the summer, when Cecile had traveled to inspect and purchase the Herefords, the weather had been warm, creeping into hot. She had packed summer clothes, never expecting tornadoes and blizzards. The only warm item she had packed was a winter jacket, to be used on cool nights. When the weather turned really bad for weeks on end, she had layered her summer clothes under her jacket.

Candy, aware of Cecile's lack of cold-weather wear, gave her a pair of long johns and a pair of her men's overalls. She also added a sweater. This combination, along with her own shirts and jacket, should be enough to keep her warm during her travel.

She was dressed and putting on her boots with Della's help. Candy knocked and entered and said, "Look what I found." She held a knitted hat. It had a cheerful ball on top of it. It was a bright red. "Belle made it. I forgot I had it."

After a struggle to pull on boots not worn for weeks, Della combed and braided her hair. Cecile had wisely decided to ignore her embarrassment and chose to wear the long underwear and men's pants. She could remove the pants and sleep in the underwear. With her hair in a long braid down her back, she pulled the knit hat over her head. It covered her ears.

"Perfect," she said. She gave Candy and Della both a hug and said, "I can't thank you both enough for all the support and help you've given me. I won't forget. I owe you. I expect both of you to come for our wedding. My hacienda and all my people will help me return your kindness."

Cecile felt a little claustrophobic. She had not had shoes or boots on for weeks since arriving in Janos. Her legs were still weak, so getting down the stairs to the saloon floor, in boots, was a challenge.

Della, noting the fear in her eyes, went first, carrying her satchel. Ready to steady her if needed. Candy followed her, carrying her jacket and gloves.

With a sigh of relief, she stepped off the last stair. Grady was finishing his breakfast. Seeing her come down the stairs, he went to meet her. He took her hands and leaned down and kissed her. She glowed. She lifted her face and returned his kiss.

There wasn't much Grady missed when it came to Cecile. He thought she looked cute as a button in her red knit hat. It mixed well with the blush in her cheeks and her long dark braid. He thought she was lovely, men's outfit and all!

He pulled out a chair next to his and seated her. Candy put her jacket and gloves on the chair next to her and went to get them both a mug of coffee, a balancing feat with one arm. If Doc didn't free her arm up soon, she would do it herself.

Della took Cecile's satchel to the porch and put it with the pile of things still to be loaded on the wagon. Lance was just tying his horse to the tie rail. He followed Della into the saloon.

He joined Grady and the ladies. "Good morning, ladies." He took off his hat and set it on the floor, by his chair.

Cecile answered him, "Good morning, Lance. You're out early."

"Yes, ma'am, I didn't want to miss you taking off. I bet you are excited to be on your way home?"

Cecile answered him, "You have no idea. I'm so impatient to get there. I can't thank you enough for all the help you've given us. You did help save my life, you know."

Embarrassed, Lance answered, "I was glad I could help out." He turned to Grady and said, "I've decided to take your advice and help my mother make the trip to your wedding in December. It will give me time to seek my vision."

Grady smiled and said, "I see you've been talking to Bear."

"Yes, sir, he makes sense. I'd appreciate your offer to collect information about the volunteers. I'll be prepared to make a decision, and I'll take your advice to prepare my mother for my moving on." Lance picked up his hat and stood. "I'll go see if I can help Bear with the horses." He held out his hand to Grady.

Grady shook it and said, "I think you made a good decision. I'll look forward to seeing you in December. Thank you for all your help. I owe you."

Embarrassed at the praise, Lance put on his hat and hurried to find Bear.

Dizzy and Jimbo came noisily down the stairs. Dizzy waved at Grady. They continued to the kitchen, where breakfast was for the taking. Lou had added oatmeal to the bacon and eggs. Workingmen needed a lot of fuel.

They filled their plates and also a bowl of oatmeal each and joined the ladies and Grady. Candy rose and went to the kitchen for mugs. She delivered them to the table on a little roll cart. She then went back to the kitchen, returned with a steaming pot, and went around the table offering fresh coffee. She set the pot in the middle of the table in easy reach.

She pulled up a chair behind Grady and Cecile, close enough to be included in their conversation.

Dizzy and Jimbo removed their hats and dropped them to the floor. Dizzy said, "Morning, ma'am, you're looking pretty perky this morning. You ready to head home?"

"Home! Isn't that a beautiful word?" she said. "Yes, Mr. Dizzy, I'm ready! Grady told me you were kind enough to delay leaving to watch over us until we catch up with the herd. Thank you so much."

"You're more than welcome, little lady. When I learned the pitiful shape my old buddy Grady was in, I couldn't say no. I hear you've agreed to marry that old cowboy."

"No, Mr. Dizzy, I did the proposing. You have no idea how much I had to beg him to marry me." She laughed seeing the expression on Grady's face.

Dizzy laughed loudly. They all joined in.

Old Lou came in from outside and joined them, grabbing a clean mug and filling it with coffee.

He said, "Bear's bringing the horses around. The wagon has to be loaded, and we are about ready to get going. Morning, Miss Ceci. You ready to travel?"

She answered, "Oh, Lou, isn't this great? We made it out of that mountain, and I'm going home!" A big smile spread across her face.

"You bet! We've got a little surprise for you out front. Grady wouldn't let any of us tell you about it."

She turned to Grady and said, "Tell me. I love surprises, but I can't wait. What have you kept from me?"

"You'll have to wait until Bear says he's ready for us." Grady was having fun teasing her. He said, "Lou let the secret out too soon."

Candy said, "Shame on you, Lou." She got up and went to look out the saloon doors. She called back, "I see him coming!" She hurried back to Cecile, picked up her jacket, and said, "Here, put this on."

Dizzy and Jimbo grabbed their hats, and Dizzy said, "Come on, Jimbo, we need to get our mules saddled." They left out the door in a hurry.

Grady took his trail jacket off the back of his chair and put it on. He took his time. Bear would have to hitch the team.

He took Cecile's hand, and they walked onto the porch. At the bottom of the stairs stood the red wagon. It sparkled with the morning dew. Lou had packed all the items from the porch.

Cecile stood eyes wide. She took a deep breath and said, "What is that?"

Grady laughed and said, "It's your chariot, my lady."

Eyes taking in the red wagon, she clung to the porch rails and went slowly down the stairs.

Bear called out, "Morning, Miss Ceci," and continued hooking up the team.

"Morning, Bear." She walked to the wagon, put out her hand, and touched its red side. She turned back to Grady, who followed her. She said, "It's red!"

"It certainly is," he answered.

She continued down the side of the wagon, her fingers moving over the painted side. When she reached the back, Grady stepped around her and opened the twin doors.

Dazed, she saw how organized it was. Her pistol hanging near the ceiling on her side. Grady's pistol on the other side. His rifle within reach, high on the wall. The little shelf holding some of her items. She saw Candy had added soaps and a jar of face cream.

The mattress filled most of the floor. Her satchel was in the corner just inside the doors. She realized all these people she had grown to love had done this for her. Tears ran down her cheeks. She turned to face them and said, "Thank you, thank all of you! It is so precious! It is such a unique size and shape. What was it?"

No one dared answer Cecile's question. All eyes turned to Grady.

Grady muttered, "Oh, it was just used to carry and deliver things." He wasn't about to tell Cecile that the things it had carried were dead bodies.

"I'm not sure whether the red color is going to attract attention or keep the Indians away because they think we are crazy," Cecile chuckled, "but this little wagon, with its personality, demands a name. I would call it the Red Cart, but we may repaint it after this trip if it does attract too much attention. I want to name this little wagon "Cart". I know it will have many years of usefulness. I am very touched that you all worked so hard to make Cart so homey and comfortable."

Bear came around the Cart and said, "I'm done, Miss Ceci. We thought maybe you would like to join Lou on the driver's bench and ride shotgun out of town."

Everyone was surprised when she let out a loud squeal, not ladylike at all, wiped the tears from her cheeks, and said, "I'd love to. Yes! Yes!"

Dr. Wilson was jogging toward them. Breathing hard, he called, "Wait up just a minute."

They all turned and waited until he stopped before Cecile, "I brought you more cough syrup and the cowboy more laudanum. You have to watch him. He thinks its whiskey."

Cecile hugged him and said, "Thank you for taking care of me." She felt like she was repeating thanks over and over. She wished she could express her gratitude more elegantly.

Lou took the bottles from the doc and crawled to put them on the little shelf. Dizzy and Jimbo arrived just then. They led their saddled mules and Grady's saddled horse.

Cecile looked at Grady and said, "You haven't been on a horse for weeks. You shouldn't do this."

He took her hand and said, "I'm just riding out of town, just like you're on top riding out of town. You're right. It's been weeks, and I really miss my horse and being aboard in my saddle. I'm going to ride a little every day and build up my strength. I'll take turns riding with Lou, riding my horse, and taking it easy riding inside with you."

She was concerned, but she smiled and said, "OK, let's get going."

Lou had already climbed up and held the reins. Dizzy stepped up to the head of the team so it wouldn't move while Grady helped Cecile to climb aboard.

She hugged everyone. She missed Della. "Where's Della?"

The girl stepped out from behind the saloon doors. Cecile said, "Come here. Let me hug you."

Della, embarrassed, came down the stairs to her. She hugged Cecile back, and Cecile whispered to her, "Thank you so much. I'll never forget you."

Cecile turned back to Grady and with his help climbed to the driver's bench. When seated, she blew kisses to those being left behind.

Bear held Grady's horse while he stuck a boot in a stirrup and swung a leg over the saddle. His horse had not been ridden during Grady's illness and was ready to move out. He sidestepped and cut up. Grady, reacting with years of experience, steadied the horse and called out, "OK, guys, let's get this show on the road." He spoke to the four left behind, Bear, Lance, Candy, and Della. "We owe you. Thank you."

He waved his hat and urged the horse on down the street. Dizzy and Jimbo followed on their mules. Lou cracked his whip over the team and hollered, "Get up. Giddap."

Some of the town's people were up and waved as they passed out of Janos.

It reminded Grady of the day Cecile had ridden her Arabian stallion, sidestepping and rearing out of San Diego.

Cecile took her gloves out of her jacket pocket. It was chilly. No! It was cold. She had been in that miserable blizzard in the canyon. Whenever she got cold, she would always be reminded of those days. For sure she wouldn't ride shotgun very long.

Back at the saloon, the four, out of habit, took a seat at Grady's table. It was like the starch had left them all. The saloon was silent. A log in the potbellied iron stove fell over. Sparks crackled. It sounded loud in the silent saloon.

Della got up and went to the kitchen. She came back with mugs of coffee. She set one in front of each of them and sat back down. She raised her mug to her lips and blew gently, steam rising. It was too hot to sip. She set the mug back down and said, "Lou made biscuit sandwiches with the bacon and eggs. It's all gone. I don't know how to make biscuits, but I can make oatmeal and toast."

Candy shook her head and said, "Don't bother. I'm going back to bed."

She rose, but before she could turn and leave, Bear grabbed her hand and got up. He said, "Wait for me."

Lance stood and said, "I'm headed home. I'll be back in the morning and get started on those packing boxes."

Della watched Candy and Bear climb the stairs holding hands. Lance passed through the saloon doors. She pulled her chair closer to the potbellied stove. Kicked her shoes off. Sipped on her coffee and warmed her feet.

It was now bright daylight. She had lit lanterns in the dark early morning so the crew could see to load. She saw they were still lit. She needed to turn them off. She felt like a rag doll that all the stuffing had fallen out of. She put her shoes on. Put wood in the stove. Turned off the lanterns and said to herself, "Guess I'll go to bed too."

Traveling for the first time with their uncle Dizzy, Ace and Elvin had gained a lot of experience. They let the six-mule team travel at their own comfortable speed but to maintain the delivery schedule had driven day and night. They had stopped morning and evening to rest and feed the mules. They prepared their meals at that time.

On this trip being able to stop for the entire evening seemed like a luxury to Ace and Elvin. When the herd stopped for the night, Ace made camp coffee first thing. Elvin rounded up enough firewood so Ace could throw supper together. Elvin's job had always been unharnessing the mules, hobbling them, and feeding them. With that done, he continued to locate burnable material to last the night if necessary. Stopping for the night would require fuel for breakfast.

Ace cut some steaks off the half beef Carmella had sent with them. He tossed four potatoes in a dutch oven, and then he went looking for four rocks about the same size. Once the campfire was established, he placed the rocks around it, north, south, east, and west. From under the wagon bed, he removed a metal grill from its rack and settled it on the rocks over the burning coals.

He set the dutch oven on the grill where he could lift the lid and test the potatoes until done. The coffeepot quickly came to a boil, and he set it on the grill's edge to stay warm.

The two young ladies had watched this activity feeling useless. Wyvon, the one who said she could cook, watched Ace, amazed. He moved with little effort. Checking the potatoes, he decided they were ready. Ace then moved the dutch oven to warm beside the coffee. He picked up the steaks and spread them evenly on the hot grill. While they sizzled, he located the container of butter and the salt and pepper Carmella had provided. He set them on the edge of the wagon. With a fork he turned the steaks. He dug four metal plates out of the supply trunk and set eating utensils next to them by the butter. He called out, "Supper's ready." He put a pan of water on the grill for cleanup.

The girls cleaned up while the young men laid their bedrolls out under the wagon. Then they sat around the fire. Ellen laughed and said, "I'm exhausted. All I did was ride in the wagon all day, and I can hardly keep my eyes open."

They all agreed with her. Ace asked, "Does anyone need a nightcap?"

"Not me," Wyvon said. "I hate the stuff. Remember we worked at a brothel. A good clean drink of water for me."

The men were not old enough to have acquired the taste for whiskey, so they all just sat awhile and watched the stars peak through the clouds. One after another they yawned.

Wyvon finally said, "I can hardly keep my eyes open. Ace, I looked over the packaged foods in the travel trunk Carmella sent with us. It has a pretty good selection: flour, cornmeal, oatmeal, necessary seasonings. I think I can manage breakfast if you leave out the dutch oven and a pan for oatmeal. I think I can find everything else."

The girls turned in. It surprised them how tired they were from simply riding in a wagon. Ellen insisted she had bruises on her bottom from bouncing around all day.

Juan's crew, familiar with each other, shared chores. They soon had the disobedient little herd under control. As the day wore on, men and animals settled into an orderly trail drive.

Deadly was the only one unsettled. He watched for Grady. Spent much of his time checking the back trail. Juan tried giving him a biscuit to calm him. He accepted it, but it didn't calm him. He had a job to do, and he did it, but he looked back often. When the drive stopped, he divided his night standing over Trumpeter and going along the back trail. His head lifted with nostrils quivering.

Five days on the trail found the travelers, animal and humans, working together. Each knew his or her job, and the small herd quit trying to escape.

Following the herd at a walk was good for Trumpeter but boring for Garcia. He sang as they traveled and enjoyed the scenery, watching for hawks and deer. Garcia composed songs in his head, and occasionally, when the boredom really got to him, he took out his guitar and worked on his compositions.

Ace's crew became a working unit. The girls, bored, riding in the uncomfortable wagon, often got out and walked. Wyvon took over the meal preparations. Burned some and learned from the experience. Ellen helped Elvin collect firewood, often picking up pieces and tossing them on the wagon when she walked. She helped him feed the mules, measuring out grain, while he removed their harness and hobbled them.

Ace continued to make camp a comfortable distance from the drovers. The young men liked the idea of keeping the two girls to themselves, but that didn't last long. Jalo, Paco, and Garcia, complete with guitar, began to visit the third night on the trail, naturally gravitating to others near their age. They all stayed on their best behavior. Evenings were times for storytelling and getting acquainted. Garcia usually ended their visit with music. Sometimes he played melodies familiar to Anglos, but he always ended the evening with a Spanish song with only his sweet voice accompanying it.

Often after their guests left, either Elvin and Ellen or Ace and Wyvon, hand in hand, took an evening stroll under the stars.

Five days out, Juan began to watch for Grady's arrival. If they left two days after the herd, they should have caught up.

The day's travel progressed without mishap. Late in the afternoon, Deadly became more agitated. He wanted to bed down the herd and go back along the trail. His instincts told him someone or something was coming.

Juan, seeing Deadly's agitation, suspected Grady wasn't far behind them. He called an early halt. Rode forward to stop Ace's wagon.

Grady's small caravan had traveled at a comfortable speed. Dizzy and Jimbo helped Lou with meals and evening chores.

Grady made Cecile his job. She wanted to exercise daily. Because it was such a task for Cecile to expend the energy to get fully dressed, she chose to stay in her robe until late afternoon. Then she would pull on her man pants, and Grady would help her with her boots and winter wear. He always dressed for the day in the early morning. He just removed his boots when he joined her in the Cart to rest.

She put her embarrassment aside. Wearing her robe, she occasionally rode on top with Lou and made necessary bathroom trips. She liked this arrangement. She could spend the evening having supper with the men and enjoying the evening comradery. It allowed her to catch up with news of her herd and enter in on travel plans.

She wanted to keep herself moving. Gain back her strength. The inside of her red chariot was so comfortable. She loved traveling in it. She had to discipline herself to leave it often during the day's travel. When she got home, she had to be on her feet. She had a ranch to run.

Like most young people in love, the recovering invalids talked a lot. Shared their histories and planned their future. Grady did his exercising on his horse or up top with Lou. He did his walking in the evenings with Cecile, hand in hand around the camp. Staying close to be safe.

Grady sometimes pushed himself longer than he should. His legs would begin to shake, and his blood pressure made itself known by the headache developing. He looked forward to removing his boots, crawling into the Cart, and stretching out next to Cecile. He put an arm under her shoulder and pulled her close. She would lay her head on his chest and hug him to her with one arm. He pulled his bedroll over them to keep her arm warm, and the best reward was a kiss from her sweet lips.

He stayed long enough to get warm and help with whatever she needed. Then he put his boots and winter wear back on and climbed back onto his saddle. Often he rode ahead and scouted the trail that had been dug up by cow and horse hooves. When he began to tire, he dismounted, tied his horse to the Cart, climbed to the driver's bench, and visited with Lou. Then he would repeat the process of removing his boots and jackets to once again join Cecile for a brief respite.

The fifth day out, Grady spent more time riding his horse ahead to scout the trail. They should be catching up with the herd. By late afternoon he was getting impatient until he saw the big bull, Deadly, trotting to meet him.

Even Grady's horse got excited. They often met in just this manner. When the bull reached them, he stopped and touched noses with the horse. Then he moved to Grady's side and with a rough swipe of his tongue pulled in the biscuit Grady held out for just such a greeting.

Grady leaned over and scratched the hard bone between the two long horns, and then he turned back to join his crew. Lou was grinning. Seeing Deadly, he knew the herd was not far ahead. Grady turned his horse in front of the team and said to Deadly, "Head them out."

Having found his friend, Deadly shook his horns and took the lead. Soon Grady spotted the camp.

Lou stopped by the supply wagon close to the campfire. They all greeted each other. After Dizzy and Jimbo shook hands around, they rode on to the freight wagon.

There was a shift in chores that night. Lou helped Fernando with supper, and Jalo took the Cart's team and Grady's horse, hobbled them, and turned them in with the remuda.

Grady helped Cecile dress and walked her to the campfire. Seating her on a log, he watched the approach of her vaqueros as they came forward, bowed to her, and kissed her hand. Their beaming faces let her know how much they cared for her.

Deadly hung around the camp, content now that Grady had arrived. He stayed until supper was served and Grady slipped him a biscuit, and then he joined Trumpeter.

For the first time since leaving Janos, Deadly calmly grazed until late at night and quietly stood over Trumpeter and dozed.

Dizzy and Jimbo rode into their camp. Ace and Elvin greeted them warmly. The girls stayed back, not knowing what to expect from Dizzy.

Elvin took their mules, hobbled them, and turned them loose with the other four.

Wyvon was fixing supper. Tonight she was frying strip steaks in the iron skillet so she could make gravy. She had potatoes cooked and ready to mash. That was Ace's job. Coffee was made. She pointed to the bottle of whiskey on the seat of the wagon if they wanted it. She had mastered the Dutch oven, and it was making loaf bread tonight.

The girls hadn't said a word. Wyvon handed Dizzy and Jimbo coffee. Dizzy accepted his and sat on a stump. He didn't say a word. Just sipped the coffee and studied the camp.

Jimbo got the whiskey bottle, removed the stopper, and held it out to Dizzy, who just nodded. Jimbo poured a shot into Dizzy's mug and then dumped an equal shot into his mug.

Jimbo put the whiskey bottle back on the wagon seat and walked off to find Elvin.

Dizzy had expected to find things in disarray. He was geared to give a tongue-lashing. His eyes were going in different directions as he looked around. He couldn't find anything to blow up about. Well! He'd shake things up a little later.

Supper around their campfire was uncomfortably quiet. Dizzy ate every bite. He didn't say a word until all had finished.

"Thank you, ma'am. Good meal. We'll be pulling out in three hours. Should give you plenty of time to get things together. We'll drive till morning and stop for morning meal. We'll feed the mules and rest them at morning and evening meal stops. Grab some sleep if you can, but be ready to hook up and travel. Jimbo and I will drive the first push. I'm going to walk over and say good-bye to Grady." He got up and walked out of camp.

Ace and Elvin stared after him. Wyvon realized her mouth was hanging open. She shut it. Ellen reached over and grabbed Elvin's hand.

They looked at each other. Ace shrugged his shoulders. He said to Elvin, "Well! It looks like we're back on schedule.

"What schedule?" Wyvon asked.

"We only stop for meals until we get to San Antonio," Elvin answered.

"You've got to be kidding!" Ellen exclaimed.

"Sorry, it's no joke. It's pretty tiring. We'd better get busy and pack up the food supplies, but remember, we'll be grabbing food on the run. Make it easy, just plan on one item a meal. Biscuits and honey, cornbread and jam, steak cooked over the campfire—get the idea? I'll store all the skillets and the grill." Ace got up and flipped the grill over into the dirt to cool.

Elvin took over. "Dress for day wear. The only time you'll be able to change into nightwear is if you do it under covers on a moving wagon. Bathroom stops are on the run at mealtimes. If you just have to go, you'll have to step off a moving wagon, and when you're through, you'll have to run to catch it."

Ace saw the stunned looks on the girls' faces. He said, "This is the warning Dizzy gave you back in Janos. He means it. He won't stop until he says so. We found that out on our way out here."

Wyvon and Ellen looked at each other and without a word began cleaning the dirty dishes and packing up all food supplies in the trunk. They spent some time in dressing and organizing their bedrolls.

Ace and Elvin climbed into their bedrolls under the wagon. Dizzy hadn't come back yet. Jimbo threw a tree branch on the camp coals, lit a cigarette, and when it was spent, tossed the stub in the fire and spread his bedroll in front of the wagon's front wheels.

Juan's crew finished supper and scattered to do chores or smoke. Grady walked Cecile to the Cart, helped remove her boots, and closed the doors. He returned to sit with Juan by the fire. He was so relieved to finally be on the move again. It seemed forever he had been bedridden and useless.

He knew he wasn't in any condition yet to ramrod this drive. He expressed his thoughts to Juan. Told him he appreciated the older man standing in for him. He shook Juan's hand and said, "If it's all right with you, you stay in charge. I'll help out when you need me." Juan rose and left Grady staring into the flames.

He was deep in thought when he was brushed against as Dizzy lifted a leg and stepped over to sit beside him on the log.

Grady said, "Want some coffee?"

Dizzy answered, "Hell, I need a drink."

Grady chuckled and said to Lou, who was cleaning up supper, "We have a bottle of Candy's whiskey anywhere?"

"You bet." He went to the Cart, rummaged around under the bench, and found a bottle. He fetched Dizzy a clean mug and poured a good slug into it. Grady held up his coffee cup, and Lou gave him a shot. Then he set the bottle where Dizzy could reach it and returned to the cleanup.

The two men sat, staring into the fire and sipping their drinks. Grady knew Dizzy had something on his mind, so he sat quiet and waited until he was ready to talk.

The camp noises were gradually ceasing as the vaqueros were gathering to visit and smoke. Soon the sweet melody of Garcia's guitar drifted to the two men seated by the fire.

Dizzy took off his hat and set it on the log beside him. He massaged his head with both hands, took a sip of his whiskey, and said, "All I've thought about for days is those women in my wagon. I planned on getting you caught up with your outfit and then taking off, driving night and day, making up time to get back to San Antonio. And then the boys drive up with two women! Hell, Grady, my wagon doesn't even have a cover on it!"

"Is that what's bothering you?" Grady asked.

"No, not really. Their camp looks good. The brunette had a kick-ass supper made tonight. They evidently made the five-day travel all right. I made a decision.

"I really need to get back. I'm worried about my mom, and I do have a business to run. I brought all my freight wagons to San Antonio, figuring to spend her last days there. I've been hiring drivers, and thank God my reputation has followed me and I'm getting some good referrals. I didn't plan on being gone so long."

Grady said, "I know you made a tough call to ride with me. I really appreciate it."

136

Dizzy said, "Glad to do it. This little side trip only took a week longer than I planned." He took out his papers and rolled a cigarette. He said, "It's those women who've got me bumfuzzled! I hate like the dickens to travel with women. If I had the time, I'd travel along with you. But I can't do it. I've got to get back. So, I told them to get ready to travel. We'll leave around midnight."

"That does sound a little harsh." Grady chuckled.

Dizzy reached for the whiskey and poured another shot. "Don't laugh," he said. "This is turning into the trip from hell." He picked up a stick and stuck the tip in the coals. When the tip turned red, he lit his cigarette.

Grady knew Dizzy from hiring on Dizzy's freight business in San Francisco in between wagon-train jobs. He knew the man was powerful. He protected his drivers from Indians and outlaws. He was an expert rifleman and a quick draw with his pistol. He said, "You're afraid of trouble. I don't blame you. It's troubling times. But I heard you warn those women. They ignored the warning. I know you Dizzy, you've got plenty of firearms, and I'll bet those boys are deadeye riflemen."

Dizzy swallowed the whiskey and set his mug by the bottle. He stood, flipped his cigarette into the fire and said, "Sure, I'm loaded with firepower, but that's a freight wagon, there's no protection there! I'll just have to stop somewhere in the morning and give those girls some rifle lessons. It's been good to see you Grady. Take care of that little lady. Now that I'm in your country, I'll see more of you."

They shook hands and Dizzy disappeared into the darkness.

The freight wagon and crew pulled out a little after midnight, Dizzy as driver and Jimbo riding shotgun. Dizzy wore a bullet belt, his .36-caliber Navy revolver holstered on his hip. Jimbo had a shotgun lying across his lap. Loaded spare rifles were under the bench and ammunition was in easy reach.

The two extra mules were saddled and tied to the tailgate. The two girls and the two young men covered with bedrolls and tarps were soon back asleep.

Early morning, Grady's camp was on its regular trail schedule. Lou and Fernando were up at four. Men fed, teams hooked up. Lou's Cart leading out by six.

Jalo had hooked up Lou's team. Lou carried biscuits and oatmeal to Grady and Cecile right before he climbed on the Cart and took up the reins. The two had remained under covers while the drovers broke camp. It was agreed that mornings they would stay in out of the way.

Grady lay on his side beside her. He studied her beautiful face. Her creamy skin had some color in her cheeks and mouth. She was getting well.

He remembered riding out of the canyon in Candy's wagon, holding Cecile in his arms. Her pale face had a blue tint to it, dark circles under her eyes, chapped lips, and a festered sore. A holdover thanks to an outlaw's wrath. He had been so afraid he was going to lose her.

He wanted to pull her close, feel her body against his. He wanted to make love to her. What he didn't want was her to be afraid of him. He knew she had been raised with the highest of moral values. He knew she loved him. What a blessing. He wanted their life together to be perfect. It was important to him that he do everything right and proper; she was a lady. He respected that. Grady counted himself lucky just to be able to lie beside this angel. Holding her in his arms without taking advantage was hard, but his love and respect for her comforted him.

He pulled his mind away from studying her face and sent his thoughts ahead to San Antonio. Marriage to Cecile. His life had taken a sharp turn. He wasn't sure what lay ahead. He had worked for years toward establishing a ranch and home. That had been his plan. He had a thousand acres paid for and many more he could lease. The property had an enormous number of wild cattle, mostly longhorns. Most were unbranded and free for the taking.

With his own hands, between trail drives, he had built a one-room cabin. It was a large log structure with adequate room for a two-person bed, a kitchen, and a table and chairs. He had built shelves on the walls and two shuttered windows. He had dreamed of slowly adding onto the cabin until he had a proper ranch house.

This year he had planned to build a barn with Bear's and Lou's help. Who knew he would fall in love with a beautiful Spanish lady and nearly lose his life to pneumonia? How quickly life can change. The only thing he was sure of was that he wanted a life with this beautiful being lying beside him. He would adjust to whatever circumstances presented itself. Take it one day at a time. Cecile was now his first priority, everything else came second to her.

He pushed his bedroll off and, moving quietly, pulled his pants over his long johns. He opened the little window Bear had provided and poked Lou in the back, signaling him to pull up.

He fastened the window, slid to the doors, and as the Cart stopped, pulled on his boots and shut the doors behind him. Jalo had saddled and tied his horse to the Cart. He untied him and climbed aboard. He would ride until he got tired. Their wagon was in the lead. He rode beside the Cart, mostly visiting with Lou. Occasionally he rode ahead to study the terrain.

When he visited with Lou, he encouraged the old gentleman to tell him about the days of survival in the canyon, while he was ill in Janos.

Midmorning they stopped for Cecile to relieve herself. In her robe she climbed to ride beside Lou. It was winter, and the weather was cold, but the day was clear. The three friends talked as the Cart followed the freight wagon's tracks.

It was noon. The sun was high in the sky when Grady pulled up his horse and said, "Lou, did you hear that?"

Lou stopped the team. His hearing wasn't good. He said, "What did you hear?"

"I think I heard gunfire." He listened, and a faint echo of three shots repeated.

Cecile said, "Yes, I heard it."

Grady said, "I'd better check it out."

Lou said, "It's probably Dizzy hunting. Don't go alone, wait for the men."

A third echo of three shots, and Grady said, "Those are 'trouble, need help' shots." He kicked his horse into a rapid run, drew his pistol, and yelled, "Call the crew."

Lou picked up his rifle and fired three shots in the air. The help signal. He turned to Cecile and said, "If we spot trouble, I'll stop. You get inside."

She started to argue, but he said, "Don't argue with me. Get inside and get your pistol. You can open the window if need be." She nodded and braced her feet. Lou slapped the reins, pushing the team into a run.

Dizzy had driven the mules until the sun came up. He stopped. Jimbo made a fire. Wyvon made oats and toast from last night's leftover bread. They all had grabbed a bite. Dizzy picked up a rifle and some ammunition. He told the girls to follow him. He spent an hour teaching them how to load the rifle. Wyvon was quick. Ellen was a complainer and afraid of guns. He didn't want to waste bullets, so he only let them take two shots apiece. He picked a tree far enough away that a ricochet wouldn't come back at them. He just wanted them to know the feel of firing a rifle.

Wyvon missed her first shot. Her second shot peeled some bark off the tree. Ellen, acting girly, missed both shots. Shaking his head, Dizzy took the rifle away from her and gave it to Wyvon. He said, "You're in charge of this rifle. She will kill one of us." His crazy eyes looked at Wyvon. "Keep it loaded and where you can reach it at all times."

"Yes, sir." She put the bullets he gave her in the pocket of her jacket. She noticed Ace had been watching her. He gave her a nod of approval.

Ellen acted crushed that Wyvon received praise. She sashayed back to the wagon and climbed on it.

This stop had turned into a three-hour layover. Ace and Elvin had a restless night. The bouncing bed of the wagon had awakened them often.

They were irritable and quarrelsome with each other. Ace took over the reins and moved the team out.

The girls settled with their backs to the driver's bench, warmly clothed with their winter wear and blankets over their legs. They were subdued by Dizzy's presence. They didn't want to incur his wrath. When he rode his mule beside the wagon, they ceased all talk.

Dizzy's mind was busy worrying about his mom. He knew he wouldn't be able to sleep. It was hard enough to sleep while a wagon was jouncing around. Add two girls who also occupied the wagon bed, and it was a sure recipe for not being able to sleep.

Jimbo had the same worries. He lived with their mother and knew firsthand her weakness. He wanted to get back as much as Dizzy and the boys.

The two older brothers chose to ride for a while, taking turns riding ahead to scout the trail for trouble. While one rode out, the other dropped back beside the wagon.

It was Dizzy's turn to ride ahead. He had ridden out of sight when the mules threw up their heads and spooked, jerking the wagon abruptly. Ellen screamed. She had hit her head hard.

Jimbo had been watching ahead for Dizzy. The scream brought his eyes to Ace and Elvin. Each had an arrow in his chest. Ace was falling off the bench to the ground, and Elvin fell onto the seat Ace just vacated.

Indian whoops and hollering began. He had put the shotgun under the seat with the other weapons. He automatically drew his side arm and was turning to fire. What he saw astounded him. It looked like ten or twelve Indians appeared where seconds before the trees had looked cool and inviting.

He didn't have time to aim. He threw up his Colt sidearm and fired at the first Indian closing in on the mules. His attention was focused ahead. Out the corner of his eye, he got the movement of a horse. He turned to see a brave almost on him. The painted face was yelling, and his arm stretched out, pointing a rifle at Jimbo. The Indian didn't aim. He just thrust the rifle in Jimbo's direction and pulled the trigger.

The bullet hit Jimbo in the thigh and traveled through the muscle and into the heart of his mule. The mule went down. Jimbo barely had time to pull his boots out of the stirrups before he hit the ground.

He managed to hold on to the Colt and drag himself under the wagon, which had come to a halt. He realized Indians had overtaken the wagon, freeing the mules by slashing the harness. He heard Wyvon's rifle fire.

The Indian who shot him jumped off his horse and was coming after him under the wagon. Jimbo shot him in his grinning face. Indians were all over the wagon. All he could see were legs of men and horses. An Indian slid off his horse, drew his knife, and bent to scalp Ace. Jimbo shot him. He fell across Ace's body.

When Ellen hit her head and heard the first Indian yell, she slid down and pulled the covers over herself to hide. Wyvon had to fight the covers to get to the rifle. With it in her hands she stood and tried to shoot the Indian standing almost on top of her while he removed Elvin's scalp. He deflected the rifle muzzle. The bullet hit one of the Indians on horseback who was holding the reins of the freed mules. He was hit and painfully so. He rode off after another Indian grabbed the reins and then rode after him, leading the four-mule team.

It seemed like Indians were everywhere. The girls were being pulled off the wagon and thrown across a horse in front of its rider. Jimbo's pistol only had one more shot. Afraid of hitting a girl, he fired his last shot at the horse that carried Wyvon. The horse stumbled, recovered, and disappeared. Now they had at least one badly injured Indian and a horse that wasn't going far.

Someone else was firing a pistol. Dizzy was almost on them. Two Indians on horseback turned to cut him off. They were guiding their horses using their legs and firing arrows. An expert pistol shot, one of Dizzy's hurried bullets knocked one off his horse. The other Indian rode to him, and like an acrobat the injured man swung behind his rescuer.

Dizzy's mule had an arrow in his lungs. The mule was ten feet from the wagon when he fell. Dizzy scrambled on hands and knees under the wagon with Jimbo. He needed to reload. Jimbo had just shoved two bullets in his pistol when a brave, out to count coup, slid off his horse. With knife in hand, he bent down to enter under the wagon. Jimbo spun his cylinder and pulled the trigger, praying the hammer would land on one of the bullets. It missed. He was pulling the trigger as fast as he could.

The Indian smiled and crept forward. Dizzy was staring at the Indian. His hands were working to pull bullets from his belt. His eyes crossed in fear and anger, each eye went its own way. The smile left the Indian's face as his eyes grew wide. He spun and ran to his horse, making a running mount.

In moments it became quiet. Not a sound was heard. This entire attack had only lasted a few minutes.

Dizzy slumped back against the wagon wheel and drew in a few deep breaths. Jimbo finished loading his pistol.

Dizzy said, "What the hell was that?"

Jimbo just shook his head.

Dizzy saw the blood oozing from Jimbo's thigh and settling in the dirt. He said, "You're hit. That don't look like no arrow wound."

Jimbo, who from the first second he saw his precious nephews killed had acted on pure, enraged adrenaline. Pain was starting to contort his face as he gasped out, "It's not, the bastard had a rifle. Looked like an old army musket. It only had one shot. I guess I'm lucky he didn't aim. Could have hit me in the heart. Kinda wish he had. I seen those kids killed in front of my eyes! That's somethin' I ain't ever gonna get outta my mind!"

Jimbo paused as a tear slid from his eye. "Best ya jest let me be and let me bleed out here. I don't wanna keep livin' this nightmare over and over again in my mind!"

Dizzy worked to free his pocketknife. "Well, ya got me to live for, so I ain't gonna listen to your horseshit!" He talked while he worked. He cut the pants away so he could inspect the wound. "A muzzle-loader's kinda hard to reload on a moving horse. Indians with rifles. That's kind of scary."

Dizzy checked the wound and saw it had passed through the flesh and exited. Jimbo pointed to his mule and said, "Bullet killed my mule."

Dizzy needed to stop the bleeding. He also wanted to check Ace. He knew Elvin was gone. He had gotten a clear picture of Elvin's scalped head as he rode in. Dizzy crawled to Jimbo's mule and cut off a couple of the leather straps used to tie a bedroll on. He tied the two together and wrapped them around Jimbo's leg above the wound. He pulled the ends tight and knotted them.

He broke off a short tree limb that was handy, slipped it under the leather strap, and turned it. He said, "Every little while loosen this, let it bleed a little, and tighten it back up. I'm going to check things out. I'll send out a help signal. Hope they're not attacking the herd." Then he added, "And don't be thinkin' about doing somethin' stupid."

He finished loading his pistol and crawled out. Holding the pistol ready, he looked closer at Elvin. He nearly threw up as he saw the young man with an arrow in his chest and a bloody scalp.

A talented Indian had shot his arrow in the heart. Instant death. Elvin hadn't felt the knife removing his hair. It was a bloody mess. Dizzy gave it up. He walked away from the wagon and threw up.

Jimbo knew things had to be bad if Dizzy had chucked. He tried to scoot over and get out from under the wagon.

Dizzy saw him and said, "Stay there. I'll help you after I check on Ace."

Jimbo nodded. Ace wasn't very far behind the wagon. The mules had been stopped about twenty feet from him. He lay on his back with a dead Indian draped over him. Jimbo had made a clean head shot, keeping the Indian from collecting Ace's scalp.

Dizzy grabbed the Indian's legs and dragged him off Ace.

When he looked down at Ace, he was surprised to see blue eyes meet his. The eyes blinked. Ace's right hand reached up to feel the arrow embedded in his shoulder.

Dizzy said, "Hold on boy, don't touch it." He yelled at Jimbo, "Ace is alive."

"Thank you, God," Jimbo answered for the blessings received.

Ace had halted the effort to feel his shoulder. His head was killing him. He redirected the arm to explore the pain.

Dizzy knelt down, stopped Ace, and felt the large swollen area. There was a wide cut dripping blood. Ace had probably hit his head when he fell off the wagon. Left him unconscious until now.

Dizzy brushed Ace's hair back off his brow and said, "Leave it be for now. I'm going to fire off some shots and see if I can get some help."

Ace nodded and closed his eyes.

Dizzy walked away from him and fired three shots, he waited a few minutes and fired three more. It was this distress signal that Grady had heard.

Dizzy quickly reloaded his pistol and returned it to his hip holster. He looked for a blanket or pillow to put under Ace's head. Everything was gone. The girls, the blankets, and pillows. Even all of their personal canvas tote bags. The only thing that was left was an empty freight wagon and two dead mules. Worst yet, all the firearms were gone from under the wagon seat.

His dead mule at least had Dizzy's saddlebag still attached to his saddle. It would have to do. He removed the saddle from the mule, unfastened the saddlebag, and was placing it under Ace's head when Grady came into sight. His horse, running at top speed, slid to a stop with an added crow-hop, almost unseating his rider.

Grady swung out of his saddle, dropping his reins to the ground. His horse was trained to stand still anytime he "ground tied" him.

Dizzy stood, and Grady walked over to look at Ace. The young man's eyes opened, and he tried to smile. Grady, studying the arrow, said, "That's got to hurt. Lou will be here soon. He'll know how to handle that."

Dizzy had tears in his eyes. He said, "Jimbo has a wound in his thigh, and Elvin is gone. Grady, they scalped him."

Grady turned to Dizzy and took him in his arms. Several inches taller and thirty pounds heavier than Grady, he welcomed the embrace and released a flood of tears.

Grady hugged him and said, "The girls?"

Dizzy stepped back, wiped his eyes, and said, "They took them. They took everything, even the firearms under the bench."

Aces eyes opened, and he spoke in a shaky voice, "Wyvon?"

"They got her, boy," Dizzy told the truth.

The red Cart came into view. The team was coming at a run. Grady shivered. Everything in that wagon would be scrambled, but he was glad to see Lou. There should be some medical supplies on the Cart, but they would be few. It pulled to a stop, and Lou joined them. He knelt down and studied the arrow as he decided on the supplies he might need.

Grady's attention went to Cecile. Her eyes were huge. She had braced her legs on the wagon and clung to the bench. She was still in her robe.

Dizzy walked with Lou to where his brother leaned against a wagon wheel. His eyes were closed, and his head leaned back on the wheel. There was a little puddle of blood in the dirt.

He opened his eyes when Lou squatted beside him and untied the leather cord. The blood flow had slowed to a slight drip. Lou asked, "This go through?"

Jimbo nodded.

Lou said, "This don't look too bad. I think I can wash both sides with whiskey, put a dab of honey in both, and wrap it with clean rags. Any other pains I need to know about?"

"No, sir, I'm feeling kind of woozy. I think with a bit of whiskey I'll manage. Rather you tend to my nephew."

The fear of the attack and grief over Elvin, added to the loss of blood, had weakened him.

While Lou was busy, Grady helped Cecile off the wagon. He took her to the back doors and suggested she get dressed. She didn't argue, just crawled in and shut the doors.

Grady went to Lou and said, "I'm going to ride back and have them bring the supply wagon here. We'll camp close for safety and so you can get to the medical trunk." Lou agreed. Grady swung into the saddle and rode back to let the drovers know what had happened. He directed the supply wagon and the cattle traveler to move forward quickly.

Lou went to the Cart and dug out the small medical box he had packed. The trunk on the supply wagon was better supplied. He located the clean rags Candy had shared and grabbed the whiskey that Grady and Dizzy had put a dent in last night.

Dizzy was squatting on his heels by Jimbo. He looked like a lost child. His crazy eyes were out of control. Lou figured the big guy was in need of doctoring for stress as much as Jimbo needed wound doctoring. At the very least, Dizzy also needed a few shots of whiskey.

He got the water dipper from the barrel on the Cart and gave both Jimbo and Dizzy a couple of swallows of whiskey and said, "Dizzy, do you feel like getting a fire started? We're probably going to need some hot water."

Dizzy welcomed the job. The shot of whiskey helped. He rounded up four stones to set the grill on. The items attached to the underside of the wagon bed had escaped the thieves.

He thanked Carmella, silently, for giving them the trunk to pack food supplies and some small pans, which included a coffeepot. The trunk had been too heavy. The Indians hadn't found the iron skillets and metal grill. Besides his thanks to Carmella, he said thanks to the Lord for these small gifts.

There was a pile of kindling and tree limbs the girls had thrown on the wagon as they walked. He didn't have to search for burnable material. He soon had a fire going, the grill on the stones, and a pan of water warming.

He went to see how Lou was doing and let him know water was warming. Lou had Jimbo's pant leg cut away above the wound so he could clean both front and rear exit wounds. Using a clean rag and the dipper, he poured some warm water over the rag. He didn't want to soil the water heating, so it took several trips, using the dipper to pour water on the rag, to clean the blood and dirt off Jimbo's leg. Once the surface wound was cleaned, Lou trickled some whiskey on the open wound.

Jimbo had to stand and lean on the wagon bed for Lou to clean the exit wound. With both wounds cleaned and dosed with whiskey, he dried the leg. Rummaging in the trunk, he found a quart of honey, the perfect thing to heal and protect against infection. He dribbled a spoonful in each opening. A clean rag was wrapped around the thigh and tied on with strips of rags.

Fernando arrived with the supply wagon. Grady had accompanied the wagon on his horse.

Grady, Fernando, Dizzy, and Lou carried Ace to the freight wagon. Lou laid out an army blanket. When the Border Patrol Army was reassigned, Candy had bought six of them and laundered them. She had given Lou two to carry as extra blankets.

Lou, using his pocketknife, cut off both Ace's shirt and undershirt, exposing the arrow's shaft.

They turned Ace on his side so Lou could see if the head of the arrow had penetrated his back. It had not! It couldn't be pulled out. It had to be driven through.

Lou stepped back, shook his head, and took a deep breath. He told Ace to relax and that he would be right back. He walked to the fire and, using the dipper, poured warm water over his hands, then dried them on a clean rag.

Dizzy and Grady joined him. He said, "We have to push it through. First we have to break the shaft off. We need to leave enough shaft to hit it with a rock and drive it through. It's going to take someone stronger than me to drive it though in one shot. If it takes more than one shot, it could tear muscle and create a problem."

They looked at each other. Grady said, "I'd better not. I've been active more than usual, and my hands and legs are beginning to shake. This can't be botched. Dizzy, are you up to this?"

Cecile joined them. She had heard Lou and realized her arrival was not welcome. She took hold of Grady's hand and said, "You've got an unopened bottle of laudanum in the Cart." She looked at Lou and said, "Would it help Ace with the pain?"

Lou said, "I think he has a concussion. He'll need the laudanum for that. Thanks, Cecile. Let's give him a dose of whiskey. Not much we can do about the pain. It's going to hurt awful, but it needs to be done and soon. It's already been in there too long."

They gathered around Ace and explained what needed to be done. He said, "Just get it done. It hurts every breath I draw in. My head is killing me."

Lou started to pour some whiskey in a mug, and Ace said, "No! I hate that stuff. I always throw it up. Give me something to bite down on."

Lou turned to Grady. "We have to secure most of his body to the wagon. He needs to hang over far enough for the arrow to go all the way clear. Can you hold his head steady?"

They shifted Ace enough for the arrow to have a clear path and not come into contact with the wagon bed. Lou got his whip out of the Cart and gave Ace the hard leather handle to put between his teeth. Now they had to break the arrow shaft.

Dizzy took out his pocketknife. The shaft needed to be broken without jerking it. The knife was sharp, and its blade glistened. He used his left hand to hold the shaft steady. With a slight upward slash, he hit the shaft. The blade cut halfway through it. The rest broke easily by snapping it with his hands.

Ace moaned. Half-crying, he clenched his teeth on the whip handle. Lou handed Dizzy a good-size stone and said, "Let's get this over with. It ain't gonna get any easier."

Without overthinking it Dizzy wrapped his fingers around the stone, turned, and sent a power blow to the broken shaft.

Ace screamed. The whip fell from his mouth. Grady struggled to hold him steady as his body stiffened. Ace passed out. Lou said, "Turn him on his side."

Grady and Dizzy rolled him over, putting his head and shoulders back on the wagon. It allowed them to confirm that the arrow had gone through. Lou was able to get a grip on the arrowhead and pull it the rest of the way out. Everyone drew a deep breath.

Lou hurriedly cleaned both entry and exit wounds with whiskey and then dropped honey in each wound. Using clean rags, he padded each wound with rag strips. He then secured them by wrapping over his shoulder and around his chest.

Dizzy and Grady moved Ace's body over more so he wouldn't roll off the wagon.

Cecile folded the army blanket and put it under Ace's head. Then she went to the Cart and got the bottle of laudanum, giving it to Dizzy.

Grady said, "A couple of spoonfuls the first dose and then one spoonful as needed."

Jimbo, by himself, had lifted Elvin. Limping painfully, he had carried him a distance from the wagons and laid him gently on the ground. Afterward, he returned and sat on the wagon bench and watched them work on Ace. A tear ran down his cheek. He said, "I'll take Ace's share of the whiskey."

Lou handed him the mug he had filled for Ace. He then walked back to the Cart and rummaged around. He found an unopened bottle of whiskey and returned to the freight wagon.

Grady noticed they had attracted an audience. All of Juan's crew except Fernando had watched the operation.

Juan stepped forward and said, "Dizzy, I'm sorry about this. Fernando is cooking a big pot of chili. If you feel like eating, please join us. You can carry some back for the boys."

Dizzy nodded and went to Jimbo. He saw Elvin had been moved. He stopped by Jimbo and dropped his head. He drew in deep breaths. Jimbo put his hand on Dizzy's head and felt his brother's body shake with sobs.

Once the herd caught up to the wagons, Deadly proceeded to circle and group the herd. With that job done he ambled over to the traveler that carried Trumpeter. Trumpeter had yet to be unloaded, and he was anxious to check on his friend. He walked around the traveler several times and then let out a brawl.

When no one answered his calls for Trumpeter to be released he decided to find Grady. Deadly trotted toward the freight wagon where Grady and the others were preoccupied.

As he neared the group, the strong scent of blood hit him. His mind and body were immediately on alert. Coming closer, he saw the dead mules. He could also smell the blood around the wagon. Something was terribly wrong.

Deadly stood perfectly still, taking in the scene. He saw Grady, which slightly calmed him. He walked quietly over to the wagon and began sniffing around, making him more agitated. Deadly began pawing the ground and swinging his horns, readying himself for battle.

Grady, afraid of what Deadly might do, casually walked over to him. Speaking in a gentle tone, he veered away from Deadly's horns and walked to his rump. He patted him there, all the while talking softly.

Hearing Grady's soothing voice quickly calmed Deadly and he quit swinging his horns. This allowed Grady to approach his massive head to pet and scratch him.

As soon as Deadly had completely settled down, Grady gave him the order to "bed them down," which meant to settle and guard the herd.

Deadly understood that, tonight, that was going to be his most important job. Grady wanted him with the herd. Whatever had happened was not good. He needed to keep careful watch over the little cows tonight and keep them safe.

Grady returned to the group. His first request was that Trumpeter be released. He knew this would help calm Deadly and keep him on task.

Everyone scattered to get evening chores done. Supper was subdued that night. Grady's crew realized they had narrowly missed an Indian attack. Weapons were dug out. Pistol holsters appeared, filled with pistols loaded and ready to fire. Rifles would be secure in saddle scabbards tomorrow.

Dizzy spent most of the night awake and restless. He was filled with guilt and remorse for putting his family at risk. He wished he had done the wise thing and traveled with the herd.

He got up frequently to check on the two injured men. He usually found Jimbo awake. He lay beside Ace on the wagon bed. The third time Dizzy checked, Jimbo said, "Cut it out Dizzy. If you can't sleep, at least rest your body. I can't sleep either. I keep seeing those arrows hittin' our nephews. Seein' Elvin's head slashed off the top. Seein' that herd of Indians attackin', and my leg is throbbing like the devil. I can keep an eye on Ace. I'll let you know if he wakes up."

Dizzy whispered, "Can I get you anything?"

Jimbo said, "I'd like a bottle of whiskey, but with what's goin' on about us, we need clear heads. I feel hot—might be a fever comin' on. You can set the water barrel a little closer."

Dizzy moved the water barrel from the tailgate and checked to be sure the dipper was in it. He patted his brother on the shoulder and walked to the dying embers of the fire. He had pulled the stack of burnable twigs and sticks off of the end of the wagon where the girls had tossed them. He threw some on the embers. They caught immediately. He sat, rolled a cigarette, and stared into the fire.

This was all his fault. He shouldn't have endangered his family. He could have hired men who knew the risk and were skilled with their guns. Now he had to go home and tell his mom her grandson was dead and her son was injured. He should have been driving the wagon. He and Jimbo might have had a chance to salvage the attack or at least save the women. He knew better. They had been struck with arrows aimed to kill. No one would have had a chance. It would have been him sitting in Ace's seat, and Jimbo would be dead.

Coulda, shoulda, woulda—he had to shake off these thoughts. He had a nephew to bury in the morning. They were helpless now. Even if he had the mules to go on tomorrow, he was scared, really scared. The two injured men could get worse: fever, infection?

Before the sun came up, Dizzy removed the shovel from under the wagon bed. He owned four freight wagons. He had moved all of them back home to Texas in order to spend the last days of his mom's life with her. He had equipped all of his wagons with those items most used when hauling freight. Racks designed to carry shovels and axes, iron skillets, and dutch oven. A small drawer for miscellaneous tools, hammers, and so on.

Built on the underside of the wagon bed, they were always available and hard to see. No thieves or outlaws had ever stolen the items. Now he could add Indians.

He carried Elvin a little farther from the camp and began to dig. Grady joined him just as the sun came up. He didn't offer to help dig. He didn't need a relapse. He would help in less physical efforts.

Dizzy had made a good start. He had a hole two and a half feet wide and six feet long. It was knee-deep. He climbed out and joined Grady. They found a spot to sit and rolled cigarettes.

Grady let him catch his breath, and then he said, "You figured this out?"

Dizzy knew what he meant but not ready to answer him said, "Nope. Don't think I'm ever gonna be right about it. I know I made a major mistake. I should have stayed with your drive. They might not have attacked. We would have outnumbered them and had more firepower. They probably would not have shown themselves. I know that's not what you asked. I'm entirely dependent on you. I hate to burden you. I know you've just dug yourselves out of a deep hole."

"Stop it. This isn't a situation where anyone's to blame. This could have happened to you if you had ridden out by yourselves. I consider it a blessing we were close behind, thanks to you traveling to accommodate us. I could have come upon you all dead and buzzards chowing down. The arrows in those boys were Apache. This is Cochise's hunting grounds.

"They were covered in war paint and struck your wagon because it was an easy target. We ran into Cochise in the mountains, and they actually assisted in capturing the outlaws that attacked our camp. I don't know how Bear convinced him that our little cows were as sacred as their 'white buffalo.' The blizzard was so bad their camp was going hungry. To thank them we offered a couple of beef. He refused the sacred cattle but accepted two mules. We gave them some of our food supplies. Thanks to Bear they let us pass."

Dizzy asked, "What's this interest in mules? They took all four of the team."

"Meals on the hoof," Grady said.

Surprised, Dizzy said, "They are going to eat my mules?"

"They won't eat their horses. They need them to conduct raids and run from the soldiers. They don't like the headset of the mules. They're too stubborn. They use their horses as trade value for wives and exchange with other tribes. Mules are worthless except for food. Speaking of mules, these are beginning to smell. I'll send Jalo over with a team and drag them away."

Grady stood and said, "Lou will have breakfast ready soon. We are staying a day or more if needed. After breakfast we'll decide what to do."

Dizzy nodded. He dropped his cigarette and stepped on it. Picked up his shovel and used it to help him stand.

They saw Garcia and Jalo coming to them. They waited until they reached them.

Garcia was carrying a shovel and said, "I'd like to help you dig that hole, Mr. Dizzy."

"I'd sure appreciate the help," Dizzy answered.

Grady stopped Jalo before he offered his help. "Jalo, we're going to have to hold over at least a day, maybe more. Hook up a team and drag these two mules away from the wagons."

Grady continued, "Don't get out of sight of the camp. Last night Dizzy and I moved the dead Indians closer to the trees. They were gone this morning. Indians don't like to leave their dead. It's a burial ceremony of some kind. The soul can't go to heaven or something. Anyway. They could be out there hanging around to pick us off one by one, so stay sharp. Keep your eyes roving."

"Yes, sir." Jalo jogged off to the remuda.

Grady went to the Cart and knocked on the door. Cecile answered, "Come in."

He opened the doors and saw she had dressed. She was brushing her hair, preparing to slick it back and form a braid to hang down her back, tied off with the leather straps. Its ends were decorated with a turquoise stone.

She said, "How are Jimbo and Ace?"

He answered, "They are still asleep. I got the impression neither of them, including Dizzy, got much sleep last night. Lou's working on breakfast."

"Grady, what are we going to do?" She finished the braid and tied it off with the leather.

"I'm glad you're up. We need to get together and decide how to carry on. The only thing I know for sure is that we are no longer two camps. We've got to move all the wagons together for safety. They got their dead out last night."

Grady pulled his travel bag to him and dug around until he found the half-full bottle of laudanum. He was reminded of Doc saying, "That's not whiskey. Use a spoon." He put the bottle back into his bag. He would save it for when his head hurt the worst. He was very stressed now but realized the medicine was not going to make things any better.

Cecile crawled to him. He helped her drop to the ground. She looked around. Were Indians out there watching her? They already had two females.

She said, "Grady, I'm afraid to go too far to relieve myself. What are we going to do? I think we need to get away from here."

"Go on the other side of the Cart between it and the supply wagon. I'll watch for you." Grady rubbed his head and massaged his neck. He also wanted to get away from here. To accomplish this, he needed to get back in charge again. So much for turning things over to Juan.

When she returned, he walked with her to the campfire. The vaqueros had cut down a tree. They had cut a few into stumps to sit on and the rest into firewood chunks.

Lou had trail-driver pancakes cooking in three iron skillets. Butter and syrup had been mixed together and left to warm in a small cast-iron pot. Finished cakes were placed in the dutch oven to stay warm.

"Cakes are ready," Lou said.

"Feed as they come," Grady said. "Jalo has a chore, and Dizzy and Garcia are burying Elvin."

"That's why I mixed pancakes. I'll hold off until they show up. Grab a tin plate, and I'll get you two fed."

Dizzy and Garcia were tossing dirt in the grave, covering Elvin. Jimbo hobbled over. He watched while they returned the loose soil to the hole. When finished, they joined Jimbo, and Dizzy, placing his arm around Jimbo, said, "We'll get together later and speak over him. We have serious plans we need to put in place right now. How's Ace?"

Jimbo answered, "He's awake, trying to move. I gave him a swallow of the laudanum. He's groaning. I think his head hurts worse than his wound."

Dizzy turned to Garcia. "Thanks for the help. Lou's got breakfast ready. You go on and eat. Tell Grady we'll be there shortly."

Garcia jogged off. Jimbo leaned on Dizzy and made it back to the wagon. Ace was sitting up. He was stretching his good arm and rubbing his head.

Dizzy leaned the shovel on the wagon and said, "How you feeling, son?"

"Like I've been shot." Ace tried to smile. It looked more like a grimace.

"You'd better take it easy today," Dizzy said. "Breakfast is at the other camp. I'll bring you some."

"I'm going with you." Ace began moving the bedroll away from him. "Where're my boots?"

Dizzy put a hand on his leg and said, "You need to take it easy."

Ace looked at him, pinning down one of his acrobatic eyes, and said, "I'm in good physical shape. If I lie around, I'll get weak. I intend to keep my body working. The sons of bitches killed my brother and took the girls. I can't just let that rest. I need to do right by Elvin, and I can't just forget about those girls. They were under our watch. I'm goin' after them."

Dizzy was speechless. Jimbo said, "OK, boy, I hear you. But you're in no shape to ride a horse."

Ace cut in, "That's why I intend to eat and move around to help my body recover from the shock. I intend to stay upright as much as I can. I can't let my body get soft. I plan on riding out of here in no later than two days. Don't even think about talking me out of it."

While he talked, he was scooting to the side of the wagon. Jimbo went to the bench where he had put Ace's boots and got them. He hobbled back to Ace and helped him put them on.

Dizzy shook his head. "All right, lean on me, and we'll go get breakfast. I'm not going to stop talking you out of this crazy idea. I want you to go on home with us. When you're all healed up, you can go Indian hunting."

Ace replied, "You're nuts if you think I'm going to let their trail grow cold."

Dizzy wasn't going to let it go, and he said, "Son, you're too young and inexperienced to take on a job this dangerous. We can report it to the army post. Your family can't afford to lose you too."

Ace was losing patience, and he said, "I'm twenty-four. I'm an expert tracker, hunter, and shooter. Let's go eat." He stepped away from the wagon. A dizzy spell hit him. He would have fallen if Jimbo hadn't caught him.

Jimbo looked at Dizzy and said, "Now's not the time to argue with him. It's good he wants to eat. Hand me the shovel. I'll have to use it as a crutch until I can make one. You take the boy."

Dizzy, shaking his head, put Ace's good arm over his shoulder. With one arm around Ace's waist, they made their way to the fire.

Grady, Cecile, Garcia, and Fernando were seated around the fire. Grady got up and helped lower Ace to the stump he had been sitting on. Dizzy and Jimbo got metal plates and utensils. Lou slapped a skillet-size pancake on each.

Cecile got another plate. Lou filled it and poured some syrup on the pancake. She held the plate on her lap, cut mouth-size bites, and fed Ace. He was in no condition to be sitting up, but he ate every bite until the plate was empty.

Garcia and Fernando finished and left to spell Juan, who was keeping an eye on the herd. Juan nodded to his replacements and rode in for breakfast. Grady had been waiting for Juan to join them. It was decision time.

Grady said, "The way I see things this morning, we need to stay together. First we need to make one camp. Juan, tell Jalo not to turn the team he's working with loose. Have him circle the wagons and place the campfire in the middle.

"They came in and got their dead sometime during the night. We've got to increase the guard until we pull out of here. They could be out there watching us so they can pick us off one at a time. I suggest we pack up and get on our way as fast as we can. Juan, have Jalo pick us out a strong team to pull Dizzy's wagon. We can't leave it here. It's part of his income. He and Jimbo can drive it, and Ace can recuperate on it."

Ace said "No."

Grady, startled, said, "No! I don't understand."

Dizzy spoke up. "Crazy kid wants to go Indian hunting."

Grady looked at Ace. He saw stubborn determination. Everyone had their eyes on Ace.

Ace stared back. Then he looked at Grady and said, "I realize I sound crazy. I'd like you to consider that I'm clearheaded. It hurts some from the knock I got, but I need to go after those girls. I don't intend to take on the Indian tribe. I want to follow them while their tracks are fresh. I'll learn where they've been taken, and then I'll turn it over to an army."

Grady was quiet. He saw a serious young man. Ace was a tall, six-foot, muscular man. He didn't see a boy. Grady turned to Dizzy and asked, "You want to say something?"

Dizzy said, "He's family. I want him to go home. If there was a chance of rescuing those girls, we would all be trying. Him going off by himself is

156

not clear thinking. I don't like it, but I also don't want to have to tie him to the wagon for weeks to keep him safe. It really boils down to you, Grady. He's going to need a horse and a weapon. We still have the saddles from the two dead mules. We're too wiped out to supply him proper, and I really don't want him goin' out an' gettin' killed. I just prefer you refuse him and then we can be done with this craziness."

Grady walked away from the fire and stared at the mountains they had just left behind them. In his head he saw Indians traveling with the two girls. Cochise's stronghold.

He walked back to the gathering and said to Ace, "You are aware you have a serious wound? A short way to the left, and that arrow would have killed you. It's going to be weeks before the wound heals. Improper care and infection will make you helpless and probably kill you. You're going to have to doctor yourself. Being alone and on horseback will increase the danger of riding to your death. With that said, I'm going to shelve this debate until tomorrow morning. I have a herd, an ill woman, and now four men almost destroyed by an Indian raid to worry over." He turned to Jimbo and said, "Do you think you can get him back to your wagon? I need Dizzy to stay here."

"Yes, sir, he's a little shaky, but he made it over here, and Lou's great pancakes should have strengthened him some."

Dizzy helped Ace stand. He picked up the shovel and handed it to Jimbo.

Grady said, "Son, I will loan you a horse if it's decided to let you do this on your own."

The two hobbled away. Grady drew in a deep breath and said, "I know how he feels. If I were in any condition to ride, I would have grabbed my rifle and taken after them myself."

"He's too young," Dizzy said.

"I know," Grady said. "When do you suppose he'll be old enough?"

Dizzy shook his head and stared at the fire.

Grady looked at Dizzy and then Juan and saw Cecile watching him. She hadn't interfered. He appreciated that. He smiled at her and turned to Lou, who had been cleaning up. He said, "Lou, please join us."

"OK, boss." He dried his hands and sat by Cecile.

Grady said to Juan, "Have Jalo include the cattle traveler also when he positions the wagons."

Grady continued, "We're going to stay at least one more day to care for our wounded. We know Indians came back during the night. Let's stay alert. Post guards. Have some of the men take day naps so they can do night shifts. Lou, we'll have more mouths to feed. I understand Carmella supplied a trunk with food supplies to help pay the girls' way on the freight wagon. Check it out and let me know if we can make it to San Antonio.

"The only thing we may be short of is meat. I loaded our supply wagon with enough to get all of our crew there. I'll check Carmella's trunk. If we're lucky, it will take care of Dizzy's three. I already miss Bear. He always keeps us in deer meat."

Cecile spoke up. "Gentlemen, I think all of you forget that I am the owner of this herd. I have hired all of you except Dizzy's crew. If it turns out we need meat, we will butcher a cow."

Grady chuckled and said, "Seems I've heard that before."

Lou laughed, and Cecile joined him. Grady cleared his throat and said, "Lou, will you please bring me the Henry and find the gun-cleaning kit. Be sure to include a cartridge belt."

"Not the Henry!" Lou said. "We got plenty of rifles." He suspected Grady's intention.

"I'm not going to let that young man leave here without the best rifle and the best horse I have," he replied.

"But, boss, what if they attack again?" Lou said.

"You just said we've got plenty of rifles." Grady smiled; Lou had tricked himself.

Dizzy's eyes were disturbed. They crossed and uncrossed. "What are you talking about?"

Lou turned to him and said, "The Henry is a rifle designed by Benjamin Tyler Henry and produced by the New Haven Arms Company. Tell him, boss. It just came out early this year."

Grady saw the excitement Lou felt talking about the rifle.

Grady said, "You're doing all right; continue."

Lou turned to Dizzy and said, "Few have been produced. We heard the first production was small, about a hundred and fifty. How Grady came onto it was through a friend. A major in one of the Union camps in New Mexico. They had acquired it in a small quantity, and Grady had a hell of a time talking him out of it."

158

"What the hell are you talking about? Just tell me, what is a Henry?" Dizzy's eyes crossed, and he glared at Lou with one of them.

Lou glared back, took a few minutes to build up suspense, and said, "The Henry is a sixteen-shot forty-four-caliber rimfire; it's lever action and breech loading."

"Sixteen-shot?" Dizzy exclaimed. "A sixteen-shot repeater?"

Grady held up his hand and said, "We're getting off the subject." He spoke to Juan, who had sat silent all this time. "Two things. Can you be in charge of condensing our camp? Second, ask your compadres if they can donate an item of clothing. All three of the freight team have lost all their belongings. All they have are the clothes on their backs."

He turned to Lou and said, "You're more familiar with our supplies than I am. They've been moved from the canyon to the saloon and now onto the supply wagon. There should be winter wear, jackets, rain gear, bedrolls. You get the idea. See if you can find my leather chaps and vest. Oh yes, I'll need my dress hat."

Lou, shaking his head, walked away talking to himself. "Of course I can find all that stuff. I packed it, didn't I? I don't like giving away the Henry. I even had a rack installed in the Cart in case we needed it in a hurry." He was still mumbling to himself as he climbed aboard the supply wagon and began going through trunks and canvas-wrapped gear.

Dizzy looked up at Grady standing before them and said, "I'm very beholden to you for all ye'r help. Only problem is we can't let that boy do this. It seems you made up your mind he's going."

Grady answered, "It's not my mind that's made up. It's his. Don't any of us want him to go. But he'd just steal a horse and disappear into the night. I believe he's got a fondness for one of those girls."

Dizzy, still shaking his head, said, "That hadn't crossed my mind. They only met those girls a week ago."

Grady smiled and looked at Cecile. He said, "Sometimes it only takes a day." She smiled back. He continued, "Besides, Dizzy, how old were you when you struck out on your own?"

Dizzy answered, "I was seventeen when I signed on with a freighter. There weren't no Indians on the warpath."

Grady chuckled. "I was on my own at sixteen. That's when I joined my first wagon train. By the time I was his age, I was an established hand at all forms of trail driving and was working for you between trail jobs. Since then I've had a few skirmishes with Indians on cattle drives. Dizzy, I'm only six years older than that young man. Could be my age being nearer to his has me understanding his intentions. Besides he's not my family. I can't imagine how hard it would be to see one of mine going off with high risk of death."

Dizzy stood and said, "Grady, he respects you. Can't you talk him out of it?"

"I plan on trying, but I believe his mind is made up, and I'm not going to wait to prepare him. He's not going to ride out of this camp without the best equipment I can pull together."

Dizzy nodded and put his hand out, and the two old friends shook hands. Dizzy said, "This evening after supper, we're going to say a few words over Elvin. You're welcome to join us."

"We'll be there. If there's anything you need, see Lou. I'm going to get my girl to lie down for a while. Tell Ace I'll see him this afternoon."

Lou saw Cecile and Grady leave the campfire and go to the Cart. They took off their boots, crawled in, and shut the doors. Cecile was still coughing. She would take some cough medicine. It usually made her drowsy. Grady would stay down long enough to ease his head.

The Henry was in the rack over Grady. Lou found the gun-cleaning kit. He added it to the pile of things he was collecting. He knew exactly what Grady was doing. He had traveled with the man for a dozen years. He found clothes and camp supplies. As he collected things, he also put together a medical kit, salt and pepper, eating utensils, and a hunting knife. Lou would wait until it was certain Ace was going Indian tracking before packing food supplies.

A camp that was stalled should take advantage of resting up, but this one had been stopped because of a violent Indian raid. Everyone was jumpy and on guard. Jalo, with Garcia's help, used the team to position the wagons. Grady and Cecile were resting in the Cart, so they tried not to disturb them as they moved the other three wagons into place. They defused their stress by joking around on the job. They laughed about placing the wagons north, east, south, and west. With only four wagons including the livestock traveler, they really couldn't circle the wagons. The way they decided to place them, a person could guard each wagon and have all four directions covered.

Per Grady's request the campfire went in the middle, with plenty of room from the wagons to be able to gather together. Garcia and Paco cut a couple of trees, trimmed the branches, cut some for firewood, and cut some into stumps to sit on. Jalo, using the team, dragged a couple of four-foot logs and positioned one on each side of the fire.

For lunch Fernando sliced ham and bread. Set out jam and butter. Each worker grabbed a sandwich. Those not on guard enjoyed a siesta.

Grady had worked on the Henry. After their morning rest, he carried the rifle to the freight wagon where Ace waited, his legs hanging over the wagon bed. Cecile made sandwiches and joined them. She handed Ace his sandwich, and Grady placed the rifle beside him.

Grady said, "I'm going to teach you how to use this rifle. Today we're just going to learn about the rifle and how to care for it. If I feel you are absorbing what I'm showing you, tomorrow we'll have a little target practice."

Ace smiled, and Grady hurried to say, "I'm not doing this as an OK for you to take off. I need to test you some, to discover your abilities and common sense. I don't intend to help you if I feel you're not capable of caring for yourself."

The smile disappeared and Ace nodded his head. The movement caused some pain. Grady sympathized.

When Ace finished his sandwich, Grady handed the rifle to him and said, "This is a Henry rifle, named for and designed by Benjamin Tyler Henry. I'm fortunate to have it. It was just introduced early this year." He saw Ace's face light up. "I see you've heard of it."

"Yes, sir! I just heard about a repeater, soon to be introduced, but I'd just bought my Spencer. I'm good with a repeater. I understand it, that is. I don't know anything about the Henry. I'm really excited to learn about it."

"I ran into a friend with the Union Army in New Mexico. Their unit was being ordered east. He personally owned this one. There weren't many Henrys manufactured in the first production. I had to beg and pay twice its cost to get him to turn this one over to me.

"The Henry shoots sixteen cartridges of forty-four-caliber rimfire. It's lever action and breech loading." Grady hesitated and asked Ace, "Are you with me so far?"

"Yes, sir, my Spencer was a seven shot. It was under the bench. They took it with all the rifles and the shotgun kept there. I've been the meat hunter in our family since I was twelve. I hate to lose that rifle. I haven't had it long."

Grady said, "That's a shame. The Indians won't know how to use it, and they won't have ammo for it. They'll end up throwing it away or breaking it. The Henry's ammunition uses rimfire cartridges, with two-hundred-sixteen-grain bullet, over twenty-five grains of gunpowder.

"This firepower has significantly less muzzle velocity and energy than other repeaters, like your Spencer. However, the lever action, on the downstroke, ejects the spent cartridge from the chamber and cocks the hammer. A spring in the magazine forces the next round into the chamber, locking the lever back into position, sealing the rifle back into firing position." Grady was watching Ace's face to see if he was understanding him. Grady said, "Are you still with me?"

Ace said, "Whew! I think so. Are you going to go over it again?"

Grady answered, "I'm going to leave the Henry with you tonight minus cartridges. Tomorrow I'll test you. There's one other thing you need to learn. It's the most important advice I can give you, and I will be repeating it over and over tomorrow."

"Yes, sir." Ace sat up and concentrated on Grady's next words.

Grady continued, "The way the Henry is designed, it lacks any form of a safety. It will actually shoot seventeen rounds with one loaded in the chamber." Grady paused and made sure he had Ace's attention. "When not in use, its hammer rests on the cartridge rim. Any impact on the back of the exposed hammer could fire a chambered round. If left cocked, it's in the firing position without a safety. Shooting yourself or killing your horse or any person is a real possibility."

Dizzy walked up. Juan and Fernando were with him. Grady knew it was time to say blessings over Elvin. He held Cecile's hands and helped her slide off the wagon. Dizzy helped Ace put his boots on. Before he got off the wagon Ace put the Henry in his bedroll and made sure it was covered.

The service by Elvin's grave was a short one. Dizzy, Jimbo, and Ace, knowing the young man, had something endearing to say. Dizzy closed the service with the Lord's Prayer.

Later they all met for supper. The added log seating pleased everyone. If there wasn't enough room on the two logs, they pulled over a stump.

Fernando had made a pot of his famous chili, and Lou had three iron skillets with corn bread.

Everyone was solemn after the service, but they chatted, went over the day's activities and joined in when Garcia brought out his guitar and played several gospel songs.

When Cecile rose, Grady walked her to the Cart. She crawled to the front wall, got the two mason jars and gave them to Grady to fill with water. The water barrel was on the supply wagon. When he returned he kissed her and closed the doors. He joined Dizzy and Juan at the fire.

Lou walked up with a bedroll and said to Dizzy, "I know them Indians took most everything. Both the mules they took had a bedroll tied to the saddles. Left you short one."

"Thanks, Lou. I didn't sleep a wink last night. Too upset. I'm weary. I'll bed down under the wagon where I can hear the boys if they need me."

Grady and Juan discussed the herd and guard duty. Juan said good night and left Grady and Dizzy staring at the fire. Paco and Garcia walked by carrying their rifles. First watch. They would circle the camp, walk down to the herd and bunch them together. Try to keep an eye on everything. The thought of Indians sneaking up on them was pretty scary, so one of them kept his eyes in front and the other behind. They had a little distance from the trail to the trees. The adrenaline of fear kept them alert.

The two men sitting by the fire rolled cigarettes and sat in silence for a while before Dizzy said, "I still can't believe this disaster just happened. I ain't ever gonna get it out of my head!"

"It's a lot to take in. Let's sleep on it. We can make plans in the morning." Grady dropped his cigarette in the fire and stood. Dizzy stood, the two shook hands and walked to their wagons.

Early, before sunup, Cecile was awake. Grady walked her behind the Cart for early-morning duty. They returned to the warmth of their bed. When she was settled under her covers, he lay down beside her and pulled his bedroll over himself. She settled her head on his shoulder. He kissed her sweet lips. She snuggled, returned the kiss, and settled back on his shoulder.

She looked up and noticed the empty place where the Henry had rested. She said, "I never really noticed your rifle. It's always been a given. Rifles are carried mostly by men."

"I know. If there were reason to, I would get one of my daddy's rifles from his gun cabinet. But I've always preferred my pistol. I'm a good shot with it because I use it and practice. After this morning I really see the need of carrying and use of a rifle. I want a Henry."

Grady chuckled and said, "Tell Santa Claus, maybe he'll bring you one for Christmas."

"Oh, you!" she said. "I thought you were Santa Claus."

"Nope, you've got the wrong man. I'm just the intended husband." He raised her face and gave her another kiss. She had such beautiful lips.

They talked about their future. Cecile shared some of the projects she wanted to get done at the ranch. When she drifted back to sleep, he moved quietly, picked up his boots, slid out the doors and closed them. He would take a turn at guard.

The day moved slower than yesterday. Juan's crew kept the cattle from spreading. The four vaqueros cut down some trees and sawed and chopped them into usable pieces. With Dizzy's approval they stacked them on the back half of the freight wagon. They cleaned harnesses and in utter boredom played cards.

Everyone had chipped in a piece of clothing. Dizzy was a big man; there was little that fit him. His brother was nearly the same size, but a pair of Fernando's long johns fit him.

Grady sat on Dizzy's wagon with the three men and talked to Ace, hoping to change his mind. Grady actually thought the young man amazing. Ace had insisted on changing his own bandage with Lou's supervision.

Lou had put together a small medical kit. He explained to Ace that the best success with a wound was to keep it open and draining from the inside out. Honey was the best for healing without infection. Honey would even cure a putrid infected wound, but the secret was to try not to get it infected. Lou said, "Honey is messy—needs a container to keep it liquid. Unfortunately we have no container small enough for a saddlebag, so you're gonna have to use carbolic acid to keep the wound open and draining."

Lou watched as Ace cleaned his wound. He started to help him, but Ace rejected any help.

Ace felt like crap. He wanted to lie down, pull the bedroll over himself, and sleep until the pain went away. He had always been an active youngster. His dad gave him a rifle at age twelve. There were three siblings in his family. Elvin was a couple of years older, he had a sister, Janet, who was younger. Elvin's interests were more those of their father. Janet of course spent most of her time with their mother.

Growing up, Ace had chores, but whenever he could he snuck away to the woods with his rifle. He taught himself tracking. He was such a good shot with his rifle that he was able to supply rabbits and squirrels for the family's meals. For this reason, eventually he was allowed to take off hunting whenever he finished his chores. By the time he was eighteen he had graduated to a muzzle-loader, and deer, wild hogs, and turkeys fed the family.

At nineteen he helped the sheriff whenever a tracker was needed. At twenty he carried a pistol on his hip. With consistent practice he was both fast and accurate. He had just acquired his Spencer repeater rifle in early spring.

When Dizzy asked him to help take this freight load to Janos, he had been approached by the rangers to join them. Looking forward to spending time with his two uncles and his brother, he shelved the decision of employment until he returned from the delivery to Janos.

Ace resented the inference that he was too young and didn't know what he was doing.

They were wrong. Ace knew exactly what he was doing. The kidnapped young women were reasons enough to pursue these Indians. A stronger reason for Ace...these savages had killed his brother, his big brother. Ace had looked up to Elvin and worshipped him all of his life. This small war party had killed his brother and taken away a big part of his heart. He would hunt them down and kill them one by one until they were all dead.

Ace knew that Grady was studying him. Ace had no intention of letting anyone know his true reason for this journey. Let them believe he would find where they took the girls and then turn it over to the army. He respected the thought that they cared for him and wanted him safe. Grady was a smart man. Ace respected him. Grady was his only chance to ride out of here with a horse and a weapon. He had to be careful or his uncle would force him to return to San Antonio, even if he had to tie him to the wagon.

Grady had acquired only forty-nine cartridges for the Henry. He cautioned Ace about shooting off too many practice rounds. Grady told him to take his time and draw a close bead. They walked away from the wagon. Ace carried the Henry. Grady had him load and unload a couple of times. He was satisfied Ace knew what he was doing. They found a felled tree. Grady collected some small pieces of wood and lined them up on the tree trunk.

Ace didn't hit wood the first shot. He was right-handed. The rifle stock rested on his right shoulder. He held the muzzle up using his arm with the shoulder injury. It hurt, and with an effort to endure the pain, his arm shook.

Before Grady could suggest a solution, Ace sat down, raised his right knee, and rested the muzzle on it. It was awkward. He adjusted his body and the rifle and pulled the trigger. The bullet hit the log just below the first piece of wood. He raised his knee a little, and the wood flew off the log. He fired two more shots to get the feel of the speed he could expect from the Henry. Two pieces of wood flew off the log.

Grady put his hand on Ace's shoulder and said, "Good. As your wound heals you'll get the aim better with that arm. Don't waste any more ammunition. You've got about forty cartridges. When you're near a fort see if they have forty-four caliber. You'll need to carry some cash. I'll talk to Dizzy and see if we can put together pocket money."

"Mr. Grady, I can't thank you enough for helping me. I know Dizzy doesn't like the idea of me going after the girls. He's known me all my life and taught me most of what I know about firearms. I'm surprised he's arguing with me. I'm probably the best hope for rescuing them. Bear is probably the only one better than me at tracking in the woods, and he's not here."

Ace was shaking, the young man needed to rest. Grady took the rifle and walked Ace to a rock close by. "Sit," he said.

Ace's legs were weak and he was relieved to get off them. Grady continued, "We don't need an audience. When you're in pain, it's hard to concentrate, and the distraction of well-meaning friends don't help. Are you going to feel like leaving early in the morning?"

"I feel pretty rotten. But I don't see much difference in riding on that wagon or a horse. At least I can stop and rest on a horse. Rest is not in

Dizzy's vocabulary. Not having any mules left, I don't suppose he will be doing things his way." Ace grinned.

Grady grinned and said, "I think you're right. I'll get a team together for him out of my remuda. I had to buy extra teams when I left San Diego. I gave Cochise's camp two mules but I think I can come up with one team. Dizzy likes to use two teams on an empty wagon but that's because he likes to hurry back. I've got four teams in use, but I always keep extra teams for backup. A strong two-horse or mule team can haul an empty wagon. We won't leave his wagon out here—I give you my word on that."

Grady squatted down so he could look Ace in the face. He continued, "OK, let's get on with Indian hunting. I'm giving you one of my quarter-horse mares to use. She's a five-year-old. She's well broke. In a full-out run, she'll stay in front about a mile. She'll start losing steam after that first mile but she'll have the endurance to outrun most breeds. If Indians are chasing you, keep your eyes looking for a place to hold them off and let the Henry do its job. "

Ace was looking forward to meeting the mare and said, "I really appreciate the use of her. I can tell you're giving me a horse that's special. What's her name?"

"I call her Sugar, and she is special to me. I trained her myself using some of Bear's techniques. Bear is one of the best horse trainers I've ever seen. He breaks his horses gentle. It's not about bucking them out or crackin' whips over them. I've been watchin' and learnin' from Bear for years. Sugar is the first horse I broke all the way and I'm real proud of how she turned out. I'm also giving you a good pack mule and a packsaddle. Lou's outfitting your pack gear. You'll have what you need for a few days. I told him not to overload you, so you'll be short on utensils. One small iron skillet, one metal dish. You get the idea. You're a hunter so you won't go hungry."

"Sir, I'm speechless. I didn't expect to borrow so much."

"Wish I could talk you out of going, but I'm convinced I'd just be wasting my breath, so pay attention. When you're following these warriors, if they stay out of sight of the Butterfield stage and head toward Janos, then they are members of Cochise's camp. They will avoid Janos and take the same trail I just came off of. You will be close enough to go out of your way and stop at Candy's. Let Doc look at that wound. Talk to Bear. He gives good advice. I'll send a letter with you so Candy can put Doc's bill on our tab. Check for ammunition for the Henry. Now, I only have one more thing to say. I'm giving you my leather chaps and vest. Do not take them off. Wear the vest under your jacket. As long as you are tracking Indians the heavy leather can deflect an arrow, could save your life. Come on, we'd better get back."

As they walked back to the wagon, Grady said, "I'm giving you my work hat. It's brown and won't be noticed easily. All right Ace, that's the best I can do for you. Don't thank me. Just don't get killed and make me feel guilty for helping you." Grady grinned and clapped his hand on Ace's good shoulder.

Jimbo was lying on the wagon. Soft snores said he was napping. Dizzy was using the gun-cleaning kit. He had spread his bandana on the wagon bed and dismantled his Colt Dragoon. The revolver had been on his hip as he rode the mule. It had escaped the Indians' raid.

Ace stepped on the tailgate and onto the wagon bed. He sat where he could watch Dizzy.

Grady handed the Henry to Ace. He laid the rifle and the cartridge belt beside himself.

They watched Dizzy clean and oil the revolver. Dizzy talked as he worked. He said, "About every other year, I made a trip back home to visit my family, and I spent time with the boys. I know Ace is an amazing tracker. I always had my weapons with me, and it was my pleasure to hunt with the boys and teach them to use any weapons I had with me.

"This Colt Dragoon is the third model introduced in '51. Ace knows this revolver. He learned its care and the variations compared with the earlier Dragoons. He's accurate with it and with some practice will be fast. I had intended to give the pistol to him this year. I've ordered the 1860 Colt Army model. It's coming with an order of firearms I have to freight to the forts in New Mexico."

He stopped talking and looked into Grady's eyes with one of his. He grinned and said, "I can't let you be the only caregiver. I appreciate what you're doing for my nephew. I'll feel a lot better knowing with the Henry's sixteen shots and the Colt's six shots he'll have some chance to come back alive."

168

That night after supper, Sugar the mare and 'Dum Dum' the pack mule were tied to the freight wagon. Lou finished packing the food supplies.

Under the freight wagon, Dizzy woke to the sounds and movement above him. Ace sat up and rolled his bedroll into a tight bundle that could be tied onto the saddle behind him. Dizzy heard Lou rattling pots and pans at four o'clock in the morning. He groaned and pulled himself from under the wagon.

He rubbed the mare's and mules' heads and ran his hands over their backs, picked up hooves, set them back down, making sure no stones had been picked up that could bruise and cripple them. He put the blanket and saddle on Sugar. He settled the packsaddle on the mule and was about to reach for the loaded pack when Lou arrived with the last-minute food supplies. Lou added them to the pack and helped Dizzy load the heavy pack and fasten it securely to the packsaddle. A lightweight canvas tarp was added over it to protect the pack. The tarp could also be used when needed, under Ace's bedroll or overhead, if a storm arose.

Lou went back to the campfire. Coffee and oatmeal were ready. He set out bowls, utensils, and honey. Dizzy came over and rummaged in the trunk on the supply wagon and found a coffee mug. He poured a mug of coffee, sat on a log, and sipped the hot brew.

It wasn't long before he heard the jingle of spurs coming toward the fire. He recognized the sound of the spurs he had given Ace last night along with his revolver.

Lou and Dizzy watched as a tall dark stranger came into sight. They didn't see Ace's face until he got closer. They could hardly recognize the man who stood before them. There was a bearing and a savage determination Dizzy had never seen before on his nephew.

Lou dished up a bowl of oatmeal and dribbled a spoon of honey on it. He handed it to Ace, who then joined Dizzy on the log.

It was a somber moment. There was nothing left to say that had not already been discussed. No one was happy that Ace was running directly into the face of danger. The odds of success were low. Everyone understood that this might be the last time they saw Ace alive. Jimbo and Dizzy both felt sick about him leaving but were unable to talk him out of it. The only noise was that of Ace's spoon hitting the side of the bowl as he ate his oatmeal.

When Ace finished he rose and shook hands with Lou. Dizzy got up and followed him back to his horse. Ace put the Henry in the saddle scabbard, fastened the ammunition belt around his waist, and settled the Colt Dragoon in its holster. He adjusted the pistol on his hip and turned to Dizzy. His uncle wrapped his arms around him and hugged him hard. Ace had already said his good-byes privately to his uncle, Dizzy, who had told him he couldn't watch him ride out of camp.

Ace took the bridle that hung on the saddle horn. He removed the halter and lead and bridled the mare. He fastened the halter to the pack, gathered the reins, and mounted the mare. This was a stranger to Sugar. She restlessly moved her weight from one hoof to the other. Ace patted her neck and soothed her anxiety.

Dizzy unfastened the mule and gave the lead to Ace, who wrapped it around the saddle horn. Turning the mare, with the mule obediently following, horse and rider rode out of sight.

Dizzy watched them leave. Not a word had been spoken. Only Paco, who was on guard, saw him leave. Dizzy returned to the fire, warmed his mug of coffee, and watched Lou prepare breakfast for the crew.

Ace didn't ride far that early morning. It was too dark to see tracks from his horse. Besides, he was certain the Indians were headed back to their mountain stronghold. They would go around Janos. It wouldn't take him long to catch up with them. He had left early to avoid the emotional good-byes that family and friends would honor him with.

As daylight dawned, he easily picked up the Indians' trail. Leaving the attack of the freight wagon they had ridden their horses hard. Afraid that angry white men would follow them they did not stop to rest until they were sure they were not followed.

Ace could tell from the horse prints there were at least eight horses and the four shod mules. They were all heavily loaded with stolen women and stolen goods.

They were at least two days ahead of him. He could tell by the imprints in the dirt that the four mules, and at least one horse, were being stubborn and combative.

Even if there had been no tracks to follow, Ace could follow the stolen items discarded along the way. The first items to be left behind were a pile of harnesses. It was probably tripping up the mules that had been wearing it. The Indians left just the bridles on the mules. They had cut the reins short enough for the Indians to easily lead the mules. Ace knew that the Indians would never have left the harnesses unless it was absolutely necessary. They could have put the harness leather to many uses, so it was a big loss.

Occasionally he found pillows, clothing, and other stolen items that had been discarded. The first campsite Ace approached showed him that the captive women were slowing them down. Two full-length skirts were abandoned. The girls would now be transported thrown facedown over the horse or tied and held in front of a warrior. Ace hoped they had worn pantaloons, popular by current fashion.

Ace was traveling much faster than the overloaded Indian horses. He figured he would catch up with them his second day out. He stopped often to rest his animals. While they grazed he rested. That night he ate the sandwiches Lou had provided. Too tired to build a fire to heat water for coffee, he drank water. Tired or not he disciplined himself to clean and dress his wound. The exit wound on his back was an exercise in patience to reach, clean, and smear salve on.

Not up to unpacking and repacking, he left the pack secured to the packsaddle. Removed both together, he hobbled the mule so he could rest and graze.

He unrolled his bedroll and, removing his boots, ammunition belt, and holster, slid into his bedroll. He laid his pistol where he could reach it in a hurry.

He was hurting. He was exhausted. This first day left him in much pain. He hoped tomorrow would be easier. He fell asleep wondering how, with his wounds, he would get his horse saddled and the pack back on Dum Dum. Silly name for a mule.

At an Indian camp, miles away, an Apache warrior named Loco Spider was losing patience with his band of thieves. Three of his warriors were on their first raid. A chance to prove manhood, count coup. They were still half-child. Their excitement of raiding the white men and carrying away all their belongings, women, and mules had gone to their heads. They were out of control, carrying on, loud of voice. Spider had given them orders of behavior before they left the winter campgrounds. Now he tried to quiet them. They were exciting the horses and mules.

Their first night he made them travel far into the night. They had been too tired to cut up. Spider, a seasoned warrior in the art of raiding the white settlements, knew that, due to inexperience, the young warriors had grabbed too much to allow for a quick escape. His first act to resolve the problem was to dispense with the harness.

They had left their winter campgrounds with twelve warriors. Three had been killed in this raid. He and two of his best warriors and friends, Buffalo Calf and Deer Slayer, had stayed behind and retrieved their dead. They had each thrown a man across his horse and had ridden most of the night.

He had given his other warriors orders to keep riding and not to wait for Spider to return with their dead. To not stop until he caught up with them. When he did catch up to them, he found his first real problem.

One of his youthful warriors was in charge of the blond-haired woman. As Spider caught up with his men, he passed them and called a rest stop. As they left their horses and began to unload their stolen goods, the young warrior pulled the woman off the horse and attempted to pull her to a tree where he could tie her. She was screaming and fighting with terrified strength. The young man had difficulty holding her as she bit and scratched.

Spider rode close, pulled his hatchet, and hit her in the head. She sank to the ground, and the boy pulled her to the tree. An expert with hatchet techniques, Spider knew he had not killed her—just shut her up. He was too tired and irritable himself to put up with any disturbances.

They ate deer jerky and drank water. All were instantly asleep. Spotted Pony, another of Spider's wise warriors, reported to him. All was well except for the loco woman. She had fought and screamed all the way. Even the dark-haired woman couldn't quiet her. The young warrior carrying her had enjoyed teasing her. Whenever she displayed out-of-control fear, his young friends were entertained. He had spent most of the time as they rode goading her with pinches and pulling her hair. He encouraged the frantic behavior by continually scaring the wits out of her. The loco woman had finally passed out from fright and fatigue.

Spider walked over to the two women. He leaned against a rock, weary himself. He needed sleep. The dark-haired woman was awake. She didn't turn her eyes away from him when he studied her.

The woman with the sunny hair was in an exhausted, restless sleep. This one would bring a good price from the female slave-traffic senior in Mexico. Yellow hair was preferred!

He hoped his young warrior had not driven her mad. The thought of losing the reward of a rifle for her irritated him. The dark-haired one was still watching him. She was a thinker. Could be dangerous.

He woke at sunrise. Using the leather he had saved from the mule's bridle reins, he tied his dead to the backs of three of the mules. Picking two of his trusted older braves, he put each in charge of two mules. They were to take their dead and the three wounded warriors to their families at the Apache winter campgrounds. No stopping except for brief rests for the animals.

174

After they left, Spider looked through the plunder they had stolen. Stealing came natural to the Apache. They had perfected thieving, and some were more talented than others. Spider was one of the talented ones.

Their raid had produce some good things and some worthless. They had three rifles, a shotgun, and a bag of ammunition—all keepers. He paused as he looked more closely to one of the rifles. It was built differently. The muzzle-loaders and the shotgun he could use. He was a smart Indian. Apache were very smart. On this raid he had surprised the white man because he was an Indian with a muzzle-loading rifle.

He played with the strange rifle and managed to open the breech. He soon realized he was wasting time on a rifle he couldn't use. It would be left behind but in no condition to work if a white man found it. He carried it to a boulder and smashed the Spencer to pieces.

With that done, he continued his survey. Some of the bedrolls were keepers. He tossed the pillows belonging to the women. He liked the bags the white men kept their sorry clothes in. White men's clothes didn't keep you warm like his deerskins did. He tossed the clothes and used the bags to pack ammunition, knives, and many of the women's things that his woman would like such as combs, brushes, mirrors.

He used the rolled blankets to wrap his treasure, including the firearms. He rolled the bundles tightly and used pieces of the discarded reins to tie them.

His braves were waking. He had started this raid with fourteen men. Now three were dead, two wounded, and two sent to escort the dead and wounded to the stronghold. This left him with seven warriors. Enough men to continue raiding if so desired or to offer protection in case of white men or soldiers coming after them.

He ordered them to mount up. They ate dried deer strips as they climbed on their horses. Spider offered the dark one a strip of dried deer meat. She shook her head. He turned to "Yellow Hair" and offered it to her. As he looked at her face, he was immediately aware he was seeing the terrified eyes of a crazy spirit woman. He stepped back with concern. He would deal with her when he was ready to mount and ride.

Each rider had a tied bundle they carried across their lap. Spider took hold of the dark woman and, with strong muscles, swung her up behind Buffalo Calf. She was cold. They had taken her skirt away from her. It was winter. She was shivering. The horse felt warm on her legs. She crossed her arms and leaned into the Indian's back. Using an elbow, he pushed her off of him. Tough! she thought. You stole me, so you can take care of me. She rammed her head into his shoulders and leaned back onto him to absorb his body heat.

He didn't protest. She closed her eyes and rested. No telling what this day would bring. Ellen had lost it. Wyvon had tried to comfort her, but Ellen was so full of fear she wouldn't let Wyvon near her.

When they were ready to ride out, Spider went to get Yellow Hair.

When she saw him coming she tried to scoot away from him. Even with her hands and feet tied she was so scared she moved with speed and rolled over several times, screaming the entire time.

Spider grabbed her by the arms and, with difficulty, stood her. She was bucking and dropping, kicking with both feet tied together. She was hysterical. He grabbed her hair and pulled her upright, drew back his arm and slugged her in the face. It knocked her out. She collapsed, becoming dead weight in his arms. Blood ran from her nose. If she kept this up and he had to hit her to keep her under control, she would be worthless. He picked her up, tossed her head down across his horse, and with a graceful swing was behind her.

Ace's arms and shoulders had stiffened overnight. He felt like crying. It was so hard just getting his saddle on Sugar. No way could he lift or handle the pack. He had to open it and remove half of the supplies. After separating it from the packsaddle, he put the saddle on and made sure it was secured well. He stuck a knee into Dum Dum's stomach to be sure he had not deliberately puffed up. He settled the half-empty pack on the saddle and, piece by piece, added the supplies back in the pack. Tears ran down his cheeks as he threw the tarp over it and tied it down.

Ace was fortunate that his anger burned so brightly inside him. His determination to seek revenge on the savages who attacked them superseded any pain he felt. He sat on a boulder and drew in deep breaths. When his heart stopped racing, he climbed on Sugar and continued following Indian tracks.

Almost immediately he came to some tracks that confused him. It slowed him down, but soon he had the tracks sorted. The mules had been shod with cleated horseshoes. The Indians had divided their loads up and were now using the stolen mules to carry some of the burden.

Ace guessed, from the pieces of harness lying about, that they had tied their dead on the mules. Two Indian horses were leading the mules, and, from the depth of the unshod horses, they were carrying double. Ace surmised that the main warrior in charge had sent his dead and injured ahead. More than likely to the stronghold in the Chiricahua Mountains.

Smart move, thought Ace. They had probably been given orders to ride straight through. Only stop to rest the horses. The leader and his braves would travel at a good speed, but they had the women and most of the stolen goods. In a sense, they would also be protecting their injured as they followed behind in case of attack.

Ace smiled. He thought, how wise you are. Here I come.

He would catch up with the braves with the women by nightfall. He would need to be careful not to come around a bend and run into them. He moved off their trail and stayed to the brush and cover. He made frequent trips back to study the tracks. By late afternoon the tracks were so fresh that he tied Sugar and the mule to a bush and continued on foot with the Henry.

He heard them before he saw them. Ellen was screaming. Indians were talking loud in an attempt to hear over her very loud hysteria.

On his stomach Ace advanced to a thick bush. The scene before him was one of confrontation. The Indian who Ace figured was their leader seemed to be ordering the Indians to abandon some of their stolen goods they were overburdened with. He was being met with arguments. One of the younger braves was teasing Ellen with a stick. She was out of control with fear.

The protesting braves ceased their arguing. A fire was made, and a couple of rabbits were skinned, gutted, and thrown on a rock in the middle of the fire.

Ace analyzed his chances. Nightfall was rapidly closing in. He was exhausted. His legs and arms were shaking. He could get the girls killed if he put the Henry to work now. No matter its rapid-fire ability if he couldn't aim steady.

Ellen's screaming was grating on his nerves. It evidently was doing the same for her captor.

Spider walked over to her, drawing his knife out of his sash. Grabbing her by the hair to hold her still, with a savage slash, he cut her throat. The screaming stopped. Spider, grabbing her arms, drug her into the dark away from the fire.

He walked back into the light and looking Wyvon in the eyes, raised the bloody knife and motioned across his neck, indicating he would do the same to her.

She was terrified, but she sat still, returning his look. She gave a small nod that evidently satisfied him. He squatted and rubbed the knife back and forth in the dirt to clean the blood off. He walked to the fire and removed the rabbit. Cut off a leg. Stuck his knife in it. Carried it to Wyvon and offered it to her.

Ace could tell she was closer to throwing up than eating anything, but she was smart enough not to tell him no and trigger his anger. The piece of rabbit was hot, and with her wrist tied, all she could do was drop it into her lap. Fortunately she had long johns under her pantaloons. She let it lie. If she could, she would eat it later. She knew she had to stay strong for whatever lay ahead.

That monstrous demonstration was obviously for the benefit of his unruly followers. It evidently worked as the area became suddenly silent. It was several minutes before even the crickets sounded.

That decided it for Ace. He was devastated, sick, and furious from the horrific display he had just witnessed, but he realized he was in no condition to take on that evil Indian tonight.

He waited for the night sounds to start up and the braves to talk quietly to each other. All the while planning his revenge. Witnessing the cruelty and heartlessness of Ellen's death fueled Ace's desire to destroy this band of killing thieves, especially their leader. Slowly he crawled away. He wanted to strike in the early morning whenever they woke up.

The sun was coming up behind him. It was barely daylight when Indians began to move. Ace had found a hiding place behind some boulders and slept soundly for a few hours. Dreaming of Ellen's head nearly severed from her body woke him. He spent the rest of the night planning his next move.

When the Indians' camp began to move about, Ace expected their leader to maintain control of Wyvon. He planned to shoot the leader first before he could retaliate by killing Wyvon. Those plans changed when a big Indian was called over by the leader. The leader pulled his knife out and toward Wyvon so quickly that Ace was unable to react. Thankfully the leader only slashed the ropes that were tying Wyvon's arms and legs together. Muscular and strong Spider lifted her up. She swung her leg over the horse, and she wrapped her arms about Buffalo Calf, as the horse lunged forward.

Spider swung onto his horse and moved the horse to the head of the braves. Plans had changed. As Ace rose with the sun behind him, his shadow stretched across to the Indian camp.

He settled the Henry into position and pulled the trigger. A bullet shattered into a head. Buffalo Calf slid sideways off his horse. Wyvon, her arms clasped tightly around the Indian's waist, was pulled to the ground with him.

Ace didn't wait to see if his shot was accurate. He moved the sight and shot the next Indian in line. The hurried shot, aimed at his head, hit him between his shoulders and separated his spine.

Moving on to the next Indian, the Henry's bullet hit solidly in the middle of his back and traveled out his chest.

When Ace dropped the third Indian, he moved on to the fourth rider. The bullet hit the horse and dropped it. The Indian whose horse was shot out from under him grabbed the loose horse of the man fallen behind him. The Indian, an excellent horseman executed a running mount.

Ace would have preferred to follow and keep picking them off, but Wyvon needed to be cared for. He knew there was a chance the Indians would return for their dead. Securing Wyvon, making sure she was safe, was his first priority. He ran to her.

She had fallen with a two-hundred-pound Indian on top of her. The Indian's shattered brain had thrown bone pieces and blood across her cheek and in her hair.

The breath had been knocked out of her. In shock she was frantically trying to drag herself out from under the Indian, while shaking the bone chips out of her hair.

When Ace pulled the Indian off her, she turned and crawled on hands and knees, struggling to draw air into her lungs. He carefully laid the Henry down and using both hands stopped her scramble to escape. He pulled her to her feet and, taking her in his arms, crooned softly, "It's all right, honey. It's Ace. It's Ace, honey, you're safe."

She quieted and looked up at his face. She trembled and drew in a large breath of air. She fought him for what seemed an eternity before she realized it was Ace and not an Indian. She sobbed and wrapped both arms around his neck. Both sobbing and struggling to fill her lungs, she collapsed in his arms. He continued to sooth her until she relaxed.

Loco Spider and two of his men escaped. Pummeling their horses, they ran them until he feared they would drop under them. The rapid fire of the Henry had convinced Spider they were being pursued by the angry men whose women they stole. That day found them well on their way into the Chiricahua Mountains.

It took a couple of days after Grady and Cecile left Janos for Bear and Candy to begin to organize her move.

The day the Cart pulled out with its inhabitants, Candy went to see Doc. He undid the binding that held her arm firmly to her body. He carefully manipulated and tested her shoulder. Candy winced a few times, due more to stiff muscles than anything else.

"OK, Doc, you're bein' too quiet." She looked at him with pleading eyes. "Do I get this darn thing off or not?"

"Well..." Doc dragged out. "I suppose, if you can promise me to take it easy, we can leave this arm freed up."

"Really?" Candy said. "I was so scared you were gonna say no! I'm so tired of this darn contraption! Thank you, thank you, thank you!" A smile lit up Candy's face.

Doc gave Candy a little smile, then quickly put on a stern face and said, "Don't start thinking you're invincible. You need to take it easy for a good long while, ya hear me? If you don't put this arm back to work very carefully, I can guarantee you will be strapped back down again."

"Oh no," she replied, "I am not going through that hell again!"

A few minutes later Candy walked out of Doc's office with a spring in her step. As she walked across the dirt road, headed back to her saloon, she stopped in the middle and did a twirl. She was happy! She was going to enjoy this small moment of time in what had become a very hectic and on-the-edge life. It was a very little thing, having her arm free, in comparison with all the dire goings-on around her.

Lance showed up and Candy put him to making wooden boxes. In August, she had sent a double order for alcoholic beverages back to her supplier in San Antonio with a freighter. It had been delivered in September, before her working girls and the bartender had quit and headed east.

She had been generous these past few weeks with both whiskey and beer. What had been used was just a small dent in her inventory. Most of it was still packed in its original freight boxes, however, she had a healthy amount of inventory on the shelves behind the bar. These were going to need packing boxes and rags to wrap each bottle so they could survive a rough wagon transport.

She was not sure what she was going to do, but she did know her alcohol inventory was cash. She could open another saloon or sell the booze outright. She was not leaving it here.

She had a dozen cases of whiskey (nine bottles per case), eight barrels of moonshine, and ten barrels of beer.

Bear began to realize Candy was planning on taking everything she could pack. It was going to take a big wagon. He had already exhausted this problem searching for a wagon for Grady. He settled for the hearse, because Janos had few wagons. Those few he knew of, the owners did not want to sell. Carmella had lent Grady her large supply wagon.

Bear had made the effort, for four days, to find someone who was selling or talk someone into it. It was a futile effort. A week and a half passed and found the three of them sitting at what they called Grady's table. Della had made a beef-and-vegetable soup and biscuits. Lance had chores and had gone home.

The three were just sitting, more tired than hungry. Almost too tired to dish supper up. Bear said, "I'm through wagon hunting. I'm going after our wagons in the canyon. We need them down anyway."

Candy studied his tired face. They were all worn out, mentally and physically. She said, "What scares me is the weather's still bad up there and we're getting more news of an Indian uprising. That canyon is too close to Cochise's stronghold, and you don't have a herd of sacred Herefords to count on."

"True, but we're going nowhere if we can't get the wagons. I talked it over with Lance today, and this is what we worked out. He can get a couple of teams, and if it's all right with Carmella, we can borrow a couple of her ranch hands. We could probably pay her in whiskey. Lance seemed to feel that would be an incentive. I'll take your team. We should be able to bring down all three of Grady's wagons. If we take a few tools, we could dismantle your buggy enough to load it on the supply wagon on the way down."

Candy said, "What if they're not there? Stolen or cut up for wood?"

"I guess we'll just have to stay in Janos until a freighter shows up," he said.

Della had been tired and sat quietly listening. Now she spoke up. "I vote you go get them. Don't worry until you have to. Candy and I can keep packing. We'll find someone to build boxes. I'll hunt down some big barrels to pack kitchen stuff and linens. We could be ready to load wagons when you get back. When Candy went up to rescue Cecile and the herd, she was gone ten days. I figure, with no loaded wagons and a herd of cows, knock a couple of days off. I think you could do it in eight days. Maybe less."

Candy said, "I guess we don't have a choice. I don't like it. I'm scared you'll get hurt or killed. I guess an Indian raid on Janos could create the same disaster. I want to get out of here. Let's make our incentive to succeed, the desire to attend Grady's wedding."

There was a sound of a horse stopping at the hitch rail by the front porch. Bear got up and went to check it out. He said, "For crying out loud, what are you doing here?"

The women jumped up and went to see who it was. Bear was hurrying down the stairs and moving quickly toward the horse. He grabbed the woman the rider was holding. Bear pulled her into his arms.

Della tied the horse, and Ace, obviously injured, lowered himself from the horse.

Bear carried Wyvon up the stairs. Candy opened the saloon doors and said, "Take her upstairs to the bath. I have warm water on the kitchen stove. Come back down and carry the bucket up. I'll find a clean nightgown, washrags, and towels." Bear was already halfway up the stairs. She turned to Della and said, "It looks like Ace has a wound. I saw blood on his jacket. Go get Doc."

"Yes, ma'am." Della ran out of the saloon.

Ace had climbed the stairs to the porch. His legs were shaking. He had taken time to pull the Henry from its scabbard. The rifle was too precious to leave it where it could be stolen. He made it to the first table and chairs. He laid the Henry on the table before him and collapsed into a chair.

When she returned, Della took over bathing Wyvon and getting her in bed. Wyvon was asleep immediately. Doc would have to check her out tomorrow. Della went downstairs to help with Ace next.

Doc arrived, puffing from his jog to the saloon. Bear helped get Ace's jacket, vest, and shirt off. Doc looked at both wounds and tsk-tsked at what he saw. "Indian arrow, my guess. Both wounds are bleeding. Not normal bleeding. The wounds have opened. The one on his back is feverish near to infection."

Della, using warm water, soap, and rag, washed all of Ace's upper body. Doc cleaned both wounds. He put on a pack of honey and wrapped it with gauze around his body to hold it in place. After supper Ace could sit his lower body in the tub of warm water and soak.

Anxious to hear Ace's story, Doc stayed for supper. Candy put bowls of soup and utensils on the table. Della added a plate filled with biscuits. Butter and honey went in the middle of the table in reach of all.

Ace was too tired to eat, but with the same determination that had driven him since the Indian raid, he forced in a few bites, set his spoon down, and told the story. Taking turns on each, he finished the tale and the soup. He remembered Sugar and Dum Dum. Sugar had carried Ace and Wyvon many miles, and the mule wore a heavy backpack. He started to stand, but his legs gave way. He said, "My horse."

Bear answered, "I'll put her up." He had recognized Grady's "Sugar." He had also recognized Grady's "Henry" and Grady's hat, leather chaps, and vests. Now that he had the story, he was greatly relieved to know his boss and crew were safe. He put his hat on and headed for the barn. His head was heavy with worry. Indian raid? With the dismantling of army posts there was going to be a serious Indian uprising. It was already starting.

Ace felt like crap! He felt so bad he couldn't sleep. He didn't have any control over his body as he got up and put on his clothes. He picked up the Henry and quietly left the saloon. In the barn he saddled Sugar and rode through town, taking the road into the Chiricahua Mountains.

After the raid on the freight wagon, the Indians were headed home. Ace had driven the wagon from Janos to where they had attacked the wagon. He knew that road back to Janos. That backtracking had been easy. When he had caught up with them and killed three, the rest escaped, riding toward Janos but circling away, around the town. He figured circling Janos would slow the Indians down. By taking the direct road to Janos and the direct road up the mountain he should meet them at some point. He hoped so, as this was now unknown territory for Ace. He had to depend on his tracking ability.

As Sugar worked to travel the uphill road, Ace looked for unshod horse tracks and ran his eyes over the scenery around him. He didn't want to get surprised. As the sun rose, making it easier to see tracks, he moved off, east of the road, and found a deer trail going up. He stayed on it until he came to a cluster of boulders high enough to see the rise ahead.

He tied Sugar to a bush at the foot of the boulders and climbed up and found a spot where he could stretch out and take a nap. The rock he stretched out on was warm. He lay down on his stomach. With the sun on his back it wasn't long before his aching body relaxed. He would depend on Sugar to alert him if anything moved. Ace had to get some sleep.

Ace was gone when Bear woke in the morning. He hurried to the barn and found the mare missing. Ace had been tired and ill last night. Bear had expected him to recover in a day or two.

Bear, listening to the details of the Indian raid, had realized Ace was obsessed with the death of the Indians who killed his brother and Ellen. He knew Ace would go after the few still running. He just didn't expect the man to take off so soon.

The Indians Ace hunted would be scared and running to reach the safety of their Apache stronghold and warriors that would help them find and kill their pursuer. Ace was on his way to cut them off and kill them.

This was bad timing. Ace on the warpath killing Indians would stir up Cochise's camp. It would jeopardize Bear's trip to recover the wagons. They needed to get organized and on their way before things really blew up! Maybe if they went direct to the canyon, they might get in and out before Cochise could retaliate.

Candy was up when he returned to the saloon. With Ace gone on horseback, she knew where he was headed. She and Bear argued until Lance showed up, expecting to build more boxes. He was informed of the Indian raid on the freight train. The death of Ellen, the rescue of Wyvon, and the killing of Indians. Ace wasn't through with his revenge on the Indians.

Lance took a moment to grieve over Ellen. The girl had worked at Carmella's bar long enough to call her a friend. Lance agreed with Bear.

They had to go now if they had any chance of getting the wagons out of the canyon. He hurried to his horse and left town on a run.

A couple of hours later, Lance returned with two teams dressed in their harness secured for travel. Accompanying him were six heavily armed ranch hands.

Bear was ready. He had Candy's team of black geldings dressed in their harness. His paint horse was tied to the hitch rail beside Ace's mule, Dum Dum, with the loaded pack. Bear had figured the pack would contain the bare necessities for meals over a fire. Della had made sandwiches to feed the men today. They hadn't figured on six gunmen.

Candy wrapped her arm around Bear's neck. She whispered in his ear, "You'd better not get killed. I'll give you six days, and then I'm coming after you."

"No, you're not! I don't intend to have that worry hanging over me. I love you, and I'll be back." He kissed her, climbed on his paint, and led Dum Dum out of town. The three teams were divided between the men. Bear realized he hadn't had breakfast.

As the men rode out of town, Candy watched them leave with a dumfounded look on her face. Bear had said, "I love you." A big smile spread across her face as she turned to go back to the saloon.

Sleep didn't come instantly. Ace's body ached. The wound on his back throbbed. His mind flashed from one disastrous memory to another. It settled on the ambush of the Indians who held Wyvon captive. He could still see her frightened face. She had clung to him, tears running down her cheeks. He used his kerchief to wipe them away. He kissed her forehead and helped her into the saddle. He had removed a blanket from his bedroll and wrapped it around her.

His entire left shoulder, including his arm, was weak with pain and numbness, even in his hand. He knew he could not use his left arm to lift himself to the saddle behind Wyvon. He was holding the Henry with his right hand. He had walked around Sugar to her right side and secured the rifle in the saddle scabbard. He said a silent prayer and, rubbing Sugar's cheeks and nose, spoke softly in her ear, "Please, girl, let me mount from this side."

He tied the reins together and laid them over the saddle horn. With both hands now free, he took a firm hold of the horn with his right hand and tugged a couple of times to tell Sugar to shift her balance. She laid back her ears but held as he put his right foot in the stirrup. With his best effort, he managed to land behind the saddle.

He reached around Wyvon and stroked Sugar's neck and told her, "Good girl, good girl." He gathered the reins and gave a soft kick to the mare. He reined her to the left. They would reach the road to Janos. He remembered laying his head on Wyvon's back.

He heard Sugar's soft snort. For a moment he thought he was still day-dreaming. He heard her stamp her feet and realized he was awake. He didn't move anything but his eyes. He could see her, and she could see him. Her head was raised, and her ears were up. He raised his eyes toward the rise in time to see a doe and fawn disappear over the ridge.

Something had scared the deer. He lay still and studied the mountain downhill, around, and up. Sugar had not relaxed. Her head was still raised. Her ears were still up, and every now and then she flicked one and returned to listening. She hadn't seen anything, but she had heard something.

He watched her. Horses are a meal for predators the same as deer and other prey. They can be trusted to stay alert. He was afraid she would nicker if horses were near, so he scooted back and slid off the boulder. He went to her head and smoothed the hair on her neck and rubbed her nose, leaving his hand over her nostrils. They were well hidden. Sugar continued to watch the path the deer had taken. After a while she lowered her head and shook her whole body.

He didn't want to catch up with his Indians. After killing three of them yesterday, they would be on high alert. He mounted, pulled the Henry from the scabbard, and laid it across his lap. Handicapped like he was, he wasn't sure he could retrieve the rifle quick enough if he were surprised.

He let Sugar pick her way up to the rise of the ridge. He shifted his eyes back and forth from the ridge to the ground under Sugar's feet. He saw tracks, mostly deer, wolves, and some small forest animals.

They came upon another deer trail headed up. The doe and fawn had been here. Now there were unshod horse tracks churning up the ground. "Gotcha!" Ace said under his breath. He recognized the tracks of the leader's spotted horse.

He saw a shady spot under a small tree. Climbed off of the mare and tied her. Talking to her, he said, "We'll rest awhile. Let them get far enough ahead so we can follow without getting too close, until dark."

As he waited, he studied the woods around him. He registered the fact that patches of snow still dotted the landscape. A shiver ran down his spine. He should have taken heavier winter wear when he left Janos. He had heard the stories of the blizzard that had crippled the Chiricahua Mountains. The higher he went, the deeper the snow would be.

When Sugar got restless and stamped her feet, Ace rose, untied her, and climbed onto the saddle. He needed to be a lot more watchful now. It would be easier for the Indians to look down on him than for him to raise his eyes from following tracks to search higher up for movement.

As the sun began to go down he moved Sugar into a faster walk. Once it got dark he would be unable to tell if they left the deer trail.

Ace hoped they would stop for the night. He would leave the mare and get close enough to make a kill shot. There was going to be a full moon tonight, and there was a clear sky.

Suddenly, Sugar threw her head up. Ace pulled back on the reins. Her ears were on alert. By trusting her instincts, she was proving to be a good partner for Ace in this hunt. He dismounted, put his hand over her nostrils, and rubbed her nose. Her eyes were glued up the trail. Ace quietly pulled the Henry from the scabbard. He tied the reins to a bush.

Dropping low, he moved from brush to whatever cover he could find. The deer trail came to a small meadow. It still had a couple of inches of snow on it. The snow was crisscrossed with animal tracks and places where the snow had been pushed aside. Spots where deer or elk had dug for dried grass.

A fire flickered on the other side of the small meadow. He couldn't see much, but he smelled roasting meat. His mouth watered.

The full moon was beginning its run across the sky. It was bright tonight. Ace wanted to position the moon behind his back. He didn't want the light in his eyes. He had to crawl on his belly, to his right, around the meadow to a spot where the moon was behind him.

Crawling, it seemed to take him forever to reach a spot he was comfortable with. He lifted his head and peered over the trampled snow. He could count three. Two men were chewing on meat held in their fingers. It was hardly cooked. Blood ran down their chins. Occasionally one would lick the juice off his fingers.

The man standing was using his knife to slice a slab of meat from a large chunk of what looked like a deer haunch.

Ace slowly sat up and quietly brought the Henry up to his shoulder. With a twinge of pain he used his sick arm to lift the muzzle and settle it on his knee. He sighted and pulled the trigger. Brains flew from the man cutting the meat.

Ace leapt to his feet as he settled the Henry's stock onto his shoulder. His shadow rose with him and stretched across the meadow like a ghost. Two Indians dropped their meat and turned to run.

The second bullet hit the closest man. The third man reached a horse and with a running mount disappeared into the woods. Ace could hear the terrified horse as it crashed through the forest and out of earshot.

Ace was cautious of the possibility that the escapee could have dropped off the horse and sent it on without him. Not caring for a surprise and possibly a knife in the back, Ace carefully retraced his path to Sugar, gathered his reins, and swung aboard.

He guided her around the meadow in the safety of the trees.

He came back to the spot where the escaped Indian mounted a horse. Two horses were tied, snorting and pulling against their braided leather reins. Ace dismounted and tied Sugar. Talking softly, he calmed the horses, petted, and slid his hand down a leg and picked up a hoof on each horse until he found what he was looking for. The leader's horse with the chunk out of the front right foot. He found it. He had hoped he had killed the leader.

He checked the two bodies. He had to pull the man from the fire. His face was blown away, but the man's build and clothing were not the leader's. Neither was the other man. "Well, darn," he said to himself. The fleeing leader had grabbed the closest horse. He was out there on an unfamiliar horse. Ace wasn't too worried about him sneaking back. The man only had a knife and the hatchet hanging from his belt.

The deer leg was beginning to burn. Using his knife and a stick, he drug it off the rock it was on in the fire, and tossed it on some clean snow.

He searched the meadow until he found the rest of the deer. An arrow was in its heart. Using his hunting knife, he cut off all three legs. He took the Indian horse's halters off and turned them loose. Using the halter reins, he tied the deer meat in a tree.

The cooked meat had cooled enough to eat. He cut a thick steak and tied the rest to the back of his saddle.

He rode back to the other side of the meadow. Put his bedroll and his saddle under a tree. Walked a ways from his camp and tied the deer leg as high as he could reach in a tree. Put Sugar's halter on and tied his lariat, one end to her halter and the other to his saddle. She had enough rope to graze at the edge of the meadow. If something disturbed the mare, a tug on his saddle, under his head, would warn him.

Ace settled in for the night. Closing his eyes, his thoughts took him back to tonight's event. Playing the scene back in his mind, Ace realized that he should feel sickened by the Indians' gruesome deaths by his hands. He didn't feel that way. He felt exhilarated that he had eliminated two more people who had a hand in destroying his family. He needed this revenge if he were ever to heal from the pain of seeing his brother killed so violently.

Spider was on an unfamiliar horse, he hadn't the time to reach his own. The Shadow was firing rapidly. He felt air from a bullet whistle past him as he entered the trees. The horse was uncomfortable with this rider and his punishing demands for more speed. In the dark, the deer path was hardly visible, and he stumbled often. When they reached the ridge overlooking the meadow, his rider slid off, led the horse behind a rock formation, and allowed it to catch its breath.

Loco Spider squatted and watched the back trail. As the horse's breathing settled, the Indian listened for night noises. Spider no longer believed several men were stalking him—just a Shadow man with a lightning stick.

The mountain creatures, night birds, crickets, and wind in the trees had gone silent because of the noise created by the struggling horse. These natural noises slowly returned. Spider was satisfied the Shadow had not followed him. A pattern was forming. The Shadow man did not continue to attack. He killed as many as he could in an ambush. He waited until the braves were at camp resting. Loco Spider could not stop—no more camps. His braves were all gone. They were his friends. Sorrow filled his chest. He drew in gasps of fresh air. He would mourn his friends another time.

He swung on his horse. With silent command by legs and lead rope, he guided the horse up, more westerly, off the deer trail. The Shadow would be coming as soon as he could see tracks.

A few miles up the mountain there was a cave. A sacred hidden cave, occupied by the spirits of the Apache ancestors. If he were careful and hid his trail, he could hide there and rest.

At midday Spider crossed the established mountain road and guided the horse into the gully that ran parallel with the road. A small mountain stream at its base ran downhill.

He let the horse drink and then guided him into the stream and continued up the mountain. An hour later he came to a group of boulders, some being bathed by the stream. He slid off the horse onto a boulder. Taking off the leather halter and reins, he whipped the horse with the reins. The animal splashed out of the stream and was rapidly on his way. Spider hoped he would leave tracks the Shadow could follow. The horse knew these mountains. Hopefully the horse would not stop until he reached the Apache stronghold.

Spider took off his leather moccasins and his britches. Along with the halter, he rolled the britches around the moccasins and tied it all together with the reins. Carrying his bundle over a shoulder he stepped back into the icy water. There was frozen ice along the sides of the stream.

He was miserable. His feet and lower legs were numb with cold. The Shadow would be looking to see if he had walked into the stream. He had to keep going up until he reached the cave or found ground he could walk on without leaving tracks. The snow, still packed in the gully where the foliage protected it, would make it hard to conceal tracks.

The Shadow had the advantage. Spider had no weapon except a knife and his hatchet. He was now without a horse, but Spider was smart. He chuckled. Spider was an idiot. He had led a raid that attracted the Shadow man. He had taken the Shadow man's women, and Spider had cut the throat of Sunshine. If someone killed Spider's woman, Spider would do exactly what the Shadow was doing.

So, Spider would disappear. He would hide in the secret cave. He was so cold. The deeper he waded into the rushing stream, the colder it became. The snow along the sides of the stream was frozen and slippery. He couldn't step out of the stream without leaving tracks in the snow. When he reached an area he recognized, he searched the walls of the ravine for the cave.

He almost missed it. A cave-in closed the entrance. A horse's rotting skeleton explained the closed entrance. Spider was shaking from the cold.

He studied the distance to the cave. In the water he saw a flat-shaped stone. He waded around until he found another stone flat enough to step on. He had to get out of this freezing water.

By putting one rock ahead and stepping on it, balancing on one leg, he was able to put the other stone a step away. It was grueling and slow work. Balancing on one stone, he picked up the stone he had just stepped off, placing it a step in front of him, but not so far that he would not be able to turn around, pick it up, and repeat the process. He finally got to a boulder large enough to crawl on.

The ravine was deep in frozen snow. There was no way he was going to reach the mouth of the cave without leaving footprints. He would have to crawl backward and brush snow over his trail. It would have to be packed down to blend in with the snow around it.

Hopefully the Shadow would follow his horse. Without his britches, his knees were soon as frozen as his feet. He made it to the cave-in and looked back over his path. Spider was an expert tracker. He admitted he could see the disturbed snow leading to the cave. He was too physically cold and tired to do more.

There was a small hole at the top of the cave-in. It didn't take him long to enlarge the hole enough to slide into. He found dry clothes—smelly white soldier clothes, but they were dry. There were three sets of uniforms. He pulled all three pairs of pants on his shivering legs. There were three saddles complete with saddle blankets. He curled up and pulled the blankets over himself. He fell into an exhausted sleep.

The men climbing the mountain, to reach the canyon where the wagons had been abandoned, were soon traveling in snow. Bear hated it. It reminded him of the miserable days struggling to save the Herefords from a blizzard that seemed to last forever.

The men made good time. Not pulling any wagons, they reached the spot where Candy's wagon crashed into a boulder. They camped there that night and, with the tools they brought, dismantled the wagon. They would load it onto the supply wagon on their way down.

They camped out one more night and would be in the meadow where Glancy's accident happened the next day. Bear wasn't about to linger where Glancy had fallen into the ravine. In no way was he going to share the cave's location with anyone. He cautioned Lance to keep it their secret. He continued up the mountain and camped at dark. They would have a short day tomorrow. They would have time to hook up the wagons and start back down.

They reached the abandoned camp in the canyon. There were some deer legs hanging from a tree branch. A red kerchief was blowing in the breeze. It was pinned to a deer rump with a pocket knife. Ace had been there and left a gift! Bear was relieved to know that Ace had made it this far. He must be having some success to have the time and presence of mind to leave the carcass.

They hooked up the teams to the three wagons. The wagons were just as they had been left months ago. The men had only to clear away frozen snow and free up the wheels, frozen to the ground. In no time they were climbing out of the canyon. Bear put Dum Dum's loaded pack and the deer legs in the grub wagon. He tied the mules lead to the back and sent Lance, driving the grub wagon first, to break a trail. The supply wagon followed, and Trumpeter's wagon brought up the rear.

As they climbed out of the canyon and drove their teams to the trail to begin their journey off the mountain, there were a dozen Indians lining the ridge. It was the same ridge where Grady's crew had seen Indians watching them leave. At that time they had put together food supplies and a couple of mules to thank Cochise and his warriors for their help during the outlaw attack.

These Indians did not look friendly. They wore war paint and carried weapons. Bear stopped Lance and ordered the men to halt and sit quietly. "Do not touch weapons. I'll be back shortly. If we are in trouble I'll take my hat off and run my hand through my hair. Then, and only then, take cover and draw your weapons. As long as my hat is on my head, do not touch a weapon."

Lance nodded, and Bear rode ahead. The paint climbed to the ridge, and Bear lifted his hand in greeting.

This was a different band of Indians from the hungry ones a month ago. These were fur-clad, big, strong warriors, wearing war paint. Their horses were decorated with feathers and war paint.

The buffalo-robed man was Cochise. He recognized Little Bear. They spoke and Bear explained that his woman, who owned the sacred little red cows, needed her wagons to continue their journey out of Cochise's territory. Bear made it clear they had no intention of causing trouble for Cochise.

Bear motioned to the warriors and asked why they were in war paint.

Lance, from the distance, could see the man in the buffalo robe using his hands to help express angry words. He quietly settled his hand high, on the front of his thigh, close to his holster. He feared by the dramatic action and the Indian's gestures that they might be in trouble.

Lance blew out a big sigh of relief when Bear gave a good-bye sign to the braves, turned his horse, and hurried back to the waiting men.

They were anxious to know what was said. Bear said, "Not now. Let's get out of here before he changes his mind. He's giving us clear passage, so get moving."

In a matter of minutes the teams were on their way off the Chiricahua Mountains. They drove nonstop until dark. Horses and men were weary, irritable, and nervous. They hung meat slices on sticks and ate them half-raw. Lance found sandwiches Della had put in the mule's pack.

Bear gathered them around the fire. Lance's ranch hands were quiet. All of them, including Lance, wished they had eyes in the backs of their heads. Bear repeated his chat with Cochise.

"He's looking for Ace. One of his war chiefs arrived in camp late last night. His name is Loco Spider. He had taken a band of warriors raiding. They attacked a wagon train and killed many. They had some dead of their own. Spider sent a few warriors ahead with the injured and dead to the stronghold. Spider and the rest of their band were traveling with captives and many plundered weapons and goods. They were slowed by their treasures."

Bear paused to gather his thoughts and continued, "Spider told a wild tale to Cochise about a shadow that walked with a lightning stick that followed him and, one by one, struck them down with his thunder. He insisted the Shadow man was close behind him and would loose his lightning stick on them all."

Lance said, "Whew, I'd hate to be Ace right now. Cochise will have the entire Apache nation looking for him."

The elder ranch hand, one of Carmella's working cowboys, took out his pistol and checked his cartridges. He said, "First time I ever saw Indians in war paint."

Bear smiled and said, "Bill, this is just the beginning. One of those painted braves was Mangas."

"Mangas Coloradas? Are you sure?" Lance, nervous, checked his own pistol.

Bear nodded. "I've met him before. It's been years, but I recognized him. He's Cochise's father-in-law. One of Cochise's sons, Tahzay, was with them."

Bear assigned guards and gave these last words, "I believe Cochise was scouting these mountains for Loco Spider's Shadow man. His name, Loco, tells me he spun some wild tale. Loco Spider told Cochise the Shadow followed Spider's tracks and killed all his braves. He said he could not follow the Shadow because the Shadow left no tracks. The Shadow was a ghost. I believe the crazy one never saw Ace's face. Cochise is looking for tracks. If he finds them, the tracks could lead the Indians right back to Janos."

Lance said, "We need to get a few hours' sleep and rest the horses. We have to get home in case what you said turns out to be true. We need to get far enough down this mountain tomorrow in case Cochise decides to pick a fight with us. The worst thing that could happen now is for Ace, the Shadow, to ride into our camp. He could lead them straight to us."

Grady was beginning to feel stronger. He stayed in the saddle a little longer each day. Cecile understood his desire to gain strength, but she was afraid he would overdo it and have a relapse. She needed to get more exercise herself and joined him in the mornings. She wanted to be strong when she reached her hacienda. There were so many things she wanted to get done before the wedding.

Jalo was asked to saddle both Grady's gelding and one of Cecile's more gentle mares. They were tied to the Cart early, before Jalo moved the remuda out. Grady was up early, got dressed, and rode around the camp checking things out. Juan was doing a good job of ramrodding this drive. Grady, once again, felt useless.

Cecile dressed and joined the men at breakfast. After breakfast she got on the mare and joined Grady. They rode along with the wagon train, occasionally going back to check the herd. They both enjoyed being together, talking with each other, out in the fresh air and away from the confines of their sickbed. Often Cecile's legs would tire, as they were weak from weeks of inactivity.

During a rare moment when Cecile and Grady rode side by side without conversation, Cecile reflected back on the many months Grady had cared for her, especially during her illness. They had grown so close. They were no longer employer and employee. They were family. Cecile now could not imagine a time without Grady. It was a wonderful feeling to have someone she loved that she could also rely on as partner. For the first time, in a very long time, she did not feel the weight of responsibility resting strictly on her shoulders. It felt wonderful!

They stopped at lunch to rest the animals and grab sandwiches. She took her lunch to the Cart, removed her riding clothes, and put on the robe Candy had given her. The robe always made her smile. It certainly wasn't the style of robe a Spanish lady would choose. It was a shiny fabric with colorful flowers and a feather boa on the collar. Cecile loved it because Candy had given it to her. It reminded her of the quirky saloon owner that was her friend.

She ate her lunch while reading the novel Candy had put in the Cart for her. Grady tied his horse and rode up top with Lou for a while. He also tired easily and, midafternoon, joined Cecile and napped. After their afternoon nap he was back on his horse in time to bed the cows. Cecile redressed and joined the men for supper.

Today had been uneventful. Although the crew found it boring, they were all more than grateful to have more days like this. The Indian attack had been traumatizing to the entire crew. No one wanted a repeat of that experience or to be a victim of a bow and arrow.

They had been on the trail for a week after Ace had ridden out. They all tried to stay alert but the slow pace of the herd made the days boring. Juan's crew took turns cleaning pistols, rifles, saddles, and chopping firewood. They also took turns riding with their eyes on the surrounding country.

Cecile dug in her trunk and got her braided long whip with the large turquoise stone embedded in the end of the hard leather handle. Grady and Lou were familiar with the whip and the deadly accuracy Cecile wielded with it.

Juan's people, all had a hand in teaching her from childhood to be accurate with the whip and with firearms. She took turns hitting an object, rocks, sticks, brush. She worked the whip from horseback and walking. When she tired, she practiced drawing her pistol.

Sometimes after lunch Grady spelled Lou driving their Cart team. With Lou's early cooking hours and cleaning up the supper mess until late at night, he needed a break. He usually lay on Dizzy's empty wagon bed and grabbed a nap.

Since Dizzy's wagon was in front of the Cart, Lou slid off the wagon and waited for Grady and the Cart to catch up. Grady climbed down, handed the reins to Lou, and mounted his horse. He had gotten in the habit of riding ahead of the freight wagon and searching the road ahead before he joined Cecile and rested for a while. He always stayed where Dizzy could see him. After the Indian attack no one wanted to take chances.

This day the weather was brisk and cold, but so far no storms. They were making good time. Grady was satisfied they would make it to Cecile's ranch by Thanksgiving.

He was searching the land around him. Often movement would catch his eye, deer, coyotes, and lots of smaller animals such as rabbits, skunks, and reptiles.

Something moved across the road. His gelding threw his head up, and his ears went forward. Grady thought he saw something. Disbelieving what he had glimpsed, pulling his pistol, he kicked the horse up. The gelding kept his ears up and Grady could feel the horse bunch under him, ready to shy.

He reached the place where he had seen whatever it was cross the road. There was nothing. No, wait! Footprints. Bare footprints. He turned the gelding to follow the prints. A boy ten or twelve years old jumped up from his hiding place and ran.

Grady kicked the horse up and was quickly on the boy. He reached down and grabbed the kid's straps on his overalls and reined in the horse.

The boy was a Negro child. He fought like a little bear. Grady held on until he quit struggling. Grady swung off his horse and said, "What's your name, boy?"

No answer. The boy wiped his nose with his arm and tried to pull away. Grady turned him. The shoulder straps over the overalls made a secure hold. Grady marched the boy back to the trail and waited for Dizzy's wagon to catch up.

The boy was shivering. Grady observed that the boy was not only barefoot but also had no coat. His nose was running, and tears ran down his cheeks.

When Dizzy pulled up, his eyes were flying all over the place. Speaking to Grady, he said, "You know what you got there, don't you?" One eye settled on Grady.

"Well, it looks to me like a boy who's cold and out here alone," Grady answered.

"You got a runaway, Grady." Dizzy leaned over and spit on the other side of his wagon.

"I figured that much, Dizzy, because he was running away." Grady smiled.

The Cart pulled up behind the freight wagon, and Cecile, in her robe, joined them. Immediately she knelt before the boy and taking one of his cold hands in hers, she rubbed to warm it. She said, "He's freezing. Lou, bring me a blanket."

Dizzy looked up and around the brush, cussed under his breath, and repeated, "He's a runaway. He's big trouble. Someone will be looking for him. Maybe a lot of somebodies." His eyes crossed and one settled on the boy. He said, "Who do you belong to?"

The boy's eyes were as big as saucers. He looked at the one eye focused on him and tried again to free himself.

Cecile put her arm around the boy and tried to calm him. She glared at Dizzy and said, "Stop it! Stop it right now! Can't you see he's terrified? He's cold and probably hungry!"

"We take care of that first, and then we determine who he is and where he belongs. If I were you, if you're so worried, I'd keep your guns handy and your crazy eyes watching for trouble," Grady added.

Lou brought Cecile an army blanket. With Grady's firm grip on the suspenders, he walked the boy to the Cart. Cecile climbed in and helped Grady lift the struggling boy in. She asked Lou, "Do we have any sandwiches left from lunch?"

"Yes, ma'am, I'll fetch a couple." He came back with two sandwiches and a mason jar of water.

Cecile said, "Grady, shut the door and put the bolt on. I don't want to have to chase him." She gave the boy a sandwich. He grabbed it and almost swallowed it whole.

"I don't like this," Grady said, "he's big enough to hurt you."

"I'll scream if that happens. He's just scared and hungry. I'll let him calm down and maybe I can get him to talk." She shut the doors, moved back, stuck her feet under the covers, and pulled them up on herself. She gave the boy the other sandwich and unscrewed the lid on the mason jar and let him drink. When he finished, she tucked the army blanket around him and also pulled Grady's bedroll over him. She then hummed a lullaby her mother used to sing to her. He was instantly asleep.

Grady climbed on the wagon and joined Lou on the Cart's driver bench. He pulled his pistol, checked the cartridges, and then settled it back in its holster. He took up the shotgun kept under the driver's seat. His eyes were searching in all directions. He noticed Lou was also watching out. "I was expecting Indians, not this."

Lou snorted, "This could be a lot more trouble. We can at least protect ourselves against Indians. We can shoot them. This pending slave war, North against South, could be one we can't shoot at."

Grady shifted the shotgun across his legs and turned on the bench to look behind, to be sure the herd was moving with them. He said, "Where do you suppose this boy came from? He's shoeless and coatless. Can't be from too far away."

"What you going to do if his owners come to collect him?" Lou flicked the reins across the team's rumps. The team walked a little faster.

"Hadn't thought that far ahead yet. Don't have enough information to form a plan. When I first saw the boy, I remembered Carmella telling us about the vigilantes. Dizzy's got them on his mind. With the Indian attack, I'm sure he is spooky about having any more troubles. When he saw the boy, he was instantly afraid of trouble from either the owners of the boy or the vigilantes."

Lou tucked the reins under one hip and rubbed his hands to warm them. He blew warm air on them and vigorously rubbed them together. He drew a pair of gloves out of his jacket pocket and put them on. Taking up the reins, he said, "I hope he's worried enough to watch for visitors, any color, black, red, or white."

With a grunt, Grady said, "There is no doubt in my mind that Dizzy is on high alert right now, given his reaction to findin' that boy."

They made camp that night with their wagons drawn up in the tight formation. Guards were stationed. Cattle circled and bedded down. They all wore their pistols or carried a rifle.

Those not on guard gathered around the campfire for supper. Lou and Fernando made kettle stew and biscuits. Cecile, holding the boy's hand, led him to the fire and asked Lou to get the boy a cup of tea.

Cecile said to Grady, "His name is Impala. His father named him after an animal far away in another land. The impala is very much like our deer. His father gave him this name because he runs fast like the impala. He prefers the short version Pala. I've tried to learn who is after him. He doesn't answer."

Grady squatted in front of Cecile and Pala and asked, "He speaks our language?"

"Yes." Cecile held up the boy's hand and raised his arm so Grady could see the raw rope burns on both wrists. She continued, "He's had a good teacher. He's not fluent, but he can make you understand. His father and Pala worked in the cotton fields in east Texas. They were often beaten by the overseers. After one savage beating of the boy, the father decided to run." She undid the boy's overalls and unbuttoned his shirt. She turned the boy so all could see.

A collective sound of indrawn breathes as they saw the red irritated whip marks lacing across his young back.

Grady's demeanor changed rapidly from curiosity to fury.

Cecile turned the boy back and fastened his shirt and the hooks on the overalls. She said, "They were becoming infected. I've cleaned them and put some lotion on them. I need something stronger. Lou, would you please get me some lard? And please don't put in any of that hellfire you mixed for me while we were on the cattle drive!"

Lou chuckled and said, "Yes, ma'am." He rummaged around in the trunk on the supply wagon and filled a mug half-full with lard and handed it to Cecile.

Grady had risen and walked into the shadows. There he paced back and forth.

Dizzy joined him. They squatted and rolled cigarettes. Dizzy finally spoke. "What are we going to do? You know as well as I do someone's after him."

"Well, I'm not giving him back to whoever did that to him." Grady threw the cigarette stub down and stomped on it.

Dizzy dropped his stub and said, "Grady, he's an expensive piece of merchandise. Legally we can be accused of theft."

Grady walked back to the camp and squatted again to look the boy in the face. Pala, his eyes big as saucers, sank back against Cecile. Grady said, "You're trouble, boy. I would have more chance protecting you if I knew who you belonged too. I'm not going to press this tonight." He rose and turned to Juan and said, "Tell Jalo to clean out the cattle traveler and put some clean hay in it and a bedroll. Lou, you get him fed, then lock him in the traveler."

Cecile started to protest. Grady put his hand palm up to her and said, "Don't argue. I'm not sharing my bed with him. I need a decent night's sleep. We will all need our wits about us if his people show up. I don't want him running away in this weather. Find him a jacket and some stockings for his feet. Get him fed and lock him up." He walked into the dark to check on the herd.

Grady looked down at Pala and added, "We are going to protect you tonight. We are going to put you in a locked wagon where you will be safe and warm. Do you understand, boy?"

Everyone sat speechless until Lou banged on the stew kettle with a big spoon. Dizzy filled his bowl and sat down beside Pala. He was there to prevent the boy from running. He wished the boy had never run into them.

Lou gave the boy a bowl of stew. Pala ate like a starved animal. When finished, Lou and Dizzy escorted him to the traveler and bolted him in for the night.

Four in the morning found everyone up and busy getting chores completed. Biscuits were all that breakfast offered. Men were eating on the run. Cecile had chosen to stay out of the way. Pala was removed from the traveler and Trumpeter was loaded.

The boy was allowed to relieve himself, then bolted in with Cecile. Lou brought them biscuits and honey and filled mason jars with fresh water.

There was an air of trouble. Everyone kept eyes searching all directions as they moved wagons, cattle herd, and remuda out on the trail.

To be safe from an ambush Grady stayed close to the freight wagon.

The cattle drive that day made good time. The animas, cattle and horses, sensed the urgency that radiated from the humans. The herd, who usually tried to halt and graze, seemed intent on running, not walking. Gaining on the wagons ahead of them created an urgency in the team horses to step it up.

Cecile, worried her little cows would suffer from the increased speed, complained to Grady. He also was concerned so he gave Deadly an order to bed them down early.

Everyone, including the little cows, was tired, dusty, and thirsty. The cattle herd, horse herd, and humans satisfied their thirst at the small creek beside their camp.

The creek flowed to join the Rio Grande. Another week and they would cross that vibrant "river of great water," as it was called by the Pueblo Indians in 1582.

Mexicans called the great river "Rio del Norte" (River of the North), as it formed the northern border with Texas, however, on most Mexican maps, the river is named "Rio Bravo." Texans preferred "Rio Grande."

Grady had trailed his cattle drives to and from California many times. His choice of crossing the Grand River was at Brackett. The town initially was a supply stop for the US Army's Fort Clark.

Grady removed the saddle and bridal from his gelding, hobbled him, and put him with the remuda.

He walked through the little herd of Hereford cows and found them all well in spite of the day's increased pace. The herd was still restless. Seemed they were picking up on the crew's growing anxiety. Some were beginning to graze. They would all settle down soon.

Trumpeter was unloaded and vigorously rolling on the ground. He was scratching and relaxing after the day's confinement in the traveler.

Deadly, relieved of the job of nurse-maiding the Herefords, waited patiently for Grady to finish his herd inspection.

Grady, aware Deadly needed some attention, went to him and began rubbing behind the big bull's head, along his neck, over his shoulder, and along the rangy back and side. A good rump scratch and reversing up the other side. Back at the head, where he started, he rubbed the hard bone between the long horns.

Grady was stressed. The day's tension had his nerves stirred. He wrapped his arms around Deadly's neck and leaned on the bull. Deadly stood still. This behavior of his friend was familiar. Many times, on many cattle drives, the trail boss had taken a few minutes to relax and regroup in this manner.

Grady released the bull, gave Deadly a pat on his neck, and headed for camp with Deadly following. Always glad to be free of the herd, Deadly spent some time hanging out at camp begging for biscuits and then wandering close by in search of grass to fill his belly. When satisfied, he returned to the herd and took his stand over old Trumpeter.

The night was restless for all. Jalo cleaned the cattle traveler and put fresh hay and the bedroll for Pala.

Guards were stationed. The boy was fed and put to bed in the traveler.

Six adults concerned about the boy gathered around the campfire. Lou brought out a bottle of whiskey. Dizzy, Jimbo, Juan, and Grady had a drink. Lou and Cecile declined.

Cecile said, "I've been thinking about this boy all day. He's very sad. Cries a lot. I've tried to get him to talk about his father. He gets scared when I ask him. I can't tell if his father is dead or being held somewhere.

"The more I thought about it, the more I wondered what he could be doing out here on the Mexican side of the river. Then I remembered something my father once told me. In 1852 Brackett was founded as Las Moras, named for a nearby spring or creek that feeds into the Rio Grande. It could even be this one we are camped by. It was named Brackett after the owner of the first dry-goods store.

"I remember these details as my father told them to me. Florida's Indian tribe, the Seminoles, often adopted black slaves, both free and escaped. Black Seminoles are the descendants of those unions. They were called Maroons. They speak their own language, a soft creole style of French, learned as slaves.

"The US government wanted to relocate Florida's four thousand Seminole people and most of their eight hundred Black Seminole allies to our western Indian territories.

"Facing the threat of enslavement, the Black Seminoles staged a mass escape to northern Mexico. The Mexican government welcomed the Seminoles and used many of them as border guards, which worked for them in aiding their fellow black runaway slaves." She quit talking and waited for someone to say something.

The men looked at each other. Grady saw they were as confused as he was. He spoke up. "Honey, I don't understand. Is Pala a Black Seminole?"

She smiled and said, "No. I'm sorry. Sometimes I offer too many words. Pala is a black slave. His father was trying to take his son to safety in Mexico via the underground communities of Black Seminoles. I'm thinking his father was caught by the vigilantes and hanged. Scared, his father probably hid him. I'm guessing, but Pala may have watched them hang his father."

Grady sat looking at Cecile. A tear left her eye and rolled down her cheek. He asked, "He told you the vigilantes hanged his father?"

A tear rolled down the other cheek. She was trying to gain control. She just shook her head. She swallowed and said, "I can't get him to speak the words. At the mention of the vigilantes, he pulls the blanket over his head and sobs. He won't talk about his father."

No one spoke. They all had pictures forming in their heads. Finally Lou spoke. "Poor little guy. I think I'll have that drink now."

They held up their mugs and clinked their drinks.

She rose, and Grady walked her to the Cart, kissed her, bolted the doors, and returned to the fire.

The men were staring into the fire. Cecile's story had them all considering the possibility of it being true.

Grady spoke, directing his words to Dizzy, "I don't have much knowledge of the pros and cons of owning slaves. I've spent most of my adult life herding cattle and hiring help. I go through or close to many towns. I always pick up newspapers and whatever gossip is current. Usually it is weeks behind current news. I've read some about the reason for this approaching war, but I've not paid much attention to news taking place elsewhere."

"I didn't figure this war would affect my life. I guess now that's changing. Can you catch me up? What's an abolitionist, and who are the vigilantes?"

Dizzy took off his hat and brushed his hair out of his eyes. He said, "Shoot, Grady! I'm as ignorant as you. I've spent my adult life driving freight wagons, and I hire my help also. I arrived in San Antonio a couple of weeks before I took on this delivery to Janos. There was a lot of talk about the burning of towns during the summer. I learned Dallas, Kaufman, and Waxahachie were nearly destroyed in those fires. And that's really all

I know. It seems there were a lot of accusations that it was a slave uprising encouraged by abolitionists?"

Dizzy's soft-spoken brother, Jimbo, cleared his throat and in his quiet voice said, "I grew up in San Antonio. Spent most of my adult life farming a few crops. Selling milk and eggs to my neighbors. Hunting with Ace. I'm not political, but I was curious about the answers to those activities. Our ma has a friend who works for the *Alamo Express*. One day I decided to stop at the newspaper and ask him to explain some of these uprisings. Besides Dallas and the towns you mentioned, Denton's town square and a store in Pilot Point burned down."

Jimbo took a swig of his drink and then continued, "I felt pretty stupid, but I wanted a clarification. Who were abolitionists, and who were the vigilantes? The man didn't laugh at me. Gave me this simple answer. An abolitionist is someone who wants to end slavery, and the word *abolition* refers to the legal prohibition and ending of slavery.

"I always read most of the newspapers, but they mostly covered the actions of both the Union and the Confederate politics and government takeovers. I did learn that white abolitionists masterminded, with the help of some blacks, a lot of these plots and lots of folks have met their deaths at the hands of angry mobs."

All eyes and ears were on Jimbo. "This caused east Texas to establish vigilance committees. Regularly constituted law-enforcement agencies stepped aside to allow the vigilantes to do their work. That work consists of searching for and punishing blacks and whites who participate in the conspiracy to launch slave uprisings. At least thirty people are thought to have been hanged by those vigilantes.

"It allowed vigilante activity some legality, but it also created fanatics, thieves, and Negro haters claiming to be vigilantes. These imposters kill, hang, and steal anyone or anything they can profit by.

"With the army posts being diverted to action in a civil war, we are not only facing Indian wars but also outlaw vigilantes." The night grew still. In a few days, they all would be crossing the mighty Rio Grande River into Texas. The fire was dying down. The stars were out.

Lou was the first to move. He said, "I've got beans to get soaked." He rose, threw some wood on the fire, and went about his chores.

Grady asked Jimbo, "What do you think about our boy?"

Jimbo shook his head and, standing, said, "Your guess is as good as mine. I just know that child didn't get out here from Texas or any of the other southern states by himself. He was running from something or someone." Jimbo said good night and headed to his bedroll on the freight wagon.

Juan said good night and left Grady and Dizzy staring at the fire.

Finally Dizzy said, "Kinda looks like our world as we know it is coming to an end. I've already been hurt by Indians. I've had enough wars of any kind, but I won't put up with a bunch of white outlaws taking what isn't theirs." He said good night and left the fire.

Grady lit a cigarette. Watched the fire flicker and replayed the information Jimbo had shared.

Lou set the pot of beans on the wire grill over the fire and joined Grady. He said, "Don't look too good, boss. What we gonna do with that little boy?"

Grady smiled and said, "Like I said, I haven't planned that far ahead yet. After hearing Cecile, we might leave him with that Seminole community at Fort Clark. Though somehow I don't believe our lady is going to leave that boy with anyone."

It was a bedraggled bunch of humans that crawled out of bedroll for a four in the morning trail-drive schedule. The threat of Indian raids and vigilante outlaws made for a restless night.

The cattle and horse herds had grazed and enjoyed a peaceful night. They were ready to repeat yesterday's fast drive. Grady, from experience, knew the drive was closing in on the big river. They were just two days from water and lush grass along the riverbanks.

Having much keener noses, the animals were receiving the moisture in the air, and excitement was starting to stir in the herd.

The drovers repeated yesterday's fast chores. Breakfast on the run. Cecile and Pala slept in the Cart. Grady helped with the herd. He intended not to have a runaway herd today. He worked the lead, slowing Deadly down, making the bull understand not to race today.

It was an effort for Deadly to slow the herd. Being larger than the little Herefords, the long-legged bull was too fast for their natural strides. His friend and trail boss wanted slower, so he slowed to a stroll. Swinging his long horns at the cows coming up on him, he let them know not to pass him.

When the herd slowed to a nice steady walk, Grady checked Cecile and Pala.

They were sleeping. Dawn was just beginning. The horse herd under Jalo's watchful eyes was still acting up. He tied Cecile's Arabians together and led them. They were high-spirited and excited from yesterday's faster pace.

By midmorning, everything was under control. Grady had visited with Dizzy and Jimbo, then ridden ahead to scout the trail. He stayed in view of the wagons. He saw dust in the air in the direction of the river. Had to be riders or another wagon train coming this way.

Grady rode back and warned Dizzy. Lou had put weapons from Grady's arsenal in all the wagons. Jimbo got the shotgun from under the bench. Dizzy lifted the pistol on his hip and settled it loosely back in his holster.

Grady warned Lou, rode on to the herd, and alerted Juan. He said, "Company's coming. Too far away to see who it is. Tell the men to weapon up. It could be trouble. If it's riders, spread out and come forward." He turned his horse and passed the red Cart. He saw Lou had his shotgun lying on the bench where he could reach it. Cecile's window was open, so she would be able to see and hear their visitors.

There were seven men coming fast toward them. Dizzy pulled up. The supply wagon and the red Cart stopped. Shotguns and rifles seemed relaxed in their hands, but the muzzles were casually pointed at the men coming to a halt in front of the freight wagon.

Two of the riders rode forward, one stopping by Dizzy, the other by Jimbo. Jimbo lifted his shotgun and aimed at the man's face. The rider pulled his horse up. For a moment it looked like the man might pull his pistol. Staring into the double muzzle of Jimbo's shotgun, he thought better of it. He was a dirty little man. He wore a filthy bandana over his hair tied behind his neck, topped off by a worn western hat. He smiled. A front tooth was missing. He turned his horse and guided it behind the riders. As soon as he turned and went back, Jimbo shifted the shotgun muzzle to the rider that had stopped his horse beside Dizzy. He motioned with the shotgun for the rider to back up.

This rider was cut from a different disposition. His clothes were clean, creases ironed in shirt and pants. His eyes were steel gray, and they looked Jimbo in the eye. He slowly put the reins around the saddle horn and laid both his hands in his lap. Each hand was lying close to a pistol on each hip.

Fernando had pulled the supply wagon up beside the back wheels of the freight wagon. Dizzy's crazy eyes rolled to the man and pointed to the double-barreled shotgun in Fernando's hands.

Jimbo held the rider's gaze and pulled the hammer back on his shotgun. The click as it fell in place was loud. The rider, with two double muzzles aimed at his face, slowly picked up his reins and backed his horse even with the other riders.

Dizzy shifted his eyes to the man who had the appearance of being in charge. Even though Dizzy's eyes were steady, only one eye was studying the big man, while his other eye wasn't quite true.

The man had the bearing of a military man. He sat tall in his army saddle. He did not wear a uniform as such, but his pants were tan, his jacket was army issue, complete with several Medals of Honor. He wore gloves, and his hat was that of a Texas cowboy.

Grady rode up and stopped beside Dizzy. He leaned an elbow on his saddle horn, he seemed to be relaxed. He said, "Good morning. Is there something we can do for you?"

The man realized Dizzy did not speak for this wagon train. It was his habit to stop the first wagon and hold it in place at gunpoint, while his men searched the wagons. Most travelers into Texas had no knowledge of the vigilantes. Now, faced with armed men, he needed to step back and use a softer tact. He was confident these cowboys would let their guard down and his men would take over.

"My name is Major Augustus Stevens. We are the elected body of vigilantes for the state of Texas. We are inspecting all persons and wagons that cross the river into the state. How many are in your party?"

Grady studied the riders as the major talked. They were heavily armed. Most held their horses still, with tight reins in one hand. Their other hand rested on or near a pistol or rifle. Grady smiled. He remained relaxed in his saddle. His eyes were steady, and the riders watching him knew they were looking at a skilled man with a firearm. His pistol, in its holster, had been pulled forward and laid on his leg in readiness.

Grady sat up and rested his right hand on his saddle horn next to the holstered pistol. He said, "I'm pleased to meet you, Major Stevens. My name is Joseph Grady. I'm trail boss, driving a herd to south Texas.

You will be dealing with me. I'll work with you as soon as I see your credentials."

The atmosphere changed. The riders looked to the major, watching for permission to attack.

Sneaky Bandana Man, his horse behind Gray eyes, pulled his pistol. A loud crack split the air. His pistol flew from his hand. He screamed. The riders started to draw their weapons.

A pistol shot got their attention. It could have turned into a gun battle. Another crack of the whip over the rider's heads and a woman stepped from behind the supply wagon. Whip in one hand, pistol in the other. She collected the whip and stood ready to use it again if anyone moved. She wore a saloon girl's robe, a holster belted around her hips. Black hair lifting in the breeze, she snapped the whip again. It hit the pistol in the dirt. The pistol skipped across the ground and landed under the feet of Sneaky Bandana Man's horse. The horse reared back, came forward, ducked his head, threw a buck, and dumped his rider.

These actions happened so fast. The riders were equally surprised and stunned by the arrival of a woman. All but the gray-eyed gunman failed to draw a weapon. Both pistols were in his hands, and his eyes of steel looked into hers.

Cecile's eyes never wavered. Her pistol muzzle was aimed at his face. Gray Eyes realized that if he pulled his trigger and shot a woman, all hell would break loose. Slowly he put both pistols in their holsters.

The rider's horses, nervous at the behavior of Bandana Man's bronc, were restless. The riders got their horses under control and looked to the major for orders. The major, his face passive, was still turned toward the woman. They followed his eyes, and now, all were staring into the faces of Mexican men lined up beside the woman. The riders were looking into the muzzles of every man working the cattle drive.

Cecile hadn't said a word. As a woman, it wasn't her place to speak up. She had been the only one to see the man go for his pistol and disarmed him. Now looking at Grady, she nodded to him and sheathed her pistol. She rolled up her whip and held it, ready to use if necessary.

The major turned his attention to Grady.

The major spoke to Grady, "Sir, as you know, our new president, Mr. Lincoln, has been sworn into office. Black slaves are riotin'. It's my job to find them and stop the burning of buildings and all the destruction from the riotin'. I would like to have your permission to search your wagons."

Grady looked the major in the eyes and without smiling, spoke, "As I said, we will cooperate if you can show us credentials." Grady drew his pistol. At this signal Juan and his Mexican vaqueros stepped forward, joined by Old Lou. Each singled out a rider to cover with his firearm.

It was a tense moment until the major held up his hand and started to turn his horse to ride off.

Grady said, "Hold it." The major stopped. Grady continued, "Starting with you, Major, leave your weapons here in this wagon."

The gray-eyed gunman rapidly drew his weapons. Cecile's whip snapped his face. He screamed and fell from his horse. Two pistols hit the dirt.

The major, seeing his men were outnumbered and heavily overpowered with firearms, realized he should have scouted this outfit first and hit it at night. All he could do now was retreat. He said, "I'll let you proceed for now. We will meet again in Texas." He motioned for his men to leave.

Grady shot over their heads. They stopped, and he repeated, "Put your weapons in the wagon."

The major carefully drew his pistol, rode forward, and laid it in the wagon bed. Five men followed his lead. Gray Eyes got to his feet and retrieved the reins to his horse. Across his face, from above one eyebrow, over his nose, and cut deep into a cheek was a slash beginning to drip blood.

He turned to Cecile. She had loosed the whip and drew her arm back, prepared to repeat an accurate lash. He looked in her eyes. Hate radiated from his entire body. His eyes never left hers as he took hold of his saddle horn and swung into the saddle. He lifted his right hand, pointed it at her, formed a make-believe pistol, and mimicked shooting. He turned his horse and left at a run, leaving two pistols in the dirt.

The major waited until each man deposited his weapons in the wagon.

Grady said, "I will leave your weapons at Fort Clark. I will let them know you stopped us across the river in Mexico. You have no jurisdiction here. Even if you had credentials, they would be worthless in Mexico. I'm taking your firearms to prevent an ambush. If I've assumed you are outlaws and I'm wrong, then I will apologize another time. Good day, gentlemen."

They turned, no longer in a hurry. Weaponless they rode out at an easy canter.

Cecile picked up the pistols the gunman had left in the dirt. She wiped them off and put them with the pile of weapons in Dizzy's wagon.

They all gathered around the freight wagon. Grady inspected the pile of pistols and rifles. They were not impressive. A few newer models. Only four rifles. There were eight pistols.

He spoke, "I'm proud of all of you. You were an impressive deterrent for what could have been a very bad gun battle." He looked at Cecile and winked. "And, woman," he continued, "that was an amazing show! I think I speak for all of us when I say we were all flabbergasted."

Cecile gave a shy half smile and looked at the ground while a blush spread across her face.

He continued, "Jalo, looking at these weapons, tell me what you see."

Jalo, the youngest member of this cattle drive, swallowed, stepped closer to the wagon, and studied the weapons. Some had landed on top. He reached in and pulled them off so he could study each one. He drug the four rifles into a pile together.

Jalo said, "Nothing special here. A couple of twenty-two caliber, a Winchester, and a Long Colt."

He sorted the pistols. Two of them he set aside. The other six he pointed at individually and said, "These two are Colt Dragoons. This one's a Navy. These two are Remington revolvers, and this old buzzard's a Walker."

He pulled the two he set aside in front of him and with respect wiped the dust off them, set them straight, and looked at Grady. He said, "I expect these are two you're interested in? I've never seen this model before. I can see they are made by Colt, they are forty-four caliber." He stepped back and said, "That's about all I can tell you, sir."

Grady smiled and said, "I'm impressed. I picked you to sort these weapons because of your youth. I was going to give you a weapons schooling." He spoke to Fernando, the boy's father, "You've taught him well."

Fernando shuffled his feet and said, "I don't know one pistol from another. I'm 'bout as surprised as you, sir."

Grady turned back to Jalo and said, "OK, let me tell you about the two you left for last. I've never seen them before either, but I've seen pictures. Colt began manufacturing them early this year. It's called the Colt Army Model 1860. Their cost is approximately twenty dollars each. The army and folks like us criticized Colt for its expense."

Grady dismounted and handed the reins to Jalo. He climbed on the wagon, facing his audience, saying, "Putting the lessons aside. These two pistols tell us a story. They are brand-new this year, and yet they have a lot of wear. The bluing is worn on the barrels. This tells us the owner is either a gunfighter or he plays with his weapons a lot. I'm going to assume he's a gunfighter."

He continued, "If so, I don't believe that fellow is going to walk away from the tools of his trade. We're going to see him again. I doubt it will be tonight, because to be a tough gunslinger, he needs to obtain a weapon, and they like a backup fellow. The thing we don't know? Was this a single confrontation, or were these men part of a larger membership, between here and the river?"

He took off his hat and slapped it against his knee. Dust flew. He ran his fingers through his hair and replaced the hat and continued, "This could just have been a scouting expedition. I'd like to handle it that way. I want all of us to stay alert and keep weapons close at all times. Most importantly we have to watch and protect our lady and that little boy at all times. Our gunfighter is not going to forget who put that scar on his face. Neither can we keep them locked up all the time. We need a disguise for the boy. Give it some thought." He gave it a thought and then said, "This cattle drive needs to get going."

It was noon as Bear, Lance, and his ranch hands arrived in Janos. They pulled the wagons past the saloon and continued to the stockyards. They unhitched the wagons at the blacksmith's shop. The ranch hands collected Carmella's teams and rode out of town.

Bear and Lance walked their horses back to the saloon and tied the horses to the hitch rail. They wearily climbed the porch steps and entered the saloon. They came to a halt upon seeing a man on a stool, leaning on the bar, drinking a beer. Ace lifted his mug, smiled, and said, "Join me, fellows?"

Lance walked over, climbed on the stool beside him, and said, "How did you beat us here?"

Bear walked to the bar and stood on Ace's other side. He said, "I figured Cochise got you. I'm sure relieved you didn't join us up there. Cochise would be wearing all our scalps on his war staff."

Ace took a big swallow of his beer and set the mug down. "I figured as much. I tracked the Indian I was after. He led me to their camp. I watched as they prepared to hunt me down. I had a pretty good head start as they did their war dance and decorated their horses and themselves."

Bear said, "Where's Candy? Save this talk while I check in with her."

"She's upstairs, Della's putting lunch together in the kitchen. Wyvon's out back washing clothes."

Bear went to find Candy. He found her sitting on her bed sorting linens. She jumped to her feet and leaped up into his arms. Her arms went around his neck and her legs wrapped around his hips. She kissed his face all over and settled on his mouth.

She withdrew and leaned her head on his shoulder. She sobbed, and he felt tears fall on his neck. She said, "I was getting so worried. I would have ridden to find you but you had both of my horses. Another day and I would have borrowed one."

He kissed both her eyes and said, "You got any bathwater warm? I'll take a rain check on this homecoming after I've soaked in that bathtub of yours."

She laughed and unwrapping herself said, "I've been keeping an ongoing bucket of water warm on the wood stove. I'll get it. You get undressed. Ace came in this morning. He thought you would get here today. He scares me, Bear. He doesn't talk much. Della took care getting him cleaned up. I hope you don't mind that I gave him a clean pair of your underwear."

"The underwear's OK. I'll just go naked." He laughed, and she left to get the water.

Della was excited, the men were back! She saw the wagons as they drove through town. Now they could load and get out of this town. She set to slicing bread and cheese. She fried bacon and eggs. She was so excited she danced about the kitchen as she worked. Lance came in and caught her. Embarrassed, she halted, and laughing she said, "I'm really excited you got the wagons. We're going to make it in time for the wedding."

He reached for her, put his arm around her waist, took her hand in a dance position, and waltzed her around the kitchen. She was giggling and breathless when he stopped and asked, "Is there any hot water left? I saw a bucket go upstairs. I need a washbasin and soap. I'm trail dirty. Too dirty to sit down at a table."

"You bet. The teakettle is full of hot water. It will be enough for the washbasin. I'll get a rag. You know where the basin is? There's soap on the washstand."

Bear lay in the warm water, his head resting on the back rim. His privates were covered with a washcloth. Candy came in with a towel. He asked, "Where's Wyvon?"

She sat in the chair placed far enough from the tub to be discreet and answered, "She's out back washing Ace's clothes. Did you see what he was wearing? Something's wrong with that man. He took those buckskins off one of those Indians he killed. Della fixed him a bath and gave him one of our robes to put on. He took Sugar out and put her in the barn. He came back with a bundle of clothes. I figured it was a change of clothes. After he bathed he walked out in those buckskins. I thought Wyvon was going to faint. He caught her before she fell. She pushed him away and backed up against the hall wall.

"Della saw this. She gathered his dirty clothes and took Wyvon and the clothes out to the back porch. She filled the washtub with water and gave Wyvon a bar of soap and the washboard. I heard her tell Wyvon that as soon as his clothes got clean and dry, Ace could get out of those Indian clothes. I think Wyvon's reaction will have him out of those clothes as soon as possible."

Bear said, "I didn't faint, but it took some effort to not show surprise. How is the girl?"

"She'll never be the same. You won't recognize her when you see her. If you remember, she stayed in bed the two days before you left to get the wagons. We carried meals to her another two days. I knew she had to suck it up and get on with it so I told her Della and I were too busy packing to bring her meals. She would have to come to the table. She missed a couple of meals, and the next morning she came down. Not for breakfast though. She had found my scissors. She stood there and picked up a handful of hair and cut it off all the way to her head. Then she handed the scissors to Della. She wanted it all off. A boy cut. You should have seen the pile of hair on the floor. Beautiful hair. A dark honey brown, slightly curly.

"That wasn't the end of it, Bear. She doesn't talk. She hasn't said a word while you were gone. I finally gave her paper and pencil, unsure she would use it. She thought for a while, and then she wrote, *They wouldn't have taken me if I were a boy. They took Ellen and me because we were women. We were of some value to them.*

"Before I could stop myself, I said, 'No! If you had been a boy they would have scalped you and left you dead.'

"She just stared at me and thought about what I said. Then she nodded, accepting it, and wrote, *I'll dress like a boy and fight like one. I'd rather die than be taken again.*"

Candy said, "Lean forward, and I'll scrub your back." He sat up and handed her the soap. She continued, "Anyway, I went across to the emporium and found boys' pants and shirts. I had a hell of a time finding boots that fit her."

Bear said, "I guess we'll never know what she experienced. I gather she eats her meals at the table now?"

Candy soaped the rag and scrubbed up and down his back, lingered on the defined muscles that ran down each side of his spine, and continued her story, "While you were gone, she became another person. She looks like a young boy. She practices her boy walk. She eats like a ruffian. She's up at daybreak and helps us pack. I hear her crying at night. She hides if anyone comes through the front doors. I needed to do something to help her fight the fear."

Bear said, "What could you do? It seems to me you've helped her a lot, just getting her out of bed was a big step."

Candy appreciated the compliment, as she smiled and rinsed the soap out of the rag. She gathered clean water, rinsed the soap off his back, and said, "I thought a lot about it and came up with an idea. I've always kept a wooden box under the bar. There have been times over the years that I've had to take a drunk's firearms away from him. The guns' owners could pick up their weapons when they sobered up. For one reason or another, some never came back and picked them up. There's a small arsenal in that box.

"The day after her transition to a boy, I brought her behind the bar and told her to go through the box and see if she could put together a holster and pistol to her liking. She chose a lightweight pistol. A twenty-two caliber on a thirty-eight frame. She had to make some adjustments to the holster.

"I found a belt at the emporium that would fit the holster. She had to cut some off the belt to make it fit her slim hips. She used the leather punch and made eyeholes. She dyed the holster and belt black."

Bear chuckled and said, "Can she even fire a gun?"

"After what she's been through, I know she'll learn. Bear, you should see the change. She's still afraid, but it's like now she has the tools to protect herself. I've even heard her laugh a few times."

He sat up, pulled the plug, and let the water flow out of the tub. She handed him the towel. He stood and wrapped it around himself. He talked as he dried. "Seems to me she owes you a lot. Woman, you've got a big heart. You've taken me in. You rescued Grady and Cecile. Della's a keeper. Wyvon's not a puppy or a kitten, what are you going to do with her?" He fastened the towel around his hips and tucked it at his waist. He stepped out of the tub and pulled Candy into his arms and kissed her.

She kissed him back and withdrew from his arms and said, "I think her fate will be decided by Ace. She spent every moment of her free time sitting on the porch watching for Ace to ride into town. She's afraid to leave the porch. She waited for him to tie his horse and climb the stairs. I thought she was going to choke him to death she hugged him so hard." She went to the door to leave so he had some privacy to dress.

"I see a job I can do to help them both. I can understand Ace choosing a warrior's clothes over a woman's feathered robe. I'll run over to the emporium and see if there are any pants to fit him. I didn't see any extra clothes in Dum Dum's pack. Everything Ace had on was Grady's. I'll hurry. We'll get him out of those deerskins before Wyvon sees him again."

Before she closed the door, she said, "While I'm thinking about guns and ammunition. We need to get as much ammunition as we can. Please, put it on your list. You can barter with whiskey."

"List? What list?" She grinned and closed the door. She could hear him groan.

When Bear came back from the emporium he beckoned Ace to follow him upstairs to the room with the tub. He handed Ace the bundle and said, "Sorry they didn't have any pants big enough. This was the only pair of overalls your size. The shirt should fit. You'll only need to wear them until your clothes dry. They will give you a change when you need it.

"We are going to be busy loading wagons for a few days. If you're traveling with us, I'll find time to teach you how to clean that buckskin. I'm half-Indian, you know. I have a lot of Indian savvy. I'll share it with you."

Della outdid herself with lunch. When Ace rode into town, she decided to make something special. She made her grandmother's companion angel-food cake and pound cake. Its major ingredient was nine eggs. The whites made the angel food and the yolks made the pound cake. The two cakes were cooling as she sliced sandwich fixin's and set tables with plates and utensils. There was a bowl of fresh churned butter, honey, jam, and home-made mustard.

When she was ready, she rang the dinner bell. The men, clean faces, damp hair, enormous appetites, found seats. Della had pushed tables together and told the men where to sit. When all had taken their seats, they realized she had seated Bear next to Candy, Ace next to Wyvon, and Lance beside her.

Candy ate quietly, her eyes watching her guests interact. Della and Lance, old friends, laughed and talked. Ace was starved and paid little attention to Wyvon. He evidently had gone days without eating. Wyvon was hardly touching her food. She couldn't keep her hands off of Ace. He didn't seem to notice. She finally relaxed, built a small sandwich, and did a good job of eating it. When Ace laid his fork on an empty plate, he put his arm around her shoulders. Candy could see the glow on the girl's face. Wyvon snuggled in with satisfaction and laid her head on his shoulder.

When all finished their last bite, Della announced she had peaches and cake for desert. She said, "I have coffee ready for those who would like a cup."

Candy spoke up, "That sounds delicious, but I'm so stuffed. I'd love to have coffee and let my lunch settle. Did you make both angel and pound?" Della said yes and Candy said, "I want both. I love your companion cakes. I'll help you serve coffee. If anyone wants something from the bar, serve yourself. If it's all right, we can catch up and have our desert later." Everyone nodded in agreement.

Bear began, "We ran into Cochise as we came out of the canyon. He was looking for our friend here." He pointed to Ace and continued, "One of his subchiefs returned to camp without his braves or their loot. The way Cochise explained it to me, a few days ago some of his men rode into camp reporting the success of the raid. Cochise didn't consider it a success as these men returned to camp with the four mules carrying injured and dead men."

Bear finished with, "They had assured Cochise that their warrior chief, Loco Spider, was following with many goods and two women."

Wyvon gasped. Ace took her hands in his and asked, "Would you like to be excused?"

Wyvon sat up, took a deep breath, and shook her head. She reached for Ace's hand and held it on the table. He shifted his hand to holding hers. He looked at Bear and spoke, "Loco Spider—that's his name?"

Bear said, "I got the feeling the name fits him."

Ace said, "Loco. He's a crazy bastard. It's good you didn't see what he did to Ellen." Wyvon shivered, Ace squeezed her hand and continued, "I really needed to kill that man. I'm glad to know his name. It will help me to find him."

Bear asked, "How did you lose him? Cochise said he staggered into camp with a wild story. He said all his braves were killed by a Shadow man. This Shadow man carried a lightning rod. The Shadow followed their tracks, and the lightning rod killed three at one time. He said he looked for the Shadow man's tracks to kill him but there were no tracks. He was a spirit. Cochise asked Loco how he was the only one that escaped. He said he could not run from a spirit, he hid in the cave of their ancestors. As he reported to Cochise, he kept looking over his shoulder, alert to the path into the camp. He believed the Shadow still followed him. That's why Cochise chose his best warriors to backtrack Loco Spider and find this Shadow man."

Ace chuckled. "I used an old Indian trick, learned from an Indian hobo that the sheriff lets sleep in the jail once in a while. I covered Sugar's hooves with deerskin booties, hair side out. When I caught up with the last three, they had killed a deer and were eating. I found it. Made booties from the skin and salvaged the meat. I hope you found it?"

"We had it for dinner," Bear said. Then he leaned forward and asked, "How did the crazy one escape?"

Ace rubbed his face and said, "I had him. He tried every trick to hide his tracks. Rode his horse hard to get far ahead of me. Sent the horse on alone while he walked in a stream for a mile. I saw right away the horse tracks were lighter. I backtracked and saw muddy water where he had stepped off the horse into the stream. I hadn't been in any hurry and that water was half-ice. He had to be miserable. I could follow the sifting dirt in the stream. I had to get Sugar out of it several times to warm up. That's where he got ahead of me. It was cold in that ravine. Frozen snow and ice in the stream."

Ace paused to take a sip of his drink. "I figure he had about eight hours ahead of me. I tracked him to where he left the creek. He was really good. 'Bout the best I've ever followed. It's really hard to hide tracks in frozen snow. It took me a lot of backtracking and start overs, but I found the cave."

When Ace said *cave*, Lance and Bear looked at each other and smiled. Ace said, "What!"

Bear said, "Was he in the cave?"

"No, but he had been there. Took a nap. Hadn't bothered to hide his tracks when he left. I realized later it was because he had just a short run to reach the stronghold and friends. When I reached their campgrounds, I found it loaded with tepees. Indians everywhere. I knew they would put together a search party. I put Sugar's boots back on her. We traveled all night downhill. They would find no tracks leading away. The spirit just disappeared."

They sat quietly digesting the story. Bear broke the silence. "If Loco never saw your face you should be safe here unless they are able to find your tracks and follow you off the mountain."

Ace said, "I wouldn't do that to you guys. I kept the mare off the road all night until her boots began to fall off. Then we traveled the road where all your teams had it churned up."

Candy spoke up. "What are you going to do now, Ace?"

He scratched his head, ran his fingers through his hair, and said, "I don't plan on taking on an entire Indian tribe, not by myself anyway. I heard about the talk Lance had with Grady about enlisting in the volunteers in New Mexico. I've been thinking I'd like to ride along with Lance. I'm in the right mind-set to fight Indians. Who knows, I might get a chance to put the killer of my brother in my rifle sights. Loco Spider is evil. He will never quit killing white men. Would it be all right if we rode along with you? I can help you load wagons, and Wyvon's a great cook. I don't like the idea of that trail by myself. When we reach the river, we'll ride on to San Antonio and spend Christmas with my family. I can meet up with Lance. We can ride the Butterfield or hitch a ride with Dizzy. He has that load of firearms for New Mexico."

They were thinking it over. Candy spoke first. "I rather like the idea of another set of eyes and a good rifle. We've also got Carmella and her gang. This train should be big enough to avoid an Indian raid. Now, with Wyvon, we are three women. Bear, Lance, and Ace evens us out, three women, three men. Grady, here we come."

The women had done a good job packing. Bear groaned when he saw Candy's lists and the volume of boxes, barrels, and furniture.

When Candy told him she wanted to take the big kitchen wood stove, the wood stove in the saloon, and her bathtub, he went to the bar and poured himself a shot of whiskey. Lance joined him. They sat with paper and pencil to make a list for loading Grady's three wagons.

(1) *The grub wagon: To be used for what it was designed for. It is enclosed and has a drop-leaf table that folds up for travel. All bedrolls and winter wear. Anything that needs protection and ease to get to. All cooking supplies, pots, and pans. A barrel of water on the back.*

(2) *Supply wagon: Furniture, including the two wood stoves and the tub. Three beds, three dressers.*
Others to be sold. Three tables, eight chairs.
Others to be sold. Washstands, side tables, coatracks, stools, aluminum tubs, buckets, barrels of linens, dishes, pots and pans, cleaning supplies.
The supply wagon can carry items that did not need to be used. A large canvas tarp to cover it, tied down firmly to hold in place, until destination is reached.

(3) *Trumpeter's small wagon: Boxes and barrels of alcoholic beverages. To be used as cash if needed. Often used: shovels, axes, toolboxes, leather goods, saddles, harness, extra barrels of water.*

With their lists made, Bear had a thought. "Now that we've got wagons, we need teams to pull them."

Lance grinned and said, "I've got that covered. You're forgetting my mom. She lent Grady her wagons. He used his teams. She's going to travel with us. She knows I'll be leaving to New Mexico. She and Glancy want to go to the wedding and then go to San Antonio to see me off. We'll use her teams going, and she'll bring her wagons home. We have Candy's black team to pull the beer wagon. Mom's driving a team with her small wagon. We are borrowing two teams for the supply wagon and one for the grub wagon."

Bear said, "Whew, that's a relief. I forgot she planned to go for the wedding. It still leaves us short of drivers."

"How do you figure that?" Lance counted on his fingers. Candy wants to drive her beer wagon. She's afraid we'll cowboy it and bust the whiskey bottles. You and I can spell her when she gets tired. We can take turns with the grub wagon. Ace and Wyvon can drive the supply wagon."

"I'm losing it. I forgot Ace. He's driven Dizzy's loaded freight wagons before. He's really experienced. We'll lose him at Brackett, but Candy, you and I can make it to the hacienda."

The trail drive the next morning found the cattle and horses still excited. They were eager to get to water. Grady gave orders for Juan to get his crew fed, then move the cattle and horses around the wagons and let them set their own pace. He said, "Keep your eyes open for visitors. I'm going to get things squared away here, then I'll join you."

Cecile and Pala slept. Grady, Dizzy, and Jimbo ate a leisurely breakfast. Lou and Fernando cleaned up the breakfast mess, stored supplies, and emptied the last of the coffee into two jugs and then joined Grady.

Grady swallowed the last of his coffee and said, "We're going to be eating dust all day. I'm sorry about that, but livestock are in charge today. We either have them pushing us from behind or us eating dirt. Also, I don't want those so-called vigilantes sneaking up and ambushing our cowboys. They will have to wade through a herd of thirsty cows before they can get to us, it will give us a chance to be prepared, if necessary."

Grady then addressed Dizzy. "Dizzy, will you do me a favor? Put Lou's Cart first. Fernando and the supply wagon second. You and Jimbo, please guard the rear." He waited for Dizzy to nod that he was agreeable. He continued, "Make use of the weapons we took from our outlaws. Lou, see if we have any ammunition that might fit any of those guns. Don't let Cecile or the boy ride on top today. If they need to stretch their legs, make it brief and lock them back up." He mounted his horse and left in a run.

The herd would reach the river sometime in the afternoon. Grady took the chance to ride ahead and study the tracks made by the major's riders. He wanted to make sure they all continued to the river crossing. After each inspection he returned to help Deadly keep the herd bunched as they hurried to reach water.

He repeated his inspection often to make sure the riders did not leave the trail and turn back. Occasionally he rode back to check on the wagons. At noon he grabbed a sandwich and spent a few minutes talking to Cecile.

It was the middle of the afternoon in the warmest part of a Rio Grande winter. Thanksgiving would soon be celebrated. Grady could see the difference in the foliage as they neared the river. Growing more abundantly were dense growths of prickly pear, mesquite, dwarf oak, cat's-claw, quajillo, huisache, black brush, cenizo. Other cactus and wild shrubs he could not name.

Across the river on the western parts of the Rio Grande plains, the growth of small oaks, mesquite, prickly pear, and a variety of wild shrubs gave it the name of Brush Country. The Mexicans called it Chaparral and Monte, meaning dense brush.

The river was still a couple of miles away when on one of his inspections he saw several small oaks, clustered together off to the left of the trail. Something was not right about one of the small oaks. He squinted and shaded his eyes. A blur, but it wasn't right. He needed to get a closer look. He moved off the trail into a fast trot. As he came close, the objects became men, black men, hanging from the trees, by their necks.

He pulled up his horse and studied the sickening sight. These men had been days hanging. Their bodies were swollen. Flies were abundant.

He rode around the trees studying the tracks in the dirt. Having followed the tracks of the major's gang all day, it was easy to recognize the tracks about the cluster of oaks.

He turned his horse and hurried back to the herd. He waved to Juan. Paco and Garcia saw him and they all rode to meet him. They knew something was up.

Grady pulled up and told them what lay ahead. He said, "Don't stop, get the herd to the river. Let them drink and bed them down. They will settle and graze. Later tonight we'll come back and bury those men."

He rode back to the wagons, passed Lou, and motioned for him to keep driving. He passed Fernando and turned his horse to ride beside Dizzy.

Talking quietly, he told Dizzy what was ahead. He cautioned Dizzy and Jimbo to keep their eyes open and continue on to the river and camp. He said, "We'll come back later if we decide it's safe and bury those men. I assume one of those men is Impala's father. I don't know yet how I'm going to handle that."

He rode to Lou's Cart and stepped out of his saddle onto the wagon. Lou moved over so he could sit.

Grady whispered. He didn't want Cecile to hear him. He told Lou enough to make him aware of the men hanging in the oaks. He climbed back on his horse and rode to help with the cattle and horses.

The cattle were oblivious to the tension of the humans, they were happy to find abundant water and good grazing. Deadly, keenly aware of Grady's moods, was the only animal who sensed that things seemed unsettled. When camp was reached for the day, Deadly took his job of settling the herd seriously. He was anxious to check on Grady, needing that contact to assure himself that all was well.

Jalo hobbled the horses, allowing the better-trained ones free to graze with the herd. He quickly had the wagons positioned. Lou and Fernando created a large pot of soup. They put Impala to peeling potatoes to add to it.

Cecile had dressed for the evening meal. It had been a miserable day confined to the Cart with Impala. There was an uncomfortable air about the camp. Men were getting chores done but the lighthearted rivalry that usually accompanied the end of the day was absent. Lou and Fernando went about their preparations. Neither would look her in the face.

Grady could see she knew something was up. He took her hand and they walked past the herd to the riverbank. He chose a rock to seat her. He walked to the rushing water, washed his hands, and collected his thoughts.

Cecile got up and came up behind him. She wrapped her arms around him and laid her head on his back. She said, "Tell me. I know something is wrong."

He rubbed her hands, parted them, and led her back to the rock. He sat and pulled her onto his lap. She was so small but stronger than any woman he'd ever known, besides his mother. "I need your help, and to get it, I need to tell you what I ran into today."

"You're scaring me."

"I'm sorry. There's a stand of oak trees back about a mile and a half. There are three men hanging off them." He felt her draw in her breath.

She turned her head to look at his face. She said, "Is it Pala's dad?"

His woman was wise. Keeping things from her wasn't easy. He said, "I don't know. That's why I need your help. I don't know what the right thing to do is. There are three black men hanging. They've been there about a week. Tracks tell me the major's boys did it."

She was stunned. "We were right, they were looking for Pala. How did that boy get as far as he did?"

He answered, "My guess is they knew they were being pursued. They probably had horses. It's possible they gave him what food they carried, sent him on, and told him to ride the trail and not look back. They probably told him they would catch up."

"But Grady, when we found him, he was horseless, shoeless, and coatless."

He answered, "A lot of things could have happened. My guess would be, at some point, the boy stopped to rest. It's possible he had a bedroll and removed his shoes and coat. The horse either got loose or maybe wolves or a bear scared the horse and left him afoot."

"Grady, why do you need my advice?" She laid her head on his shoulder.

"What should we do? Tell the boy or just ride on?"

"Oh dear! Grady, I don't know. I had to deal with the death of my parents. I hated they were gone but I had to arrange their burial. It was terrible but I at least knew I had taken care of them. Buried them properly, with respect. Even now I can visit their grave. I don't know how I would have handled not knowing what happened to them. I also don't know how I would have handled a hanging, it would have left me with nightmares." Tears were running down her cheeks.

Grady used his bandana and wiped the tears. He said, "I understand, because I felt the same about burying my family. I actually had to dig the holes and prepare them, lay them out and cover them. I was sixteen and alone. What I'm wondering is if the right thing is to tell the boy and let him help bury his dad or just keep going and let him believe his dad will show up. Another question, does he have family somewhere and how do we find them?"

"Oh, Grady, let's don't worry about that right now. Let's get past tonight. Maybe we should tell Pala his dad is dead and let him decide if he needs to see him."

"Cecile, his dad is hanging by his neck. His body is swollen." He felt her shudder. "I'm sorry, honey. I should not have said that."

She got off his lap and looking him in the eyes said, "My family was broken into pieces lying in a gully. It took my dad days to die. We couldn't move him. I stayed by his side and watched him die. I was no longer a child. I became a woman with responsibilities. We all have to overcome things. Let's see how supper goes."

Grady stood and said, "I've already told the men we would ride back and do a burial."

"You're a good man, Joe Bob Grady." She took his hand and they walked back to camp.

Before they got there they heard loud voices and the child screaming.

They ran and found Dizzy and Jimbo holding a fighting, screaming boy. Lou and Fernando were trying to talk to him.

Cecile ran to Impala and wrapped her arms around him. The boy quieted and leaned into her.

Grady said, "What's up?"

Dizzy answered, "It's my fault. Jimbo and I were talking as we made our way to the fire. I didn't know the kid was anywhere near us. I guess he had left the fire to relieve hisself. He heard us talking about the night's work. We had just been gathering shovels."

Grady looked at Dizzy and Jimbo. He asked, "How much did he hear?"

Jimbo stared at the ground. Dizzy shrugged. His eyes crossed and uncrossed. He said, "I'm really sorry, Grady."

Grady helped Cecile up and walked her and the boy to a log by the fire. Cecile kept her arms about the boy. He snuggled close to her, tears streaming down his face. Grady knelt on one knee and looked Impala straight in his eyes.

He said, "I guess you know I found your father today. He's dead, boy. I plan on taking some of us back after supper and giving him proper burial. I'm truly sorry, boy."

Impala wiped his eyes, straightened his back, and looked steady into Grady's eyes. He said, "I want to see my paw. I was going back, and these men won't let me go."

"Well, I guess that settles that. OK! Impala, you listen to me. I'll take you to your father, but we're going to do this like men. There're three fellows hanging from a tree. I believe one of them to be your father. I don't know because I never met your father. You are the only one here that knows these men and can identify your father. This will be a nasty trip for all of us. We plan on digging holes, burying all three, and speaking words over their graves."

He continued, "The job will take us most of the night. We could be in danger of being ambushed by the riders that hanged them. You may stay here with Miss Cecile or ride with us. We are going to eat a big supper so we have the energy to do this sorry job. If you know these men, it will be a big help in giving them a proper burial. I'm hoping, if you decide to go with us, you eat to be strong, for what's waiting for us." He walked away to the Cart.

Cecile thought she saw tears in Grady's eyes. She hugged Pala to her and kissed his brow. He turned his head into her shoulder and she felt him sob.

Supper was early. Grady wanted to get back to the hanging tree before dark. They would take lanterns for later, but there were jobs to do, like searching the men for identities and letting Impala see his father.

Lou encouraged them all to dig into the soup. They were all hungry and not looking forward to the night's work.

Jalo ate quickly and gathered horses from the remuda. Paco and Garcia helped him saddle seven horses. Cecile informed him she would ride the seventh horse with Impala.

Jimbo, with his gunshot leg, stayed behind with Lou and Fernando. They would guard the camp and the herd. They had weapons loaded and in easy reach.

After Grady had given Deadly the command to stay with the herd, he turned his horse and set a fast pace. It didn't take long to reach the oak trees. The sun was going down. It would be dark soon.

Cecile pulled up her horse and tried to hang back. Impala slid off the horse, and before she could catch him, he darted around bushes and ran to the hanging man on the left. The boy's head reached the man's knees. He wrapped his arms around the swinging legs and cried.

The men were trying to be men. They got busy rolling cigarettes and gave the boy time. It was an emotional moment for everyone, seeing Impala's pain. They cleared their throats and wiped tears away.

Grady said, "Well, I guess that clears up the mystery."

Dizzy said, "We'd better get busy or we'll be here all night."

Cecile dismounted and went to Impala. She put her hands on his shoulders and said, "The men have a job to do. You and I can ride back to camp if you would like."

"No, thank you, Miss Cecile, I'm going to bury my paw." He picked up a shovel, found ground clear of brush, and stomped the shovel into the ground. The men put out their cigarettes and joined him.

While Impala struggled to break ground, Grady supervised the release of the dead from the tree.

Impala soon tired. Cecile talked him into letting the men take over. She unsaddled her horse and placed the horse blanket on the ground, close enough for him to sit and watch them dig.

The men concentrated on the father's grave. The ground was hard, so they took turns. Soon the hole was large enough. Dizzy and Paco Mendez carried the body over and laid it beside the grave. Juan crossed the man's arms across his chest. Garcia and Jalo used their lariats and lowered the body into the ground.

Tears were running down Impala's cheeks. He wiped them away and picked up a shovel. He threw the first shovel of dirt over his father. Dizzy and Paco helped him fill the hole.

Cecile, using fallen tree branches, fashioned a cross, and Dizzy hammered it into the dirt, at the head of the grave.

They gathered around the grave. Cecile stood by Impala on one side, her arm around his shoulder. Grady stood on the other side. Juan led his vaqueros in a Mexican burial prayer.

Garcia, who was never without his guitar, played a gospel song. They all joined him, their voices soft and sweet in the silent night.

Dizzy put Cecile's blanket and saddle back on her horse. He said to Grady, "You need to get your lady and the boy to bed. You need to do the same. You've pushed those cowboy legs too much today. We'll get the rest of this job done."

Grady didn't argue. His legs were trembling. His breathing was heavy. Fatigue was taking over his entire body.

Dizzy helped the boy climb behind Cecile.

It didn't take long to reach the campfire. Jimbo took their horses. Hobbled and left them with the remuda.

Lou made kettle tea for the three. Impala drank his, and Lou walked him back to his bed in the cattle traveler.

Grady and Cecile sipped their tea. Grady said, "There goes a brave little fellow. Can you believe how he took over?"

Cecile said, "Remember how confused we were over how to handle the death of his father? He took it out of our hands." She sipped her tea and hesitated before saying, "I've been thinking about those riders. We sure dodged bullets there. You did the right thing taking their weapons. And you're right—we haven't seen the last of them. We had plenty of experience on the cattle drive with men of that caliber. He is going to come after me. I saw the hatred in his eyes."

She swallowed the last of her tea and continued, "With the disbanding of the army, and the rangers overloaded with local violence, outlaws are making a living killing, hanging, and robbing all over Texas. I don't want him to follow us to my home. Grady, I don't want to cross the river here."

"What do you mean you don't want to cross here?" Grady set his mug on the ground and turned more so he could see her face.

She answered, "If we cross here and go inland to Brackett, we will be going thirty miles out of our way."

"I realize that, but we turn south on the river road that follows the Rio Grande and ends on the gulf. As I understand it, your ranch is approximately halfway between the turn off at Brackett and Laredo. The road will be easier on the Herefords, as it is well traveled."

"I agree the roads are better, because the traffic is heavier east to San Antonio and south to Laredo, but I don't want that man following us to Hacienda del Ciela. I'm hoping they ride on to Brackett and wait for us there to collect their weapons. They don't know who we are, and we could gain a few days as they wait for us to arrive at the fort at Brackett."

"What do you have in mind?" He rubbed his eyes and the back of his neck. Lord, he was tired.

She reached for his hand and said, "I know you're tired. So am I. Let me just throw this at you, then we'll get some sleep. In the morning we'll do whatever you decide is best."

He nodded and she continued, "I haven't told you much about Hacienda del Ciela. I did tell you it was a land grant awarded to my great-grandfather by the Spanish Crown in the seventeen hundreds. I'm so looking forward to showing it to you. The grant itself is four thousand four hundred twenty-eight acres. One league. The property is divided by the Rio Grande. Fourteen hundred acres are in Texas and three thousand acres in Mexico. The hacienda, barns, and fenced pastures are in Texas. My people live across the river, We call the settlement Ciela Grande. There is a lot of rich river bottomland. We farm many acres there."

Cecile paused in order to gather her thoughts. "I think we should turn south here, on the Mexican side of the river. I'm not too sure of the terrain, but we have a small herd. They can handle some brush travel if we go slowly. We will run into Ciela Grande. We have a river crossing that has been maintained for generations. It is small, but the float will carry five or six cows. It's designed to carry workers back and forth between the two properties. If need be, we can pen the herd at Ciela Grande while I warn my people. I also need to move a herd of Black Toros from one of the pastures and move the Herefords closer to the hacienda."

Grady was in another one of Cecile's rambling explanations. He was a little confused. He said, "We've got those guns to drop off and that gang to report to the army. We also need to see if we can find out anything about Pala's father. We need to check out the Black Seminole community. It might turn out we can leave Pala with people who deal with this problem of runaway slaves. Or at least learn what to do with him." He knew immediately he had said the wrong thing.

Cecile's face changed. Her eyes flashed and her mouth hardened as she said, "He goes with us, there are other ways to learn about him." She clamped her hand over her mouth and took a minute before saying, "I'm sorry. Dizzy and Jimbo are leaving us. They will cross here and drive through Brackett on their way to San Antonio. I think Dizzy is as curious as we are about Impala. He can inform the army and the rangers about the murdered men and the vigilantes."

Grady stood, took her hands, and pulled her to her feet and into his arms. He hugged her and said, "Sounds like you have it all figured out."

"No! No! You must talk to Juan. He and his vaqueros hunt that area. I know there is some hill country and savage brush. He will know if it's the right thing to do."

He kissed her, stopping the anxious flow of words. She relaxed in his arms and returned his kiss. He pulled her around, his arm around her. They walked toward the Cart. With a chuckle Grady said, "May I go to bed now?"

"Oh! I am so sorry for bending your ear that way. I have just been so worried ever since that encounter with the vigilantes."

"Honey, you can bend my ear anytime." Grady turned Cecile and gave her a kiss, lingering for a moment so he could enjoy the softness of her lips.

Cecile was sound asleep when Grady heard Lou start the morning meal. Coffee would soon be ready. Grady's head still hurt. Sleep had been fitful. His mind had a hard time shutting down. It was filled with Cecile's late-night request, the threat of vigilantes, worry over Ace pursuing the Indians, and the night's memory of hanging men.

He rummaged around in his pack and located the near-empty laudanum bottle. He swallowed the last of the syrup and saved the empty bottle. Bottles of any size were treasures. He joined Lou at the fire. Lou got two mugs, filled both with coffee, and joined Grady.

They sat quietly and sipped the hot brew. They had spent many mornings on many cattle drives like this. Good times, bad times. Lou finally said, "I heard Miss Ceci last night. She's really worried. I'm not real anxious for us to run into that bunch again. But we're still in Indian country. Indians are not as apt to raid us on a traveled trail."

Grady sipped coffee and stared into the fire. He swallowed the last of it and set the mug on the ground. He rubbed his brow and massaged his neck. Removed his hat and set it beside him on the log. With both hands, rubbed his head vigorously with his fingers, stopped, and shifted to his temples, giving that area a good massage. Grady put his hat back on and with one last rub on his eyes said, "Hell, Lou, have we ever had a drive where so many things go wrong?"

Lou chuckled and said, "Well, I can't think of any that didn't have some problems. After losing my son, I'm just kind of doing what comes next. Don't seem no end to what keeps on coming next, and I miss Bear."

"Me too. I sure hope he catches up soon. To answer you, I need to talk to Juan before we decide what's best. My job is to get this herd to her ranch in as good a shape as possible. Even if it means fighting our way through a gang of vigilantes. I'll make that decision after I've talked to Juan."

Lou picked up Grady's mug and stood up. He said, "He should be up soon. They were a tired bunch when they came in last night. Before I went to my bedroll, I fed the fire and left the rest of that bottle of whiskey out. It was empty this morning. I imagine they might sleep in a little. I'm not much better off. I'm just making oatmeal and toasting the last of our bread."

Cecile walked up and said, "Sounds good to me." She sat by Grady and asked, "How's the head?"

He said, "It's better this morning. You could have slept in. It seems the men are. Nasty night work. We won't hurry to get on with the drive until after we talk to Juan."

Lou handed Cecile a mug of coffee. She smiled her thanks. He handed Grady a refilled mug and went to begin breakfast.

"I have some concern about getting our wagons over heavily brush-covered ground," Grady said. "We could make better time on the Texas bank." Before she could protest, he continued, "I know, I remember your words. It's not important how fast we go. It's just best to get there safely with the Herefords. It's not the speed that I'm worried about. It's the men. They are tired, physically, and have worked under the threat of Indian raids and gun battles with outlaws. Clearing brush a hundred miles might do us in."

She sipped her coffee. It was still hot. She reached for Grady's hand, and holding it, she gave it a light squeeze and said, "Let's hear what Juan thinks."

He returned the light squeeze and said, "Let me ease your mind about Impala. I already figured you wanted to take him with us. I've no problem with that. I just want you to understand he's not ours. Someone actually owns him. I may not be able to keep them from claiming him. However, I will make some strong objections before I'll let him go to the person that tore his back up like that."

She wrapped her arms around his neck and said, "You're my hero."

Jalo was the first of the vaqueros up. The endless energy of youth had him out of his bedroll and gathering teams that he hitched to wagons.

Juan, hearing the noise, and needing less sleep as he aged, crawled from his bedroll. His tired old body complained loudly as stiff muscles unwound.

He made his way to the campfire and found Cecile and Grady waiting for him. Lou handed him a mug of coffee and they waited for him to adjust from waking. He drank half the coffee in the mug before he looked into Grady's eyes and said, "What's up?"

Grady looked to Cecile and nodded. She had been given the job of asking Juan his opinion on changing travel plans. After explaining her reason for the change—mainly her fear of the outlaws following them home— Juan contemplated as he drank the rest of his coffee. Lou filled the mug again.

Juan said, "I've been giving this some thought myself. On this side of the river, there's a traveled path to Piedras Negras. It's a sister community to Eagle Pass across the river on the Texas banks. There is an adequate crossing shared and maintained by both communities. Our fields at Ciela Grande, for many years, have provided those communities and Fort Duncan with fresh produce and have traveled the river road enough to have a trail adequate for the wagons. Once we cross over to the Texas bank we may lose a little time repairing the trails, but we have the advantage of being thirty miles ahead by not going to Brackett."

Grady spoke up. "Fort Duncan? How close is the fort? Is it still occupied? If so, we can notify the army about the so-called vigilantes and the hangings. It might be of help to alert the army of the possibility of that group of outlaws becoming a threat to Hacienda de Ciela and the neighboring communities."

"Si, Senor, it's been an army post since the Mexican War in forty-eight or forty-nine. During the fifties the fort provided merchants and traders protection from outlaws and Indians. They would have information about the boy. Since 1855 both forts, Duncan and Clark, became involved with the rangers in capturing runaway slaves. At that time, Mexico's Seminoles beat the army back all the way to Piedras Negras."

Cecile's hackles rose. Grady thought she was going to explode but when she spoke she was in control and used a soft voice. "Juan, Impala stays with us. I don't want anyone to know he is with us. I trust you. You are like a father to me. We need to send someone to the fort to report the outlaws and the hangings. Without mentioning the boy, they will make a discreet inquiry on current information on runaway slaves."

Juan set his mug down, taking time to form an answer. When ready, he said, "Secretary of War John Floyd ordered Fort Duncan abandoned early spring last year. We lost a lot of produce sales with that closure. Then in early 1860, Lieutenant Colonel Robert E. Lee ordered the fort reoccupied. I've had a chance to meet the officers in command. I believe I can do as you ask, but, Ceci, as you favor me as a guardian, I am telling you this with love. This boy is not a pet. Keep your wits about you. You have a big heart. It would be a shame for you to lose your judgment. You could miss an opportunity to do what's best for the boy." He rose, got a bowl, and filled it with oatmeal. He carried his breakfast with him, eating on the way to waking his vaqueros.

Cecile's eyes were large. Her mouth hung open. She shut her mouth and said, "Well, that's twice I've been scolded. Am I being overly protective of Impala?"

Grady took his time to analyze her question. He picked up her hand and twined his fingers in hers and said, "I believe it's safe for you to be as protecting as is needed to keep the boy safe. I think our concern is for you. I know, as I watch you with him, you are becoming more than a protector. You care for him, and that's a good thing, but the child has no one here. You are becoming both his protector and a mother figure. If we have to give him up, I feel more for the boy's loss, with all else he is suffering." Grady was quiet for moment, deciding to give Cecile an example. "If for any reason I were to lose you, I don't believe I would recover." He raised her hand and kissed it.

Dizzy walked in, grabbed a bowl and spoon, and served himself oatmeal and honey. Chose a large slice of bread, spread a spoonful of honey over it, and joined Grady and Cecile. He said, "Am I intruding?"

"Not at all. I need to talk to you. How did it go last night?"

"About how you'd expect. The ground was hard rock caliche. My upper arm muscles are screaming this morning." Dizzy's eyes rolled, and he closed them and savored the mouthful of honeyed toast.

Grady said, "I appreciate all the help you've given us. With all the sorrow you've encountered, you still took time to help us when needed."

"Grady, this has been the trip from hell. If anyone is owed a thank-you, it's you. I'll never be able to pay you back for all the help you gave my nephew. Also the loan of a team to salvage my freight wagon."

Grady answered, "Let's call it even. I was truly glad to have you hang with us. If you had elected not to stay and protect us, you might have avoided that Indian raid."

Dizzy looked at Grady. His eyes crossed. He said, "That's not the way I figured it. We could have been out there with no backup and those varmints would have killed all of us, four men and two women, with arrows. At least because of your backup I still have a brother, one nephew, and my life."

Cecile had stayed quiet, still uncomfortable with Juan's reference to her treating Impala like a puppy. She shook off her thoughts and said, "I want to add my thanks and my sorrow for your losses. I am very glad to have met you and Jimbo. You must come and visit us."

"This sounds like a good-bye. I figured we would get to that at Brackett." Dizzy set his empty bowl down on the ground, and one eye settled on Grady's face.

Grady smiled and said, "Yes, it is a good-bye. That's what we've been sitting here trying to decide. We are going to turn south this side of the river and cross over to Texas at Eagle Pass. Once we are on the Texas side, we will continue south to Cecile's ranch. We don't want the major or any of his bandits following us to the ranch."

"I approve that detour. That two-gun bandit had his eye on Cecile. I think he will come after her. Probably with both pistols. Well, I really do wish you youngsters the best. I'll see you get your team back. Also the Henry. I've got that order of weapons going to New Mexico whenever it reaches San Antonio. If there's a Henry in the bunch, I'll send you one." His eyes were watering, and Cecile stood up, leaned over, and gave him a hug.

Jimbo walked up and said, "Hey, can I get one of those?"

She laughed, as tears entered her eyes. She wrapped her arms about his neck. He lifted her off her feet and gave her a bear hug. Kissed the top of her head and set her down. She returned to her seat by Grady.

Jimbo, his face a big smile, said, "Now then, what was that all about?"

Dizzy spoke up. "They are trying to get rid of us. We're being cut loose." He undid his bandana and wiped the tears from his eyes. He continued, "Get some breakfast down you and sit. We'll get our traveling orders."

They waited for Jimbo to serve himself. Lou was busy getting another pot of oatmeal ready for the second breakfast rush. The toast was gone, so he quickly made biscuits, put them in the dutch oven, and set it on the grill. He put another pot of coffee on and poured the last of the first pot into two mugs. He gave Jimbo one and took the other to a stump and sat to listen to the day's drive orders.

Grady turned to Dizzy. "We are afraid the major's men or certainly his one gunslinger will be waiting for us probably, hopefully in Brackett, not on the other side of the river.

"If I thought they were waiting to ambush us across the crossing, I wouldn't send you on alone. But just in case, Lou has loaded as many of their weapons as we had ammunition for. If they do try an ambush, blow them away. They were told their weapons would be in Brackett or the fort. I believe the major's men would rather sit around waiting for us in a cantina in Brackett than try to ambush us without any weapons. That gunman is not going to come after us without the tools of his trade.

"Dizzy, I'd appreciate it if you took the time to drop off the weapons, and be sure you don't talk about the Hereford herd, its owner, and the little colored boy. If you find time, you might drop in at the fort and inquire about the vigilantes. Tell both the army and the rangers about our experience. Tell them about the men hanged and where they are buried. The telling might make it hard for those boys to get their weapons back."

Dizzy said, "I'll manage. The holidays are coming on. There's snow in the passes. Even if that load for New Mexico is in, I can hold off that trip for a while. I'll find time to get some information on both the bandits and the runaways."

"Thanks, Dizzy. Don't worry about the team. You lost six mules in that raid. If you need them for the New Mexico haul, use them. I'm not planning a drive this spring. I can pick them up anytime I'm in San Antonio." Grady rose and walked with the brothers to the freight wagon.

Jalo had hitched the team. Lou put the loaded weapons under the driver's seat and the rest in a gunnysack he found.

They shook hands, and then Dizzy pulled Grady into a big bear hug. He said, "Take care of that little lady. She's a keeper."

The river crossing was a simple pulley system, operated on both banks. Grady watched as heavily muscled men pulled the wagon across on a sturdy platform. The mules were tied to the back of the platform and swam when not touching river bottom. When the platform halted on the Texas side, the mules were hitched. Dizzy and Jimbo climbed aboard, waved to Grady, drove the wagon off the platform, and continued out of sight.

Juan woke the vaqueros and gave them the day's drive orders. He advised them of the change of plans. Not knowing the terrain ahead of them, they were to try to maintain a fifteen-mile-a-day drive. In two and a half days they should reach the Piedras Negras crossing.

The men were relieved to be back on schedule. They were excited! Home was just a week away! Jalo and Paco hitched teams. At Grady's request, when they got to saddling horses, saddled his horse and one of Cecile's Arabian mares.

The men laughed and kidded through breakfast. When finished, Jalo moved the remuda out. With Deadly's help, Juan and Paco followed with the herd. Garcia, with his guitar stored behind the bench, followed with Trumpeter in the carrier.

Lou took his time cleaning up. He packed supplies, first in the trunk on the supply wagon so Fernando could get going. He hung clean pots on the sides of the Cart, put the fire out, and with Impala riding shotgun moved the Cart out.

The lifted sprits of the drovers was felt by the livestock and most of the morning's drive was covered at a strong walk.

Grady, worried they would exhaust themselves early, called a lunch break. They let the animals spread out and graze along the riverbank. Paco watered the teams and put a small amount of oats in their nose bags.

The teams remained hitched to their wagons. They rested while the men made sandwiches and drank cold tea from the cold river water.

The trail along the river was adequately defined. The occasional brush that had grown over the summer had to be cut back so the wagons could pass. The path itself was rough. Ruts formed by summer showers needed filling, but in all, this first day on their way to the crossing was passable.

By noon on the third day, the small community was in sight. Many of the children ran to meet them.

Much of the land around Piedras Negras was river irrigated by water canals. Even with the dead days of winter, Grady could see there were many small garden plots.

A few of the men in the community helped swim the animals across the river. The wagons were strapped to floats and pulled across onto the crossing yard at Eagle Pass. Grady was surprised to see the vaqueros greeted by many of the people who gathered to watch the crossing of the strange-looking Hereford cattle.

Juan signaled his men to settle down. He ordered them to drive horses and cattle to the south side of the Eagle Pass community. The wagons were arranged in the regular order for the night.

After supper he permitted the young vaqueros to walk into town to a cantina. They had orders not to drink too much and be back by midnight. Tomorrow they would be headed home. They hurried to town laughing and carrying on. Garcia carried his guitar.

Fernando and Lou helped Juan keep an eye on the livestock. Impala took turns helping to keep the herd bunched and joining Grady and Cecile at the campfire.

There was a restless and excited air about the camp that night.

Cecile said, "I can't believe it. I'm nearly home. It will take us a couple of days to get to the hacienda, but by tomorrow night we will be on Hacienda de Ciela property.

247

She turned to Grady, and he could see the glow in her cheeks. She radiated excitement as she said, "Thank you, Joe Bob Grady, for getting us here. You were right at San Diego when you tried to turn me down and when you told me that trail was too hard for a woman. Knowing what I know now, you were right, and I have so much respect for you. You took me on and accepted the added worry I would cause you."

He took her hand, and she quieted. He said, "You have no idea how close I came to turning you down. Your spirit and drive were an added surprise. No matter how hard times got, you didn't complain. Besides, I had unexpected help from Juan and your men and from Candy and Lance. This trail driver learned a lot on this small cattle drive. I want to express how proud I am of you. I'd ride the trail with you any time."

Impala ran up breathing heavily, got a drink from the dipper in the water bucket, and ran back to the herd. He had taken a liking to Lou who spent time with him. He helped to fix meals, and Lou gave the boy other chores to do. They had become buddies.

With both of them suffering a terrible loss, Grady and Cecile agreed it was good for them to find a friendship with each other.

They sat quiet a few more minutes, and then Grady squeezed her hand and said, "Lady, you're right, you're almost home. It's time for you to take a serious look at this marriage business. You need to make a decision now that you are back on familiar ground. Do you really want to marry me?"

A shocked look came over her face, and she said, "Grady, are you trying to break our engagement?"

He chuckled, moved from the log, and knelt in front of her. He took both her hands in his and said, "Grace Cecile McNamara, I love you. Will you marry me?" He grinned and said, "Now's your time to get out of this. If you say yes, you're stuck with me the rest of your life."

She freed her hands, said yes, and took his head in her hands and joined their lips. He had no doubt this was his woman.

Wyvon shivered. Her entire body moved. The air was brisk. It was a cloudy November day, but the shiver was not caused by the cold.

She stood with her arms wrapped across her breasts. Terrified, her eyes moved around the small clearing at the edge of Janos. Out there were brush and trees. Beyond that, the Chiricahua Mountains rose high above the small town. In those mountains, the evil one, the Spider, lived.

She shuddered. Her body shook. Her mouth was dry. A scream lay trapped in her throat. She forced her eyes to come away from the mountains and return to watch Ace, who was sixty feet away from her. He was placing empty bottles, gourds, and other items along a fallen log.

This was her seventh day of pistol practice. She wanted to throw up, but she didn't want Ace to know how totally scared she was. That first day, last week, after they both had completed their chores, Ace had saddled a horse. Loaded his saddlebag with .22-caliber bullets. She had been scared he was leaving again.

She stood on the saloon porch and watched as he packed the ammunition. Her heart sank to her feet. She nearly fainted with fear. Ace was her savior. Her strength. She was so weak with fear that she didn't struggle when he climbed the porch stairs and picked her up. He carried her to Sugar and lifted her up into the saddle. He then put his foot in the stirrup and swung up behind her, just as he had done when he rescued her from the Indians.

He took up the reins, moved the horse onto the road, and trotted out of town. He headed the horse toward the mountains. The fear spread. She wanted to get off the horse. She tried to tell him *NO*. But she had no voice. She had lost her voice on the mountain. Ellen had screamed and yelled until the evil Indian had drawn his knife across her throat. Ellen's head was nearly severed. It fell back, exposing bones and blood. Blood flew everywhere. That was when Wyvon lost her voice.

That day a week ago, when Ace sat her on the horse and rode out of town, she had been terrified. He had carried on a one-sided conversation. They were nearly to this clearing when she realized he had been talking to her about her pistol. The items on the log had already been set up. He must have done that before he removed her from the porch. Her porch, her safety net, was far behind her.

He didn't give her a chance to refuse getting off the horse. He tied the horse and pulled her off. He walked her to a distance of fifty feet from the log and pulled her pistol from her holster. Without looking at her he pointed the pistol at the log and fired off three shots. Three targets flew off the log. He stood behind her and put the pistol in her right hand. His right hand around hers, his trigger finger on top of hers. With his left around her waist, he sighted the pistol and, pressing on her trigger finger, fired three rounds.

Only one item flew off the log. He pulled her to the horse, ejected the spent cartridges, and reloaded. He pulled her back to the firing line and repeated the previous exercise. He reloaded again and stood her at the firing line. This time he put the pistol in her right hand, but instead of covering her hand with his, he brought up her left hand and wrapped it around her right hand and the pistol. Her eyes had glazed over. Her hands trembled and threatened to drop the pistol. His voice was controlled but firm as he said, "Pull the trigger."

She tried to look at the items on the log, but she saw the mountains behind it. He told her again to pull the trigger. His voice was just a roar in her head. She knew he wanted her to fire but her muscles were weak with fear. Not of the pistol but the distance around her. The mountains were the home of the Apache and the evil Spider. She wanted to kill him. She wanted to shoot his vicious face off. Suddenly anger and adrenaline shot through her at a cellular level in her hand and fingers. She squeezed the trigger. She couldn't stop. She continued to pull the trigger until empty clicks were all she heard.

She felt Ace remove the pistol from her hands as she sank to the ground.

Every day after that, Ace taught her by example. He taught her how to draw her pistol and how to replace it in the holster. He made her repeat the lessons of each day over and over.

Today they were going to practice the fast draw. Ace was setting up the items on the log, six for him, six for her.

He finished arranging the items and returned to her. He withdrew the Colt Dragoon from his holster. He lovingly rubbed his hands over it. His uncle Dizzy came to mind. He started to think about folks at home. He shook his head, spun the barrel, and replaced it in his holster. He lifted it up and reseated it a couple of times. Wyvon repeated his actions.

Ace said, "I'll count to three. Draw on three." She smiled and nodded.

He said, "One, two." He hesitated. "Three."

He was a few seconds ahead of her. His items all flew off the log. Like it was intended, her first item flew off after his last shot, and all of her items followed.

He returned the Dragoon to its holster and held up his hand with thumb up. She holstered her pistol and flung herself into his arms.

On Thanksgiving Day they were all invited to Carmella's for the big dinner. The saloon was stripped. All of Candy's possessions were packed on wagons. All they had to do was get up in the morning, harness the teams, and take off.

They were all tired but so relieved to have all the work behind them. They felt like celebrating. Ace wanted to show everyone the success his student Wyvon had with her pistol.

Lance led them to the hay barn where he had a canvas with a circle painted on it. There was a bull's-eye painted in the center of the circle. He hung the canvas on the side of a stack of hay. The large haystack would accept the bullets and not allow them to pass through and do damage.

Wyvon was uncomfortable away from the saloon. Ace had gradually been weaning her away from the saloon. He never asked her if she wanted to take a ride with him. He knew she would say no. He just saddled his horse, tied it to the tie rack, and hunted her down. He picked her up, carried her to the horse, settled her in the saddle, swung up behind her, and rode around town.

Sometimes he packed a lunch and found a place out of the winter's wind to eat. He talked to her all the time. She knew he was trying to get her to talk to him. She really wanted to talk to him, but when she tried, the fear crawled up her throat. She pictured Ellen's head falling away from her neck and the blood shooting out like a fountain. She couldn't scream. The Spider would cut her throat. She was safe now, but the picture of Ellen's beheading never went away.

Today she clung to Ace's arm and determined to enjoy this Thanksgiving outing. If Ace wanted to show off her pistol skills, she could do this. She was getting pretty good with her pistol.

A bale of hay was placed fifty feet from the target. Ace spread his bandana out on one end of the bale. Wyvon ejected her bullets from the pistol, put them together in a pile on the bandana, and laid her pistol beside them.

Ace asked Lance to do the same. Lance was eager to show off his fast draw. Quickly he had his bandana off and spread on the other end of the hay bale. He ejected his bullets and laid his pistol beside them.

Ace said, "I'll count to three. You'll start when I say three. You'll load your pistol and fire six shots at the target. Lance, your pistol fires a larger-caliber bullet than Wyvon's twenty-two. So we will be able to see which holes are hers and which are yours."

Lance grinned at the crowd standing around. He patted his chest and raised his arms in a victory pose and danced around.

Wyvon, who was only as tall as Ace's shoulders, stood with hands in her pockets, head down. Ace reached to her head and ruffled the short haircut. "Come on, girl, chin up. Make me proud."

She straightened, took her hands out of her pockets and moved to her end of the bale. She didn't look at her audience. Her eyes stayed glued to her pistol.

Ace asked, "Ready?"

Wyvon and Lance both nodded, and Ace began his count. "One, two..." And he hesitated before "Three."

Wyvon was first to her pistol, the bullets fell accurately into their slots. She snapped the barrel in place and fired six rapid shots at the target.

Lance was right behind her. They all heard his last shot fired because no other bullet sound accompanied it. They all realized Wyvon had loaded faster and fired first.

Now they all needed to see how accurate both shooters were.

They all walked to the target. Lance, eager to see how well he did, stepped up to count the holes.

Dead in the center of the bull's-eye were two of Wyvon's .22 holes. Lance had three in the bull's-eye. Wyvon's four other shots had landed on the edge of the bull's-eye and just outside the edge. She put all six of her bullets in a tight circle. If shooting at a man, all six of her bullets would have killed him.

Lance's last three shots were scattered high and low a foot from the bull's-eye.

Ace said, "You're dead, Lance. She beat you to the draw. She's more accurate than you are." He turned to Wyvon and said, "That's my girl." He walked to her and, hugging her, swung her around. When he set her down, the audience was all over her with praise.

Lance whined and said, "Aw, that wasn't fair; she's been practicing while I've been loading wagons."

Candy hugged her and said, "I'm glad my weapon of choice is my shotgun. I'm pretty poor with a pistol. You would have shot me dead."

Ace said, "That's the idea. She hasn't realized that yet. She can protect herself now. She will get better with practice."

Their Thanksgiving Day dinner was outstanding. Carmella's housekeeper and her three daughters did all the cooking while Carmella, Lance, and her ranch hands traveling with her, finished packing. Glancy sat in his wheelchair visiting with everyone, wearing a broad grin on his face. He had been packed and ready to go for a week.

When Candy's bunch headed back to the saloon for their last night, they took three of Carmella's teams. Heavy draft horses, bred first by her long-dead husband and continued to be bred by her boys.

Her guests, Bear, Ace, Della, and Wyvon, gathered at the bar, and Candy pulled up a bottle of peach brandy. She filled five glasses. She raised her glass and said, "I'm so grateful to all of you for the help you've given me to pack up. I'm looking forward to this trip to meet up with dear friends over the holidays. Let's bow our heads and with silent prayers ask the man up there to help us have a safe journey." She drank her brandy and bowed her head.

Juan was up with Lou at four in the morning. Jalo heard Lou gathering pots and pans to begin breakfast. Jalo knew Juan was making an early ride to Fort Duncan to report the hangings and the outlaw vigilantes. Miss Ceci wanted Juan to request that the fort keep an eye out for any suspicious riders and to check in at the hacienda whenever they were on patrol.

Fernando didn't want Juan to make the trip alone. He gave Jalo orders to ride with Juan. Jalo crawled out of his bedroll, pulled on his boots and cut two horses out of the remuda. He saddled and tied them at the supply wagon.

Juan had finished a trail-driver pancake and was mounting his horse. Jalo grabbed a pancake, poured some honey on it, folded it over, climbed on his horse, and licking honey off his fingers followed Juan out of the camp.

Short on crew to drive cattle and horses, Paco saddled Grady's gelding and Cecile's mare. With breakfast over they left Lou and Fernando to pack up camp. Paco and Garcia moved the Herefords out.

Grady climbed on his horse and turned the gelding toward the herd. Out of the corner of his eye he saw Impala standing by the fire with sad eyes. He called the boy over. Removing one boot from the stirrup, he motioned the boy to climb behind him. Impala was up in a flash, a smile from ear to ear.

Cecile smiled at Grady, and they cantered to catch up with the herd.

Paco was having trouble with the remuda, normally Jalo's job. The horses were testing Paco to see what they could get away with. In spite of long travel, and hobbles, they were doing pretty much what they wanted to do. Paco's patience was wearing thin. Cecile's Arabian stallion was out of control.

Cecile shook out her lariat and settled it over his head. She soon had him quieted. She caught her other mare and a couple of the younger geldings on lead ropes. They all calmed down and settled into a comfortable walk. Cecile took over the remuda, and Paco, with a deeper admiration for Jalo's and Cecile's abilities with horses, went and helped Grady with the herd.

Cecile looked back to see how Paco and Grady were doing with the herd. She spotted Grady as he turned his gelding and kicked it into a run after a cow who left the herd. She caught her breath, worried about Impala, but seeing his arms were tight about Grady's waist. A grin was plastered on his face. He was having a ball.

She trailed after the remuda. The horses had settled down. She drew in deep breaths of fresh river air. She was home. She began making a mental list. Diablo was first. As soon as Juan and Jalo returned, she would send someone ahead with orders to put Diablo in his special corral. If Diablo was loose in the pasture with Deadly, Trumpeter, and Reginald coming onto his territory, there would be bloodshed.

Second, Thanksgiving. She wasn't worried about the dinner. Maria, Fernando's wife, and his daughter would have it all under control. She just needed to tell Maria of the extra dinner guests.

Three, she needed to have a room prepared for Grady. Thinking of him, her thoughts drifted to her wedding. Hours passed while she was deep in thought.

It surprised her when Jalo rode up and relieved her of the string of horses. She rode back to the wagons and found Grady unloading Impala to the seat of the Cart with Lou.

Juan was getting ready to join Paco at the herd. She called him over and waved at Grady to join her.

Sitting their horses, she said, "Juan, we need someone to ride on to alert the ranch we are coming. We need to have Diablo corralled. Whoever you send, they need to let Maria know we have three guests for Thanksgiving. We need the guest room across from mine prepared. We also need the messenger to spread the word the ranch is on lock-down. Explain the danger to our people. No one is to be allowed on the property unless they are known. Who should we send?"

256

Juan looked at Grady. Grady nodded, giving Juan the job of picking the messenger.

Juan said, "We can't send Jalo. He's the only one who can control the remuda. Same as the herd. We need Paco. If we send Garcia, someone's got to drive Trumpeter's carrier."

Grady said, "Sounds like the solution. I can help with the cattle or drive the carrier."

Juan said, "Senor, forgive me, but you have done my job with the cows this morning and you look exhausted."

Grady smiled. "I feel exhausted, but I think I can drive a wagon."

Cecile swung off her horse and handed the reins to Juan. She said, "I'll climb in the Cart and rest for a while, and then I'll drive and Grady can rest."

Juan took Grady's horse and stopped the Cart and the carrier. He gave Garcia orders, led the horses to the remuda, and told Jalo to saddle a fresh horse for Garcia.

Jalo saddled a horse for Garcia and delivered it to him where he stood by Cecile and Grady. She was giving Garcia her orders. He had his pack and guitar. Jalo took the pack and tied it to the saddle and returned to his job with the remuda.

Shortly Garcia cantered his horse past the remuda. He yelled at Jalo, "See you at home." Then with a "Hee-haw!" and hat waving in the air, Garcia pushed his horse into a run. He was going home!

At camp that night, Cecile climbed off the carrier and gratefully handed the team to Jalo. She almost staggered to the campfire and sank on a log Jalo had pulled close enough to sit and feel the heat.

Fernando and Impala were working on a stew. Lou had just mixed corn bread and poured it into three iron skillets and set them on the fire grill.

Grady wasn't in sight. Lou saw her looking for him and said, "He's asleep. He's not gaining his strength back as fast as he would like it. You either. Neither one of you needs to be doing a thing but getting well."

She answered, "We're almost home, Lou. You have to be as tired, or more so, than us. We'll have help at the ranch and we can all get rested. We just have to hang in there a couple more days."

Cecile was right. When they drove the herd through the front gates to the hacienda, a crowd was gathered in the barnyards. Immediately three horsemen opened gates to a pasture and drove the Herefords in. The cattle separated and appreciated the lush pasture grass.

A corral gate opened, and the remuda locked in. People were running everywhere. Hay was thrown to horses and wagons unloaded.

Grady and Cecile sat on the carrier while Trumpeter was unloaded and disappeared into multistall stables.

Children were running everywhere. They surrounded the carrier and were calling, "Welcome home, Miss Ceci." Cecile occasionally gave an order in Spanish. Impala was kidnapped by the children. Laughing, they grabbed items and delivered them to rooms in the hacienda or the stables.

A man Grady didn't know unhooked the horses, placed a couple of young boys on the backs of the carrier's team, and let them ride to the stables, where he set them off, undressed the harness, and turned the horses in with the remuda. The man came back and repeated the action with the Cart team.

Grady helped Cecile off the cattle carrier. Juan came by and motioned for them to follow him. He led them to an area across the back of the hacienda. It was covered with trellises that were winter dead but would sprout grapes in the spring. There were several groups of chairs. A table was filled with glasses and pitchers of lemonade. Beside them was a large insulated urn of coffee, a stack of mugs, sugar bowls, and cream pitchers.

Juan waited until Cecile and Grady sat before he removed his hat and sat down. Fernando crossed the lawn and joined them. A little middle-aged Mexican woman dressed in black lace, with a starched white apron, came from the house with a plate of cookies. She stopped by Fernando and kissed his cheek. She set the cookies on the table and walked behind Cecile, wrapped her arms around her, gave her a kiss on her cheek, and said, "Welcome home, Miss Ceci."

"That's Maria, she's Fernando's wife, and she is in charge of the casa."

Grady was in shock. Occasionally someone would address Cecile as Miss Ceci and quietly ask her a question in Spanish, and she would answer in Spanish, which Grady understood a little.

The respect shown her did not surprise him, but the love was evident. All of them addressed her as Miss Ceci, even the children. This was what she had fussed about on the cattle drive. She told them she preferred Ceci, but the men on the drive felt more comfortable with the more formal Cecile. Evidently she had been given the nickname at birth. He determined to respect her wishes and use her nickname. He smiled to himself as he thought of their marriage. Senora Ceci, Senora Grady. Shoot, he'd stick to Cecile.

Lou found them and poured a cup of coffee, sat, pulled off his hat, and laid his head back on the chair. It wasn't long before Jalo, Paco, and Garcia joined them. A young man brought out a pan of frosted flat cake and set it by the cookies.

Cecile called the young man to her and introduced him as Diego, Fernando's youngest son. She asked him, "Would you mind getting Senor Grady and me a cup of coffee." He grinned like he was of major importance. He poured a cup and looked to Grady for cream or sugar. Grady shook his head and thanked Diego when he handed the cup and saucer to him. The boy knew Cecile's preference and added both to the cup he handed her. He asked if they would like him to serve cookies or cake. They both declined, too tired to bother.

Jalo spoke up. "Hey, boy, I'll have the same, only I'll have cake also." Diego cut a piece of cake, picked it up in his hand, and threw it at his brother. The cake landed frosting first in his face. The young cowhands laughed and kidded Jalo as he used his fingers to scoop up some frosting and taste it. Diego ran for the house and Mother Maria's protection.

A group of children, dragging Impala with them, hit the cookie platter and ran laughing out to the stables. Someone had used a team and hauled off all the wagons to an area behind the stables. Occasionally a man or woman, sometimes both, came to Cecile, bowed, kissed her hand, and disappeared. Even Impala and children disappeared. It became quiet.

Juan said, "Senor Lou, I would be honored to share my home with you."

Lou answered, "The honor would be mine, thank you."

Juan turned to the vaqueros and said, "You boys get. These people need their rest."

They rose and also disappeared. Cecile and Grady were left nursing their coffee. They were both wrung out. Grady didn't know what to do, he said, "Is it always like that around here?"

"Pretty much." She smiled, took his empty cup and saucer, placed it with hers, set them on the edge of the table, and took his hand in hers.

"Where did they all go?" He was bewildered.

"Juan's house is between here and the river crossing. Paco and Garcia live in the bunkhouse out past the stables. Fernando's family lives across the river in the Ciela Grande community. Most of the people in the community are descendants of the ancestors that came with my ancestors who were rewarded this land grant.

"Many generations live in the community and share the care of the entire ranch. You probably are familiar with the word *peon*. Most of the workers that live on the property are called peons. When my grandfather died and my father became the head of the grant, he made a lot of changes. He detested the name *peon*. It reminded him too much of the bondage of the Negro slaves. He made sure their houses were well built and comfortable. He turned the produce fields over to the community. Not the ownership—just the right to work the fields and receive the moneys they earn. The community pays the Hacienda de Ciela a percentage. As the grant stays with the hacienda, we have the credit when we use the bank for suppliers. It helps us to govern the outgo and income for the community. It helps us to help them. We do the purchasing for the community and can determine its solvency. With the community running its own business we see a better return and a pride in the community. They are not peons.

"The livestock are the sole income of Ramone and myself. I will go into that another time when we are not so exhausted. To answer your question, there are always a few people working here at the main ranch. Fernando's wife and daughter are here most days.

"We have our own ferry. We maintain it and replace it when needed. It is heavily used, and all those who came to help today have now gone home across the river."

"Amazing" was all Grady could say.

Just then a young woman came from the house. She dropped a curtsy in front of Cecile and said, "Miss Ceci, both waters are heated and the guest room is ready. Is there anything else I can do?"

"No, Gina. Thank you. Where is Ramone?"

"OH OH! I'm sorry, ma'am. He told me to tell you he would see you in the morning. He knew you would be tired and he did not want to get in the way with his wheelchair."

"Thank you, Gina, run on home. We will be OK tonight. We are very tired."

Gina ran off, another person gone like a puff of smoke.

Cecile laughed and said, "You can help me up. Or I'll help you up. If we can, we need to hurry or our bath water will be cold."

Laughing and leaning on each other they made it into the hacienda. The inside décor was early Spanish with an influence of Southwest Indian. Cecile said, "Tomorrow I'll give you a tour." They went down a long hall and stopped at a door. Cecile opened it. A large carved wooden bed with a canopy overpowered the room. "This was my parent's room. It will be ours after the wedding."

She pulled him further to the last two doors on the long hall. She opened the door on the right and said, "This is my room. It's been mine since I was born. One day it will be our daughter's."

She turned to the door on the left and swung the door open. The room was more masculine. The girl's room was softer, with florals and a dressing table. This room contained another strong carved wooden bed, minus the canopy. The walls retained the adobe soft cream color. The furniture was heavy dark mahogany. There was an oil painting of a magnificent Arabian stallion over the fireplace.

Cecile said, "This was my brothers Ramone's room before he was crippled. He doesn't like manipulating around the house in a wheelchair. We built an addition off the east wing of the casa to provide him ample room for himself and his hobbies."

"This will be your room until the wedding," Cecile said with a blushing smile.

"Will he resent me using his room?"

"I think not. He doesn't know anything about you other than I was to meet you in San Diego. You have a lot of people to meet tomorrow. Will you be all right if I leave you to care for yourself? I do find myself quite exhausted. I have Diego bringing you a sandwich tray. If you need anything else, just let him know."

Now that they were in Cecile's domain he felt a bit awkward. He, once again, mentally questioned how he had gotten so lucky to have a woman like Cecile love him?. He pulled her into his arms, gave her a soft kiss, and said, "You run on. Don't worry about me. I might even beat you to sleep. Welcome home, honey."

She hugged his neck. With a smile she turned and walked to her door. With her hand on the doorknob, she whispered, "Good night, Grady, and thank you for getting me home." She turned back to the door, opened it, walked into her room and closed the door.

To say he was stunned would hardly express how he felt. He had expected Cecile's ranch to be well established, but he hadn't expected it to be so steeped in Spanish history and elegance. He realized this ranch had two centuries of time to build and grow the manicured buildings and fenced pastures he had seen coming in that long drive from the entrance.

It was evident that Cecile was not only his woman, but she was connected to all of those people that had swarmed about her and paid homage to her.

He was so tired. He walked forward in the room. There was a pair of French doors, mostly squares of glass. He opened one and saw a small private patio. There was a seating area with a small side table. He closed the door and went to the other door in the room. Opening it, he found a bathroom and bathtub filled with water, towel and wash rag waiting.

Someone knocked on the hall door. He went and opened it. Diego stood with a tray, covered with a napkin. He walked in and set the tray on a table with two chairs. He said with a Spanish accent, "Senor, is there anything I can help you with?"

Grady smiled and said, "I'll be fine tonight. Thanks for the tray."

Diego ducked his head and hurried from the room. Grady smiled at his thoughts. This boy would disappear like everyone else. He lifted the napkin on the tray and saw an open-faced sandwich, fresh sourdough bread, butter, mustard, ham and cheese on one side, and sliced garden tomatoes and lettuce on the other side. Grady's mouth watered. He had been so tired, but this looked like a meal fit for a king to him.

He walked into the bathroom, tested the water, it was cooling. He dropped his clothes on the floor and stepped into the tub.

He sank until his head slid into the warm water. He held his breath and lay still until he had to breathe and slid back up. He settled, laying back on the slant of the tub. It was a large porcelain tub with four legs. There was a brass water spigot and a drainage hole in the bottom of the tub. He wondered where the water went. He had stayed in first- class hotels that didn't have indoor plumbing.

He enjoyed soaking. He studied the room. There was a permanent washbasin. In a corner was a commode. No outhouse? He thought about his dirty clothes lying on the floor. He spotted his pack. One of those many kids probably delivered it to his room. All the clothes in it were dirty but the pack did hold his shaving gear.

He continued checking things out. By the clean towel was a stack of clean clothes. He wondered whose they were. They had definitely been left for him. He quit dawdling, soaped and rinsed, washed his hair, climbed out, and dried himself.

He eyed the full-length mirror hanging on one wall. Stepped in front of it and studied his six-foot-two-inch reflection. There were muscles where they needed to be for a man who spent most of his time on a horse. They looked more impressive than he felt. After weeks recovering from pneumonia, he still had not toned up his muscles or gained back his weight. Whatever did that beautiful woman see in a cowboy like me?

Evidently the man whose clothes he pulled on was the same size as Grady. The pants would be a little loose on him for now, but they would hang just right with his boots on. A pair of soft leather slippers with a clean pair of socks lay under a clean western shirt and, yes, a pair of underwear.

He picked up his food tray and took it onto the balcony. It was cold, the middle of winter. It looked like snow clouds were forming. It was hard to believe they had made it to her ranch in time for Thanksgiving.

He stacked the sandwich and really enjoyed it. The cup of coffee had grown cold. He washed the sandwich down with it anyway. Leaving the tray, he went inside, closing the door behind him, and removed the slippers and pants, climbed in bed, and pulled the covers over him. His last thoughts were of Cecile. She was in a comfortable, warm bed also. No more Cart.

Deadly was feeling out of sorts. He had been shuttled into an enclosure with Trumpeter. Once Trumpeter settled down, Deadly checked out the parameters of the enclosure.

First of all, he did not like being fenced in, although it was a large area. He was searching for a way out of the enclosure.

Secondly, he needed to find Grady. He worried that Grady had not been there when he had been separated from the herd. Grady usually came to instruct him. Today he had not seen Grady after being put in the pasture. Was Grady OK? That was what Deadly needed to know. Grady hadn't even come later to scratch him and give him biscuits, at the very least!

One of things adding to Deadly's anxiety was the smell of another bull. He could not see the other animal, but the smell was strong. He picked up his scent all over the pasture. Could Grady be in danger?

Deadly continued walking the edges of the fencing, looking for a way out. It didn't usually take him long to free himself. With his size and weight, it was usually easy for him to find a weakness. This enclosure was different. It was very strong. He pawed, pushed, and poked at this enclosure for hours, all the while catching the scent of a potential threat.

In the early hours of the morning he finally gave up. He was tired and needed to rest. There was a chance he would need to battle an enemy. Deadly walked back to Trumpeter and settled down. He closed his eyes but kept his head and neck up, staying alert. Just in case.

It was early morning, before sunrise. Grady woke with a strange feeling. He didn't know what to do. He was displaced. He had not slept well. The bed was new to him. It was wonderfully comfortable, but anything would be comfortable after years in a bedroll on the ground or a month in the Cart. He missed the Cart.

He knew it wasn't the rattling old hearse he missed, it was Cecile sleeping beside him. He missed hearing her breathe. He missed feeling her move.

It had been hard lying next to her and not romancing her, but when they first left Janos and shared the Cart, they were weak from illnesses. Grady, narrowly escaping death from pneumonia and concussions. Cecile, completely run-down, still coughing and weak from colds and exhaustion.

It had been a comfort for both of them just to be together. They were on their way to her home. She was safe under the pallet's covers and he in his bedroll beside her. He could still take her in his arms, and she could nestle her head on his shoulder.

As they had gained strength there were too many serious events happening outside the Cart to occupy their minds and further exhaust their bodies. Indian raids. Vigilante outlaws and hanging men. At times it was enough to know they were both alive and safe in each other's arms.

Now that they had reached their destination, Grady didn't know what to do. What was expected of him as Cecile's husband-to-be? He had been surprised as her people took over the minute they drove in the barnyard. Many adults and children unloaded the wagons. He had sat by Cecile, on the Cart, as people came to her for orders and then scurried away to do what she had bidden. That was yesterday.

Now he sat on the edge of his bed, scratched his head, and realized it still hurt but possibly not as much. Grady massaged his neck and shoulders. Still not knowing what to do, he got out of bed and pulled on the pants someone had provided him last night. Found his boots by the tub and pulled them on. He picked up his dirty pants and removed his belt and other items from the pockets. He ran his belt through the borrowed pants and stored the pocketknife and other items in the pockets. Well! Now what?

It was just beginning to get light as he walked quietly down the hall and slipped out the back door. He sat in the same chair he sat in the night before. It was the only thing he was slightly familiar with. It was quiet except for a constant clatter that came from a corral on the west side of the stables. Concentrating, he tried to determine its origin. He realized he had been hearing this sound off and on ever since they had driven into the large barnyard.

As he listened to the rhythmic clatter, his eyes wandered, taking in the cultivated lawns and the white-fenced pasture where the Herefords had spread out and were grazing peacefully. He spotted Reginald standing by a cow laying in the grass, both were dozing.

There was a central road leading out of the large barnyard toward the river. It had to be nearly a half a mile as he could not see the river, just the trees that bordered it.

That road had to be the path to the crossing, where on the Mexico side of the river was the rest of the property Cecile had described and called Ciela Grande. All of yesterday's greeters had disappeared down that road except the men housed in the bunkhouse.

He also remembered Juan had a house. There was a small white house about halfway down the road on the left side. The trim on its windows and doors matched the blue trim on the white stables and bunkhouse.

As he looked around at all the established grounds and buildings, he realized this property had not been put together by Texas's early pioneers. There was a century-old ambience with a Spanish style that was slowly being lost as Texas was being occupied by Anglos.

The cream-colored adobe hacienda showed signs where additions were created as the generations needed. The stables and bunkhouse were to his right, on the road to the river. Juan's house was to his left. He thought about her brother Ramone, whose bedroom he occupied last night. Cecile said she had a building added to accommodate his studio and his wheel-chair. He couldn't spot another building that might be Ramone's.

Enough of this sight-seeing from a chair. He rose and walked toward the clatter coming from the corral to the left of the stables. The walls of this corral were over his head. They were made of the thick adobe, like the hacienda. He couldn't see over them, but as he drew nearer the stables, he saw a small set of benches built like risers. They would hold several people, and they could look over into the corral.

He wanted to identify the clatter so he stepped up to the second riser. Instant silence as an enraged black bull ran at the wall Grady was looking over and slammed into it.

The bull reared up on his hind legs. Grady fell back onto the next riser. The bull screamed a raucous roar. Once he realized the bull could not reach him, he straightened up to where he could see the animal.

What he saw was a beast that radiated power. Black as coal and well muscled with a prominent complex of muscles over the shoulders and neck that would give the bull strength to use the horns, which were longer than most breeds, except the longhorn cattle of Texas. This bull's horns were wide and thick and curved forward. The horns were sharp and pointed, to penetrate as the mighty shoulders shoved into its target.

As this animal's target was Grady, he backed up, launched himself, and slammed into the adobe wall again. Dirt sifted to the ground. Grady was getting ready to step down to keep the bull from destroying the thick adobe corral wall.

Just as he turned to step down, Cecile joined him. She had her whip with her. She smiled at him and said, "I see you've met Diablo." She motioned Grady to move over. She sat and shook out her whip and snapped it over the enraged bull. Diablo stopped instantly.

Diablo glared at her and decided the man had a protector. He made a round of the corral, shadowboxing with his horns. There were several thick tree stumps that had the appearance of receiving savage attacks by sharp horns. There was one such heavy stump close to the wall where the two humans watched him.

He stood in place across the corral and threw dirt over his shoulders as he pawed the ground. Then he charged the stump, rammed his horns in it, and tossed the stump into the wall.

Cecile yelled, "Cut it out!" and sent the whip whistling over Diablo's head, snapping it on a horn. The bull shook his head and thought about another attack. Decided against it.

Diablo was not a stranger to this woman with the whip. She had never drawn blood, but occasionally when he refused to cease his tirades, she let the tip burn. He turned, flicked his tail, and trotted to a large round pole buried in the ground in the center of the corral. A chain with what looked like an iron cannonball hung from an iron eye pin at the top of the pole. Diablo settled to moving his head back and forth, catching the chain with one horn and moving it back to be caught by the other horn.

Every time it was caught by a horn, the iron ball hit with a clatter. The sound was amplified due to an iron sheath bolted around the wooden pole.

Grady put his arm around Cecile. He said, "Sorry, did we wake you?"

"No, I didn't sleep much. I missed you." She leaned her head on his shoulder and said, "Let's sit awhile. I've asked Maria to send coffee here. I intended to introduce you to Mr. Aggressive Diablo and show you the ranch. I heard you leave. I took a shower and dressed. I knew when I heard Diablo I would find you here."

"Is he always this combative?" Grady asked.

"Fighting bulls are judged by their aggressive behavior. Diablo fills that category but is so loaded with the breeding urge he cannot stay still. When Diablo was a novella, old enough for bullfighting, he was trained and became the best of our bulls for corridas de toros, full matadors.

"Under Spanish law the bull must be at least four years old and reach the weight of four hundred sixty kilograms to fight in a first-rank bullring. There are other restrictions for second rate and third rate, they must have fully functional vision and even horns that have not been tampered with.

"Diablo is number one in all requirements. He has entered the bullring with the highest-ranked matador. As you know, or maybe not, these bulls usually die in the bullring.

"Once in a while a bull will be indultado, or pardoned. Meaning his life is to be spared due to outstanding behavior in the bullring. They are chosen by the audience to petition the president of the ring by waving white handkerchiefs."

With a proud smile, Cecile looked at Diablo. "The matador joins the petition, as it is a great honor for a bull one has fought bravely to be pardoned. That bull is returned to the ranch where he was born and will live out his days in the fields. He is mated once, to about thirty cows, and his offspring are tested after four years for worthiness in the ring."

"You're telling me Diablo is that special bull?" Grady returned his attention to the crazy, maddened bull he had met. Now Grady felt some pride looking at the animal.

Just then Diego arrived with a tray. Large colorful mugs with cream and sugar. He set the tray down beside Cecile, who said, "Thank you, Diego." The young man grinned and ran back to the casa.

Cecile gave Grady a mug of black coffee, as he liked it. She dosed hers with cream and sugar. She sipped her coffee and watched Grady as he studied the bull with different eyes.

In a lowered voice, she said, "My grandfather, on his deathbed, made my father promise to keep Diablo's breeding line true. My father gave that job to Juan. As a young man, Juan helped my grandfather develop and maintain the Hacienda de Ciela's Diablo bloodlines. I have nothing to do with this except support Juan monetarily. As you probably know, raising Spanish bulls for the ring is not very profitable. To respect and honor my grandfather's wishes and help relieve the financial burden on the ranch, I heavily culled the Toros to thirty or forty cows and a couple of Diablo's sons. We care for many people on this ranch. I have to get it profitable. I hope you will help me do so."

"Oh! I see you want to marry me for my financial wizardry. Not for my muscles?"

She laughed and answered, "I love you, Grady. You would be surprised by all the good I see in you. I believe we will achieve anything we work together on, even a second Texas ranch. Let's go get breakfast, and then we'll saddle up and I'll show you our ranch."

Their ride that morning was a brief one. Cecile was eager to show Grady her ranch. There was so much to see it was frustrating. They agreed to continue taking brief morning rides before breakfast.

After breakfast she wanted to see her brother and introduce Grady to him. She grabbed Grady's hand and took him down the east wing of the hacienda.

On the way she opened a door and let him look in at a large library. Shelves of books lined the walls. A fire crackled in the fireplace. The flames were cheerful. There was a comfortable seating area and a serious desk and wooden file cabinets.

"This is the office. We'll spend some time in here later this afternoon." She closed the door and pulled him to the next stop before beautiful carved double doors. She swung them open to reveal a large empty room—or at least it looked empty, but as he stepped inside he saw tables and chairs stacked in a corner. Across the room was a raised platform, and he realized this was a stage for a band. The shiny wood floor was for dancing.

"This is the room we will be married in. When my parents were alive, this ballroom had many gatherings, parties, holiday dinners, prayer meetings, and weddings of my family and those from the community. This was a happy room. I'm looking forward to us returning it to that special ballroom, and hopefully our children will be married here!"

For a moment Grady digested her words. They were not married and already she talked of children. Looking around the room, he had a vision of Cecile dressed in white, in his arms, waltzing around the room. He lightly squeezed her hand, bent his head, and kissed those sweet lips.

She pulled him into the hall. Three doors were left, two were across from each other. When she pulled them open, there were two more bedrooms. Both were complete with bathrooms and commodes.

She closed the hall doors and walked him to the doors at the end of the hall. They were like the double doors of the ballroom. Elegant carved wood. The carvings pictured a child's stuffed bear, there were two, facing each other.

She swung them open, it was another large room. At first, it also looked empty, but as he looked around, he saw there were shelves on one side filled with packing boxes. Stacks of what looked like children's books. Toys rested, collecting dust. On a children's rug in front of the shelves was a large wooden rocking horse and several tricycles and toys too big to fit on the shelves.

"This was our playroom. It was our mother's before us. The east wing was built during my grandfather's life." She walked to another door without any carvings, very wide and built with strong lengths of two-by-sixes. Its iron door handle seemed low to Grady's eye. Cecile knocked.

A voice answered, "Come in."

She opened the door and they entered another room larger than the playroom. It was mostly open. No clutter on the floor. A bed with a wood rack that had a chain with a hand ring. It was designed for helping a person get himself or herself onto the bed.

There was a small kitchen area, built so that a wheelchair-bound person could slide under and work at the sink and counters. A water pump handle was proof of indoor water. There were closets along one wall and shelves filled with supplies. Grady figured they were silversmithing supplies, as he had seen much of Ramone's work on the items Cecile carried with her on the trail drive, especially her saddle. The closets were low so a wheelchair-bound person could reach hangers.

Cecile was pulling him around the kitchen area to another corner of the room where a specially built table stood. It was ten by ten feet. Again built to allow the wheelchair patient to run his knees under it. It was piled with tools. Many in easy reach. Deerskins and hairy hides were stacked on a corner. Half-finished leather quirts, like Cecile's, with the end showing a beautiful turquoise stone.

A young man backed his wheelchair and turned it to meet them. Cecile released Grady's hand and went to the beautiful young man. She climbed on his lap and wrapped her arms about him. She kissed one spot after another until he playfully slapped her leg and said, "Cut it out!"

She laughed and ran her fingers through his gleaming black hair. It fell in soft waves onto his neck. She said, "You need a haircut."

He removed her hand from his hair and said, "Don't start on me."

She gave him a big hug and removed herself from his lap. She pulled a couple of stools out from under the table. She pushed one to Grady and sat on the other one.

She said, "Did you miss me?"

272

"All you do is nag on me when you're here, why would I miss you?' He reached for a rag amid tools and colorful rocks. He dipped the corner of the rag in a pan of water and scrubbed his hands. Some dust on his hands turned to mud. He scrubbed until his delicate hands and fingers were free of whatever had bothered him.

"Did you get my letters?" She took his hand and held it in her lap.

"You mean the one you wrote six months ago in San Diego?"

"Was it that long ago? I guess it was. It seems like it was forever. I was so homesick, and I missed my baby brother."

He turned his hand over and held one of hers. He petted it with his other hand and said, "Are you going to tell me who this person is? You've lost your manners." He looked at Grady and smiled.

"I'll tell you who he is if you promise not to scold me." She pouted a little.

"If you deserve to be scolded, I will do so. No promises. What have you done now?"

"Just exactly what I set out to do. I bought the Herefords. I told you that in my letters."

"That was about all you told me. Do you have any idea how worried I've been?" His eyes teared up, and Grady thought, the young fake—he really loves his sister.

Cecile reached over and brushed a tear away. She said, "I told you I was waiting for my trail driver to arrive. Well, this is my trail driver, Joe Bob Grady. Grady, this is my brother Ramone."

Grady smiled and said, "She's told me a little about you, and I've seen the incredible silver and turquoise items you made. You are very talented." He held out his hand and said, "I'm pleased to meet you,"

Ramone took his hand. They shook, and Ramone said, "Thank you for getting her home safe. I guess you've had plenty of time to find out what a pain she can be."

Grady ducked his head, grinned, and said, "I've met that Cecile." He stood and said, "I'll leave you two to catch up. I have a bull I'd like to check on. Do I just go back the way we came?"

Cecile answered, "Yes, or take that door over there. It goes outside and you can walk around. I'll see you at lunch."

Stepping out the door he saw the pasture where the Herefords were settling in. There was a nice covered porch where Ramone could sit and watch the cattle. A brick path took him to the trellis-covered backyard. From there he walked to the stables. He passed the risers. No sense in stirring up the black devil.

Inside the stable he studied the layout. There was a large tack room. He started to walk on, but a saddle caught his eye. It was his saddle. He hadn't been surprised their horses had been saddled and waiting for them this morning. If he thought about it at all, he figured Jalo had saddled them as he had on the trail. He saw his saddle was beside Cecile's. They were becoming a couple.

There was an office where pictures of Arabian horses and Toro black bulls hung on the walls. Awards and ribbons on shelves. Desks and more wooden file cabinets, and there was a cot. Probably for whoever sat up with a sick animal or a baby delivery.

He didn't walk the west wing of the stables, as it would take him to the iron gate that opened to Diablo's corral. No sense in antagonizing the bull.

A couple of the stalls down that hall had horses, their heads hanging over the stall gates watching him. Expecting food or treats. All the other stalls were empty. Grady figured no one wanted to upset Diablo. All the stalls down the east wing had horses in them. Most were hanging their heads out watching him.

Grady was impressed. There were twelve stalls in both the west wing and the east wing. The stalls faced each other and were separated by a ten-foot hall. Twenty-four stalls in all.

Next to the office was a feed room adequately stocked with grains, medications, grooming supplies, and shavings for the stalls.

He walked on to the east gate, to the enclosure Deadly and Trumpeter were in. Deadly was waiting for him. Trumpeter stood beside him. Both waited patiently for him to reach them. He opened the gate, entered, and closed it behind him. He walked to the enclosure fencing. It wasn't adobe like Diablo's. It was sturdy and painted white, with an iron railing. He climbed up and seated himself on the top rail.

Deadly followed and nudged Grady's leg with his muzzle. The enormous horn spread prevented him from swinging his head, as there was discomfort when the horns hit the iron rails, so he stood still and occasionally nudged Grady's knees. Grady occasionally scratched Deadly while he sat on the fence rail deep in thought. He had left Cecile to explain their relationship to Ramone. There was nothing to be gained by all three being embarrassed if there was a negative reaction.

Deadly nudged again and brought Grady's thoughts back to his faithful friend. Grady reached over to the large bull's head, inches from his knees, and once again scratched the hard area between the two long horns. He moved down the face between the bull's eyes, scratching as he went. Deadly closed his eyes and enjoyed a good scratching in areas he couldn't reach himself. Around the heavy cheeks, back up the head, and around the ears.

Grady talked as he scratched. "Well, old buddy, How do you like these digs? Pretty classy, huh? I fully understand if you're feeling a little out of place. I'm feeling a lot out of place."

He took a biscuit out of his shirt pocket and held his hand out with the biscuit on it. Deadly's talented tongue swept the biscuit into his mouth. Grady always carried two biscuits for Deadly. He held the second one out to the bull and watched while he swept another biscuit expertly into his mouth. Deadly remained where he was but closed his eyes and dozed while Grady spoke his thoughts out loud. For many years on many trail drives, Grady had talked out bad times and good times with Deadly patiently listening.

Occasionally the big bull nudged Grady's knee with his nose and continued to doze.

Grady continued to ramble on. "I feel like I'm in over my head. Which reminds me, I don't have a headache today. Imagine that! You would think meeting all these people and not knowing what to do with myself would have brought on a humdinger. Only thing I figure is reaching our destination and putting our girl on safe ground has taken a load off. There's got to be a connection."

Deadly raised his head, opened his eyes, and smelled the air. He saw something behind Grady. Grady turned to see Cecile cutting across the yard toward him. He smiled as she climbed on the fence and joined him.

She spoke, "I thought I'd find you here. How are these old scalawags?" She reached over and scrubbed Deadly between the eyes. He blinked, closed his eyes, and continued to doze.

Grady put his arm around her and said, "I think he likes it here. How did it go with Ramone?"

"I think it staggered him. I had to tell him about most of the drive. After I relayed all the dangerous events, he gained some respect for my trail boss. I told him we were getting wed."

Cecile scanned the herd, out beyond Deadly, "You should have seen his face. Poor baby. Especially when I told him I wanted the wedding Christmas day. He argued with me. I told him, with the country unsettled with talk of war and the Indians on the rampage, our future is unsure. I am sure about you, and I don't want to waste time getting our life started. He's kind of a recluse, I guess you noticed. He works in that room. I don't believe he reads the newspapers we pick up in San Antonio. I don't think he even knows of all the conflicts going on now.

Grady asked, "How did you leave it with him?"

"I think he realizes I met a man I wanted in my life. I'm not a naive young girl. I'm old in the eyes of Mexican marriages. He knew I would take this step someday. I just had to convince him that I was happy. He said to tell you he would join us at supper tonight."

"Maria has lunch ready. Let's go eat and this afternoon we can spend some time in the office. I have strict orders from Lou, for both of us to rest before supper."

Lunch was a quick meal of soup and biscuits. Grady was realizing he was a guest now but would soon marry into this atmosphere. Cecile was a woman he cared for. He needed to learn quickly his part if he expected to be useful or even needed. Having always been in charge of his own world, this world was not going to be easy, as it was already highly efficient.

He was always observing and analyzing Cecile's surroundings. He felt great relief when just he and Cecile entered and closed the door to the office.

She took his hand and pulled him to the sofa in front of the fire. She said, "I had forgotten how suffocating it could be with all the activities and constant attention from all the people involved. It must be overwhelming for you."

Grady laid his head back on the sofa and said, "Overwhelmed! So that's what I've been feeling. I haven't had time to develop a headache. Do you suppose I'll have to stay 'overwhelmed' to be free of the headaches?"

He pulled her to him and kissed her. She kissed him back and then settled against him and answered, "I don't think so, it's probably relief at having my ridiculous Hereford cattle drive completed."

He chuckled and said, "That is certainly a relief. I've been wondering what I was going to do next. I feel at loose ends. I expected to have some difficulty just retiring from the drives. You have got to realize a marriage is also going to change the dynamics around here for both of us. Maybe we can spend whatever time we do get alone discussing it."

"You're right. I realize you had planned on retiring and developing your own cattle ranch. You still need to do that. There is no reason why we can't have two ranches."

He hugged her and said, "Now who's the ambitious one? If you are in the financial straits you say you're in, we don't need the time and expense of developing another ranch."

She turned, looked at him, and said, "Maybe not, but I believe we both have an emotional need for that ranch. It's a longtime dream of yours. For me, a need to escape the guilt I would have if you gave up your dreams to aid me with mine."

It was no wonder he loved this woman. She was not just a beautiful woman, she was a beautiful human being.

Their lips met. The kiss was soft and full of promise. When she pulled away she said, "We must make plans. I have a secret I will share with you. Have you noticed no one has interrupted us? This was my father's sanctuary. I didn't know it then, but I was the only one allowed in when he was working. I had to sit very quiet and read a book on the sofa until he spoke to me.

"After my father died, I was overwhelmed with serious new responsibilities, much like you must be now. My father hired an older woman as a schoolteacher for the community. She was a great teacher, and one or two days a week after classes, she worked in the office for my father. Most of the time by herself. I was banned from the office on those days, and often my father spent that time with Ramone and me. It was always quality time. I later learned she kept the books for him.

"It wasn't until after he died that I realized what a help she had been. She spent many afternoons teaching me the mechanics of running this ranch and the necessity of keeping good books. She is elderly now. To help me be able to leave the ranch, she offered to continue the job until I returned, and then she wanted to retire. Which means not only that our first job will be to hire a bookkeeper, who can also teach the children.."

Cecile saw the confused look on Grady's face, and she said, "I'm doing it again. I see the lost look on your face. The short of it is this office is a sanctuary. You and I will be the main occupants, but the rules apply to both of us. If the door is closed, you must knock to be offered or refused entrance.

"If the door is open, people may greet you, chat, or do necessary jobs such as tend the fire. If the door is closed, no one is to bother you, except in an emergency. If you need to order something from the kitchen, there is a pull cord by the door that rings a bell in the kitchen. Someone is usually there. If you need to speak to an individual, that person will relay your message. If no one answers you, you're on your own. This is our sanctuary. When you get overwhelmed, retreat here. If I can't find you, I'll look for you here, and I will knock."

Grady grinned. "One question. How does the bell ring in the kitchen?"

Cecile laughed and said, "Most of the hacienda has a flat roof except over the entry hall that goes through from the front doors to the back door. The walls are higher on both sides of that wide hall. My father had the ceiling lowered a few feet over the hall so he could run a rope to the kitchen. Fortunately both the office and the kitchen are on either side of that raised area. He really wanted a sanctuary."

Cecile was getting tired. He could see it in her face. It made him aware of his own fatigue. He kissed her and stood, pulled her up, and wrapped his arms about her. "Old Lou told you to rest after lunch."

She hugged him and answered, "We have to get a routine that allows us to rest every day. We can take our ride early and attend to other duties. Then we can meet with Agnes a couple of hours after lunch. We'll rest before supper each day. Sound OK?"

"Yes, ma'am." With arms around each other they traveled the long hall and separated at their doors.

Supper was an easy meal of chicken and dumplings. As Grady came to the table he realized there was a flurry of activity in the kitchen and all through the hacienda. Tomorrow was Thanksgiving! Turkeys were being stuffed, and the smell of apple pie drifted into the dining room where Cecile waited for him. She had informed Maria to plan on just her, Grady, and Ramone. She wanted Grady and Ramone to get to know each other.

She poured three wineglasses with a fragrant red wine. She said, "This comes from our own vines. A hobby of Fernando's." They talked and sipped while they waited for Ramone.

It wasn't long before he arrived.

A pretty young girl pushed his wheelchair into the dining room and left him to wheel himself to the table. She disappeared into the kitchen. Grady recognized her as the young woman, Gina. He had met her briefly the night before.

Ramone, using his hands and arm power, wheeled the chair and stopped beside Grady. He held out his hand and Grady shook it.

Ramone said, "I've been informed I'm to have a brother-in-law. When I was a youngster I always wanted a brother. Instead I had this brat of a sister. She beat me at everything, and she was smarter than me. I hope you can put up with her. Take some of her attention off of me."

He wheeled himself to Cecile, kissed her cheek, and settled himself at the head of the table. Cecile was to his right and Grady to his left.

Cecile was all smiles as she said, "Grady, don't believe him. He was the brat. Following me all the time, tattling on me, pulling my pigtails."

Grady, getting into the teasing, said, "Yes, I've met that side of your sister. She can be a brat, and she is smarter than me, also."

Ramone raised his wineglass and said, "Welcome, brother." Grady clinked their glasses.

Cecile said, "That's not fair. You two are ganging up on me."

Ramone raised his glass again and said, "Welcome to Hacienda de Ciela, Mr. Grady."

The three clinked glasses just as Gina came from the kitchen with a large bowl of chicken dumplings. Diego followed with a platter of sliced tomatoes and lettuce wedges.

Conversation was light as they ate. Occasionally Diego came in and removed items from the china cupboard and buffet. Cecile saw Grady watching the boy and said, "We will have Thanksgiving in the ballroom tomorrow. It's being cleaned and the table set.

"Our custom has always been to invite those who don't have family in the community to our table. Which also includes Fernando's family, as Maria's children are all helpers in the kitchen."

Ramone said, "I enjoyed all the gatherings when I was a child, but after I landed in this chair I dread big get-togethers. I usually have a plate sent to my studio."

Cecile laid her napkin beside her plate and said, "This is such a special Thanksgiving for me. Won't you please join us tomorrow?"

He looked at Grady and said, "Now she begs me. Usually she orders me. I think I'm going to like this married situation." He wheeled his chair back and prepared to turn and roll out.

Grady put his hand out and stopped him. "I'd like to visit you. I've always wanted a silver buckle, and I'd really like to watch you work—that is, if it doesn't bother you to have someone looking over your shoulder."

Ramone smiled and looked at Cecile while he answered. "I would be honored. It's best we make appointments. It's my way of getting back at my sister for the hours she got to spend with Father in the sanctuary. Now, I have my own sanctuary, and the same rules are applied. Tomorrow is our holiday. The next day at ten in the morning." They shook hands, and Gina came out of the kitchen and wheeled him away.

They began their daily routine with the scheduled horseback ride. Cecile told Grady their planned routine would go on hold for a couple of days until the holiday was over.

He understood as the morning moved on and frantic people hurried in and out of the hacienda. Some carried covered dishes and deposited them in the kitchen. Others were getting chores done early, animals fed and watered, so they could spend the afternoon with family.

Cecile and Grady retreated to the office out of the way. They sat relaxed in the leather chairs by the fire. They talked of many things past, present, and future. Remembered friends in Janos and wondered if any would be here for the wedding.

Diego was often confused as to who his boss was. His mother called on him to do any job she needed doing. Run here, run there. Miss Ceci was much nicer, asking him "please" and thanking him. Fernando, his own dad, gave him orders. Juan often gave him a list of things to do. His brother Jalo always made him angry, and right now he wanted to hit him, but Jalo hadn't given him time. He had given an order and was gone before Diego could punch him.

Diego had been cleaning and polishing the table and chairs in the ballroom. Mother's orders. Jalo stuck his head in the door and told him to feed the animals in the stable. That job was one of Jalo's chores! Jalo said their mother was sending him across the river to get some dishes and pies prepared for the table in the ballroom.

Jalo hadn't given him time to refuse the order. Diego ground his teeth. He had six chairs left to do. Rebelling, he finished the furniture before he went to the stables.

Feeding all the horses and the three bulls was not a quick job. Usually the shoveling and collecting the manure was part of the feeding routine. Well! It was not going to get done by him today. He began by throwing hay to Deadly and Trumpeter.

There were fourteen horses in the stalls. There were written directions on each stall door as to pounds of hay and portions of grain that each horse was to receive. There were scales in the feed room to accomplish this tedious job. That wasn't going to happen today either. He picked up a pitchfork and threw the hay over the stall door. Faster than putting it in the manger.

Diego was beginning to sweat from the hurried work. The hay being thrown from the pitchfork caused hay dust and little slivers of hay to catch in his sweat. It made him itch and he was uncomfortable. He was angry with Jalo and feeling guilty about doing a lousy job. Too bad! He was getting them fed.

He went to the feed room and got three ears of dried field corn. He went out of the stable to the stair riser and stepped up where he could see Diablo. He hollered, "Come and get it, Black Devil." He tossed the corn over the wall on the ground, jumped down, hurried back in the stables, and got a pitchfork full of hay. Using one hand to manage the pitchfork, he took the bolt off the gate to Diablo's iron corral. He swung the gate open and with two hands stepped inside and tossed the hay. Quickly he turned back to get out the gate and bolt it. As he turned to replace the bolt, he heard and saw the maddened black bull slam into the unfastened iron gate.

Both the gate and the bull hit Diego, sending him sprawling back onto the stable floor. The bull passed over him, cloven hooves landing on Diego's body and one hoof hitting his head.

Terrified and dazed, he couldn't breathe. Blood was running into his eyes. He struggled to get air into his lungs. Scared the bull would turn and come back at him, he rolled onto his hands and knees, gasping, wiping the blood from his eyes with his hand. He saw a bleary disaster in the making as Diablo charged the iron gate at the end of the east wing where the Hereford bull and the longhorn bull stood watching the maddened animal plow into the iron gate.

Diego was gasping, in spite of the pain from the damage Diablo had inflicted. He managed to crawl out the stable door to where the iron emergency bell hung on the outside wall. He could just barely reach the end of the chain that rang the bell. He jerked it back and forth, sending ragged clangs from the bell screaming over the landscape.

Deadly was bored. He was used to more freedom. Being penned up with Trumpeter, he was restricted to sleeping and eating. He was getting in the habit of standing in one place, the place where his friend Grady came to sit on the corral fence and give him his biscuits.

He had discovered he could watch all the activity coming from the road to the river, and he watched the comings and goings while chewing his cud. Even that got boring.

He moved his cud back in a cheek and turned to go and check on Trumpeter. The old bull was a slow eater and was still standing over what was left of their hay.

Diablo thundered into the gate. Trumpeter, surprised, turned toward the gate. He realized immediately there was another bull challenging him.

Diablo backed up, kicked dirt into the air, and charged the gate again. Trumpeter answered the black bull with a scream from his own lungs and pawed at the dirt.

Deadly had been at the far end of the corral but instantly leaped into motion. Trumpeter had answered the stranger's challenge. He hurried to put himself beside the old bull and watched the fury of Diablo battering the iron rails.

The chain on the gate was holding, but a post holding the gate was being pulled out of the ground. The post was loosening with each strike. The enraged black bull was ignoring the pain of ramming the iron gate.

Deadly moved toward the gate being destroyed and put himself between the gate and Trumpeter. His appearance was noted by Diablo. Instead of the small red bull he was challenging, he was now faced by a long-legged, powerful brush bull, with horns so long they could not be ignored.

Diablo let out another vicious roar and hit the gate. The post with the gate and the iron fence attached to it were leaning far over into the corral. It was low enough that Diablo could step over the rails. He snorted and moving his rear end back and forth studied the longhorn bull in front of him.

Deadly stood still, his head lowered. He waited for the next move of the black bull. His horns gleamed in the sunlight. The silver ornamental balls on the tips flashed when he moved his horns.

Neither big bull knew the strength of the other. As fierce as Diablo was, he had rarely fought anything but a matador in the ring. Butting heads with a wooden stump was not going to prepare him to challenge a Texas longhorn brush bull.

Deadly was a lead bull over thousands of cattle on trail drives. He had survived many such challenges over many years. He had also been disciplined to behave himself. He knew there were times when he had to ignore such challenges. The care of the cattle on those drives, including cows, steers, and bulls, was his job.

This challenger, Deadly figured, was one he should ignore. As long as the black bull stood on the other side of the gate, Deadly stood and watched the posturing and the gate coming down.

Trumpeter was ready to do battle. The Hereford bull was bred as a food animal, but bravery had not been bred out of him. He was ready to help Deadly and tried to move around to stand beside his friend.

Deadly just moved his rump to block Trumpeter. He swung his horns a little to discourage Trumpeter, who knew how much a blow from those long horns hurt. Trumpeter moved back just as Diablo stepped over the fallen rails and skirted around the longhorn to put himself in the middle of the corral.

From here he could make a forceful charge driving his curved horns forward into his target.

Deadly moved around Trumpeter and stood in front of him again. He continued to stand passive. He didn't return the challenge. He gave the irate challenger time to cool off. Didn't happen. Diablo pawed the ground and, while still screaming, charged.

Deadly held still until Diablo was ready to connect. Deadly stepped to one side, swinging his master horn. Diablo missed his target and continued straight. The horn Deadly swung hit Diablo on the bone that ran from Diablo's eyes to his nose. A loud crack was enough to suggest it was broken.

The clanging of the iron bell could barely be heard in the office where Cecile and Grady had closed the door to escape from the Thanksgiving activity. It took a moment for Cecile to recognize what she was hearing. She leaped to her feet and ran yelling, "Trouble, trouble."

Startled, Grady ran after her. She was screaming as she ran, "Trouble!" People were pouring out of the kitchen and from the east hall. Not stopping, she grabbed her whip off the rack by the back door. She didn't know what the emergency was, as the bell continued to peel, but it was the stable bell. She saw Diego frantically jerking the pull on the iron bell.

Grady saw Garcia and Paco run out of the bunkhouse. Farther down the river road Juan and Lou were coming.

When Cecile got close enough that Diego knew she was coming, he stopped tugging on the bell rope. Having recovered his breath, he yelled, "Diablo!" over and over while he pointed toward the east corral. The corral that the prized Hereford bull was in. Her heart felt like it was thudding in her chest. She was running as fast as she could and almost fell to her knees. No! No! No! No! Cecile screamed in her mind. This could not be happening! They had sacrificed so much to get the old bull here safely. Please, God, do not let this be happening! Cecile sent up a silent prayer as she ran toward the corral.

Grady heard Diego and instantly knew the problem. Diablo was loose and in the corral with Trumpeter. He continued to the stables, ran to the tack room and grabbed a lariat off the pegs and ran for the corral. He yelled to Garcia, "Get a rope. It's Diablo."

Diablo was more than enraged. He was in pain and determined to destroy the long-horned bull. This was Diablo's territory. He skidded to a halt, spun around, and lunged at Deadly. He was so close that Deadly barely had time to swing a horn and deflect the sharp forward thrust of Diablo's sharpened horns. One of the black horns cut a swath across Deadly's shoulder.

Diablo thundered to the center of the corral and turned to face his enemy. He was breathing heavily. With each exhale of breath, he sent angry screams.

He dug up the ground under himself and, with his horns, tossed dirt over his head. He leaped out, intent on another run at the longhorn bull.

A sharp pain shocked the already injured nose of Diablo. He came to an abrupt halt. He shook his head to shake off the pain. He saw Cecile, with the whip, on the iron fence rails.

Cecile drew in the whip and prepared to send out another strike. Diablo didn't hesitate. He lowered his head and charged her. She jumped backward off the fence and landed on her rump in the yard. Diablo hit the iron rails and tried to punish them by jerking his head, sending the hard horns clattering onto the rails. Hitting the rails hurt! He redirected his anger, backed up, turned, and charged Deadly. This time Deadly ran to meet him.

Deadly, like Diablo, had years of experience swinging and shadowboxing his horns to know how to successfully use them. However, Deadly's horns did not curve toward the front, so he didn't stand a chance in a head-on collision.

Diablo charged, head down, the sharp horns pointed straight at Deadly's chest. A few feet from collision, Deadly altered his path just enough for Diablo to pass on his right side. The black bull, his head lowered nearly to the ground, the sharp horns prepared for contact, was too late to readjust his path, when Deadly dodged away. Deadly expertly swung his long horn, with the silver ball tip, directly into the already injured face of the black bull.

Diablo went insane with rage and pain. He spun around, screamed, and charged Deadly. The long-legged bull easily avoided him. Next, Diablo turned and charged the old bull. He was hit with a severe snap of Cecile's whip. It struck his rump and slid down to wrap around his hind leg. It slowed him enough to give Deadly time to get between Trumpeter and Diablo.

Diablo wheeled around toward the direction of the whip. His spin was fast and powerful. With Cecile holding onto the now taut whip, the momentum jerked her over the rails and into the corral. Because Diablo was wary of being hit with the whip, he hesitated. Cecile was instantly on her feet, trying to untangle the whip, as the strap was firmly wrapped around her wrist. It clung to the bull's leg and slowly unwrapped, but not in time to draw back her arm and send it out again. Diablo charged.

Deadly was already in motion. No longer making the calculated and controlled movements to avoid Diablo, he leaped forward, lowered his head, and charged into the side of the black bull. Without any hindrance from his wide horns, he was able to slam into Diablo's side with all of his power. He hit hard and continued to shove. Diablo wheezed as the breath was driven from him.

Grady's rope settled over Diablo's head. Help was on its way! Deadly moved to get out of the way of more ropes he knew would come. A daily occurrence on a cattle drive. He moved over to stand beside Trumpeter and watched while lariats snaked out. Another around the black bull's neck by Garcia and one around his hind legs by Paco.

The lariats pulled tight. Garcia pulled hard toward the center of the corral, while Grady pulled hard to the fence. Paco's rope stretched, threatening to pull Diablo's hind legs out from under him and dump the bull on the ground.

With the lariats around his neck threatening to choke him, he still swung his head, and his horns would grab the rope and nearly pull it out of their hands. Juan added his strength to Grady's rope, and Lou helped Garcia.

Jalo had been returning in a small buggy, bringing back pies and casseroles for the Thanksgiving dinner. On his way back from the community, he heard the stable bell and turned the horse for the barn, encouraging a run, and pulled up by the east corral.

Grady yelled at him, "Unhook the horse. Go inside the stable and undo the chain on the gate. Hook the horse up and pull the gate and fence back up and brace it as best you can!" In minutes Jalo had the horse loosened and headed into the stable.

Diablo was not ready to give in. He was thrashing and trying to reach the men in the corral, holding his head. His strain on the lariat Grady and Juan controlled by the fence was taxing Grady's weakened condition and Juan's age.

Grady yelled at Lou to go through the fence and help them pull the bull to the fence so they could tie its head up to a rail. The three men gradually pulled the bull toward the fence. Garcia dropped his rope and climbed through the fence. Once he added his strength to the lariat, Grady and Juan were able to climb to the outside. The four men, each with one foot braced on the bottom rail, hand over hand, pulled the bull's head tight to the rail.

Diablo was trembling with rage. Paco's rope on his hind legs slipped off. It freed the bull up to add swinging his rear to the stomping and hooking the lariat around his head.

People were gathering from the hacienda and the community. A couple of the men helped secure the lariat. Grady sank to the ground and said, "That's not going to hold him for long. You saw what he did to that post by the gate? He'll have the entire corral down."

Juan sat down beside Grady and said, "Garcia, get me a nose chain." Garcia ran to do so.

Cecile had sunk to the ground, her whip coiled in her lap. She had been so scared, not for herself but for Trumpeter. As Garcia ran for the nose chain, she rose and went to Deadly. She wrapped her arms around his neck. She whispered into his ear, "Thank you, Deadly. Once again you are a hero. You are so very special."

Uncomfortable, he shifted his weight from one rear leg to the other but stayed until she turned him loose.

"Oh! Deadly," she exclaimed when she saw the deep tear in his shoulder muscle. Blood had run in a thin stream down to his knee.

Garcia returned with the nose chain. Juan stood up, took the chain, and climbed back through the rails and went to the black bull's head. He stood back where the sharp horns didn't reach and showed the bull the chain. Diablo's eyes walled. He tossed his head. It slammed the bruised head bone into an iron rail. Pain shattered his head and for a moment he was still. Juan snapped the ring into his nostrils.

Immediately a different Toro bull stood before them. All the anger went out of him. He shook his head, trying to lose both the head pain and the nose ring.

Grady stood and looked for Cecile. He saw her standing by Deadly. He climbed through the fence and went to her. As he got closer he saw the blood on Deadly. She looked up from inspecting the bull's wound and saw Grady. She wrapped her arms around his neck, and he pulled her to him. She was trembling. He held her tight until the trembling stopped.

He asked if she was all right. She nodded her head yes and said, "Deadly's hurt."

"Let's take a look." He released her and bent down to inspect the wound. It was deep enough to need a few stitches. He doubted Deadly would stand for that. They would have to wait until all this ruckus was over and take care of the wound later, after Deadly had calmed. He patted the bull on his neck, scratched the hard bone between the two horns, and said, "Good boy, Deadly. Glad you were on duty."

He looked over to see how they were doing with Diablo. His jaw dropped in amazement as he saw Juan removing the lariats from the bull's neck. When both were removed, Juan patted Diablo on the neck and said, "You're in deep trouble with me." Juan turned Diablo to lead him into the stable.

Diablo saw Deadly. He snorted and turned toward him. Juan gave a gentle snap to the chain. It put pressure on the nose ring and Diablo lowered his head and followed Juan through the stable. He was turned loose in his own corral, then the gate was closed and bolted.

Everyone stood around and discussed the close encounter. Gradually they all drifted back to what they were doing when the bell rang.

Cecile remembered Diego. She saw Fernando talking with Garcia and Paco. She called to him, "Have you seen Diego? I think he's hurt."

Fernando came to her. "Hurt? Where is he?"

"I saw him by the bell." She ran through the stable to the front opening and found the boy still slumped on the ground.

Grady and Fernando were right behind her.

Fernando started to raise the boy's head.

Grady said, "Wait, and don't move him until we know the damage. Let's see if he can open his eyes."

Fernando said, "Diego, son, can you open your eyes?"

Diego gasped, raised his head, and opened one eye. The other was swollen and turning blue. A wound on the side of his head had quit bleeding, but blood had run down his face and dried. He looked ghastly. Cecile drew in a deep breath. "Where's Lou?"

Grady went back into the stables and found Lou talking to Juan in the tack room. Juan was replacing the nose chain where it belonged. Grady told them Diego was injured, and they followed Grady back to where the boy lay slumped against the stable.

Lou spoke to the boy to let him know he was going to look him over. With gentle hands he explored the open cut on his head and the swollen lump under it. He asked Diego to move his head. Diego tried, but he began gasping for breath. Lou asked him where it hurt. Diego's arms were wrapped over his chest. He slowly lifted one and patted his chest. He tried to speak. "Can't breathe—hurts."

Lou gently moved his arms and with one finger carefully traced a few ribs. He said, "Two broke." He checked the boy's arms while he had them unwrapped. "A few bruises—the same with his legs. The bull left places all over the boy that will be sore, but I can't find any other breaks. I don't think there's any internal damage. Head is damaged enough to be a concussion. It will let us know for sure as the day goes on. Let's get him in the house so I can wrap the ribs."

Fernando, Lou, Garcia, and Paco carried the boy into the hacienda and laid him on a sofa in the formal living room.

Grady and Cecile followed them in. Grady held her hand and could feel she was still shaken. He spoke quietly to Juan, "When the boy is stable, tell Lou to join us in the office, please come with him." Juan nodded, and Grady walked Cecile to the office, closed the door, and went to one of the big chairs. He sat and pulled her onto his lap. Her whole body was shaking. She laid her head on his shoulder. Tears ran down her face, and weeping she said, "I was so scared."

Grady rubbed her arm from shoulder to elbow and back and said, "It's over. You're safe now."

She gulped, tried to control the trembles, and said, "Not me. Trumpeter. What if he had gotten to Trumpeter?"

He understood. Keeping Trumpeter safe had been a high priority on the cattle drive. He said, "He's all right. Deadly took care of him." He moved her over in the chair and slid out from under her. "I'm going to order us some coffee. I've got Juan and Lou coming to give us a report on Diego. After that I want you to take a bath and lie down until dinner."

She watched him walk to the rope pull. This was her Grady. The in-charge man she loved.

Gina answered the bell that rang in the kitchen. Grady requested coffee for four and took the other big chair by the fire. He laid his head back on the leather headrest. The headache was back. His body was weak from overexertion and fear. He didn't have the strength to hold Diablo. He had been the first to toss his lariat and was nearly pulled off his feet as the crazed bull hit the end of the lariat. When he first saw Cecile in the middle of that corral with that black devil charging her, he knew he wasn't close enough to save her. Fear had blinded him. Thank God Deadly was there!

Cecile watched Grady as he sat back in the chair. She realized that Grady was doing his best to be brave for her, but she could tell he had been scared.

She wasn't the only one who had been scared. She said, "Grady?"

He held up a hand and stopped her from continuing. He put the hand over his eyes. His voice was trembling as he spoke, "Do you realize if Deadly hadn't been there, you would be dead now? I was too far away. I watched that devil charging you. I wasn't close enough, I couldn't get there in time."

Grady rubbed his forehead, appearing to be gathering his thoughts for a moment before he continued. "I know how important your Herefords are for you to hang on to your ranch. But if you get yourself killed trying to protect them, then what's the point? Without you running this place, it will probably be sold off, piece by piece. Then what happens to the people in the community?"

He lowered his hand, sat forward in the chair, and looked her in the eyes. "I should turn you over my lap and paddle you."

Her eyes grew large, and her mouth dropped open.

Someone knocked on the door. Grady said, "Come in." Juan and Lou entered. They felt the tension in the room.

Grady pointed to the coffee. "Pour yourself a cup and have a seat." They filled their cups and sat on the couch.

Grady poured a cup, added cream and sugar, and handed it to Cecile. She took it and said a quiet thank-you.

He poured himself a cup, black, and sat back down. He looked at Juan and said, "Will you please tell me how a bull as angry as Diablo was, could turn into a pussycat when attached to a nose ring?" He noticed Juan's hands were shaking. The man was not young, and he had also seen his goddaughter nearly get killed. Grady took a sip of his coffee and set the cup on the side table. He sat back in the chair and tried to relax.

Juan drank some of his coffee and set the cup on the end table by him. "Senor, when a Toro bull calf is born, the aggression is born with them.

"You must realize he has to be handled at times. The day he was born, I attached the ring to his nose. The nose is very sensitive. Every day I work with him while he is small. It's early training, much like his own mother would do.

"While he is small and I can train him that there is pain when he disobeys. He is ground trained, trailer trained, and bathing and grooming trained.

"Remember, Senor, the Toro bulls are bred for the show ring. We have to be able to bathe and care for hooves. They must be trailered many miles and sometimes stalled in the trailer. Here on the ranch he has to be moved from stable to pasture. Sometimes we bring a cow to him for breeding, and sometimes we must go to the cow.

"When the nose ring and chain are attached, the pain of disobedience from his baby memory kicks in. Now that he is a mature bull, he fights to keep from being attached to the ring. We often have to throw several ropes on him and take him down. Today, for him, was a normal experience with one exception. Jalo typically takes care of Diablo and the animals in the stable. While he was on the trail with us, others had to do his job. It would seem Diablo was waiting for someone to slip up. Diablo is very smart. He knows there are other bulls in his territory. It has made him more aggressive and looking for ways to get at them. I wasn't even sure he would allow me to attach the nose ring."

They sat quiet for a while and Grady looked Juan in the eyes and said, "He nearly killed Cecile today. If that had happened, his aggressive days would be over." He turned to Lou. "How's the boy?"

"Mild concussion, two broken ribs, set and wrapped. He's in some pain."

"We're out of laudanum unless Miss Cecile has some?"

Cecile said, "Sorry, I don't, but someone in the community might. Fernando will handle that."

Grady turned back to Juan and Lou and said, "I guess the immediate concern is to get the corral gate repaired. Trumpeter can go in a stall. Leave Deadly out. He's not used to being stalled. He won't bother anyone unless they bother him. He will still spend most of his time near Trumpeter." He held out his hand and said, "Thanks for your help today and especially you, Juan. That took guts to control that bull." They shook hands, and the men headed for the door.

Cecile said, "I'm going to tell Maria to stall dinner a couple of hours. I'm going to take a bath and rest until then. Thanks again for all your help."

The two left and closed the door. Cecile walked to the pull and rang to the kitchen. She picked up the coffee cups and put them on the tray. It was Gina again that knocked on the door and stuck her head in. Cecile gave her the message for Maria to delay the Thanksgiving dinner. Gina picked up the tray and closed the door as she left.

Cecile turned to Grady and said, "Would you have really spanked my bottom?"

"I'd like to think I would, but I've yet to hit a woman. Cecile, if that bull had killed you today, there wouldn't be a bottom to paddle. There would be a dead bull. I just want you to promise me you won't take any risks like the one you did today. I couldn't handle it if you died, especially on my watch."

He pulled her into his arms and kissed the top of her head and said, "Let's go get that rest. I'll be ready for Thanksgiving dinner. I know what I'm thankful for. I have you alive and in my arms."

The smell of Thanksgiving dinner drifted down the hall from the kitchen. Neither Grady nor Cecile had napped. She looked at her pale face in her mirror. Rarely did she wear rouge on her cheeks and lips, but the reflection looking back at her from the mirror needed some color. She still had occasional body shakes. She had to pull herself together.

She had to get through this dinner. After that she could fall apart. She stood and studied herself in the mirror. She had chosen one of her better winter garments. One that had autumn flowers on a warm brown background. The dress would go well with the Thanksgiving garlands of colorful gourds and pumpkins that decorated the table.

She picked up her small perfume bottle and touched some on her wrist and behind her ears.

She closed the door behind her and knocked on Grady's door. He saw her standing there with a wary expression on her face. He smiled and said,

"You look wonderful." He stepped close. "You smell good enough to eat. Let's forget turkey and spend the rest of the afternoon under covers."

She giggled and said, "Behave yourself." She took his arm and pulled him down the hall. She said, "You look good enough to eat also."

He did look magnificent. He was wearing a slimline black suit. The cut and style had the modified look of a Spanish gentleman. The shirt, under the jacket, was a shiny cream satin. The only items he wore that showed he was a cowboy were his boots. Someone had used a black dye and hand rubbed them to a high gloss.

He recognized the hungry look in her eyes as she admired him. He was embarrassed. He said, "I'm uncomfortable wearing your father's clothes. I would have put mine on, but all I have is trail worn. I don't want you to be ashamed of me."

As they walked she laid her head against his shoulder and whispered, "I love you very much. Never would I ever be embarrassed by you. I'm sorry—I don't want you to be uncomfortable in the clothes I lay out for you. They are not my father's. He was as tall as you, but he was heavier.

"What you are wearing today were my grandfather's. When he died, my mother could not bear to destroy his things. I knew, the moment I saw you in San Diego, you reminded me of my grandfather. Lighter in hair color but built like him. Today you look so handsome."

They walked into the ballroom and all heads turned to them. Grady stood tall and escorted his lady to the side table that contained pitchers of lemonade, cold tea, and bottles of wine. He poured her a glass of wine and handed it to her. He bent and kissed her, and she smiled and went to where Diego sat. His head was bandaged, he had a frightened look on his face.

She said, "Are you all right?"

"Yes, ma'am, I'm so sorry about Diablo. I got careless and turned my back on him."

She smiled and said, "I guess you won't do that again? Besides, you were only half to blame. The stables are Jalo's job. What happened there?"

"He asked me to feed for him. He had to run an errand for Ma."

She could tell he was uncomfortable telling on his brother. She kissed his cheek and said, "I'm just glad it wasn't worse. He could have killed you."

She saw Grady talking with Juan and Lou. Latisha, Maria and Fernando's daughter, wheeled in a tea cart loaded with covered dishes. She watched as the girl emptied the dishes to the table where all the food but the turkey would be served as a buffet.

She stopped the girl as she turned the cart to return to the kitchen. She gave the girl a one-arm hug, careful not to spill her wine, and said, "Where have you been?"

Latisha was beautiful! Cecile was surprised at the change in Latisha. She had grown into a woman during the months Cecile was gone. She said, "You were a teenager, and now look at you. You are gorgeous!"

Latisha smiled, ducked her head, and said, "Miss Ceci, I wanted to come welcome you back, but Senora Angela had a baby the day you arrived. I have been taking care of her twin boys and helping her out."

"My goodness, Latisha, I've lost track of time. I forgot she was with child. Well, I'm proud of you, helping out. Try to sneak away sometime and we'll get caught up with each other."

As Latisha left, Ramone and Gina arrived. As before, she pushed him in the door, then left him and walked with Latisha toward the kitchen.

Ramone took over the job of wheeling himself to Cecile. He said, "What were you thinking?" He was frowning and she knew someone had told him about Diablo's escape.

"Please don't scold me. I'm so glad you're joining us for dinner. Thank you."

"Don't change the subject. I came down here to lambast you. I haven't decided to stay for dinner." He wheeled to the beverage table and half filled a large tea glass with red wine.

"Ramone, you'll get drunk! What are you doing?"

"I'm getting drunk! What does it look like!" He looked her in the eyes and swallowed several big mouthfuls. "Now! Tell me you were not in the pen of a maddened bull with that ridiculous whip of yours!"

"Who told on me? I didn't want you to worry. I promise, Ramone, it was just a bad accident. I admit I was being careless." She reached to take the glass away from him.

With one hand he turned the wheelchair away from her and nearly ran into Grady, who was standing watching the exchange between sister and brother.

"I'm only going to say this once, so you listen to me. I came very close to taking my pistol down there and putting a bullet in his head. I was so scared I was weak. That's the only thing that stopped me. I didn't have the strength to wheel this miserable piece of shit all that distance." He threw his glass at the wall and used both hands to beat on the arms of the wheelchair.

Cecile climbed on his lap and wrapped her arms around his head and shoulders. He grabbed her, and with closed eyes they soothed each other.

Grady knelt down before the wheelchair where he could address both of them. He said, "Well finally, I've met someone who thinks like I do. I'm with you little brother. There'd better not be a next time. Today was too close."

Latisha, hearing the glass hit the wall, appeared with two look-alike five-year-old boys and Impala. She gave them rags, and while she picked up glass the boys wiped up the wine. When finished, Impala went to Cecile and waited for her to sit up. Surprised when she saw him, she reached out and hugged him. "I'm so glad to see you! You just disappeared! I figured all the children in the community would be more fun than hanging out with me, but I miss you."

"I missed you too, Miss Ceci." He had picked up on the nickname all the community called her by.

She took his hand and said, "This is my brother Ramone. Ramone, this is Impala." She was surprised to see Impala grin and duck his head.

Ramone said, "We've already met. Impala wants to learn to be a silver-smith, and he's working for me when I need someone to wheel me around the ranch."

Grady stuck his hand out and shook Impala's hand and then held his hand out to Ramone and shook his. He said, "I'm proud of you, Pala. I admire you, Mr. McNamara."

Latisha, finished with the cleanup, said, "Dinner's ready." Then she turned to Fernando and said, "Papa, Mom wants you to bring Juan and get the turkeys."

When they returned with two golden-browned turkeys, they set one down in front of each of their table settings. Juan sat at the head of the table at one end. Fernando sat to his right. They would be in charge of carving the turkeys. Ramone wheeled himself to the head of the table at the other end. As before, Cecile sat to his right, Grady to his left.

When Maria, Latisha, and Gina joined them, Juan said, "Let's pray, please bow your heads." He gave a blessing for the meal and a special thanks for the Lord watching over the loved ones. He ended the prayer with, "Please continue to protect us. Amen."

A collective amen was expressed. As Juan and Fernando carved the turkeys, Latisha helped the three young boys fill their plates at the buffet table and put them at a table set just for them, where they could cut up and enjoy being boys.

Grady was surprised when more people arrived. Two women came from the kitchen. Garcia, Paco, and Jalo had been waiting in the backyard arbor with a couple of older gentlemen.

The carved turkeys were set on the buffet. Soon everyone filled their plates and were seated. The stressful event of the day was put aside.

Ramone was a gracious host, and after his explosive entrance he became animated, talking with everyone, singling some out and asking their opinion on current events, especially the talk of civil war and the newly elected Republican, Abraham Lincoln, and his defeat of Breckenridge, Douglas, and Bell. Conversation also included the talk of some states seceding from the Union and speculation about President Lincoln's upcoming inauguration on March 4, 1861.

It was a beautiful meal and a wonderful time. Grady started to relax and enjoyed getting to know Cecile's "extended family."

Everyone pulled away from the table with stuffed bellies, feeling very content. After the meal many of the adults gathered by a large fireplace, back in the large living area, and spent the rest of the winter day visiting.

Grady and Cecile were the first to retire, before even Ramone, who was still enjoying catching up on news and debating politics.

After Thanksgiving holidays, the ballroom's decorations were packed up and stored.

As the Thanksgiving boxes were carried out, Christmas boxes were carried in. Daily activity of some kind was conducted in the ballroom. The hacienda's halls were decorated. Wreaths appeared on doors.

Cecile and Grady retreated to the office with Agnes. She came with a box of ledgers. They ordered coffee, and Agnes started with the ledger that began the month that Cecile left on the Butterfield Coach out of San Antonio to San Diego.

Grady sat quietly and listened as Agnes talked cash in, cash out, supplies ordered, produce sold. Crops from orchards, vineyards, fields, and winter gardens, both sold or canned for winter use.

He sat, lost, trying to understand and trying to keep up. He finally realized Hacienda de Ciela was not just a cattle ranch. It was also a successful farming community.

Gradually he began to draw from his years working with his father. Crops of corn and wheat raised from seed, planting, harvesting, and sold. The care and use of farm animals. His mother canning garden produce for winter use.

He realized he needed to learn more about the physical use of the ranch. He asked Juan to ride out with him and teach him the many commercial activities of the ranch and their location.

He was surprised at the established size and selection of the fruit orchard. Grapefruits, oranges, limes. Along the valleys near the river were acres of pecan trees. There were grape vineyards, blackberry and boysenberry gardens. Crops were endless. Beans, peanuts, soybeans. Potatoes, onions, sweet-potato fields. Summer produce, watermelons, cantaloupes, honeydew, peppers, and cucumbers.

In his amazement and surprise, as he viewed each endeavor, he had to keep reminding himself this ranch was over 150 years old. The families living on it were descendants of the original people brought with Cecile's ancestors. Year after year they learned from their parents, and they improved upon the knowledge handed down for generations.

There were many small backyard gardens that produced table vegetables, carrots, cabbage, squash, spinach, and much more.

Besides cattle and horses, there were goats, hogs, milking cows, and chickens that also made commercial sales. The chicken houses raised fryers, broilers, and eggs.

As the days passed and Agnes patiently taught Cecile the job of keeping the ledgers, with his head looking over their shoulders and listening, Grady began to get an understanding of the workings of the community and their very large participation in supporting the ranch.

He also began to understand Cecile's dream and determination to strengthen the cattle ranching with a better beef animal. Texas was growing, and now was the time to begin developing cattle to feed that growth.

He had paid attention to the brush cattle that he observed all over the ranch. Cecile had sold some, but to be able to make room for her new beef cattle, there were plenty more that needed to be rounded up and moved out. He had some direction. With a war brewing, and with his contacts, he could gather a herd to drive to market. Confederate or Union. So much for retiring.

After several weeks, Agnes closed the last ledger and hugged Cecile and Grady. She wished them well. Her bags were packed and she left on the community wagon headed to San Antonio with Christmas produce.

As Cecile and Grady said their good-byes to Agnes, Grady got to actually see one of the ranches produce wagons. It had cages built on it to hold chickens, turkeys, and rabbits. There were sacks of potatoes, sweet potatoes, peanuts, onions, pumpkins, and dry beans and jars of shelled pecans packed in freight boxes. All a holiday treat. Money coming in to be entered into the ledgers made Grady remember the tally books he had kept for ranchers he had worked for.

The activity in the ballroom did not slow down. A beautiful sixteen-foot tree stood in one corner of the room. Boxes of ornaments sat waiting to be hung. There were two weeks until Christmas Eve. It was children's night in the ballroom.

Fernando made his famous Mexican chili, and Lou made pans of cornbread. After supper many hands hung paper garlands, colored balls, and candy canes. Popcorn garland was strung and hung. The Spanish angel was placed on the top of the tree. The children laughed and clapped.

Each child went home that night with a candy cane.

There was one young black boy in the midst of Mexican children. Impala had helped the twin boys hang decorations. He had become just another community child. He belonged, accepted by all the children.

Grady, Cecile, and some of the parents and elderly had shared a glass of wine and watched the children decorate the tree.

As he watched the children, Grady thought of all the Christmases he had spent alone after his family died. He was overwhelmed, not just by this ceremony in the ballroom, but also, by how the hacienda had been transformed. Doors, halls, and bedrooms shared holiday decorations and spirit.

There was a constant odor of baked goods. Cookies, candy, pies, cakes, and many varieties of breads. These odors drifted through the casa's halls.

As Grady watched the children decorate the tree, he realized how quickly he had gone from having no one to being a member of many families. From now on he would be sharing the responsibility of these children and their families. Although it felt odd after years of being alone, he welcomed it and realized this feeling of family and responsibility was exactly what he had been missing.

He shook off those thoughts and turned his eyes to a corner of the large room and saw what looked like an arbor. It was white and had satin ribbons woven in and out of the wooden trellis. He asked Cecile what it was. She told him it was part of the wedding decorations.

After the children were sent home to bed, some of the adults grabbed bowls and finished the chili and corn bread.

Cecile asked Maria to please send some warm cider drinks to the office for her and Grady.

They were both exhausted. These days had been busy, both physically and mentally.

Cecile coughed a little. She took a sip of the cider and said, "Where did that cough come from? I really did forget the coughing. I've been so busy stuffing my head with those ledgers that I haven't coughed for days. In fact I feel pretty good. I do get tired but I don't feel weak and sick anymore. How are you feeling?"

He smiled. "I'm tired tonight, but like you, I'm not headachy and sick with it. I feel more like the old me. Our morning horseback rides and the trips with Juan to learn the ranch workings have helped. I'm glad to be back in the saddle again."

"Yes," she said, "I like being able to climb on a horse again. We've been tied down with Agnes and the ledgers, and we haven't had much time together. I've missed you."

He kissed her and said, "You're right. We haven't had much time alone together. I've missed our long talks. Seeing that wedding arbor tonight made me realize our wedding has kind of taken a backseat. There are probably things I ought to be doing. Don't we need to make plans?"

She took a swallow of her cider. It was cooling, so she emptied the mug and set it on the side table. She said, "You're right. I've totally set aside thoughts of my wedding dress. One of the ladies in the community is making it. I guess she would have sent someone to get me if she was ready for a fitting."

Grady said, "Do you have a minister in that bunch?"

Cecile sat up. "Didn't I tell you? It seems like months since we came through Piedras Negras. I requested the justice of the peace, Mr. Thomas, visit me at our camp. I persuaded him to spend the Christmas holidays with us. He gave me a wedding certificate. We have to fill it out, and he will sign it after the ceremony. We can take it into San Antonio to register it."

"Does he conduct the ceremony? I've never been married before but I have always presumed the ceremony was conducted by a minister or some connection to a church."

Cecile sat back and picked up his hand and said, "We've run into this before. Sometimes we have someone representing the church. But our congregation is small, and they move on. Right now Fernando holds gatherings, and they study with him. We learned that a judge, mayor, or justice of the peace may perform civil marriages. All states require a marriage license issued by a local civil authority, which Mr. Thomas is, for Texas. We may, if we choose, have a religious ceremony, but we still have to obtain a marriage license issued by a civil authority."

Grady said, "I'm beginning to understand how smart you are. A small community is like a small town. You have the legalities, and the problem solving, of all these people. Is this Mr. Thomas a personal friend? How did you talk him into coming over Christmas? Doesn't he have a family?"

She giggled, "I'll tell you if you promise not to scold me."

"Cecile, what have you done now?" He studied her face.

"You have to promise not to scold me."

He took her hands and said, "Cecile, what have you done?"

"Well, he's not married. He has married children, but they live in San Antonio. I had to bribe him." She hesitated.

Grady said, "Cecile, give!"

"I gave him a two-year-old gelding." She held her breath.

He said, "That sounds a little much for a wedding service."

She ducked her head and laughed. "It was worth it to me. How often does a girl get married to a Texas cowboy? Besides, I'm getting overbred with Arabian stud colts."

He exploded. "You gave him an Arabian? Have you lost your mind?"

She snuggled back into his arms and said, "I knew you would have a fit. I promise, after we're married I won't do anything until I talk it over with you."

Little Bear's wagon caravan was small but well guarded. Candy led out with her black geldings pulling Trumpeter's wagon full of alcoholic beverages and tools they might need to access easily.

Lance followed with a four-horse team, pulling Grady's supply wagon loaded with all of Candy's possessions. Della rode shotgun.

Ace and Wyvon followed with Grady's grub wagon, filled with all of Candy's food supplies, along with beef and ham donated by Carmella.

Carmella followed in her small fancy family buggy with Glancy, who was being very serious about his job of being on lookout with his shotgun in hand.

Carmella knew she had two wagons to bring back, so she had provided horses for Candy's supply wagon and Grady's grub wagon. She wanted strength in weapons in case of an Indian raid. She brought six of her young ranch hands and plenty of ammunition.

Two young men stayed in the rear to watch the back trail. Four spread out, two on each side of the wagons, and they rode with rifles ready.

Two days out Bear spotted several Indians seated on horses on a rise to the north of them. He stopped Candy and called one of Carmella's men to him. He said, "Go back and tell each one not to pick up a weapon. Tell Ace not to touch his rifle unless I run into trouble. You tell him there's to be no Indian killing today."

Bear rode out to meet the Indians waiting for him. As he drew close he raised his hand in greeting.

The Indian wearing the buffalo robe answered with a palm raised and in Apache said, "I know you, Bear Man. I know the woman that drives the wagon. She is not your woman."

Bear, remembering he had told Cochise that Cecile was his woman for her protection, answered in Apache, "We had to leave our wagons in the canyon. I sent my woman to drive the red cows to the big water. She is to wait there for me. We salute you, Cochise, and thank you for allowing us to pass through your hunting grounds. The woman driving the wagon is also moving out of Cochise territory."

Cochise said, "She is the woman that fed my people. She is wise. She respects our land and our ways. I saw this small wagon train and thought I might raid it. I counted the men who carry guns. I have a small band with me, and when I see you, Bear Man, leading this little wagon train, I think maybe the woman will share some more food. If so, I will not have to raid your wagons."

Bear smiled. He saw the twinkle in the Indian's eyes. "Cochise is a wise chief. I will go parlay with the woman, and maybe we can avoid a raid by Cochise's skilled warriors."

Bear stopped by Candy's wagon and told her the Indian's request.

"I don't think sharing the alcohol is wise. It might cause someone else to get raided. We packed two fifty-pound sacks of pinto beans. We'll give one to them. I don't think we'll be doing any cake baking, so give them the can of sugar. We'll leave enough sugar for coffee. There's a sack of cornmeal. We'll get by with biscuits." She saw the look on Bear's face and said, "Oh, all right. You stay here with the team. I'll go back to the grub wagon and find things." She climbed off the wagon and onto Bear's horse.

He said, "Be sure Ace doesn't have Cochise in his rifle sights."

Candy laughed as she rode back to the grub wagon. It had taken her a moment to realize that it would demean Bear in Cochise's eyes if Bear were to gather the food, as that was squaws' work.

Her laugh died when she saw Ace sitting with his rifle across his lap. She handed him the horse's reins and said, "Hold this and keep your hands off that rifle."

303

Candy, knowing Wyvon's hatred and fear of the Indians, said, "Wyvon, I need you to stay calm right now. They only want some food, and we are all goin' to get out of this alive. I know you're good with a gun, but please just help me and keep your hand away from your holster right now."

Wyvon was shaking but listened to Candy. She gave her a small nod and climbed down from the wagon.

With Wyvon's help she rummaged around until she had the supplies that she wanted. She put them in two gunnysacks and tied them together. They hoisted them over the horse, behind the saddle, and tied them with the leather saddle ties to hold them. She returned to Bear.

After she got off the horse, she waved to the bunch of Indians. Cochise raised his hand.

Bear rode back and handed the sacks to one of the warriors before turning his attention to Cochise. Bear said, "I realize you weren't on a raid. No war paint. What's going on, Chief?"

Cochise said, "I think there is going to be bad trouble with the white men who dig up Mother Earth for her yellow rocks. These men are in Mangas's homeland. Land he loves. They are tearing up the hills. He wants to go to the Pinos Altos area and ask them to move away. We went to tell Mangas this could bring trouble. I don't think he will listen to me."

Bear turned his horse and said, "Well, he should. That could be very bad trouble."

Bear's little wagon train began to get into a routine. He kept his paint saddled and spent most of his time scouting ahead. He often tied his horse to Candy's wagon and spelled her. She rode his horse or just sat next to him, and they talked.

Bear called it her "beer wagon."

They didn't see any more Indians. Bear was bored, really bored! Driving cattle, he had cows to chase and return to the herd. Other cowboys to laugh and joke with. Changes of remuda horses. Hunts for meat to feed the crew. Encounters with deer and wild brush cattle. And he missed Grady.

He had traveled with Grady for four years. He considered the man his best friend and his boss. He was beginning to realize it was not as much fun being a wagon master as it was being a cowboy. However, Grady didn't have to deal with women. Miss McNamara had been a first. He loved Candace Murray, but at times she made him loco.

They had two weeks behind them. There were, at best, two more weeks to go to reach the river.

The right rear wheel on the supply wagon developed a squeal.

He had inspected it, even crawled under and checked the inside rims. While he was under the wagon, he looked to see if there was a spare wheel attached to the underside of the wagon floor.

There was! Bear was relieved. Grady, from his time working with Dizzy, had copied his way of storing items that m ight be needed in a hurry by attaching them to the underside of the wagon bed. There were spaces for the camp grill, shovels, hoes, and saws. Small tool drawer and hooks for water barrels and large skillets. All the items except the wheel had been removed when they left Grady's wagons in the canyon. It had been too much a job to undo the wheel then.

Bear had forgotten to check on the wheel after rescuing the wagons. It would have been difficult for someone to steal the big wagon, but it wouldn't have surprised him if the wheel had been stolen. Bear had tasked Lance with replacing all the underneath work tools but forgot all about making sure the wheel was in place before they left Janos.

Bear mentally cussed himself for forgetting something so important. It could have been a serious error. Although he couldn't respect Grady more than he already did, it made him realize the huge responsibility that weighed on Grady's shoulders as head trail boss.

Bear hoped they wouldn't need it, but the wheel kept squealing and getting louder. The noise kept up for three days, then it began to wobble.

Bear called an immediate halt. They all stood around and looked at the wheel. A shiver ran up Bear's back. The wheel was threatening to collapse. No way would they be able to lift the heavy wagon up to replace the wheel. Worse yet, if it collapsed, heavy iron household items could crush anyone working underneath the wagon.

He explained this to Lance and Ace. Carmella's ranch hands just stood around and shook their heads. Bear said, "We've got to get something under there to keep that wagon up in the air. We can't remove the wheel until we secure the wagon"

They were getting further away from the mountains and the pine trees. They were entering the subtropical dry lands of Mexico and Texas. The vegetation included shrubs, cactus, weeds, and grasses.

When the wheel first started to protest, Bear began to worry and form solutions. The supply wagon was fifteen feet long and ran on four wheels. The wagon always carried a heavy load, but the iron stoves and bathtub had been loaded last directly over the axle. Good and bad.

Grady always had his wagon axles reinforced with iron. They probably wouldn't bend, but could drop that side of the rear wagon. He hated the thought of having to unload the wagon to fix it. There was no way they could release the wheel without bracing the wagon from underneath.

With the squealing wheel getting steadily worse, he had frantically been scouting ahead for a hardwood tree. They didn't have any lumber with them. They would have to make do. He preferred an oak. A live oak or a post oak. Mesquite was increasing, and so were cactus, cat's-claw, several species of brush, and an occasional dwarf oak.

Bear finally thought he spotted a good-size oak way ahead of them. As he got closer, he saw it was twin oaks He kicked up his paint and rode to inspect them. They weren't as thick as he would have liked, but they would have to do.

He hoped the wheel would hang in until they reached the oaks. The wobble finally stopped the wagon train. He couldn't risk driving the wagon to the trees. He would have to bring the trees to the wagon.

He put Lance to carefully unbolting the wheel attached to the underneath of the wagon bed. He put Ace to setting up camp and caring for the horses. He said, "We need Candy's geldings to pull the logs in, so don't undress them. When Lance finishes releasing the new wheel, have him bring the team to me. Have Wyvon work on supper."

With the tree saw, he hurried his horse back to the twins. It wasn't long sawing the hardwood before he removed his jacket and shirt. Soon he was glistening with perspiration.

Candy walked with Lance, each leading a black gelding. Long before they reached Bear, she saw his body shining with sweat. It brought back memories.

When she saw him in the mountain canyon for the first time, he had removed his shirt and was cutting firewood. That was three months ago or longer. She had thought him handsome then. Watching him now, he was not only handsome but also a special person. She had fallen in love with him in that canyon. A moment of fear shook her. It wouldn't be long until they reached Cecile's ranch. Bear would be influenced by his friend and boss. She hadn't made a decision as to where she was headed with all her possessions. She wasn't ready to give up this beautiful man.

Bear measured the distance from the bottom of the axle to the ground and mentally added another foot. He cut four logs, and just to be safe he had added a foot and a half to each.

Back at the supply wagon, he explained what he had in mind. Directly under the axle close to the back side of the wheel, they were going to dig a hole a foot and a half deep. They would slide a log into it and straighten it up under the axle. They might have to adjust the hole. Dig deeper, or add to it, to make it work. They were going to put another one under the axle close to the first one on the back side of the wheel. Right against them, between the two logs under the axle, they would put one close between the two to brace the ones under the axle, hoping to hold make them secure. Can't have the axle slip off the logs.

Bear continued explaining his idea. "When the logs are set, we'll pack the dirt around them. We just have the one shovel so we'll take turns digging the holes. When not on the shovel, the rest of us will rock hunt. That includes the women. Carmella, please put your ranch hands to work."

He used the shovel first and struggled to dig under the wagon. The long handle of the shovel prevented use under the wagon bed. Tired and pissed, he got the ax and chopped it in half.

As Bear dug, he prayed to his spirit father to help make this work. The logs wouldn't have to hold the wagon up but a few seconds, as he removed the old wheel and slid the new one on. He expected some drop as the weight of the loaded wagon settled on the log brace.

It would probably sink the wheel itself into the dirt a bit, and he would have to dig the old wheel out a little to remove it and install the new one. Please, log brace, don't collapse. He almost said it out loud. He knew the danger and intended to be the one switching the wheels. He would be prepared to move quickly if push came to shove and the stove did topple out of the wagon.

They struggled to stand the first log up in Bear's hole. They couldn't stand the log upright without digging a slanted hole in the side of Bear's hole. All three men were sweating profusely before they got the log upright under the axle. Bear threw some small rocks into the hole and tamped them down tight. Ace dug the hole next to it, struggling to be careful not to hit or jostle the log already placed or get so close to the existing hole that he caved it in.

Bear watched Ace's predicament and called a halt. This wasn't going to work. They were going to have to dig a large hole, put all the logs in, wrap them all together with baling wire, and then wedge them with rocks and packed dirt, and stack more rocks around the outside of the logs.

Wyvon hated to interrupt, but the beans were warm and the biscuits done. Bear needed a breather, and he knew his helpers were about to collapse. They grabbed tins, dished up, and joined the ranch hands who had already started to eat.

Bear finished eating and went to check the rock pile. It was adequate, but to be safe, Bear asked the ranch hands to find two or three big rocks that two men working together could roll to the wagon.

With full bellies, and renewed energy, it didn't take long to get the large hole dug.

Lying on their backs and sides was a killer, but they managed to get the logs in the larger hole. When they were placed under the axle, where they wanted it, Bear wrapped several strands of wire around them. He knew where the fireplace pokers were packed, close to the stoves. Bear had to unpack several items to reach the iron poker. After retrieving it he ran the poker between the wire and the logs. It took both Bear's and Ace's muscles to twist the wire and tighten it until the multistrands bit into the logs. Bear pushed against the logs. They didn't move.

Bear, Ace, and Lance sat back. Bear put tobacco in his pipe, and Lance rolled two cigarettes and handed one to Ace. They rested and watched the six ranch hands while they stacked the heavy rocks around three sides of the logs. The side next to the wheel left plenty of room to work with the wheels.

The women cleaned up the supper mess. Put more beans to soak, enjoyed spit baths, and then curled up in bed. Carmella and Glancy had been spreading their bedrolls under the supply wagon. They made do, closer to the fire. Wyvon and Ace under the grub wagon. Bear found Candy laying against a log. They had always thrown their pallet a little ways out of the light from the campfire for privacy, but tonight she hadn't wanted to go into the dark alone.

The ranch hands always made themselves a separate campfire and spread their bedrolls around it.

Before she went to bed, Carmella got a couple of railroad lanterns from her camp equipment. She lit them and put them where it helped the workers most.

The log brace worked. There were times when either the wagon bed groaned or the logs shifted a little. Bear held his breath when he heard these settling sounds. The bolts were stubborn, both on the old wheel and on the new one. He poured linseed oil on them hoping to loosen them. They were rusted from the frozen snows in the canyon.

The wooden rims had saturated with moisture in those snows. The last weeks in this dry western climate were not kind to the wooden wagon-wheel parts. Low humidity and hot sun removed that moisture from the wood, shrinking it in size. The wheel, with loose parts, caused the trouble with an overloaded wagon. There were still some rough trails of unsettled land ahead. The three companion wheels attached to the wagon, and the spare had also come from the frozen and melting snow in the canyon.

As Bear banged and wrenched on the wheel, he hoped he would make it to Cecile's. He wondered if they would have more wheel trouble before he reached Grady's land. With his mind wandering while he worked, he nearly fell when the bolt loosened. Cheers accompanied the success of loosening the bolts and quickly making the exchange of wheels. The last strenuous job was to get the log brace out from under the axle as the heavy wagonload was settled hard on the logs.

They were all tired. It was decided to hook up the teams in the morning to pull the wagon off the brace.

The men all headed for their bedrolls. Bear sat on the log Candy was leaning against and pulled his pipe out of his shirt pocket. The ritual of filling the pipe with tobacco and lighting it was going to be an effort tonight. That was how tired he was. He just held the empty pipe in his jaw, put an arm around Candy, and pulled her against his leg. She laid her head on his knee.

A man came toward them out of the dark, into the fire's glow. They saw it was Ace. He sat on a log next to them and rolled a cigarette. He smoked until half the cigarette was gone before he broke the silence.

"Bear, let me throw something at you. Maybe you can help me make a decision."

Bear just nodded. Ace said, "You've been around Wyvon and gotten to know her some. I've been worrying about this for some time. You notice, I'm pretty much stuck with her."

Another nod from Bear. Candy just watched Ace's face and waited for him to go on.

Ace said, "Don't take that wrong. I like the girl. Hell, I probably love her, or this decision wouldn't be so hard to make."

Bear began to stuff tobacco in the pipe and waited.

Ace continued, "When we hit Brackett, you guys will turn off. I had planned to go on to San Antonio and spend Christmas holidays with my family." He drew in on the cigarette and slowly released the smoke. He said, "She's not getting better fast. I had hoped she would put her fears behind her and enter back into our world. It's not happening. There's no way I can put her in a hotel and leave her alone. I can't risk taking her to my parents. They are good people, but Indian lovers they're not. They would treat her like she had been Indian raped, and she doesn't deserve that."

He dropped his cigarette and stepped on it. And he said, "Can we ride on with you to Cecile's? I admire Mr. Grady, and I really would like to be there for the wedding. Wyvon knows all you guys. She's comfortable with you. Would it be imposing on Cecile to have unexpected guests?"

Bear took a pull on his pipe and said, "I've thought about this a lot. All you'll be doing is postponing the inevitable, but I can't see you taking her back into society. She may never recover. You're going to have to make a decision sometime, but I agree now is too soon. I think Cecile meant it when she invited a gang to the wedding. I think she'll welcome you, and I know Grady will want to hear how you did with his Henry. Besides, you're a good wagon driver. Candy, wouldn't you like him to continue looking after your belongings?"

Crossing the Rio Grande was an act of utter frustration. There was no trouble loading the grub wagon and the beer wagon on the ferry raft and floating them across. It was the supply wagon with Candy's possessions that presented problems. It was too heavy to drive it across. It threatened to sink to the bottom of the riverbed.

The men gathered to decide what to do. Candy sat and listened. She felt a little guilty, as it was her possessions causing the problem, but she wasn't going to agree to discarding anything.

The men argued for about an hour and kept coming back to the same conclusion. The only thing they could do was to back up to the ferry and unload as much as the ferry would hold.

The hardest job was unloading the huge iron kitchen stove, the smaller iron heating stove, and the bathtub. Those three items made the first trip.

They loaded as much as the ferry would hold. Pulled it across, unloaded on the Texas bank, and went back and got another load. It took three trips to get all the boxes and barrels across.

Once the wagon was unloaded, it half floated across the river. Reloading the wagon didn't take long. The boxes and barrels were easy. With Carmella's ranch hands helping with the larger, heavy items, Bear, Lance, and Ace made quick work of the smaller things, but they were tired. It had been a long, exhausting day.

The men sat in the shade of the supply wagon and rolled cigarettes. Bear lit his pipe. They sat and stared at the three heavy iron items still waiting to be loaded.

Candy was tired too. She had worked alongside the men, making sure everything was handled properly, tied down, and secured. It was a lot like having to put a puzzle together. Everything had to be reloaded exactly the way it was originally packed to fit everything. She didn't smoke, but she needed a drink of water, and that gave her an idea.

She had a small picnic barrel of beer on the beer wagon. Most of the barrels of beer were large and sealed. The picnic barrel had its own spigot. She had loaded it on the wagon last, where she could get to it if needed.

She decided, with this overly frustrating day, that beer was definitely needed. Della helped her get mugs out of the grub wagon. A rousing cheer broke out when she set the small keg of beer on the tailgate of the supply wagon and began filling mugs. It was the middle of winter. The beer was cold and frothy.

Cigarettes were passed around, and a much needed beer party was under way. After they filled their mugs a time or two, the iron monsters didn't look so daunting. All the men helped grapple with the huge stove to get it on the wagon. The two lighter items were loaded by men who were feeling great and harmonizing "Ninety-Nine Bottles of Beer on the Wall."

It had taken all day to get everything over the river. They made a campfire. Sliced some ham and slapped it between two pieces of bread spread with mustard. Swallowed this makeshift supper with another mug of beer.

It wasn't long until most of the men had found their bedrolls and passed out. The ladies had turned in, and the only ones left by the fire were Bear and Candy. Too tired to move, they sat leaning against each other and staring at the flickering fire.

"That beer did the trick, you did good." Bear lifted her hand to his lips and kissed it. "What gave you the idea of the beer party?"

She hesitated and said, "Besides getting my possessions into Texas, I had something else I wanted to celebrate." She sat quiet.

He waited for her to go on. When she didn't, he said, "Woman, is this a surprise? What are you celebrating?"

"Bear, I think I'm pregnant."

"Pregnant! How the hell did that happen?"

"Bear, you do know how children are conceived?"

"Hell yes, but we haven't even discussed marriage." He sat up and turned her shoulders so she faced him.

His lips were moving. Candy figured he was forming an answer. Possibly a denial. She said, "What are you thinking? I didn't ask you to marry me. I said I think I may be pregnant."

He stood up and said, "It's too soon. We haven't been together that long."

She said, "It's been a couple of months, almost three. I'm guessing our meeting in the canyon is possible. I've missed two months and am expecting to miss the third now."

He began walking back and forth. He looked terrified and said, "What are you going to do?"

"What do you mean? What am I going to do? I'm going to have a baby!"

"Candy, I love you. I'd be proud to be married to you, but I'll understand if you don't want to marry an Indian."

She was fuming. She said, "Oh, will you knock it off? I'm trying to discuss a pregnancy with you."

"Girl, I'm the child of parents that had two wedding ceremonies. A civil one and an Indian ritual. Any child of mine needs to carry my name."

She stared at him in astonishment. She swallowed and said, "Bear, are you trying to tell me you don't want this child? I'm a saloon girl. My parents weren't married. I don't even know who my father is. But I love you, and I already love this child. I'll understand if you don't want to acknowledge this baby."

He stopped pacing, walked over, and picked her up in his arms and sat holding her. He said, "Woman, what I'm trying to tell you is I want this child to have two legal parents." He kissed her neck and said, "This baby will always be my son or daughter, but it's a dangerous path for a white woman to marry an Indian or a man with Indian blood. We've taken this walk together knowing that at some point we were going to have to make some final decisions. This announcement is my time to make that decision. I want to marry you. Your being a saloon girl and not having a father has nothing to do with the woman I want to marry. I know you, Candace Murray. You are kind, loyal, and brave. I'll repeat, I want to marry you, but I will understand if that is not your desire."

Candy was grinning, she decided to tease him. "Will you just show some excitement? We're having a baby, ya big oaf!" She playfully exclaimed as she smacked his shoulder.

"Of course I will!" Bear exclaimed, as he picked her up in his arms, and twirled her around while yelling out a loud "WOO HOO!"

Bear's wagon train rolled into the long road to Hacienda del Ciela, three days before Christmas Eve.

One of the vaqueros spotted them and alerted the casa. Instantly people poured out to greet them. Grady stopped the wagons on the entry road. He recognized his wagons and knew they would have to stay loaded until after Christmas, when Bear would travel on to his ranch in northwestern Texas.

Juan climbed on Carmella's wagon and directed her through the hacienda's courtyard onto the river road to his house. There Carmella and Glancy were unloaded and shown to their room. After their bags were unloaded, Juan unhitched her sorrel geldings. He walked them to the stables and stalled them next to each other in the west wing.

Cecile was so excited. She had to hug everyone. The community and the children arrived. They ran from Cecile to grab items and run to deliver them where she directed.

Ace and Lance stood around, feeling a little self-conscious, waiting for someone to tell them where to put horses. Grady rescued them. He had Ace help Wyvon down. She looked bewildered. Lance helped Della off the grub wagon. Grady led them to the grape arbor where they could watch as people appeared and then horses and people disappeared.

Miraculously lemonade, hot coffee, and cookies appeared on the table. Grady enjoyed seeing the amazed looks on their guests as the vaqueros took over the teams. Harness was removed, and the horses were stabled in the west wing.

As quickly as they had arrived, after the children grabbed cookies, children and adults disappeared down the river road.

Cecile had never met Wyvon, but she did know the girl was one the Indians had carried off when Dizzy's wagon was raided. The first sight of her with the pistol lying easily around her hips had startled her. Candy drew Cecile aside when she saw Cecile's curious look. Candy explained the fear the girl had from that raid.

Candy said, "This is your home. If you're uncomfortable having Ace and Wyvon, just tell me and we'll supply them with horses and let them go on to San Antonio."

"Candy, it just surprised me to see a woman packing a pistol. Tell me about her. She dresses and acts like a young boy."

"It's a disguise. She thinks the Indians took her and Ellen because they were women. I told her they would have killed her if she were a boy and scalped her. She says she'd rather die as a boy than have them take her as a woman. It must have been a horrible experience."

Candy continued, "She plans to fight with the men if she's ever in a raid again. And, Cecile, she doesn't talk. She hasn't said a word since Ace rescued her. She's very territorial. She stays with Ace. Wherever you settle them, she will spend most of her time there. She's not good with crowds. She's not ready to stay alone at a hotel without Ace, and he doesn't think his family will welcome her. We didn't want to impose on you, but she is comfortable with the six of us."

Candy took a deep breath and said, "Well, I guess we need to get them comfortable and let her get to know us."

Cecile asked Latisha to show Candy, Wyvon, and Della to a bedroom in the east wing. Bear and Lance were shown to the bedroom across the hall.

She asked Juan to locate a double-person mattress and exchange it with the cot at the stable office.

Juan accomplished that by exchanging his double mattress for the cot. He and Lou located another cot and put it in the guest room so Glancy wouldn't have to double up with his mother.

Lou moved his things to the bunkhouse and was surprised the twelve-bed bunkhouse was suddenly occupied as Carmella's ranch hands moved in.

She saw Grady had directed most of the guests to the grape arbor. She asked him to go with her to the stable and bring Ace with him. As they walked to the stable, she suggested moving Trumpeter to a stall and leaving Deadly loose so they could put all the guests' saddle horses in that corral.

When that chore was done, she had the two men sit in the office. She said to Ace, "Candy was kind enough to tell me a little about Wyvon. From what she told me, I admire you, Ace, for taking care of her. I wanted you to know you're both welcome and I'll work with you to make her comfortable."

"Thank you, ma'am. We don't want to be a bother." Ace was not comfortable. He sat on the edge of his chair and twisted his hands. He continued, "I wanted to be here for your wedding. I wanted to thank Mr. Grady for all the help he gave me."

Cecile smiled and said, "We'll get a time when we can sit down together. We're both eager to hear about you tracking those Indians. Right now we need to get everyone settled in. I sent Wyvon with Candy so I could confer with you on your room accommodations."

Cecile saw Juan and Lou had brought the mattress. They had left it standing against the wall.

She said, "I thought she might be more comfortable away from crowds. The hacienda is a madhouse during Christmas holidays. I had this mattress brought in. Do you think she'll be comfortable here? I don't want her to think we're banishing her from the house, but from what Candy explained to me, she needs to be with you. The stable is off limits to everyone but the men in charge of feeding the livestock during the week of holiday activities, so there is privacy."

Ace sat back in his chair and visually relaxed. He said, "Ma'am, this is perfect. Thank you so much for understanding and welcoming us."

Cecile reached over to Grady and took his hand and said, "We're glad you are both here. Let's go to the casa and get linens, pillows, and blankets." She hesitated for a minute and remembered the small stove in the corner of the room. She said, "We are in a barn with hay and burnable materials everywhere, but that small stove is surrounded by and on top of firebricks. It's small, but it does heat this room. I had it installed because I often have stable bookwork. I'll have wood sent out. You can share baths with Bear and Lance. Wyvon can share with Candy and Della."

They found the three ladies laughing and unpacking. Wyvon was sitting in the middle of a double bed. There were two double beds in each bedroom. Both beds in each room had soft feather mattresses.

Ace picked up Wyvon's bag and said, "Come on, woman. We've got to get our space set up."

They followed Cecile to a linen closet. She loaded them both with bedding.

Cecile hugged Wyvon and said, "I'm so glad you came for my wedding."

Wyvon, with her arms loaded, couldn't move away. She ducked her head and smiled shyly.

Grady grabbed an armful of pillows and walked them back to the stables.

He left them setting up their space and went to find Deadly. He found the big bull by the east pasture where Reginald had come to the fence to touch noses. They both were grazing on opposite sides of the fence close enough to visit.

Grady said, "Thought I'd find you here. Too many people for you?"

Deadly raised his head and smelled Grady's shirt pocket. There usually was a biscuit in each pocket. Grady pulled out a cookie from the grape-arbor platter. A sweet sugar cookie. Reginald knew this routine. Deadly was getting something good. Begging, he came to the fence. Grady pulled another one out of the other pocket, broke it in half, and gave each bull half. To pacify Deadly, he gave the big bull a body scratching. He rubbed Reginald's face between the eyes and headed back to the hacienda.

The afternoon was spent unpacking and visiting. Latisha was busy heating bathwater. Della, seeing the overload on the bathtubs, stepped in to help.

They gathered dirty clothes, and all the loads disappeared. They went down the road and across the river. The ladies in the community would launder and iron them, and then return them to the assigned rooms.

Latisha was assigned the men's room to heat water and fill the tubs. Della cared for the women. Latisha's first bathwater was for Bear. She knocked on their door and waited for permission to enter. Bear said, "Come in." She opened the door. Both Bear and Lance stood as she entered. She kept her head down and went straight to the tub in the small bathing room. They continued to stand until she left. As their door closed, Bear, looking forward to a good soaking, hurried to get out of his clothes and into the tub.

Lance just stood there. He was entranced. He had just beheld the most beautiful woman he had ever seen. She had glanced at him when she first entered the room and quickly ducked her head. He had seen the soft brown eyes with a flash of gold flecks. Her eyelashes were so long they curved over her cheeks.

Her mouth was full, and her face flushed as she hurried to empty the hot water. She moved quickly but gracefully, and on her way out she lifted her eyes and met his. She went through the door and closed it behind her.

Lance stood there spellbound. He hoped she would be the one to bring the hot water for his bath. He needed to see this dream girl again.

When not bathing or napping, groups would gather in the grape arbor. An outdoor firebox had wood burning, giving off a fragrant cedar scent. Benches and chairs circled it.

Grady and Cecile stuck with their routine. They rested, each in his or her own room. They were too excited to sleep but got the body rest needed to recover and hold up under the rigorous daily activities of the holidays at Hacienda del Ciela.

Maria knew guests were coming. She just hadn't known when. The minute she heard the wagons had arrived, she began making large pots of soup. One chicken noodle and one vegetable beef. A couple of women from the community came to help. Soon pans of biscuits appeared. There w plenty of Christmas breads, cakes, and cookies already baked and waiting.

These guests would be tired this first night off the trail. Most of them would go to bed early. All Maria had to do was fill their bellies.

317

They were a different bunch of people as they entered the ballroom for supper. The warmth of the room with its Christmas decorations, colored lanterns, and a roaring fire in the huge fireplace set the comfortable ambience of Christmas holidays.

Grady and Cecile each gave a welcoming address. Ramone had chosen to avoid the crowd. Carmella and Glancy sat at Juan's end of the long table. Carmella's ranch hands and Juan's vaqueros were getting acquainted, and some table talk of a poker game in the bunkhouse later was heard.

Ace had requested a tray sent to the stables. Maria packed a decent sized pot of chicken-noodle soup, plenty of biscuits for two, a loaf of pecan bread, and a bottle of wine.

Halfway through the meal in the ballroom, Garcia got his guitar and played Christmas carols. When some began to say good night and head for bed, he disappeared, probably to join the poker game in the bunkhouse.

Most of the wagon-train guests slept in. Grady and Cecile stuck to their routine. Up at six in the morning. Horseback ride. Coffee sent to the office.

When breakfast was announced, they joined their guests in the ballroom. Tables were loaded with bacon, ham, and sausage, scrambled eggs, hash-brown potatoes, biscuits, and gravy.

The guests wandered in at different times. As a platter emptied, another full one took its place. The guests were told that, due to a late breakfast, lunch would be served in the ballroom at two.

Lance's eyes searched the room for Latisha. She had busily helped with serving supper last night. He thought she might serve breakfast. He was disappointed when she did not show up. He finished his breakfast and joined the men at the grape arbor.

Grady and Cecile retired to the office. The fire was lit. A table had been loaded with Christmas desserts. They left their door open and welcomed those who joined them. The morning was comfortable catching up with each other.

Some took walks. Lance joined the ongoing poker game until his mother pulled him away. Juan loaded Carmella and Glancy in his wagon. He told them he would be driving them back and forth. He loaded Glancy's wheelchair. He suggested they leave it at the hacienda. Glancy was doing well on short walks. The long halls of the hacienda would be difficult.

After breakfast, Juan drove them to the river crossing and crossed over into the community, where they spent the early part of the day, until it was time to return to the hacienda for lunch.

Lunch was easy. Baked beans, potato salad, cold ham, sliced tomatoes, and sliced bread. They had a choice to make a sandwich or fill a plate.

Everyone showed up for lunch. Ace and Wyvon looked rested. She had attempted to curl the longer hair on the top of her head. It softened her face. She had even added a little rouge to her lips. Candy figured she felt comfortable enough with this bunch to put the boy disguise away. Today anyway.

Glancy was in his wheelchair filling his lunch plate when Ramone was wheeled in by Gina. As usual, she left him at the door to wheel himself to fill his plate. The two wheelchair occupants saw each other, and big grins spread across their faces.

Ramone wheeled himself to the buffet table. He stopped by Glancy. He stuck his hand out, and Glancy took it. They shook, and Ramone said, "Are you stuck in that thing, or is it temporary?

Glancy laughed. "Temporary I hope, but I've pretty much lost the use of this leg. It's about three inches shorter, and the muscles and ligaments don't work too well. I can walk short distances, like from the bed to the chamber pot."

Ramone laughed. "Come over with me. We'll eat lunch, and I'll tell you my story."

Cecile saw them coming and moved her plate over by Grady. Glancy wheeled in on Ramone's right. The two spent most of the lunch hour talking and laughing.

Grady stole a kiss every now and then. He said, "This is some party house.

Cecile answered, "I love it. The hacienda was like a big old sad barn after my parents died. You realize you are the person who's brought it back to life."

"What do you mean?"

She took his face in her hands. She said, "I left here to buy cows. I met you. Look around. What do you see? Bear and Lou, your friends. I love them. Candy, Carmella, Lance, Glancy, Della, Ace, and Wyvon. You brought all these people into my life, and I can share my people with you.

319

This is a happy casa. We are going to have a big family and many more gatherings of people we love."

He kissed her and then got up to join the men, who were leaving to smoke in the grape arbor.

The men got settled with or without a cigarette and pipes. They encouraged Ace to tell them about his Indian encounters.

The women were in the kitchen helping Maria and Latisha clean up. Carmella was storing leftovers and said, "Cecile, I'd like to see your prize-winning Toro bull. Juan's been telling me about him."

"Of course, Carmella. The men will be busy with their tall tales for a while. Anyone else want to meet Diablo?"

Della and Candy both said yes and followed Cecile and Carmella out the back door. Cecile waved to the men and pointed, indicating the ladies were headed to the stables.

The men were caught up in Ace's story. Grady waved and dismissed the ladies as he returned to Ace's tale.

As they reached the risers, Cecile asked the women to halt by them and cautioned them not to step up on them until she got back, explaining that she had to get her whip in the tack room. She needed it to keep Diablo from charging the adobe wall. She would also check to see if Wyvon wanted to join them.

The door to the stable office was closed. The room stayed warm with the door closed, and the little stove was lit. Cecile knocked, and Wyvon opened the door. She held a book. She was in her stocking feet. Cecile could see she had been sitting in a chair by the stove. She had removed her boots and was reading and warming her feet.

Cecile greeted her and said, "The ladies are waiting by the risers. They want to see Diablo. Would you like to join us?" Wyvon nodded, her face lighting up with a big smile.

Cecile said, "I'm going next door to the tack room to get my whip. I'll be right back. Put on your boots and I'll walk out with you."

Cecile knew exactly where the whip was hung. She had put it there herself. She had been a little annoyed at Grady. He had talked her into changing the location of the whip. She had always hung it on the coatrack by the hacienda's back door.

Grady had been so upset when she had climbed up onto the corral rails with her whip, making it easy for Diablo to unbalance her and pull her into the corral. He suggested she move the whip to the tack room. That distance would give her time to think and make a better decision before risking her life. She thought it a silly move, but he had been so worried that she agreed to move the whip.

She took it from the hook, shook it out, rewound it, ran her arm through it and then settled it on her shoulder. She left the tack room to pick up Wyvon at the office.

Behind her a gruff voice said, "Bitch! Face me. I want you to see what you did to my face. You touch that whip and you're dead."

She turned slowly and saw the silhouette of the man between her and the bright sunlight at the end of the long east stable. She was going to die. The only weapon she had was her whip. She straightened her arm and let the whip slide off her shoulder. She caught it in her hand.

He pulled the trigger.

Wyvon stepped out of the office. Heard the shot. Saw the black silhouette of the man and pistol. At the same time as she screamed, "Gun!" her pistol left the holster and fired six bullets. The first hit the outlaw in his heart. The rest hit close together, one after the other, as the silhouette sank to his knees and fell face forward.

Wyvon sank to the dirt of the stable walkway. She was trembling violently. Wyvon's arms were limp. She dropped the pistol in her lap.

Women were screaming. Men were running from the bunkhouse. Garcia rang the stable bell. People were already spilling out of the hacienda.

Grady had run at the sound of gunfire. A couple of the men from the bunkhouse had pistols drawn but hesitated entering the stable's dark interior, unsure of who was shooting.

Candy, standing by the risers, saw Grady running toward them. She screamed, "Cecile, Cecile," and she pointed at the stables.

Grady pushed through the men hesitating at the entrance. He grabbed one of their pistols and flung himself into the stables on his stomach. His eyes strained coming in from the sunlight. He couldn't see. He yelled, "Cecile!"

A weak voice answered, "Gun, gun."

His eyes adjusted. He could see the girl, Wyvon. She was repeating, "Gun," over and over. She was holding Cecile's head on her lap, rocking back and forth.

He knew this woman carried a pistol. His first thought was that Wyvon had shot Cecile, until he realized the girl was pointing down the aisle at a form lying facedown in the dirt.

He crawled to Wyvon and took Cecile out of her arms. He placed his fingers on her neck and felt the beat of her heart. She was alive. He saw the blood on her shirt—possible shoulder shot.

He yelled, "All clear, get Lou!"

As men entered the stable, Grady strained his eyes to inspect the man Wyvon had pointed at. Ace came through the stable entrance and immediately saw and recognized the scene on the stable floor. Wyvon saw him and pointed at the fallen man. She said, "Gun!"

Ace registered in his mind that Wyvon was voicing her first words in a long while. He kissed her on her forehead and put his fingers over her mouth.

Wyvon shuddered and quit repeating herself.

Ace went to the gunman and turned him over. The body was riddled with bullets. He saw right away what had happened. The man's pistol laid beside him. Ace picked it up and spun the revolver. One bullet had been fired. Wyvon's pistol had destroyed the man before he could fire a second time.

Lou arrived. After checking Cecile, he determined the bullet had hit just below the collarbone and exited out her back. A few inches lower and her heart would have exploded.

Grady carried Cecile to the casa. As he walked, she came to and opened her eyes. She saw Grady had her. She hurt and tried to lift her arm to feel her shoulder. One arm didn't work and the other was pinned against Grady.

He felt her move and looked down into her open eyes. He said, "Relax, sweetheart, it's just a shoulder wound." Just a shoulder wound! His thoughts ran wild. The bastard almost killed her. He could be carrying a lifeless Cecile. Tears ran down his cheeks.

She said, "Don't cry. Lou will fix me."

Lou was walking beside them. He said, "Damn right, honey, you're going to be fine."

The hacienda was quiet. Word had spread that their patron had been shot and was being cared for. People were whispering so as not to disturb her and the people caring for her. They collected at the grape arbor and made trips to the stable to view the outlaw that nearly killed her. Jalo and Paco put the body on a horse and with shovels disappeared down the river road.

Ace took Wyvon into their office bedroom, removed her clothes, put on her nightgown and put her to bed. He took off his boots and pants and climbed in beside her. He took her in his arms. She wrapped her arm around his chest and laid her head on his shoulder.

She was still trembling. Ace said, "You did well. It's all right, you did the right thing. You saved Cecile. Relax now. Close your eyes and go to sleep." He kissed her and tucked the covers around her. The trembling slowed. Soon she was sleeping.

The same scene was being repeated in Cecile's room except Grady sat in the bedside chair and watched Cecile sleep.

Lou had cleaned both the entry and exit wounds, packed them with honey, and wrapped the shoulder with clean, soft rags.

Maria got some knockout powders from the casa's medicine cupboard. Mixed in warm tea, and Cecile was out. Her face was relaxed, so Grady sat quiet and studied her. He wasn't sure he was going to recover from the fear he felt when he saw her being held by Wyvon. He was sure she was dead. He had seen the whip lying beside her. If she died, it was his fault. If she had taken the whip off the coatrack, she wouldn't have gone into the stable to retrieve it from the tack room.

He knew he was being unreasonable. The conflict with the outlaw was inevitable. It could have taken place anywhere, and probably there would be no one to protect her. He owed Wyvon big-time. He was going to the tack room to get Cecile's whip and return it to the coatrack.

Both Juan and Ramone came to see how Cecile was. To keep from having to get up and down Grady decided to leave the door open. When someone looked in, he smiled and put a finger to his lips.

Maria came by late. She walked in and set an empty glass with some powder in it on the side table. She had a pitcher of water in the other hand. She stood by Grady and squeezed his shoulder. From a pocket in her apron she took out a bottle of laudanum and set it beside the glass. She said, "If she wakes she may need the pain medicine. She may need the powdered drug to sleep. Just add water to it—a full glass. I put a bedpan under the bed earlier. Supper's about ready. I gave her a pretty strong dose of the powder. She may sleep through the night. Come get some supper in you. You can stay with her tonight."

He patted her hand and asked, "Have you seen Ace?"

"No, Senor, Juan says he's in the office with the girl. He put her to bed."

"I'll walk out there, and then I'll join you for supper."

"OK, ask him if he wants a tray out there."

"Yes, ma'am, I won't be long.

He knocked softly on the stable office door. Ace opened the door. Seeing it was Grady, he stepped out and closed the door. They moved away from the door and leaned on one of the stalls. Grady rested his elbows on the top rail and one booted foot on the bottom rail.

He asked, "How is she?"

"She's pretty shook up. She's never shot at a person before, just targets."

Grady said, "She saved Cecile's life. He got Cecile in her shoulder just inches above her heart. It's a serious gunshot wound, but if it doesn't get infected, she'll live."

Ace brushed the hair back out of his eyes and said, "Well, that's a blessing. Didn't look good to me in the barn. I recognized him, Grady. He was hanging out at the crossing at Brackett. He helped the river guys pull us across. I got a good look at him.

"We were all so glad to be on the Texas side of the river, he might have heard us asking the tow guys how much farther to the hacienda. He had to've followed us."

"We expected him to show up sometime. Not your fault. At least his ambush failed. I owe you one, Ace."

Surprised, Ace said, "You don't owe me nothing, Mr. Grady. I wanted to come this way to thank you and return your Henry."

"I definitely owe Wyvon, but you seem to be in charge of her. Can I do something for her?"

"I can't answer for her, sir. Let's let things cool down and enjoy the holiday and see how that goes."

"Suits me." Grady stood away from the stall and said, "Supper's ready. You can join us, or Maria will send you a tray."

"Tray sounds good. I need to be here when she wakes. She'll probably regress some after this. She lives mostly in a world of fear."

They shook hands and Grady went to the tack room and got Cecile's whip. When he entered the casa, he hung it back on the hat rack. He washed up and checked on Cecile. He found supper being served in the ballroom. Nearly everyone, from Bear's wagon train to Juan's vaqueros and the hacienda's regulars, was there, working on baked beans and ribs.

Everyone looked up when Grady entered. He knew it wasn't him they were interested in. He said, "She's asleep. Wounds doctored. Unless it gets infected she will recover."

Carmella spoke up. "What was that all about?"

He turned to her and asked, "Do you remember the conversation we had about vigilantes?"

"Yes, I heard you ran into some on your way here."

"We think we ran into outlaws claiming to be vigilantes. We had a small altercation with this bunch. This man drew a pistol, and Cecile slammed him with the whip. Cut his cheek open. She made him give up his weapons. He wore two guns, gunfighter-style. We took his and all the gang's weapons. He only had one pistol today. I gather he didn't get his dual pistols back. If he had, Cecile would be dead. Two bullets fired at the same time would have killed her."

"That day he threatened her, and we've been expecting him. We usually have someone with her. When she went outside with the ladies, I figured she had plenty of protection. I messed up."

He took his seat beside Ramone. The young man was pale. Grady had kept that 10:00 a.m. appointment with the young silversmith. That visit had turned into regular lessons. Ramone was talented in many disciplines. One of them was hand tooling designs on leather.

Grady told him about the conversation with his sister. About her desire to wear her mother's rings. Grady explained he needed to give her something in place of engagement and wedding rings. With Christmas coming he wanted to give her something special.

Ramone helped him to make a small box covered with hand-tooled leather. Her name was tooled, dyed black, and buffed to a high shine. Grady's lessons included a turquoise stone set in an engraved silver disk.

He learned how to make silver hinges and a closure catch. This jewelry box was nearly finished and would be ready by Christmas morning.

Those hours spent with Ramone created a friendship that may not have occurred by just becoming in-laws.

Ramone was not a physically strong person. He dealt with his crippled legs, and Grady learned Gina did more than push him around in his chair. She had been hired by Cecile when Ramone left the hospital in San Antonio. She was a nurse trained in working with crippled and damaged bodies.

She spent two hours a day massaging and working his body. Because his small silversmithing hobby was sedentary, she not only worked his legs but also his shoulders and back. She supervised his meals, bathed him, and when necessary dressed him.

Now, seeing his pale face, Grady worried and asked, "Are you all right?"

Ramone picked up his glass and swallowed a big mouthful of red wine. He said, "Grady, my sister is the only family I have. You see all these people around here? They are not my family. They do represent a responsibility. As the male heir of this community, I'm supposed to be the ruler and caretaker. When my father died and I became broken, my sister stepped in to shoulder that responsibility. My responsibility. Do you have any idea how scared I get when she takes on a man's job? My job! And the fear she will die. She's my strength and the last family I have. I wish she would walk away from this place and take me with her! I know she loves this ranch, and I will never ask her to give it up. I just die a little when she risks herself." He was shaken with this confession. He took another swallow of wine, closed his eyes, and drew in a deep breath to calm himself.

Grady reached for the wine bottle, filled his glass, topped off Ramone's, and said, "I'll tell you a secret, little brother. If anything happens to her, you won't be the only one lost. I have to keep telling myself how fortunate I am to have this wonderful creature in my life. We don't get a notice when it's our time to die. We get a nine-month notice for a birth. I think it rude we can't plan our lives and have no indication of death. I just have to keep telling myself how lucky I am for the time I'm allowed to live with her in the life she loves and to know that she loves me."

Grady picked up his fork and said, "Now eat your dinner. We'll put on our game faces, and no one will know how scared we are that we nearly lost her today."

Cecile woke sometime in the early morning. It was still dark but someone had lit a lantern. In its dull glow she realized part of her body was confined. One arm moved, and she raised it to dislodge the covers she thought held her bound. Her movement sent sharp pain. She gasped, and Grady, who had stretched out beside her raised his head. Someone had thrown a blanket over him as he slept.

He said, "Hold still, honey. Give me a minute and I'll help you." He moved the blanket so he could stand and walked around the bed to her side. He moved her arm and put it back under the covers.

Cecile groaned and said, "Pain. Hurts."

"Honey, you were shot. Don't you remember?"

Her eyes closed. Her face relaxed as memory returned. She asked, "How bad?"

"It's not as bad as it could have been. He put one bullet in your shoulder. Wyvon hit him with a revolver full of bullets." He filled a small glass with water. Maria had left it with a measure of knockout powder in case Cecile needed it to put her back to sleep. There was a bottle of laudanum beside it. She even left a spoon. He used it to dissolve the powder in the water. He set the glass aside and looked at Cecile. She had opened her eyes.

She said, "It really hurts." She wanted to rub it, but it might start it bleeding again.

"Honey, Maria left some laudanum. You think you could swallow a spoonful? It might help with the pain."

He filled the spoon and held it while she swallowed. She smiled, though it came out as more of a grimace, and said, "I understand now why you didn't want to use a spoon. Right now I'd swallow the whole bottle if it took away this pain."

He chuckled. It was good her head was clearing. That was her sense of humor surfacing.

He picked up the glass and said, "Here's a chaser, rinse your mouth out and drink it down."

"You think you're pretty smart. I saw that powder in that glass. You're going to put me to sleep again."

He grinned and said, "Whatever works."

With a straight face, she said, "I'll fix you. I'll drink the drugs if you'll help me use the chamber pot."

"Ha-ha, gotcha there. Maria left a bedpan. You lie still and I'll get your nightie up. I'll lift your knees up with one arm and slide the bedpan under with the other. Don't you try to help—might start the bleeding."

He pulled the pan from under the bed and set it on the bedside chair. Carefully he pulled the covers down and got her settled on the pan. Pulled the covers back over her. Leaned down and kissed her forehead.

He said, "I'll make a trip to relieve myself and give you a little privacy. Do not get off the pot until I get back."

"Yes, sir," she said. Her face had flushed red. This was intimacy she hadn't expected until her wedding night, but she realized Grady had been taking care of her since her encounter with the outlaw on the trail who had crushed her breasts.

When he returned, he removed the bedpan and put it in her bathroom. He covered her and held the glass while she drank the drugged water.

He said, "It might take a little while for that to work. Let's talk awhile."

She worked her undamaged arm out of the covers and held her hand out to him. He took it in both of his, bent over, and kissed it.

She said, "Are we ever going to have a peaceful life? It seems there're always some perils—storms, Indians, outlaws, Glancy's accident, concussions, illnesses and animal attacks."

"I've wondered that myself. I've decided loving someone can be hurtful. It's scary. I've nearly lost you twice to outlaws and once to a bull. The pain it's cost my heart is bad. I don't believe if I lost you it'd be a pain that would ever go away. All I know to do is appreciate the time we have together and look forward to loving you forever."

She smiled and squeezed his hand. She was beginning to feel drowsy. She asked, "How's Wyvon?"

"Ace is taking care of her. He put her to bed. Said she was pretty shaken up. Not to change the subject, but do you realize our planned wedding is to take place the day after tomorrow? We'd better call it off until you're better."

Her eyes widened. "No, please don't. I'll be good. I'll stay in bed all day tomorrow. That's Christmas Eve. We always have presents under the tree for the children. I can borrow Ramone's wheelchair. Christmas Day I'll stay in bed until the dinner. We'll have the ceremony after the dinner. Mr. Thomas will arrive tomorrow."

Grady cut her off. "Are you nuts? Do you hear yourself? This ongoing party is too much. You were just shot, Cecile!"

She whined, "I can do it. I'll be good. I'll rest. I love you, Grady. I want to marry you. I'm sleepy. Lie back beside me. We spent many nights beside each other on the trail, and I miss you next to me." Her voice faded out, her eyes closed.

Grady turned off the lantern and lay beside her. He pulled her covers over her. Pulled his blanket back on himself and listened to her breathing as it slowed to a rhythmic cadence. She should be out for a while.

They needed to postpone this wedding. What kind of wedding night were they going to have if he couldn't touch her?

He mulled that thought over. It was too early to know the results of the gunshot. She might come down with a fever. He wanted to bundle her up and take her to a doctor in San Antonio. She was in no condition to make that trip. He didn't know what to do. A two-day wagon trip to San Antonio could create what he was trying to prevent. He would wait and see how she was tomorrow.

Glancy and Ramone sat together eating breakfast. It was Christmas Eve, and the buffet was simple fare, as the kitchen crew was busy preparing the evening meal for the children's opening of Christmas presents.

Everything else was on hold until Maria got word on how to proceed or cancel.

The two young men in wheelchairs were eating mouthfuls of oatmeal, toast, and fruit. They were fast becoming friends. Everyone was trying to keep busy. They all wanted to hear how Cecile made it through the night. The young men, both solemn and anxious to get some news, planned to spend the day in Ramone's hideaway. Ramone was going to show Glancy how to make beaded earrings, Christmas gifts for the important people in both their lives. Later in the day they wanted to visit Miss Ceci.

Juan and Carmella were having breakfast at the kitchen in his house. They had shared cooking duties, and when the meal was over, they stayed seated and talked over coffee.

Carmella was talking. She hesitated and said, "I heard you leave early. I figured you went to check on Cecile. How is she?"

"She was still asleep. Grady was up. He joined me in the hall and said she woke during the night. Lot of pain. Said he thought they should cancel the wedding but she had a fit. He said to check with him later when she was awake."

Carmella was surprised. She said, "The wedding is tomorrow, isn't it?"

"Yes, and the community children's Christmas party is tonight. The Christmas dinner tomorrow is at two o'clock, and the wedding is scheduled for six."

Carmella rolled her eyes. "That's a lot of activity for a person that just took a bullet. My sympathy is with her. Rotten timing. I can just imagine all the planning that's gone into the holidays and the wedding. Maria has got to be pulling her hair out."

"Maria doesn't let much bother her. I stopped at the kitchen and asked if she needed help. She said she was carrying on with the orders she had until told otherwise. She knows our girl as well as I do. I can bet Cecile's going to have her wedding."

They both chuckled. Carmella refilled their coffee mugs and changed the subject. "You've told me a little about the black cattle. Sounds like they are becoming a problem?"

"Yeah, I thought Grady was going to shoot Diablo when he found Cecile in the corral with the bull. I respect him for refraining from doing so. He's a good man, but he doesn't have the experience of dealing with the aggressive dispositions of the Toros. Miss Ceci would continue breeding the Toros because she promised her father, but her focus is on the Herefords. The two breeds won't do well together, and with attention unfocused there's always an accident waiting to happen. You have to be on guard always with the Toros.

"Miss Ceci has been turning the Toro cattle over to me entirely." He swallowed the last of his coffee and reached for Carmella's hand.

He continued, "I've got a little problem. I need someone to talk it over with, would you mind?"

She smiled and said, "I believe I know the problem. You've been in charge of this ranch for many years. Long before Cecile was born. She's taken a husband, and you're caught in between."

"You've noticed? I haven't said anything to anyone. What I tell you is between the two of us," he said. "I was born in the community. I grew up with Cecile's mother, Estralita. I loved her all my life. I knew always that she loved me like a brother. I knew we would never marry. I had to be content just to take care of her. Then I had Cecile and Ramone to care for. Under their father I had respect. I was manager of the ranch and the community. The Toros have been my responsibility since the grandfather turned them over to me for breeding and training for the ring. I have held that position through Estralita's marriage, and now Cecile's, my patron and godchild. I am the responsible breeder of the black cattle."

Carmella started to speak. He stopped her. "Hear me out. I approve of this man for Ceci. I like him. I've ridden the trail with him so I know his character. He is right for her, and right for the changes this ranch needs to be successful in the future, and in a possible civil war. I'm tired, Carmella. I'm ready to turn this ranch over to Grady and Ceci. I want a life of my own. Please don't be offended when I tell you you're the first woman I've met in all these years I respect and admire. I'd like to court you if there's a possibility you could feel the same toward me?"

She took his other hand and smiled. "I would be honored to be courted by you, but let's take this one step at a time. As I see it, the black cattle are the problem. They will tie you to this ranch where you are no longer in charge. As for your Toro's, given Grady's reaction to Cecile's encounter with Diablo, were it left to him, he would serve them all up on a platter."

He looked startled. She continued. "I'm glad you trusted me enough to tell me you need a change. I need a foreman. Edward, my oldest son, wants to develop a guest ranch on the property where you and I met. The many cabins and the lodge are perfect for that. He hates ranching. He will depend on my ranch to entertain his guests, but he's getting married and no longer wants to run my ranch. Lance can't wait to leave home. Looking for more excitement."

Juan didn't say anything, but she could tell he was thinking.

Carmella said, "Do you think Cecile would sell the Toros?"

He blinked and rubbed his face. Carmella rose and refilled their mugs. He hadn't answered.

She continued, "To me?"

331

He grinned. He understood what she had in mind. He said, "I can't answer for Ceci, but I know Grady would. But, Carmella, you would be taking on Diablo and a small herd of aggressive cattle. The very worries that we need to get rid of here."

"Juan, I'm Mexican. I was born in Mexico. Until I was eighteen and married Mr. Smith, I grew up watching the bulls. It is part of my past. The Toros are in my memories. I'd love for my ranch to be the home of the award-winning Diablo and his ladies. If you agreed to move to my ranch and be in charge of it and the Toros, I would be honored."

He leaned over. She met him halfway. They kissed.

He got up, put his hat on, and said, "Come on, woman. Maria gave me a job. We're to take the wagon across the river and pick up the presents that go under the tree in the ballroom."

Grady woke to a soft knock on the door. He moved slowly so he didn't wake Cecile. He opened the door to find Jalo holding a tray with a coffee carafe and fixings. He took the tray from him and said, "What are you? The new waiter?"

Jalo said, "It's Ma's doing. She says it's my fault Diego got hurt. I gotta do his jobs. Paco's been put in charge of the stables. She wants to know if you want a breakfast tray sent up."

"Yes, tell her Cecile will be confined to her bed. As soon as she awakes and I can talk to her, tell Maria I'll come down and share with her how we're going to handle the next two days."

"Yes, sir." Jalo left.

Grady poured himself a cup of coffee. He sat and studied Cecile's face. It looked peaceful. She hadn't moved after the midnight glass of powered drug. It reminded him of the time Lou gave her a drug and it took her a day and a night to come out of it. He had been worried then. It might be how she would always react to a sleeping powder. Might be wise to use half a dose. Better yet, no more traumas were what he needed.

She moved. She groaned and opened her eyes. "That smells good." She tried to turn to him. She was caught in the covers. He set his cup down and held the covers so she could free her right arm.

She groaned again. "I'm so stiff." She grinned. "I feel like I've been shot."

He shook his head and said, "I'm glad you can joke about it. I don't think it's funny. I'll get the bedpan, and when that chore is done, I'll pour you some coffee."

He looked in the bathroom. The pan was gone. Someone had come in while he slept, emptied it, and put it back under the bed. He got her settled on it, walked across the hall to his room, and looked at himself in the mirror. He needed a shave. He needed a bath. He relieved himself, washed his hands, filled them with water, and soaked his hair and face until he felt he could take on the day. He returned to get Cecile settled. He helped her sit up. Stuffed a pillow behind her and fixed her a cup of coffee with her preferred cream and two spoons of sugar.

"How do you feel?" A normal inquiry of someone with a bullet wound.

She smiled at him and said, "I'm not going to tell you I feel terrible. You're just waiting to find a way to get out of marrying me."

"Cecile, that's not funny. I have to be able to make some decisions. I need to know what we're up against."

There was a knock on the door. Grady said, "Come in." Jalo entered with a breakfast tray. Grady could tell it was a tray for one. Oatmeal, toast, and fruit. Maria was expecting him for breakfast. He realized everyone was looking to him for answers. He wasn't even married yet, and he was lord of the manor. King of all he surveyed. He figured he was picking up on Cecile's morning sense of humor. He moved the coffee tray, and Jalo set the breakfast tray in its place.

Jalo said, "Miss Ceci, are you all right? All the fellows said to tell you they are rooting for you."

"Thank you, Jalo. Tell them it's not fun but I think I'll be fine in a day or two and thanks for their concern."

"Yes, ma'am." He took the coffee tray and left.

Grady had a frown on his face, "A couple of days, huh?"

"Don't I get a good-morning kiss?" Her mouth pouted.

He couldn't help but smile. He got up, leaned over, and kissed her on the forehead. "You don't get a mouth kiss until I've had a bath, shave, and tooth brushing."

"Oh dear, a bath sounds glorious. I can sit in the tub." She looked longingly at him.

"Oh no you don't. I'm not going to bathe you. Bedpan's my limit. Della's here, remember. I'll see if she wants the job." He put some butter, cream, and sugar in her oatmeal and settled the tray in her lap.

She struggled a little with the oatmeal. He could tell she was hurting but wasn't going to show it.

"You can relax and moan if you need to. I spent time mulling over how to handle this and decided the only way was to take it step by step. It could do more damage if I put you in a wagon and drove a couple of days to town to a doctor. Could kill you.

"So, if you'll promise me when you feel the need and I mean tired, sick, pain, whatever, so I can put you back to bed. We'll play this out for a few days. If we make it through the wedding, I'll have some real power and maybe make some better decisions." He smiled to let her know he was kidding. "My worst fear is fever and infection. You've got to be truthful with me, or I'll wrap you in a blanket and take you to San Antonio."

She set her spoon down. A tear ran down her cheek. She picked up her napkin and wiped it away. She smiled and said, "I promise, Grady. I do feel pretty awful, but I'm going to feel awful in this bed. I'd rather feel awful and get married to you. I need you to be in charge. You see to the next few days while I get on a laudanum routine. I could use a mouthful now."

He used her spoon and gave her a dose. She ate her breakfast and slid back down in the bed. He pulled the covers over her and kissed her forehead. Took the tray to the kitchen.

Maria hadn't slowed down or stopped the preparations for the children's Christmas Eve dinner, their favorite, fried chicken, mashed potatoes, and gravy. No vegetables. Chocolate pie for desert.

People came and went in the kitchen and the ballroom. Presents were placed around the tree. The community ladies had knitted the boys' caps and the girls' mittens. Now all were wrapped and under the tree. The gifts from Cecile and Ramone were store bought. Marbles for the boys and jacks for the girls. They all got fudge and divinity. Linens with a Christmas print were added to the tables. The buffet was set up with dishes and silverware. This special night they got to use the hacienda's special silver, brought from Spain many years ago.

The Christmas brunch would be the adult package opening, and after the two o'clock Christmas dinner, the wedding arbor and decorations would be set up. There would be dessert and coffee after the wedding. Fernando, with his violin, Garcia, with his guitar, and a couple of the other community musicians, would play for a couple of hours. All adults were invited.

Grady found Della and asked her if she would help Miss Cecile take a bath.

Della was not one of his charges, but she had taken care of Cecile in Janos. She was pleased to be asked to help. Grady found Jalo and requested hot water for himself.

Lou was asked to remove the bandages and allow Cecile time to take a tub bath and then doctor the wound and rewrap it.

Grady went to his room and collapsed on his bed. He woke when Jalo came with hot water. He bathed, shaved, and brushed his teeth. Looking through drawers, he found his trail clothes washed and ironed. He put them on, and for the first time in days felt like himself, as he pulled on his western boots.

Grady was ignoring the fatigue his body felt. He realized the fatigue was mostly stress related. If not careful, he might relapse. He would stick to his and Cecile's routine. He would get a nap this afternoon.

Right now he had to get Cecile through the next two days.

As it turned out, Maria was the one in charge. He realized she had been supervising the Christmas holidays for many years.

When he told her the events were to be carried out as planned, the activity in the casa increased. He retreated to the office, where he found Bear and Candy, Juan and Carmella, and Lou and Lance.

When he entered, Juan got up as if to leave. Grady said, "Sit, sit. I was going to send for all of you. This makes it easier." He pulled the rope to the kitchen and took a seat.

He said, "Did I interrupt?"

Carmella spoke, "We were looking for a room out of the way after breakfast. The fire in here was inviting. It was a good time to plan our departure after the wedding. But first tell us how Cecile is this morning."

"She hurts, but she's determined to get through the next two days. Della's helping her get a bath, and she has promised to stay in bed until the children's Christmas Eve party tonight."

Latisha walked in, and Grady asked for coffee around. She said, "Yes, sir," and left.

"I'm glad you're all here. If Cecile gets worse, I intend to take her to San Antonio to a doctor. Even if she gets through these next few days. I want to get her checked out by a doctor."

Bear said, "Our trip to San Antonio was what we were discussing when you came in. Candy and I are going to need some supplies before we continue on to your ranch."

"We stocked that wily old Indian chief when we left Janos. We need to replace those supplies. Carmella will take her supply wagon, get ranch supplies, and replace the hay and grain she sold you out of Dizzy's delivery. Lance and Ace plan to take the Butterfield to New Mexico to join up with the regulars. Carmella wants to see her son off."

Grady looked to Lance. "So that's still on?"

Lance smiled and said, "Yes, sir."

Grady looked around this room full of friends and said, "Well, it looks like we'll be traveling together again. Besides the doctor, I've got business to do myself. Lance, you remind me when we get there to introduce you to a friend who can help you." Lance nodded.

Lunch was announced. They rose and headed out. Juan hung behind and asked Grady to stay a minute. He said, "I need to talk some business with Miss Ceci. I'd like you to be present. Please let me know a good time to visit her."

Grady figured it was ranch business and important or Juan would not bother Cecile while she felt so bad. He said, "I'm headed to check on her now. I'll let you know when."

He found her sitting up in bed drinking a mug of chicken broth. There were a couple of pieces of toast on a saucer. He sat and said, "How was the bath?"

She set her mug down and said, "Wonderful. It helped the stiff muscles." She broke off a piece of toast and dunked it in the broth.

Grady watched her put it in her mouth. For a moment she closed her eyes. She enjoyed the simple bread soaked in broth.

He didn't see any signs of fever. "Did Lou get your bandage changed?"

Eyes opened, she picked up her mug and swallowed some broth. Set it back and broke off another piece of toast. "Yes, the entry wound doesn't look bad. It's cleaned up, and there's just a very small hole."

She dunked the toast. "Lou says the exit wound is more torn up. I'm having a little trouble with pain when I sit up."

He sat and watched her finish the one piece of toast. He could tell she was tired. She drank the last of the broth. Pushed the saucer with the second piece of toast away.

He got up, took the tray, and put it out in the hall.

She was fighting to stay awake. She said, "If I had a spoonful of laudanum, I think I could sleep."

He filled a spoon with laudanum, and she swallowed. "Yuck," she said. "It's pretty awful, but it does help."

He sat down and said, "I'll help you get settled. Juan needs to talk to you. It's nap time for both of us. I didn't get much sleep last night either. I'm going to grab some lunch and some shut-eye. How's three or four for Juan?"

"Four sounds good. I'll have to get up then to dress for tonight." She slid down.

Grady removed the extra pillow. She turned to her right side and curled into a fetal position, taking the pressure off of the exit wound. He kissed her cheek and said, "Sleep tight."

He returned to the ballroom where lunch was set out. Sandwiches and soup. He gave Juan Cecile's message and informed Juan and Maria he would be in his room in case of an emergency. He needed some sleep.

Juan knocked on Grady's door at four in the afternoon. Grady pulled on his boots and opened it to see Juan and Carmella waiting at Cecile's door.

He knocked and stuck his head in. She was sitting up. Della was brushing her hair.

Cecile waved him in.

He asked, "Are you ready for company?"

She invited them in. Della pulled a chair over from the dressing table for Carmella. Grady sat Juan in the side chair, and he walked around the bed, sat, and leaned against the headboard.

No one spoke. It got uncomfortable. Carmella looked from Juan to Cecile and said, "Juan's been telling me about the Toro cattle." She continued to explain to them her Mexican history. Her love of the Spanish traditions, including the running of the bulls. She ended saying, "I'd like to buy your Toro livestock, including Diablo."

Cecile almost said *no* automatically. She turned her eyes to Juan and back to Carmella. Juan had a hard time keeping a straight face.

Cecile said, "What's going on? Juan, did you put her up to this? You know I can't sell the Toros. I promised my father."

Juan got serious. "A foolish promise. The Toros have always been my responsibility. Times change. Texas is no longer the place for fighting bulls. The only way you can make a living with them is with a bull-riding attraction or butchering them. And neither of those efforts will pay what they are worth. Diablo will kill your Hereford bulls if he gets loose, and you've had a taste of that. I recommend you sell the Toros and concentrate on the Herefords."

Cecile sat eyes wide. She was anxious as she absorbed Juan's words. Her breathing increased. She looked to Grady.

He said, "Don't look at me. You already know how I feel about that bull. This is not a decision for me. He's your bull."

Carmella talked to fill the empty void. "I couldn't pay a lump sum, but I understand you made a payment arrangement with the lady that you bought the Herefords from. I could manage some down and monthly payments. If we could settle on the amount for the bull and all of the cows."

Cecile just looked at Carmella. Her head was full of thoughts. She didn't know how she could honor her father. She said, "Carmella, these cattle have been on Hacienda del Ciela's land for generations. There are long bloodlines. I don't even know them without looking in the ledgers."

Juan raised a hand and said, "I know the promise you made your father, and I admire your determination to honor that promise, but let me be blunt. You have never been interested in the Toros. Your main interest is in preserving this ranch. These black cattle have been mine since I became your grandfather's majordomo. Long before you were born. I'm the only one who knows in my head and in my heart the bloodlines of these cattle."

The room was still. Cecile sat speechless. Grady suspected there was more than the sale of the cattle occurring here and said, "Juan, you've just given a real reason not to sell and remove them from your management. Cecile would never do that to you."

Juan reached to Carmella, and they held hands. He said, "I go with the Toros."

Cecile gasped. She said, "You would leave me? Leave Hacienda del Ciela? You have been like a father to us. You are the heart of this ranch!"

Juan got a stern look on his face and said, "Stop this. Do not throw one of your tantrums. I am like a father. I have loved and cared for you and your brother and your mother all of my life. I have taken care of you since birth. You are now a grown woman. You can take care of yourself. You have found a good man. He will care for you and this demanding ranch. I'm finally going to have a life of my own. I'm going to court this beautiful lady. If you agree to sell the Toros, I'm going with her and help her manage her ranch."

The room was silent. Grady saw Cecile was in shock. She had been scolded, and a tear ran down her cheek.

He said, "You've given us a lot to think about. I suggest we put this on hold until after the wedding. We need time to think about it. We will give you an answer."

Juan stood. Holding Carmella's hand, he said to Cecile, "I love you." They walked out the door and closed it behind them.

She sobbed, and one tear turned into many. He couldn't comfort her on this side of the bed. He walked around and took her in his arms. He let her cry. After all she had been through, she probably needed a good cry.

When she finally stopped, he went to the bathroom and wet a rag. He gave it to her to wash away the tears and cool her face.

She hiccupped and said, "It's just been one bad thing after another since my parents died. You're the only good thing that's happened to me in years."

"Well, let's call this a beginning. I don't think this move of Juan's was a bad thing. I'm kind of proud of the old boy. At his age he's going courting. Do you realize he will have someone taking care of him for a change? And getting that bull off this ranch is the best thing he could do for you. He's still taking care of you. Now you lie down and rest for an hour. If you look this upset an hour from now, you're not going to that kid's party."

He kissed her, tucked the covers, and left.

The laughter of children was what everyone needed. There were more adults in the room than children. Maria had planned on it. Platters of fried chicken, bowls of mashed potatoes, and pitchers of gravy were loaded on the buffet table.

Cecile and Grady sat in their usual places beside Ramone and across from Glancy. Glancy had given up his wheelchair to Cecile. Ramone took turns filling a plate for Glancy and then one for himself.

Grady filled a plate for Cecile. She requested a chicken leg. With only one arm free, she picked it up and gnawed the meat off the bone. The children laughed at her and followed by picking their pieces of chicken up and eating it with their hands.

After supper the present opening went fast. The children were excited. They laughed and ran to show their parents their gifts. They had been warned not to hug Miss Ceci, but they all came to thank her for their gifts.

As soon as they ate their fudge and divinity, they were eager to leave. They got their parents that had come to watch and headed home.

Grady wondered why the hurry, until Cecile explained. They had to go to bed early so Santa could come. They would get their special gifts under their trees at home in the morning.

Cecile whispered to Grady, "I'm tired."

He said their good-nights and told Glancy he was taking Miss Ceci to bed and would be right back with his wheelchair.

Della walked back with them to Cecile's room. Cecile had her nightgown on under her robe. He helped her out of the chair and into bed. He left them both, with Della taking the pins out of her hair and undoing the braids. It seemed Della had taken over the care of Cecile McNamara. Soon to be Grace Cecile McNamara Grady.

When Grady got back to the ballroom, most of the kitchen staff were filling plates, talking, and laughing. They were taking a break and finishing the leftovers.

Ramone and Glancy were having their chocolate-cream pie and chuckling over something.

Grady barely got to the buffet and rescued the last piece of pie. He sat with the young men and learned Juan had moved Glancy's cot to Ramone's room. When they finished their pie, they said good night, and Ramone turned his chair and said to Glancy, "Beat you to the room. Loser has to read the story."

He needed this fun atmosphere. His chest had been locked up since the moment Cecile was shot. He got a cup of coffee and ate his pie slow. Every now and then someone came by, but most realized he needed some quiet time.

He finished the pie and was working on the coffee when Gina came over and sat beside him. He did not know her as well as some of the men and women who came and went in the hacienda. He associated her with moving Ramone around in the wheelchair.

He said, "Kinda lost your job," as they listened to the wheelchairs racing back and forth in the hall.

"Yes, isn't it wonderful? I've never seen Ramone so happy. He needs friends. This Glancy, also in a wheelchair, has been good for him."

"Yes, you're right. They are both good young men. It's a shame they live so far apart."

She clasped her hands on the table and said, "This ranch is pretty isolated. Not so much in distance as the fact that it is a small community. The ranch cares for most of their needs. Seldom do people come here. These youngsters are even schooled here. I guess, with Agnes gone, you'll be looking for a new teacher?"

Grady smiled and said, "Are you looking to add to your duties?"

"No, sir! I needed to speak with Miss Ceci, but this is not a good time for her."

Gina continued, "Mr. Grady, I'm getting married."

Grady relaxed, he had expected bad news. "That's wonderful, who's the lucky young man?"

"He's a major. A doctor in the Confederate Army. He's being transferred east and wants me to go with him."

It was bad news. "What's your schedule? When are you leaving?"

"I just can't pack up and leave. I wouldn't do that to Ramone, but I'm giving you notice. I'll stay on for a couple of weeks so you can find someone. I need to train whoever takes over the job, so I'm hoping you can find someone soon."

"Thank you, Gina. I appreciate the notice. I know this marriage is a happy time for you. Have you said anything to anyone?"

"No, sir," she answered.

"Let's keep this between the two of us. I'm planning on taking Miss Cecile to the doctor. We will travel with our friends when they get packed up and leave. I'd like you to stay on until we get back. I have business that will take a couple of days, and I'll inquire about someone to take your place, but I don't have much hope. Most qualified doctors and nurses will be headed to war or overloaded due to shortage of medical personnel.

"While we are gone. I'm going to ask Miss Della to work with you. She may want to travel on to the city. I'll talk to her and let you know."

"Thank you, Mr. Grady. I will stay until you return, and I think Miss Della could turn out to be the answer for both of us."

Grady was having a hard time hiding his irritation that her notice had given him. It seemed to Grady that the mice were leaving the ship. He wondered if he had created this sequence of events.

Leaving Janos, Lance and Ace both traveled with Bear's little caravan. Both young men were looking forward to joining the regulars being recruited by the forts in New Mexico and Arizona. The Union Army and the Confederate Army were being summoned east, leaving the regulars to control the Indians, free now to raid, steal, and kill the settlers unprotected by the army.

Ace had never had a personal reason for fighting Indians until his uncle Dizzy's freight wagon had been raided. A dozen or more painted warriors had ambushed the wagon, killed his big brother, and kidnapped the two women.

Wounded himself, he had tracked the raiders and picked them off, leaving a blood trail as the Indians struggled to escape his accurate rifle shots. He had followed them to their campgrounds. He saved one woman. Wyvon. He left his obsessive need to kill Indians to get her to safety.

He joined Bear's caravan with the intention of hooking up with Lance and joining the regulars. His desire was to have a legal right to kill Indians.

The time spent on the trail to Texas gave the two young men a chance to form a friendship. Wyvon had clung to Ace. Smothered him a little. But she helped the women with chores, and this allowed the two to join Carmella's ranch hands, visiting, playing cards, telling tales, and discussing the pending war.

The first day after they had arrived at Cecile's ranch, the outlaw shot Cecile. Wyvon had killed the man before he could fire a killing shot. Ace was again taking care of Wyvon.

Lance wasn't missing his friend Ace. He was occupied with someone else. The daughter of the cook. She was stunning. She was tall for a woman. Lance was six feet. She came to his nose. Their appearance was alike. He had brown eyes rimmed with long black eyelashes. Her brown eyes had flecks of gold, and her lashes were longer than his. His hair was almost black. When not pulled back and controlled by a leather tie, it had soft curls. Her hair fell down her back. It was silky black with tints of lavender that flashed when firelight hit just right. It waved and ended in soft curls.

Her name was Latisha. He said it over and over. It was a beautiful name. He said it often in his head. Sometimes he just chanted, "Tish, Tish, Tisha."

He took to hanging out where she worked. She helped her mother in the kitchen and was often in the ballroom setting tables, clearing tables, and helping with holiday decorations.

To spend time with her, he often offered to carry things. Trays of dirty dishes to the kitchen. Boxes of decorations to the ballroom.

Latisha had not noticed she had an admirer. She was on the move most of the time. When not working in the casa, she was babysitting the terrible twins with Impala's help. The two five-year-olds were constantly up to some kind of mischief. Impala was a lot of help, but he had times he spent with Ramone, and often the twins got away from her.

It was one of those times that she first noticed Lance Smith. He offered to help her look for them. They found them in the stable loft. They had swiped a deck of cards from the bunkhouse. They didn't know how to play cards but were having fun throwing one card at a time onto the horses in the stalls.

They had the horses excited. Ace had yelled at them. His yelling alerted Latisha to their whereabouts. She and Lance each grabbed a boy. Lance helped her walk the boys to the river raft.

They turned the boys over to their mother and walked back to the casa together. They introduced themselves. Lance begin to appear wherever she was. He even washed dishes for Maria just to be near Tish. His nickname for her was often on his lips.

Latisha thought he was handsome. She was often fending off the vaqueros. She was attractive, but she didn't believe she was beautiful. Latisha just figured there were few young women on the ranch, and she kidded the cowboys. She knew how to control a flirt. Lance didn't flirt. He just wanted to be near her.

They took their first walk together the day Cecile was shot. They were both afraid she might die. They did evening chores, and Lance walked Latisha to the river raft. This walk turned into a nightly occurrence as they got to know each other.

Christmas morning arrived with a white Christmas. Four inches of snow fell during the night. Grady, an early riser, got to see the yards and buildings covered in snow. A beautiful winter spectacle. Soon it would be trampled from the constant activity at Hacienda del Ciela. He went to the kitchen and begged a cup of coffee. Maria poured him one and then poured herself one and joined him at the kitchen table.

Grady said, "I want to thank you for helping me fit in here. It's been quite a ride. Different from driving cattle. I see the care you give to everyone and especially to Cecile and Ramone."

She smiled. "My job, Senor Grady. I have taken care of Cecile from the day she was born. She is like my own child. I raised her with my children. I take this opportunity to assure you this is like my child getting married. I want it to be special for her. I will see to everything so it is special."

Grady swallowed the last of his coffee. "I appreciate all you're doing. I need to check on her. If she's fever-free I'll bring her down for brunch and the present opening. She may have to stay in bed until the wedding. She won't want to miss the dinner, but if it looks like too much I'll let you know, and you can send a tray. I'll eat with her."

"Si, Senor, let me know. I think dinner and wedding are too much. She stubborn child. You be boss man. I send dinner tray."

The casa was beginning to stir. Grady went back to his room and shaved. He saw Della leave Cecile's room.

He asked, "Is she awake?"

"Yes, sir, I'm going for coffee. I'll bring enough for two."

He knocked and opened the door to find Cecile sitting up in bed. She grinned and said, "Christmas gift." A puzzled look on his face made her laugh.

She said, "It's a family custom. If you say, 'Christmas gift' first, the other person owes you a kiss. You owe me a kiss."

"I'll gladly do that." He bent over and gave her a kiss. His lips lingered on hers, tasting the freshness of a mouth clean from salt and soda.

He exclaimed, "I like this custom!"

The door opened, and Ramone, in his wheelchair, stuck his head in and said, "Christmas gift."

Cecile laughed and said, "Oh, you! How do you always get me first? Come here and get your kiss."

Grady moved the bed chair so Ramone could wheel up to the bed. Ramone could not reach her, but she took his hand and kissed it.

Grady laughed and said, "I'll shake your hand. I won't kiss you."

Ramone said, "Good enough," and they shook hands.

Ramone studied Cecile's face and said, "You look good. How do you feel?"

She frowned and answered, "I think I feel better. I can't really tell this early in the morning. I wake up stiff and sore."

Della came in with a coffee tray and set it on the side table. She said, "Mr. Ramone, I'm headed back to the kitchen. May I wheel you back?"

Ramone said, "I'd appreciate the ride." He turned to Cecile and asked, "Are you going to make it to the brunch and present opening?"

"Wouldn't miss it," she answered.

Della wheeled him out, and Grady fixed Cecile a cup of coffee and doctored it with cream and sugar. He poured a cup for himself and moved the chair back and sat.

They were quiet for a moment, and Grady asked, "Have you given some thought to Juan's request?"

"That's all I've thought about. I just can't imagine the hacienda without Juan. I know that's selfish of me. He deserves, as he put it, a life of his own. If I don't sell the black cattle, he will have to remain here to care for them. It's a perfect solution for us to sell them to Carmella. It makes immediate room for the Herefords and relieves us of the danger Diablo represents. So, I guess the answer is yes. We'll sell them to her, but how much to ask for them?"

"OK, let's not worry over that today. I'll get together with Juan. With his knowledge of the price of the Toros and my knowledge of cattle prices north in the gold fields, we'll come up with a fair price. We'll sit down with both of them tomorrow. First, let's get through this wedding tonight."

Grady borrowed Glancy's wheelchair, and Cecile, in her saloon robe, had a smile on her face as she entered the ballroom for the Christmas brunch. Many voices called out, "Christmas gift."

She laughed and said, "I owe kisses. Let me get well. I won't forget."

They all clapped and went about filling their plates. Brunch was over quickly. Today it was just adults, but there was a childish desire to open gifts.

Grady was amazed to see everyone had one or two gifts. He tried to guess who had done all the shopping for the ranch hands and house servants and the many guests invited for the wedding.

Ramone and his crew, Glancy and Impala, had made earrings for all the ladies. The men had new western hats.

Candy, not knowing what to expect at Cecile's hacienda, had paid Belle to knit some items for Christmas gifts, before they left Janos. Metta Maybelle Moore, the owner of the hearse, was happy to get the work. Candy had a small trunk packed with ladies' matching hats, scarves, and mittens.

She gave Bear, Lance, Juan, Ace, Lou, and Grady a bottle of bourbon. She donated a barrel of beer to be served after the wedding at the reception.

Grady was overcome with guilt that he was unable to give as many gifts, considering all the gifts coming his way. He opened a small wrapped gift from Ramone to find a beautiful silver and turquoise belt buckle. He cataloged his intention to purchase in town a piece of jewelry equipment Ramone didn't have.

Cecile had gifts pile up around her. Many were items made by the community women and men. She was getting tired. She opened Grady's jewelry box. He could tell how much she liked it. She kept running her hands over it.

She opened Ramone's gift. The light flashed as a sparkling silver and turquoise squash blossom spilled out into her lap. The silver was polished to a high sheen. The stones had the deep color of the Kingman turquoise. She held it up to lie across her bosom. There were oohs and ahs, and many clapped. She kissed Ramone and put it into her beautiful jewelry box. The boy's earring gift joined the necklace in the jewelry box.

She looked to Grady and nodded. She needed to go. He stood and apologized. "Our lady is getting tired. Would someone put her unopened gifts back under the tree? She's looking forward to opening them when she regains her strength."

She was put in her bed. Grady kissed her and said, "Get some rest. Big night tonight." He took the wheelchair back to Glancy and went to the office. He had plenty of things to think over. He left the door open so anyone who cared to join him could. He pulled the bell cord and took a seat in what was becoming his big leather cowhide chair.

Diego entered in summons of the bell. Grady said, "You get your job back?"

"Yes, sir. Mom says we don't have time for me to slack off."

"How's the head?" Grady asked.

"It's better than the shoulder." Diego used his good hand to run through his hair.

Grady said, "Think you can handle coffee for two?"

"Yes, sir." He started to turn.

Grady said, "Please find Little Bear and send him to me."

"Yes, sir!"

Bear arrived with the tray of coffee. Grady laughed and said, "Maria put you to work?"

"I needed something to do. I'm not used to so much leisure time, and I'm uncomfortable with people waiting on me. I think I could get used to it though." He grinned.

Grady leaned his head back on the soft leather of the big chair. He said, "I've wanted to talk to you, but things went to hell so fast. I feared Cecile was dead, and she's not out of the woods yet."

He closed his eyes and said, "We have both concentrated on recovering from our illnesses. You see how they go all out for the holidays. With a wedding thrown into the mix, it's overwhelmed me. She was just cruising through it all until this gunshot."

Bear said, "It will be a while before she gets over that. Bad thing with her body already worn out from those weeks in the canyon." He refilled their coffee mugs and said, "I needed to talk to you also but figured it could wait until after today."

Grady swallowed some of the coffee. It was growing cold, so he downed several swallows and set the mug aside. "I had asked you to stay and winter with me at my Texas cabin. When I saw you arrive with two loaded wagons and Candy, I wondered if that arrangement was still on?"

Bear drank his coffee and set the mug aside. "I guess that's up to you. If you've changed your mind, let me know."

"No, no, I haven't changed mine. I see how close you and Candy are and thought maybe your plans had changed." Grady laid his head back, rubbed his eyes, and said, "I've ended up having more responsibilities than I expected right here."

"Hell, Grady, let me tell you about responsibilities. Candy's pregnant."

Grady sat up, opened his eyes, and said, "How did that happen?"

"That's what I said when she told me. Do you realize it's been three months, almost four, since we all met in the canyon?"

"Well, well," Grady laughed. "Why, you sly old teddy bear. So we're going to have a little Bear Junior?"

"Don't laugh, it's not funny. I wish it were me getting married tonight instead of you."

Grady thought a moment and said, "I can arrange that if you're serious?"

Bear looked stunned. He swallowed.

Grady said, "The justice is here. He can marry the two of you. There won't be all the hullabaloo like for ours, but it will be legal and can be registered in San Antonio."

"I wasn't sure about you making it to the cabin. Seeing the job around here and now Cecile down, your hands are pretty full. Candy had decided to winter with me if you had to bail out."

"That sounds good. It fits into why I asked you to meet me here." Grady got up and closed the office door. He said, "Cecile and I have had a lot of time together while we both recuperated. We've tried to look at the big picture, and it's a scary scene."

"We will have two ranches to manage and build. Hers is in financial straits. Big loan on the Herefords. It's going to take some juggling to keep it from going under, and mine isn't even started."

Grady paused, deep in thought, then continued, "I've thought of selling mine, but when I suggested it to her, Cecile put her foot down. She gave me an idea, and I think it will work if we can pull it off. I'll need your help to put it together."

"My help? You know I'll do whatever you need. You hired me on when no one else would hire me." Bear sat forward, eager to hear what Grady had to say.

"I need you to sign on as a partner on the north-Texas ranch." Grady waited.

Bear just looked at him. Then he grinned and said, "I thought Deadly was your partner."

Grady laughed. "That's a good one. If you sign on, he will be your partner too."

They were both quiet. Grady waited for Bear to digest his offer.

"Boss, I don't have much to offer to be made a partner." His voice was quiet but strong.

"That's funny. I don't have much to offer either. A piece of Texas soil, a small log cabin, and an unknown number of brush cattle, though I've got plans to change that. I don't want money from you. I need someone I can trust to live on that land and help me build a ranch house and a herd of beef cattle."

Grady continued, "Tell you the truth, Bear. I haven't had much sleep. The holiday and wedding preparations. A month of studying the ledgers for this ranch and riding with Juan to learn the lay of this place. I'll welcome someone to help me carry the load for the 'Double D' ranch. Someone I can depend on and trust."

Bear grinned. "The 'Double D.' I like it. Old Deadly is our third partner. I don't know how well I can organize, but I can work cattle and build a ranch house." He looked directly into Grady's eyes and said, "I want to thank you for asking me. I've never felt I'd have much, being a half breed. I'll work my hands to the bone. You won't regret asking me to be your partner."

"I know you will, Bear. I have respect for your work ethic. I'm aware of how talented you are. There's only one thing we have to clear up." Grady was serious.

Bear swallowed and said, "OK, hit me with it."

Grady grinned and said, "I'm going to write up a contract and have it registered at the land office when we get to town. I can't register a contract with 'Little Bear.' Man, what's your real name?"

Bear was speechless, then he laughed, "You'll be sorry. My father was a sergeant with Colonel Doniphan's soldiers at Bear Springs. The treaty was not honored by many young Navajo raiders. I was fourteen when my father died policing one of those raids. His name was Anthony Ambrose Newcastle the Second. Both my white grandfather and my father are dead. When I was born and they were alive, I was the Third. With them dead I guess that makes me Anthony Ambrose Newcastle the First? I don't have any idea how it works."

Grady said, "Good grief, are you sure there wasn't a 'Sir' at the beginning of that moniker? Do you sign all of that?"

"No, I just used 'Tony Newcastle,' but the kids in the white man's school teased me, so it's been the name my Navajo grandfather gave me. My father was a big man. Big gruff voice. Grandfather always referred to him as 'the Bear.' So I became 'Little Bear.'"

Grady said, "Well, I prefer Little Bear, but we probably need to use the moniker. Do you have that birth certificate?"

"My mother is still alive. She was very proud of that piece of paper. When we get to the city I'll send a letter to the reservation with Butterfield. It might be documented in the army's register. I never needed it, so I guess we'll have to wait and see."

Grady said, "I've got to see a lawyer on other things. I'll ask him."

Bear said, "Boss, what do I call you? I don't think I can say 'partner.'"

"Grady's good." Grady rose and said, "Come with me. I've got an idea."

Bear followed him down the long east wing of the hacienda to Ramone's door. He knocked. Ramone answered, "Who is it?"

"It's Grady. I've got company. I need to ask a favor."

Ramone was giving a leather-crafting lesson to Glancy and Impala. Grady explained the reason for the visit and said to Ramone, "I saw you had some rings completed in your display drawer. This man needs a ring. I'll see you get paid for it. You may need to size it, but he will still be here for a few more days. We need it for tonight. We may have a second wedding after mine and your sister's. He has to ask her and needs the ring to seal the deal."

Ramone didn't hesitate. He took Bear to the display drawer and let him pick out a smooth silver band with one small beautiful turquoise stone set into the silver.

Grady looked over Glancy's and Impala's shoulders. They were working on stamping a design into the leather. Grady had learned this craft making Cecile's jewelry box. He said, "Hey, guys, you're getting good at this. That's really nice."

They grinned at the praise but continued on their projects. Ramone handed the ring to Bear, who thanked him. Ramone returned to the worktable. Grady and Bear left.

As they walked back to the main hall, Bear said, "This has been some holiday for me. The company and love of a woman I admire. An offer of partnership with someone I respect. The possibility of a family and a home for them. And now I have a ring, hopefully for the bride-to-be. From now on I'll just call you Santa Claus."

They laughed as they walked out the back door and went to the bunkhouse. They found the justice playing cards to pass the time until the ceremony. They explained the situation to him. The justice then assured them he had additional wedding certificates in his briefcase and could perform the required nuptials. With that accomplished all that was needed was for Bear to see if Candy would agree to marry him.

Grady left Bear with orders to meet him at the office first thing before daybreak to go over his plans for the Double D. Bear agreed. He still had to report to Grady on the repairs needed on the supply wagon.

This was her wedding day. She was determined to get through this day. To do so she had to eliminate activities that would tire her. She was looking at one of those activities. Her wedding dress hung on the door of her closet. It was beautiful. The ladies of the community had done a grand job. It looked like they had followed her request as to the design perfectly. The problem was it needed a fitting. She could tell it was a little large in the waist. Struggling to put it on and standing while it was pinned to her was not going to happen.

She would be in the wheelchair most of the time anyway. Della had just brought the dress in and stood patiently waiting to see if Miss Ceci had a request before she left. Cecile smiled at her and said, "It's lovely. Please tell the ladies 'thank you' for me. I'm really tired from opening presents, Della. Would you please give me a dose of laudanum? I'm going to rest the rest of the day. I think I'll skip the dinner. Please tell Maria I would rather have a tray in my room. Something light."

Grady looked in on her several times during the afternoon. She slept. Her breathing was regular. When Christmas dinner was served in the ballroom, he got their dinner tray from the kitchen and joined her. Della had given her a sponge bath and combed her hair.

As he set the tray on the side table, she smiled and said, "The groom is not supposed to see the bride before the wedding."

He answered, "The bride's not supposed to get married with a bullet hole in her either. How are you doing? And don't fib to me."

"I've felt better, but I've been good. I'm rested and a little excited. We're finally getting married."

He leaned over and kissed her. He sat and fed her the vegetable soup and crackers Maria had decided she needed to give her the strength to get through the evening. She did not protest being fed. Lifting her arm was painful, and she needed all her strength to get through this evening. She just watched this beautiful and thoughtful man take care of her. This was her man, soon to be her husband.

Maria had put a some of the Christmas dinner fixings on the tray for him. When the food was gone, he set the tray in the hall and came back and sat. He took her hand in his and asked, "Well, Lady McNamara, are you ready to be my wife?"

"I'm so ready," she replied.

"I'm going to my room to get beautiful. I don't want you to outdo me. Tell Della to knock on my door when you're ready. She's bringing the wheelchair." Grady bent down and gave Cecile a light kiss on the lips before leaving the room.

When Della knocked, he was admiring himself in the mirror. His wheat-colored hair was clean cut to shoulder length. His face glistened with a close shave. His black Spanish suit adorned with leather and embroidery fit his body like a glove. Never in his entire life had he ever worn finery like he wore tonight for his wedding. Satisfied with what he saw he went to get his bride.

She was beautiful. Even with her seated in a wheelchair he marveled at the sight. She was radiant. Della had braided her long hair and wrapped it around her head. The white wedding dress was designed where her neck and shoulders were bare. She wore a short white veil. She had it lifted over her face, and she blushed to see Grady's hungry look as he stared at her. She reached with her good arm and pulled the veil over her face.

Grady was startled when he pushed the wheelchair through the ballroom doors. The transformation from dining room to wedding chapel was amazing. The lattice arch had been woven with white satin ribbons. A pedestal was set in front of it. Justice Thomas stood behind it. His Bible and wedding-ceremony literature was waiting for the bride and groom. The dining-room chairs and extra seats were in rows on each side of the aisle made down the middle leading to the altar.

Grady drew in a deep breath, lightly squeezed Cecile's shoulder, and walked down the aisle to stand beside Lou, his best man. Juan went to Cecile and kissed her on the cheek. Garcia played a soft Spanish melody on his guitar as Juan pushed the wheelchair down the aisle and stopped beside Grady. He set the chair's brake and took his seat by Maria.

Justice Thomas said, "We are gathered here today to celebrate one of life's greatest moments, the joining of two hearts, and to give recognition to the worth and beauty of love and to add our best wishes to the words that unite this couple in marriage.

"Should there be anyone who has cause why this couple should not be united in marriage, speak up now."

The room was silent except for a rustle of clothes while some looked around.

The justice cleared his throat and said, "Today we have come together to witness the joining of these two lives. For them, out of the routine of ordinary life, the extraordinary has happened. They met each other, fell in love, and are finalizing it with this wedding. A good marriage must be created. It is never being too old to hold hands. It's to remember to say 'I love you' every day. It's not just marrying the right person—it's being the right partner."

The justice turned to Grady and said, "Joseph Robert Grady, what say you to this woman?"

Kneeling on one knee in front of Cecile, his face flushed, he looked into her brown eyes, and said, "I, Joseph Robert Grady, take you, Grace Cecile McNamara, to be my wife, my partner in life, and my true love. I will cherish our friendship and love you today, tomorrow, and forever."

Cecile took Grady's hands in hers. Love radiant in her face repeated, "I, Grace Cecile McNamara, take you, Joseph Robert Grady, to be my husband, my partner in life, and my one true love. I will cherish our friendship and love you today, tomorrow, and forever."

Grady, still holding her hands, lifted her gently to her feet. With one arm about her, he helped her turn and face the justice, who said, "Joseph Robert Grady, do you take Grace Cecile McNamara to be your wife?"

"I do," said Grady as he stared into Cecile's eyes.

The justice continued, "Do you promise to love her, cherish and protect her, forsaking all others and holding only unto her?"

"I sure do!" Grady exclaimed with an eager smile.

"Grace Cecile McNamara, do you take Joseph Robert Grady to be your husband?"

"I do," said Cecile, as she stared up at Grady with a face full of love.

The justice motioned Impala to step forward with his pillow of rings. He continued, "Wedding rings are an unbroken circle of love, signifying to all the union of this couple in marriage."

On the small pillow lay Cecile's mother's engagement and wedding ring.

Grady picked up the engagement ring and slid it on her ring finger. He picked up the solid gold wedding ring. Holding it, he said, "These rings are a sacred gift with my promise that I will always love you, cherish you, and honor you all the days of my life. With this ring I thee wed." He slid the gold band on her finger to rest beside the diamond engagement ring.

Impala, a wide grin on his face, lifted the pillow for Cecile to remove the solitary gold ring from it.

She said, "This ring is my sacred gift, with my promise that I will always love you, cherish you, and honor you all the days of my life. With this ring I thee wed."

Justice Thomas said, "I now pronounce you husband and wife. You may kiss your wife."

Grady put his arm under her knees, lifting her and settling her against his chest. Their lips met. Their audience clapped. They could all see Grady's and Cecile's relief as they held that kiss, finally able to express the depth of their love.

Grady returned her to the wheelchair and turned to Impala and said, "Good job."

Then he shook Old Lou's hand. "Thanks, buddy, for always being there for me." Lou beamed.

He turned to Ramone. "For sure now you're my little brother." He bent down and gave the young man a hug.

The kitchen crew filled the buffet table with breads, pies, and in the middle a three-tiered white wedding cake with two handcrafted wedding dolls on the top layer. The girl doll was in white dress and veil. The boy doll was in the black Spanish suit, but that doll wore a cowboy hat.

A few more musicians joined Fernando and Garcia, and they struck up a waltz. Grady bowed in front of Cecile, scooped her out of her wheelchair, and lifting her up in his arms waltzed her around the room.

Bear and Candy joined them. The couples laughed and moved to the music.

Lance took a big breath and asked Latisha to waltz. Other couples rose, and Grady waltzed to the wheelchair and settled Cecile back in it. He was gasping for breath, and she was laughing joyfully.

Bear and Candy joined them, and Candy showed them her wedding ring. Amid congratulations she hugged Grady and whispered in his ear, "Thank you."

Bear told them they had tied the knot in the stables in the afternoon. All their close group from Janos was there. Bear apologized they hadn't included Grady and Cecile because they knew the two were overwhelmed with their own preparations for the night.

Grady hugged Candy and said, "You've got a good man. Congratulations." He whispered in her ear, "For the little one on the way, also."

Latisha left the dance floor dragging Lance with her. She asked Cecile and Grady to cut their cake. She pushed Cecile close to the table and pulled the cake to the edge where Cecile could reach it. Grady put his hand over hers, and together they cut the cake. They shared bites of the sweet cake, and the crowd yelled and clapped. The band struck up again, and couples danced onto the floor. Latisha pulled Lance back and they joined the revelry.

Their wedding night was torture for both Cecile and Grady. They had agreed to postpone the consummation of their marriage. Cecile's pain when she tried to turn over or lift her upper body to rise or sit up in bed alerted them to cool any sexual drive.

Cecile, exhausted from the activity of the wedding itself and the delightful dance in Grady's arms, cried. Tears ran down her cheeks as they prepared for their first night together as man and wife. She wanted him under the covers with his arms about her.

He wiped the tears away and assured her he fully intended to join her in her bed and hold her in his arms. He had been "on hold" from the first day he met Grace Cecile McNamara. He fully intended to stay "on hold" until he had her seen by a doctor.

He suggested she concentrate on getting well. The trip to San Antonio could act as a honeymoon.

Fighting pain and exhaustion, she quickly fell asleep in his arms.

Careful not to wake her, he removed his arms and rolled over. It made the abstinence easier not feeling her body stretched out against him.

He couldn't get to sleep. He got up and sat in the chair by the bed. He finally fell into a restless sleep.

After the wedding the small band played for an hour. The men and women of the community gradually left down the river road.

The band dissolved and Garcia joined the vaqueros and Carmella's ranch hands in the card games at the bunkhouse.

Old Lou sat and visited with Fernando while the kitchen crew put food away and cleaned up. Lance rolled up his sleeves and washed the dishes. Latisha dried.

They had been the last two off the dance floor. It had been an opportunity for Lance to hold her in his arms. During the slow dances she laid her head on his shoulder and wrapped both arms around his neck. Both his arms were around her waist.

Now as the kitchen chores were done, Fernando's family, walked down the river road. Jalo joined the card game.

Lance walked with Latisha, holding her hand. The two slowed and fell behind her parents. They didn't want to say good-night but Fernando called Latisha to join them on the river raft. She turned to Lance, rose on her toes, and gave him a quick kiss.

Fernando frowned. Maria grabbed his arm and shook her head.

Lance was both surprised and delighted. She had done what he had wanted to do since the day he first saw her. She kissed him. In front of her parents. As far as he was concerned, she had expressed her feelings for him. He whistled a tune as he headed back to the bunkhouse.

Pain and a stiff neck woke Grady. He went to his room, shaved, and dressed in his trail clothes.

He was surprised when he opened the office door. The room was full of people. Bear had alerted the guests. Someone, probably Maria, had provided coffee and cinnamon rolls.

He filled a mug, picked up a napkin and a roll, and sat in the large leather chair left vacant for him. He said, "Good morning."

They answered in unison, "Good morning."

He continued, "I see Bear called a meeting. I'm glad you're all here. I know you're eager to get to San Antonio. So am I." He turned to Lou and said, "Will you please clean up the Cart. You'll drive."

Lou answered, "Yes, sir."

Grady turned to Bear and said, "I gather you're having trouble with the wagons."

Bear told him about the trouble they had on the way here. He finished by saying, "Our wagons were left in the canyon in the snow and bad weather. The wood swelled, and now the dry air is drying them out. The back wheels that are carrying the heaviest load are breaking down on the supply wagon. Trumpeter's Cart and the grub wagon are holding up. I think we can make it to the Double D with them, but the supply wagon with its heavy load may not make it out of the yard."

Grady turned to Carmella and said, "I believe your intentions are on hold until we settle our business. I don't have the sale price figured, but we are accepting your offer. We will get together with you this afternoon and work out a reasonable sale price. Knowing this, can you give me an idea of your plans for the trip to the city?"

Carmella smiled. She took Juan's hand, squeezed it, and said, "Yes, sir, you used my cattle carrier to haul Trumpeter here. We'll take Diablo back in it. You also used my supply wagon. It's here. I need to pick up supplies in town. Lance will drive it. Juan's going to stay here with most of my men to gather the Toros. Juan will give us a week to get our business in the city done. Glancy and I will drive my buggy. I'll need it to carry food supplies for nine of us on the trail back to Janos. As Lance will leave us, I'll take one of my men to drive the supply wagon. When we leave the city, we will take the road to Brackett, cross the river at Ciudad Acuna, and meet Juan and the herd on the Mexican side." She drew a deep breath and sat back.

Grady felt like clapping. This lady was a take-charge woman. He said, "As you will have an empty supply wagon going to town, would it be all right for us to shift some of our loaded wagon to yours? It might help our wagon reach town and a wheelwright."

Carmella nodded yes, and Grady turned to Bear and said, "With Carmella's ranch hands and ours, you can shift some of that load. Lou can show you where the wagon is.

"Lance, you go to the remuda. You know both your mom's teams and mine. We will need two for the supply wagon and one for the grub wagon. Get Candy's black geldings for her beverage wagon. Your mom will need two teams for her supply wagon and one for her buggy. Bear will be in charge. I have things to get done. You can all get started, I need to have a few minutes with Bear." Everyone got up and excused themselves except for Bear.

Grady refilled his mug and settled in to reveal the program he and Cecile had planned. He said to Bear, "As a partner in the Double D, you'll be included in all decisions. I'm laying out a program we've had time to discuss and develop. This will all be new for you, and I will be looking forward to any ideas pro or con from you when we reach San Antonio. This will give you time to mull it over and point out any direction you feel is good or bad.

"I'm telling you this now so you will have an idea of our future. You can plan your projects to coincide with ours." Grady stopped to take a sip of his coffee.

Setting the cup back down, he continued, "Cecile's ranch is large. She has acres of the ranch feeding wild brush cattle. For several years she has increased that herd using Toro bulls to add size and weight to the brush cattle."

"The Herefords are in the only fenced pasture available. We will have to do more fencing to hold the brush cattle we round up. In May we will move the cows to the Double D. We will have them branded. We will keep the bulls and culls here.

"The Double D will need some fencing. Once that is done you will collect the bulls, young and old, and the culls." Grady watched Bear absorb this.

Bear shifted his feet, stood up, walked to the coffee pitcher, refilled his mug, and said, "Any idea how many head she wants to move?"

"She figures she has about two thousand head scattered about. She doesn't expect to move that many at once. In time she will build her Hereford bloodlines up and sell off all the brush cattle. The cows we send you will be turned loose to range wild. You will continue to gather bulls and culls in your fenced pasture.

"I'll be pulling together our beef calves, bulls, and culls and add your collection to ours. I'll trail them to whichever is the most profitable market. North to the gold fields or east to the Union or Confederate Armies."

Bear sat back down. "This sounds like a lot of work. What happened to getting well and retirement? If we're going to be branding cattle, we need a brand for the Double D."

Grady smiled. "Already done. Old Lou's been making branding irons for us." Grady drew the Double-D brand. The two Ds faced each other.

Grady continued, "I realize you are going to be alone for a while, getting settled in. We'll hire you a couple of hands, and when we deliver the first herd of cows, we'll build a bunkhouse. Retirement's off the table. We will be losing Juan, her ranch foreman. That job will fall to me. We need funds to save her ranch and to build our ranch. I'm counting on the Double D collecting a thousand head. We should do that here. Between us we could trail two thousand this summer."

Bear stood and said, "I'd better get busy."

Grady said, "Hold on a minute. Considering our third partner, Deadly, my desire is to keep any long-horned cow we run across. Longhorns have adapted to the heat, the bugs, and tough grasses. They can fend for themselves, but with the coming of better beef cattle, the longhorn will disappear. Through natural selection, I would like to preserve the breed."

Bear grinned, two deep dimples appearing in his cheeks. He said, "How about buffalos? Can we preserve them too?"

"Now that's talking like a real partner." Grady laughed. "Which reminds me. Our produce wagon came back from the city with a stack of newspapers. I haven't had time to sort them out, but I did read a small item concerning Mangas Coloradas. It seems after some trouble provoked by miners, led by James H. Teves, Mangas went there to convince the miners to move away from his campgrounds and go to the Sierra Madre to seek gold. They tied Mangas to a tree and whipped him badly."

Bear sat back down. "You know what that will cause? Cochise will arm himself and go to the aid of his father-in-law, and I can tell you right now Chief Jus and Geronimo will be right with him."

"It means our Double D ranch will be closer to their raids. You'll have to keep your eyes open. Cochise is not a friend. He's an acquaintance. One who will put an arrow in you if you forbid him anything he wants. My advice is give him a cow if it saves your life."

"South Carolina seceded from the Union on December 20. Looks like Texas will follow. That's all I had time to read about. When do you think we'll be ready to drive out of the yard?"

As Bear rose and headed for the door, he said, "I'll let you know later tonight."

Grady sat back and rested his head on the leather chair back. He had things to do. He closed his eyes and tried to organize his jobs.

Find lawyer to make contracts legal *Register the Double D brand*
A contract for Carmella *Hire a replacement for Gina*
A contract between him and Bear *Take Cecile to doctor*
Go to the Land office

He kept remembering things he had only a day to organize. His head began to ache. He said out loud, "To hell with this." He left the office in search of Maria. He would give her the job of getting Cecile ready to travel.

The next two days, Lance continued to assist Tish with her jobs. They packed up Christmas decorations and helped prepare meals. They worked steadily. Eager to get chores done so they could have some quality time to explore the feelings they had and possibly practice that kiss.

Lance was left weak in the knees after they had practiced a time or two.

Latisha called a halt to the practice and asked him, "Are you really going to join the Regulars and fight Indians?"

He cleared his head and answered, "It's my choice. I don't care to fight in this civil war."

"But your mother has a cattle ranch. Why don't you help with that? You could get killed fighting Indians." She pulled away, took his hand, and walked with him to the grape arbor where a fire still burned in the open grill.

They sat. He put his arm around her shoulders and pulled her close.

Lance was hesitant. He knew what she was thinking. It would be embarrassing to explain his reasons. He really wanted to escape cleaning the saloon after a bunch of drunks all the time. That couldn't be his answer.

So he said, "I've been nurse aiding cows all my life. I'm not sure I want to choose that for a lifetime. Joining the Regulars will give me a salary while I go adventuring."

Looking him straight in the eyes, she said, "Have you set any goals for how long you chase Indians?"

He had to tread carefully answering this. He sat back, put his arm in his lap, and said, "Latisha, I'm crazy about you. I think I'm in love with you. If you love me, I'd be put in a position of wanting to marry you. In my way of thinking, I need to be able to take care of a wife and possibly a family. Army life is not for everyone. I might learn it's not for me. I might discover I'm a better rancher. I just need to get out there and explore a little."

She sighed, took his hand, and held it in her lap. "I understand wanting to move out or escape. You have seen my life. I'm pretty much at the beck and call of my family and the entire community. I feel like a slave. I need to see more too. I'd even go out and fight Indians if it were allowed. Being a woman, I don't stand much of a chance of becoming anything but a slave. Being married and having a family sounds like more of what I already have here."

"Golly, Latisha, you sound like the way I feel. Honey, if I were in a position to care for you, I'd take you out of here. But you are right. Marriage is caring for a family, doing the same for them as you do here. At least I can join an army. What is it you want to do with your life?"

She laughed and said, "I've talked with Miss Ceci about it. She's going to look into some schools in the city. Most professions for women are the same jobs I do here. I'm very experienced. Boring, yes, but at least I'll be paid. She suggested I become a teacher and come back and work with the community kids. How's that for escaping?"

They kissed. It was late. He walked her to the river raft. Lance realized they were just a couple of kids seeking an adventure. Now was not the time to take on a wife. It would be a pretty tough job in the regulars just staying alive.

Latisha was depressed. She thought she was falling in love with Lance. If it was true that he was in love with her, they were in a real pickle. They might have had a chance if he stayed on the ranch.

She certainly had the skills to be a wife. She'd make a darn good one too, but she, like Lance, yearned for something more. Oh well, they were young, and time was on their side. If they ended up going their separate ways for a while to find out what they each wanted, it was possible that it could strengthen their relationship or prove it to be just a fling.

The hacienda was at it before sunup. The kitchen crew was getting breakfast together. Teams were being hitched to wagons, and last-minute items loaded. Carmella's team was hitched, and she and Glancy had eaten. Ramone had made an effort to join them to say good-bye to Glancy. He wheeled himself to the back courtyard to wave good-bye as the boy and Carmella climbed onto their buggy and moved out of the yard.

The Cart was ready. Lou waited while Grady got Cecile settled inside. Grady's horse was tied to the Cart. He planned to ride and direct traffic until the caravan settled to a steady pace. Mounting his horse, Grady and the Cart moved out to catch Carmella's wagon.

Bear's half-empty supply wagon followed the Cart.

Carmella's supply wagon, driven by Lance, was next in line to move out. He was still fiddling with the harness. He kept looking for Latisha. He had almost given up when he saw her running from the river road. He ran to meet her. She was out of breath and tears ran down her face.

He kissed her and said, "Write me, please write me. I'll send you an address as soon as I know where."

She sobbed, "Yes, I promise."

They walked arm in arm back to the wagon. They kissed again, and Lance climbed in the wagon, took up the reins, released the brake, and moved the wagon out.

The grub wagon, with Ace and Wyvon, passed her. Candy's beer wagon was the last to drive out of the yard.

Latisha lifted the hem of her apron and wiped the tears from her eyes. She sent a little prayer after him, *please, Lord, don't let an Indian kill him.*

As the last wagon pulled out of the yard, Lance looked back and waved his hat. She was still standing in place watching him drive away.

Impala and the twin terrors joined her. His last memory would be of her standing with one arm over Impala and the other across the twins. The children were laughing and waving back.

This wagon train and the people riding out of Hacienda del Ciela were destined to go many directions. Grady, Cecile, and Old Lou would be the only ones to return to the hacienda.

The *Deadly Deadly* saga continues. "Like" M. J. Vigna's Facebook page at facebook.com/mjvigna. We will send you notifications about the release of *Deadly Deadly* book III.

You can follow her Twitter at @mjvignabullbook.

If you have enjoyed this novel, please leave a review. Reviews by readers are the best advertisement for authors. Your review is very important, and M. J. Vigna is delighted to read each one. (Click here to leave a review.)

Thank you for spending time reading *Deadly Deadly*. Much of the history and people mentioned in this book are factual. M. J. Vigna loves to research the early history of our nation and include it in her writings..

INFORMATION ON THE APACHE WARS FROM WIKIPEDIA

The Apache Wars were a series of armed conflicts between the United States Army and various Apache nations which were fought in the Southwest between 1849 and 1886.

The Confederate Army participated in the wars during the early 1860s in Texas, before being diverted to action in the American Civil War. After the Civil war began in April 1861, Mangas Coloradas and Cochise, his son-in-law, struck an alliance, agreeing to drive all Americans and Mexicans out of Apache territory. Their campaigns against the Confederates were the battles of Tubac, Cookes Canyon, Florida Mountains, Pinos Altos and Dragoon Springs.

Mangas Coloradas and Cochise were joined in their campaign by Chief Juh and the notable warrior Geronimo.

In January 1863, Mangas met with military leaders at Fort McLane. He arrived under a flag of truce. Armed soldiers took him into custody. That night he was beaten, shot and killed.

After many various skirmishes with the Army, Cochise and his men were gradually driven into the Dragoon Mountains. Cochise evaded capture and continued his raids against white settlements and travelers until 1872. A treaty was negotiated and Cochise retired to his new reservation, where he died of natural causes (probably abdominal cancer). He was born in 1805 and died June 8, 1874.

Geronimo is probably the most notable Apache warrior of that time period, but he was not alone. After Cochise died in 1874, The U.S. government decided to move the Chiricahua to the San Carlos reservation in 1876. Half complied, the other half, led by Geronimo, escaped to Mexico.

In the spring of 1877 He was captured and returned to San Carlos. In 1881 he fled the reservation with seven hundred Apache back to Mexico.

On April 19, 1882, Chief Juh attacked the San Carlos reservation and forced Chief Loco to break out. Juh's warriors killed the Chief of police and an Apache policeman. Juh led Loco and seven hundred Apache back to Mexico.

Juh (also known as Ju, Ha, Whoa and sometimes Who) was a warrior and Chief of Janeros, a local band (The Ndendai) of the Chiricahua Apache.

They were named Janeros, after the town Janos in northern Chihuahua, which they were usually at peace with and traded their goods. Juh died in 1883, near Casas Grandes, Chihuahua. Some say he was drunk, fell off his horse, and broke his neck. His son said he had a heart attack.

The Chiricahua were sent to Florida as prisoners. In 1870 they were settled at Fort Sill in Oklahoma.

Geronimo, after many escapes from the reservation to Mexico, a Brigadier General named Nelson Miles, deployed five thousand soldiers, five hundred Apache scouts, one hundred Navajo scouts and thousands of civilian militia, against Geronimo and his twenty-four warriors. They found Geronimo in 1886 and persuaded him to surrender.

In his final days Geronimo went to the World's Fair, and other public events, as an exhibit of himself. He attended President Theodore Roosevelt's inauguration and in 1905 dictated his autobiography. He died of pneumonia on February 17, 1909, at the age of eighty.